Memory Reclaimed

Book Six of *Tales of Tasimu*
By
Celu Amberstone

MEMORY RECLAIMED

First edition. March 23, 2025.

ISBN: 978-1990581274

Written by Celu Amberstone.

Note to the Reader

Memory Reclaimed is a work of fiction. I hope you'll read and enjoy it as such. Though I've drawn material in the abstract from places I've lived and from my own mixed race background, any resemblance to people, places, cultures Indigenous or other, and languages in our world is purely coincidental.

One Further Note to the Reader
about Pronoun Usage

THE CHARACTERS FROM another dimension who can shift to be either male or female when assuming a physical form in Tas's world, I have chosen to adopt the pronouns ze and zer instead of the, they/them usage more commonly used to determine a person's non-binary gender. The ze/zer as well as the word "per" have been adopted by other SF writers in the past, and I personally have chosen to use these terms because I find, they them, confusing and I suspect others might as well.

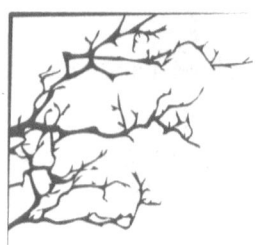

Dedication

This book is dedicated to all the refugees and displaced indigenous peoples around the world. It is also dedicated to my children and grandchildren. Not being a woman of material wealth, my writing is my legacy to boththem, and all the children who are our cherished future. Also in dedication, I offer my eternal gratitude for the traditional teachings of my grandparents, aunties, and the other Elders I've met over the years who have taken the time to teach me. The wisdom and strength of my Elders has always been, and will continue to be, an inspiration in my life.

Acknowledgements

I WOULD LIKE TO THANK for their support, my four sons, my daughter, and my friends when I needed them. Paula, and Lila, your friendship and help with proof reading, cover design, and other editing was greatly appreciated.

Daniel, your edits and suggestions were beyond price for the first edition of the first book in this series. I would also like to thank the folks at Kegedonce Press for their dedication, hard work, their vision, and their fearless determination to encourage Indigenous writers of all types.

A Brief Summary of the Earlier Books

In book one, *Taste of Memory*, Tasimu, a youth with special gifts he has inherited from his mysterious father dwelling in another dimension, is forced with his family to move away from their ancestral home when the invaders discover gold in their northern mountains. Tribal members who converted to the invaders' religion signed a treaty in which all the northern peoples were forced to relocate to a newly created Tribal Preserve.

During their traumatic journey south to the desert Preserve, Tasimu finds a man who knows of his unique heritage, and can teach him how to use his magical gifts, if Tasimu will agree to help with his own quest for revenge against the converts whom he blames for giving away tribal lands.

Book one ends with Tasimu morning the loss of family members and fearing what will await them in this new southern land.

IN BOOK TWO, *When Memory Dies,* Tasimu and his people finally arrive on the barren, water-starved land they have been allotted only to discover that the treaty goods they were promised are slow to arrive or never show up at all. Conflicts between different factions grow and fester, ending in violence. In retaliation for their agent's thievery, a faction of warriors leaves the Preserve to raid enemy settlements nearby to feed their starving relatives.

Caught in the middle between two warring factions, Tasimu endures beatings and scorn by both sides. When he is contacted by the outlaws who need a person with power to help them, he agrees. The desert war leader, who starts to see Tasimu like a son, is badly wounded. He and Tasimu barely escape with their lives during a raid on the agency to rescue his mother and grandfather.

IN BOOK THREE, *Abandoning Memory,* The war leader is told to seek out the Prophet. In the Prophet's camp the war leader does receive healing and he and Tasimu's mother marry and Tas will have a baby sister before spring. While living with his new family the Kukiya war chief Golannah is summoned to a peace negotiation. Tas is included in the delegation. Once at the fort they discover the soldiers and government men plan to jail the delegates and force them to sign a new treaty, giving up more land.

By invoking his Gift Tas and the Kukiya delegation are able to escape the soldiers trap, and another ambush in the desert, but by his use of power another man, a malicer and old enemy of the war chief is alerted and seeks revenge that will set into motion events that will end in a massacre of innocent women and children and the hanging of Tasimu's beloved adopted father and Tasimu's capture.

Book four, *Bitter Echoes of Memory*, is the story of what happens to Tasimu and the other youths captured and sentenced to the live-away school, where the students endure hunger and beatings and Tasimu is forced to use his Gift many times to save his warband of friends and relatives from cruel, sadistic priests and bullying boys.

When a high official comes to investigate accusations of witchcraft, Tasimu is jailed in an underground cell at the school where he is beaten and tortured. But this priest is far more than a temple official. He, like Tasimu, is not completely human. He is a creature in alliance with the enemies of Tasimu's Benefactor. He wants Tasimu to turn traitor and join him. Fortunately the otherworldly being, who is Tasimu's true father, arrives and together father and son escape into another dimension, leaving the burning school behind.

BOOK FIVE: *Reawakening Memory*, begins the story of Tasimu, now a man grown, his magical lessons learned, who wants to go home. He bargains with relatives to return him to the world of his birth, but his tricky cousins bring him back to a place and time of their choosing, in a confusing future, and then they abandon him. They promised him that he has friends and family living in the strange city, so he searches for them and tries to adjust to his new life. He marries a granddaughter of an old friend from his youth and seeks others, but the few who remain, like his sister have become old in his absence.

Knowing that he is hunted by the ancient enemy who is seeking his death for his part in the killing of their favored agent, Tasimu must survive several attempts to murder him and try to make a new life for himself in the unfamiliar world of his future.

A Tribal History of Long Ago, Rushton Archives: Sixth interview with Indigenous Zacatik subject 297

Until being forced to change by the Empire and its soldiers and priests my Qwani'Ya people always traced their descent through their mother's lineage. There were no bastard children among us. All our little ones were loved and cared for by uncles and aunties as well as their parents.

That is not to say that our fathers or men in general didn't play a significant role both in a child's life and the life of the tribe. Our men were the fierce face we presented to outsiders, both in peace and in war, but our chiefs and warriors showed a gentler face to their wives and children. They always took their guidance from the council of clan mothers. A woman is one who holds the life giving force within her body. She has her roots sunk deep into the Earth Mother herself, and can know what is the best path for the people, so the old ones reasoned.

I think the chamuqwani have become so aggressive and crazy, in their endless wars, their harsh religion and their constant striving for personal wealth and new technology, because they don't listen to the voices of their wise women anymore. Allowing only men to rule they are unrooted and ignorant of the true blessings of this world.

As tribal people the most important thing we can do is to keep alive and teach our traditions, not only to our own people, but to all people of good heart. There are forces massing in the Beyond, powerful beings dwelling within the worlds of the Starry River who won't let us survive to infect others with our disharmony. We are doomed unless we set aside our destructive ways and learn once more to walk in balance with all creation.

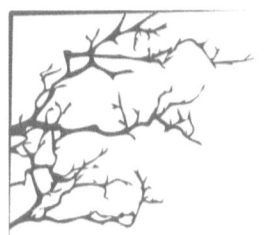

Chapter One

My emotions were still raw. It had been hard to lose my sister so soon after I discovered her in the modern world in which my tricky otherworldly cousins had abandoned me. Kitahtla was no longer the tiny baby I left behind, when I was captured by the imperial soldiers; she was an old woman with an incurable illness when I found her again.

I escaped my live-away school prison, trying to return to her earlier in my life, but I was recaptured by a priest with otherworldly Gifts, similar to my own; and my true father the Qwa'Nayhi Seal man, had to rescue me from his torture and took me with him into the Beyond, where I had remained till a man grown. For that reason, our time together was much too short for my liking.

My new family and I arrived home from my sister's funeral with heavy hearts only to find more trouble waiting for us. Because a spring snow storm in the pass had delayed our return, we had missed the start of the children's school classes and those at the lectorium were already in progress, too.

Meeting us at the door, my brother-in-law Stakaya informed us that a goldy and a new social worker had been around looking for Gahji. Someone has filed a complaint about the children not being in school.

"What?" Leaving Mathrom and Saskina to finish unpacking the vehicle I followed Gahji and her brother back into the house. "What does anyone have to complain about? We went to a funeral; we are caring for our children just fine," I said as I sat down to release the fussing O'siyan from his cradleboard.

"The woman didn't say, but she was angry when I told her you guys had gone back to the Preserve."

"And did you tell her why we took the children out of school and went back to the Preserve?"

He shrugged. "She didn't want to listen."

Barging past us into the kitchen to make a fresh pot of kaf-tea Gahji snarled, "It's Win's damned parents again—I would put money on it."

She was angry, by the sounds of thumping and banging she was doing as she made the kaf-tea and put away the leftover food from our trip. Her Bear was snarling, but I could also see the snaking lines of fear writhing through her spirit fire.

When the baby now freed crawled to an open cupboard and began pulling out his favorite pans to stack and bang she yelled at him to stop when she stepped back and nearly tripped over a pot lid. That, of course got him crying to add to the din.

I could see the tears glistening in the corners of her eyes, so I picked up our crying son and left the kitchen, saying I was going to change his nappy. Stakaya too had prudently left for his room, and Mathrom and the other children had decided it was not a good time to beg for a snack and had plunked down on our sagging couch and turned on the picta-view.

I took the fussing little one into our room and did what I said, changed his nappy. By the time we came back into the living room he had calmed down, so I asked Angika and Saskina to watch him while I went to talk to Gahji. For her to be this upset I knew there was more behind the visit, than she had told me about.

Daring to confront the bear woman in her den I entered the kitchen and closed the door behind me. Coming up behind her where she was washing the cub's dirty dishes and muttering curses under her breath I put my arms around her and rested my chin atop her soft black hair. "Tell me what you have been so successfully trying to keep from me."

Turning in my arms she buried her face against my chest. I could feel her whole body trembling as she clung to me. I reached over her shoulder and turned off the tap over the sink, then I guided her to a chair at the kitchen table and sat her in it. Pulling over another chair I sat down beside her and took her hand.

"What's going on, Gahji?"

She dried her eyes on a shirt sleeve, sniffed and began, "You know Tuunac's grandparents have always been after me to give them Win's children. Even after the divorce was finalized and I got custody they kept after me. They've already had me investigated by the Imperial Ministry for

Child Protection a couple times, claiming that I was an unfit mother. The worst was when Stakaya got arrested. Thank all the ancestors for our tribal attorneys. They were able to block their attempts in the past but now..."

She broke off reaching for a napkin to blow her nose. "Until now," I prompted, "what has changed?"

"You and our baby have changed things."

I jerked back as if hit by an unseen fist. "What do you mean, me and the baby? Please explain, my heart."

"When I was here with the children and just going to school and work, those awful people couldn't find fault with me. The kids and the house were clean—or reasonably so, every time they checked on me. The Imperial Ministry had nothing to base a case on and our attorneys made sure they knew if they tried they would lose in court. But then—"

"But then I came along and we fell in love and now we have O'siyan."

She nodded. "When school started again an old classmate who transferred into social work warned me that there were rumors that I was a loose woman who was seeing lots of men and had had another baby by one of them."

"You and other men? Were they as handsome as me?" I joked, trying to make her laugh.

Instead she punched me in the arm—hard. "This isn't funny, Tas. Don't be a stupid mud worm."

"I'm sorry, my heart. I know it isn't funny—not really," I said and rubbed my arm. Did your friend say anything else about us?"

"Win's family is very religious. My not attending their Djoven temple was always an issue with them, even when Win and I were a couple. Win didn't care; he hated the temple anyway, so it wasn't a problem for him, but after the divorce they wanted the children raised in a proper 'civilized' manner. When I refused to let them take Tuunac and later Bijah to the temple with them is when all the trouble with them really started.

"My friend told me a while ago that I should get married to you in the temple and that would stop their claims that I was a whore and unfit."

"Gahji, why didn't you tell me this?"

"Because I know how you feel about Djoven's temple after what they did to you. And we are married already in our Qwani'Ya traditional way."

"What happened to me when I lived among those damned priests doesn't matter now. No, I don't like the idea of giving any priest that kind of power over our lives, but as you and others keep telling me it isn't the same as a hundred years ago. I will marry you in the temple if that will stop all this nonsense of trying to take away our children.

"In fact I can go see the old reverend at the Mother of Mercy temple tomorrow. He would be happy to do it, and we can even go to his meetings every once in a while to keep the appearance that we have changed our evil heathen ways. Why, we can even invite those mean-spirited dog humpers to the wedding to prove it."

She did laugh at that, and I breathed an inward sigh of relief, knowing I had eased her worry somewhat.

I'd like to meet them anyway. Just so I will know whose throat I'm going to rip open if they try to take Tuunac and Bijah, I thought to myself.

Reverend Cal was delighted when I stopped by to ask him. We set a date of a ten-day later when I explained about the Imperial Ministry visit. Though it was short notice and we wanted only a small quiet ceremony I was amazed at the crowd of well-wishers that turned up for the ceremony and the feast afterward that Auntie Megara took charge of. My Gahji looked beautiful in her wachidai regalia and we had a good time visiting with our many friends and relatives.

The grandparents didn't show up but I learned later that some cheeky relative had sent them an invitation. At the advice of Chief Rickson and the tribal attorney Gahji did return the social worker's call and set up a meeting to which Rickson the attorney and I also attended.

When she learned that the reason we had taken the children out of school wasn't to go to the Preserve and get drunk, as she'd been told, but we had gone to attend a beloved elder relative's funeral and that a late season blizzard in the high pass had closed the roads, she had to back down. The chief and the attorney also produced documents and signed reference letters stating that we were both employed and, "of good character."

The whole situation angered me almost to the point of madness. I hated that we had to prove our worthiness to keep our children, because I also knew a chamuqwani couple without a temple-blessed marriage wouldn't have had to suffer through such a humiliation, or live with the fear that their children could be snatched away at the slightest whim of the imperial government and their zaunk-hating minions.

I hoped our compliance to their rules would put an end to this, so my sweet Gahji could sleep peacefully and not wake up crying when the nightmares came to torment her. And it seemed to be—for a while, anyway.

But then...

About a moon after we had our meeting at the Imperial ministry for Child Protection a strange man and woman dressed in business clothes showed up at our door, looking for Gahji and the children. Stakaya and I were the only ones home at the time. Gahji and auntie were planning a surprise birthday for Uncle Samul. She had taken the children with her to Auntie Megara's for the afternoon, growling for Stakaya and me to do a thorough clean of the house, because our house was going to be where the party would be held.

We had just finished and were having a well-deserved cup of kaf-tea when a hard knock sounded at the front door. At the same moment Aqwissa hissed a warning into my mind. Walking into the living room I peeked out the window and saw two unknown chamuqwani on the porch.

One was a tall thin man in an old fashioned black jacket and trousers with a broad-brimmed hat, similar to what the old-time priests used to wear when I was a child. He had a neatly trimmed white beard and hard gray eyes. He reminded me of Director Harriscot and I shivered in spite of myself.

The woman with him was younger, but equally grim in her appearance. She was dressed in a long dark skirt and jacket, her mousy brown hair pulled back into a severe bun.

I opened the front door and stepped out onto the porch, closing the door firmly behind me. "How can I help you?"

The true reason for Aqwissa's warning became clear when I saw that each of our visitors had little red-eyed demons, perching on their shoulders. They grinned at me when they realized I could see them.

<<Have a care, little pests, what you whisper into the ears of your hosts if you want to live. My companion is always hungry.>> I warned.

"I am intercessor Fredderton and this is Celibress Joan. We are from the Temple agency dedicated to the welfare of children. May we come in? We would like to talk to you and, uh, your wife."

"No, you may not." My voice and my stare were as cold as a winter ice storm as I looked them in the eye and I spoke.

They were surprised that I refused them, the woman stepping back a pace when I caught her gaze and held her in my power.

The intercessor was made of sterner stuff; he scowled but held his ground and stared right back. "It would be in your family's best interest to talk to us, young man. We only want to assure ourselves and our patron that the children are being raised in accordance with the teachings of Mighty Djoven."

"And according to Imperial law that isn't up to you or Win's parents to decide. The Imperial Ministry for Child Protection has already done their investigation and made their report. They found nothing to show that my wife and I are unfit parents.

"As a 'private' agency, neither you nor the Temple has any say in the matter, and I don't care how big a donation to your agency the grandparents have promised you to bring them our children. They can't have them."

<<We see you, walking dead man, our power is greater than yours,>> their demons taunted. <<You have powerful enemies and your enemies are our friends. When they kill you, we will take what belongs to Djoven's stupid priests.>>

I allowed my lips to curl into a snarl. <<Come closer and say that to me again, little pests. I can't hear you.>> When Aqwissa hissed at them they screeched and disappeared.

The intercessor studied me closely for a long moment before speaking. "I don't understand why you are resisting the inevitable, young man. Most men would be happy to get rid of children that aren't his, especially now that the woman has given you a son of your own. Why deny the old people the children born to their lineage?"

"You don't understand me, because your people never have taken the time to understand my people and our ways. Among my Qwani'Ya people children always belong to the mother and her family. In keeping with our traditions Tuunac and Bijahgwi are my children and I will love and care for them as well as the child I sired, but even he belongs to his mother's family, not to me.

"And as to Win's parents visiting with their grandchildren, if we could trust them not to send people like you to kidnap them, arrangements could be made through the tribal attorneys and the Imperial Ministry for them to visit. But the children stay with their mother—with us, until they are old enough to decide otherwise." I opened the door and stepped inside. "And you can tell them that, too."

Listening through the door Stakaya had heard enough to know who our visitors were and what they wanted. "When Gahji and the children get home don't blurt out to her about our visitors," I warned. "No need to get her upset after she has had a nice relaxing day at auntie's. I'll tell her later after the children are in bed."

He agreed with me and soon after that he decided to go to his girlfriend Jula's place, and that was probably for the best. When he was gone I went into the now clean kitchen to see what was in the ice box I could cook for our dinner.

As I worked peeling and chopping up potatoes and then frying bacon and deer meat my mind kept mulling over the problem these convert grandparents posed for us. I wasn't going to let them take our children, but what had the demons meant when they taunted me by saying my enemies were their friends? Had the Crokno found another way to carry out their revenge? I shuddered and hoped it wouldn't come to that.

When the family arrived home to the good smells of my cooking all excited to tell me about their day Gahji sensed my joking mood was a diversion. She knew right away that something was wrong, but waited till the children and the baby were asleep before questioning me about what was troubling me.

I knew what I had to say was going to worry her so I waited till we had made love and I could hold her close in my arms before telling her about our visitors. When I finished I could feel her trembling and held her tighter. "I'm not going to let them take our children, my heart. I will sacrifice my own life before I let that happen."

She made a rude noise in her throat and looked into my eyes her mouth hardening into a grim line. "And what good will that do if you go and get yourself killed, eh? Then I will only have four fatherless children to raise and the Imperial Ministry will probably take all of them away unless I find some other idiot zaunk to marry—and I don't want that. Damn it, in spite of your stupid and heroic words, you can't use your Qwakaiva to solve all of our problems. So don't talk to me about your Gift and dying for the family, you stupid mud worm!"

I thought about it for a while just holding her close and stroking her hair. "You are right about me using my Qwakaiva. I will draw too much of the wrong attention if I try to fix everybody's problems that way. What do you suggest we do then?"

"I don't know, and that's the problem."

"Tomorrow I think I will go after work to talk to Chief Rickson—and maybe I wil go see the reverend as well. Rickson can alert the tribe's attorneys and Reverend Cal might know about this agency and how to deal with them."

And then again, he might not, I thought privately, I also suspected that if the modern hierarchy of the temple was similar to what it had been when I was a youth, the Mother of Mercy priests would have little authority to stop the more ruthless dealings that Djoven's devotees were famous for a hundred years ago.

"That sounds like a good idea but..." she hesitated, not wanting to voice her worried thoughts.

"What is it? My beautiful bear woman, please tell me."

She hesitated a while longer then said, "I'm almost ashamed to ask, because I know your Crokno enemies are always looking for you, but it would ease my mind if Aqwissa could go with the children when they are away from us at school."

I posed the question to Aqwissa, before I answered her. <<It is very possible that these treacherous people might try to steal away the children from their school. If you want me to protect them for you then I will form myself into a choker for Bijah to wear.>>

<<Yes, I think that would be best. We will do that in the morning.>>

<<If I go with the children then you will have to be especially vigilant. And don't forget what those little demons said to you.>>

<<I will remember.>>

When I told Gahji she was relieved and soon after fell asleep.

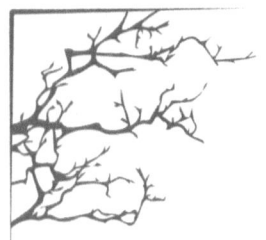

Chapter Two

Two afternoons later I was coming home by way of the shortcut across the homeless encampment and the railroad tracks when a slight noise behind me was the only warning I got before a green arm snaked across my neck and began choking me.

"Traitorous Crokno scum, what have you done to your kin? After we took you in, has your weak human nature finally won out and you have betrayed the ones who sheltered and taught you," Dathna snarled next to my ear.

"Let me go! I don't know what you are talking about!"

"I don't believe you. Where is Zeiva, and your father, for that matter? Have you secretly become the Crokno's new agent among us? Tell me where they are and I will make your death easy when I kill you."

"I-haven't-betrayed-anyone." My hands over zer's I tried to pry zer clawed fingers loose. But with all my Qwakaiva I couldn't. Zer grip was like a vice of iron. "If you want me to speak, Dathna, stop choking me," I finally gasped out.

Giving me an extra hard squeeze ze at last let me go. I doubled over choking and coughing. Barely concealed behind the semblance of a human form, the irate otherworldly being's aura facing me pulsed with murderous fury. I cringed, aware of how close I was to death right then. When I at last could catch my breath, I wheezed, "After what Sabisa's warped child Hoyt did to me I could never betray my father—never! Didn't Zeiva tell you about my sending?"

Ze scowled. "What sending?"

"When you came to the wachidai last summer looking for my father and Utreal I had a sending. Zeiva took it from my mind, because ze wasn't sure I had interpreted it correctly. Ze couldn't believe that Utreal had succumbed to the Crokno's power and imprisoned my father. I begged zer to tell you and the elders. Star Swimmer is in trouble!"

Zer scowl deepened as ze thought. "Ze did mention something about a sending you had, but after ze thought about it more ze also decided that it meant nothing, and when next ze saw Utreal ze would ask zer about it."

My heart churned with the maelstrom of emotions I dared not express lest I anger zer beyond reason. Arrogant and stupid beings from the Beyond! My paternal relatives had always mistrusted my half-breed human Gift, not because I was wrong, but just because I wasn't truly one of them. They thought because of their power they were invincible and humans were an inferior life form.

"The sending was true, and Zeiva thought so at the time when I showed it to zer. Ze promised me ze would tell you and the elders. Star Swimmer has been imprisoned by the Crokno and Utreal is his jailer. And now you tell me Zeiva is missing, too? I wish someone would believe me."

"Hmm..." Then without asking Dathna took my arm firming up zer grip, so I couldn't pull away. "Show me what you showed zer."

I shuddered, bracing myself for what was coming. "It's been nearly a year; I don't know if I can, or how clear the memory will be," I warned.

"Then I will just have to 'take' it, Siyatli worm."

Knowing ze wouldn't care if I was damaged in the process I relaxed as best I could, surrendering to zer probe. Ze took all the information about my sending last summer that ze wanted, but then absorbed far more. Ze plundered the memories of my fights with the Sabiyan hunters and then dug through my childhood making me remember the happy and painful portions of my earlier life including my resistance to my imprisonment and torture by Hoyt, which interested zer the most. At last ze released me and I sagged to the earth, drained and exhausted.

Standing over me ze studied me with a cold penetrating intensity that left me naked and vulnerable. There was no pity or apology in zer gaze. Finally ze spoke, "Unless you are far cleverer than any half-breed I have ever encountered or heard of, you appear to be telling me the truth. I will believe you—for now—or until I learn otherwise. That still leaves me with several unanswered questions, however."

"I know, and I have no answers to offer you. I don't know what has happened, but I will do anything within my power to help them, I swear it, cousin. Please consult with Kunai, Co'yeh, and the other elders of our clan. Tell them what you have learned from me. I beg you. Star Swimmer—and maybe Zeiva, too are in trouble!"

"Yes, I will do that, little siyatli cousin." Dathna turned and without another word ze disappeared.

Unable to regain my feet and continue home I crawled to the side of the trail and threw up in the bushes after ze left me. Even though my house was nearby I lacked the strength left to make it the rest of the way home. I let out an ironic chuckle and dropped my cheek into the grass. If my Crokno enemies found me now... Well, they would have no trouble putting an end to me—that was for certain. Taking deep breaths I lay, hoping the world would stop spinning, before that happened.

I just needed to rest a moment more, and then...

It was growing dark when a worried Mathrom and Stakaya found me and carried me home. I was regaining my strength by then but I was grateful for their help.

"What happened?" a grim-faced Mathrom wanted to know when he threw my limp arm over his shoulder. "Did the Crokno find—"

"N-no Crokno enemy, it was Dathna who came for me. Zeiva didn't take my warning seriously and now ze is missing, too. Dathna thought... Never mind, it's not important."

Mathrom swore, but I ignored him and slipped out of their hold. We were home and I was determined to walk up the back stairs and into the kitchen on my own, so my Gahji wouldn't worry.

My lame effort didn't fool her. She took one look at me and burst into tears and rushed to hug me, nearly knocking me over. "This is all my fault," she sobbed. "If I hadn't begged you to send Aqwissa to guard the children—" she burst into tears again as she clung to me.

"It's alright, my dear one. Aqwissa couldn't have helped me this time. I was being shielded. I probably look worse than I am. I'm not hurt much—mostly just tired," I said as I pushed her gently away. The dizziness was returning and I needed to sit down.

Stepping away she folded her arms across her chest, looking me over for blood and other signs of a struggle. There was no blood, but she must have noticed the bruises around my neck, because she growled, "Just tired, eh? I was worried and your neck is all purple with bruises. What happened to you?"

I sighed and waved a hand in dismissal. I really did need to sit down, but she was blocking my path to the chairs at the table. "Nothing much, it was just a misunderstanding on the part of one of my cousins, and no real harm done."

Seeing my bruises for the first time in the brighter kitchen light, Stakaya's eyes popped wide and with a note of awe coming into his voice, he said, "Wow! With relatives who can do that, who needs enemies?"

"Shut up, Ky, and go clean your room. It's a pig mess," Gahji snapped still glaring at me and not bothering to look at him.

"But Tas and I already gave it a good clean yesterday," he protested.

"Shut up and go do it again," she growled.

The cub murmured something and hastily retreated. I plastered what I hoped was a convincing smile on my face. "I will be alright after I eat and have a good rest—truly."

She made a disgusted noise in her throat that was almost a growl. "Was this 'misunderstanding' with that bitch Zeiva?"

"No, the other one, Dathna, Zeiva is now missing, too—"

"And that stupid bitch thought you were to blame, eh?"

"Something like that—but it's all straightened out now—please, my love can I sit down?"

Gahji snorted, motioned me to a chair and returned to the cooker to pour me a cup of kaf-tea. Still muttering angry curses under her breath, she plunked the cup in front of me and returned to the cooker to retrieve my warming plate of food from the oven.

My throat hurt and the hot drink felt soothing. The meat was too rough, but I was able to smash up the potatoes with my fork and swallow them down. Pushing my plate away, I said, "The meal is very tasty my love, but I'll have to finish the rest later. Right now I need—"

"Need to go lie down," she finished for me, muttering some insulting comments about me and my paternal relatives under her breath as she opened a cupboard door containing our herbs and spices. "I'll make you some lemon and honey tea for your throat and a warm herbal compress to put over those bruises." She made a shoeing gesture. "Go lay down then."

As the spirits in the ceremonial house had warned me this was turning out to be a year of many changes. As the winter storms were waning and sap was beginning to flow up into the tree limbs again Director Rabbitson called Kutima and I into his office to give us some bad news.

"The Imperials have denied our proposal for another year of funding for the Qwani'Yan portion of our language programming," he announced as soon as we were seated. "When we finish for the summer holidays that will be the end of the classes, unless I can find another funding source, before the fall."

The chief had warned me, but it still came as a shock, nonetheless. "Did they say why they were cutting the program?"

Rabbitson shrugged, toying with the paperweight on his desk and not looking at me. "They said that there aren't enough Qwani'Ya people in Seatown and the number of people enrolled was too low for the expense. They want to focus on the coastal languages and maybe introduce Kukiyatan instead."

That made some sense, but it wasn't good news for me personally. I might have to take up fishing—or smuggling with the chief's shady cousin after all.

"You know, director, Tas speaks Kukiyatan, too. Would you be thinking of hiring him for that program if it is approved? He has learned a lot from me and Preceptor Rushton about how to layout lessons for Qwani'Yan that could easily be applied to Kukiyatan," Kutima said.

Still not looking at me, Rabbitson said, "We shall have to see about that. I'm told the tribe has in mind a couple fluent speakers from the Preserve they would like to see teach that program to their members living here in the city."

And that, too made perfect sense, I had to admit. And I also knew the director wasn't going to push very hard for me to be hired for that program. I wasn't sure why, but Rabbitson and I had never gotten along.

"I am sorry to hear about the lack of funding, but I was thinking on turning over the teaching to Tas by summer anyway. I'm getting too old to continue and with Tas here to take over I had planned on retiring.

"But surely if the language program has been canceled you can find something for him here at ZFH," Kutima argued. "He is a good reliable worker with a young family to support."

Looking up at last the director said, "Elder, I can make no promises, but I will see what I can do." And with that vague assurance floating in the air between us, we were dismissed.

Back in our classroom I slumped into a chair and rested my chin on my hands atop the table. "I hate to admit it, but I can see the imperials' point in a way."

"What do you mean? Please explain."

I sighed. "If we are honest here, you would have to admit that most of our students aren't learning much at all."

"I would have to agree, though, like you, I don't like to admit it. There are too many other things like programs on the picta-views that we have to compete with."

"Yes, even with my own children it is hard and I speak to them all the time in our language. They usually understand me, but getting them to actually speak to me in Qwani'Yan is a totally different matter. I wish I knew the answer, because it is so important that now in this time we pass our traditional knowledge on to the next generation, and we can't truly do that if they can't speak our language."

"Then we will just have to learn to teach in a different manner, brother, eh?"

"Hmm, I agree, Kutima, but how?"

"Think about how we learned the two languages we know, Tas. We learned our Qwani'Ya language by listening to our relatives and by doing things where the words we were learning made sense, because they were associated with actions that were important to us and our survival."

He thought about it for a while then chuckled. "And in a more brutal fashion that is how you and most of our people had to learn the chamuqwani language we use today."

I made a disgusted sound deep in my throat, and I couldn't keep the bitterness out of my voice when I said, "Yes, it was a matter of survival, true enough. You learned or you were beaten—or even killed if you didn't speak the enemy's tongue."

"So maybe in a more modified fashion that is the way to teach our young people our beautiful language," Kutima mused.

I stared, I could tell he had been giving this idea some thought, and I was curious. "Tell me what you are thinking, war brother."

"I haven't thought it through completely, but you got me thinking when you took those young people out on the land to teach them the bush skills we all had to learn as children. What if we combined those teachings with the language? Instead of studying a dry book lesson in the class room the students could apply what they learned to their daily activities. I'm sure the words they learned would have more meaning that way and they would absorb our language faster."

I gave him an evil grin. "Especially if they got no food or I smacked their hands with a willow rod if I heard them speaking the imperial tongue, like those damned priests did to us when we spoke Qwani'Yan."

I laughed when I saw his horrified look, then he laughed, too, thinking I was joking. I wasn't joking—not completely, anyway.

Still chuckling, he said, "Well, I don't know if the imperials would let you go to that extreme, but there certainly could be consequences for using the imperial tongue, and rewards for speaking our language."

We discussed the idea further over the next few days and when we had a rough draft of a grant proposal laid out we decided to take it to Rabbitson for his approval.

When we finally had it polished enough to show to the director and a few interested members of the board and we sat around an empty table in the quiet dining room at the appointed time, to my surprise, our proposal, received only a lukewarm reception from them.

"It is an interesting idea," one of the older board members finally said. "But I think it is well beyond the mandate given to our Friendship Houses in our charter from the imperial government."

Pleading on my behalf Kutima said, "But, how can that be so? Doesn't the mandate state that we are to promote and revitalize our traditional languages and cultures? I don't see how this proposal would be a problem for that."

When he finished and looked around the table no one met his eye. "We don't have either the funds or the staff available for such a time consuming project," Rabbitson finally said, still not looking at us.

"Then add those needs into the grant," I said, impatient with their evasions. Like murky pond water I sensed something else was going on here I didn't understand.

Rabbitson's head jerked up as if I had hit him. Taking a deep breath, he said, "It's not that simple, Tas. What you want would take far more funding than the imperials are likely to grant us. And I've already submitted a big proposal to build some badly needed renovations in our kitchen and ramps needed to improve the accessibility for our Elders. I can't ask them for anything else right now."

"Director, surely you and the other board members here can see that a program like Tas and I propose would be of great value to all our Zacatik peoples. Not just those who want to learn Qwani'Yan.

"The program could be broadened to include Kukiyatan and the coastal languages, too. Combining language lessons with traditional bush skills is a natural way for our youth to learn our languages and learn their people's traditional teachings as well."

"And of course, Elder, you would like us to hire your assistant to head up this project, eh?" one of the board members said.

"He would be a logical choice for one of the instructors, so yes. Why not hire him?" Kutima said.

"And this circles back around to our original point about not having the staff or the money to implement such a program at this time, no matter how much we would like to help out a Zacatik brother with a young family."

Leaning forward I rested my arms on the table and looked each of the men rudely in the eye in the chamuqwani fashion. "That isn't the true reason why we are proposing this language and bush skills program for our young people.

"And what we do to preserve our cultures and languages is far more important to the survival of our people—of our entire world than a new cooker for the kitchen or a ramp to the front door," I said, my voice quivering with my emotions.

I was finding it hard to keep the anger and bitterness out of my voice when I tried to explain our reasons to these short-sighted, ignorant people. "This program is important; believe me when I say this. Our very survival may depend on what we do in the next few years."

Rabbitson could see I was growing upset but he misunderstood the cause. Maybe he had heard some of the stories about me, because he let out a nervous laugh and tried to sooth me. "Surely things aren't all that bad in another couple years we can revisit this again—and in the meantime we can probably find at least part time work for you here—"

"Damn it! This isn't just about me and my personal need for a job and money to support my family. I am trying to prevent the destruction of not only our way of life but our world."

When they stared at me as if I had just grown a set of moose antlers on my head I sighed and tried to calm down and explain. "There are beings in the Beyond who are watching our destructive power grow. If we don't return to our old ways and relationships with Earth Mother and the natural world, along with the new technology the Empire's people are developing, they won't *let* us survive to spread our destructive imperialistic ways to other worlds among the stars.

"If you have heard the stories about me as a Puhani, a man with special power and knowledge. It is me, the Puhani, who tells you these things. For our survival we must teach the old languages and the old skills if we want to survive. We have no choice and we must work to convince imperials the truth of that. This is the true reason why Kutima/Keveneth and I are fighting so hard for this program."

The meeting lasted for a while after that, but I could tell by their glazed expressions that they thought me crazy and they couldn't be persuaded to change their minds.

"Maybe Chief Rickson or one of the other Zacatik organizations will be interested in our proposal, Tas, so don't give up hope," Kutima said as Martin settled him in the front seat of his mecho-cart.

I smiled and told him I wouldn't, but I was in a frustrated mood when I hopped on the mecho-transit and headed home.

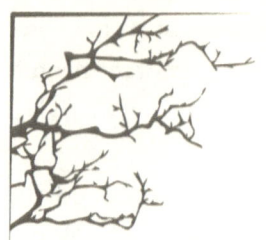

Chapter Three

I didn't tell Gahji right away about the program's termination. I knew she would worry; we were barely getting by since our landlord raised our rent. She would want to extend her work time at the infirmarium, and our son still needed her too much for that. I did ask Rickson about other jobs, hoping that something else would turn up before the classes at ZFH ended.

Somehow Mathrom found out, too, and one afternoon when we were alone and I was cooking some fish over a small fire in the yard he came out and sat down on a log round near me.

He watched me in silence for a while, but I knew he had something on his mind, so I just focused on my cooking and let him tell me when he was ready. At last he blurted it out, "Neko called yesterday when everybody was at school or work. He says he has a job on the rancha till fall, but then he wants to come to Seatown to live with me, because his mom let Rafton come back home and he doesn't want to be there if he starts drinking again—which he probably will."

"I'm sorry to hear about my niece. It's sad, but beat-down women often can't find the courage to be on their own. I guess we can hope that Rafton's fear of my vengeance will keep him sober for some time yet.

"Do you two think you can manage on your own? If the landlord here raises the rent again we will probably have to move as well. We could look for something bigger with a lower level where you and Neko—and maybe Ky could have your own space," I offered.

Truth be told, though not so much the modern custom, I liked having the young people living with us. It was a comforting reminder of my childhood when several related families lived together in the same earthen lodge. I would be sorry to see him go—and Stakaya, too if he ever married the girl he had been seeing for the last year or so.

"We would get allotment stipends from the tribe and the imperial mining companies left on the Preserve, so if we took in at least one other guy we could manage." Then thinking about what I'd said, and didn't say, he offered after a moment's hesitation, "When I wanted to register for your language class next fall I was told it was canceled due to lack of funding. If you need me—and Neko to stay, we could do that, for sure."

I sat down on another round and gave him my full attention. "I am enjoying having you stay here, nephew, and I hope to always be here if you need me. But I also want you to do what is right for you at this time in your life. So, don't make your decision based on my looming unemployment. Like last summer I will have some work at the wachidai dances and the bush school Chief Rickson plans, and I'm sure something will turn up for me by the fall."

He nodded, accepting my answer, but I could tell there was still something on his mind. When he remained silent for a long time, I grew impatient, because the fish was nearly done, and I would have to take it into the kitchen, so I said, "You better tell me the rest of it, nephew."

He sighed. "I heard from a friend in the Kukiya Action League that they were the ones who got older relatives on the tribal council to pressure Rabbitson and the ZFH board to cancel the Qwani'Yan portion of the program. And, probably to get back at you—and maybe me, too, Rody was the one singing the loudest for the change."

He seemed surprised when I only nodded my agreement with the board's decision. Expecting me to fly into a rage if he told me, and afraid of what I might do with my Qwakaiva, that was probably why he was so reluctant to tell me, so I offered him a further explanation.

"Yes, it will be hard for me personally, and Rody may have done his part hoping to cause me ill, but if so, it's not going to work, because I happen to agree that Kukiyatan should be taught here."

When his mouth dropped open I laughed. "Wasn't it you who told me when we first met that your student group was going to 'make' the imperials listen to your demands. Well, they have, and I'm glad of it. Though Qwani'ya by blood on your grandmother's side and chamuqwani on the other, mam Sagila was smart enough to enroll her adopted daughter, my sister, on the

Kukiya tribal roles, which is why you are still able to get those nice stipends to help with school."

"But tribal politics being what it is they won't hire you if Rody's family has anything to say about it, which they will," he angrily complained.

"Yes, I know that, but it's still fine with me," I said patiently. "My Qwani'Ya people were settled in the north and east of the Preserve, so when people left they would have gone to the imperial cities like Prairietown or others further to the east. The Zacatik Friendship Houses back there should be offering that language, not out here. It's alright, nephew, truly, I'll find something else."

Worried about me as well Kutima must have talked to Rushton about my upcoming unemployment, because Rushton called me a few days later to tell me he could offer me some money as a paid informant for his history projects if I wanted to take him up on his earlier offer. I told him I would think about it, and that I appreciated his concern.

At that time in my life I still was reluctant to share my story, but I would do it if I had to help my family. For the moment I was content to wait and see what might happen. I had work lined up for most of the summer so I wasn't in a panic to take the first thing offered. I sensed something was coming and I didn't want to be confined by obligations I might have to break if I was called for some other purpose.

Then along with higher rent and my looming unemployment to trouble our hearts and minds, a neighbor Gahji and I were friendly with told her that she had seen a strange black vehicle driving through our street and often parking where the bushes from the abandoned house across the street would partially conceal it, and its occupants.

"Sometimes they stay hidden over there for a long time, watching your place," the old chamuqwani woman told me when I dropped off a couple bags of groceries I picked up for her at the mission. "And once I saw them taking pictures of the children when they were going somewhere with your wife's brother." I thanked her and told her to call us, if she saw the vehicle again.

Though I knew my news would worry Gahji, I couldn't keep it from her. Though we'd been left alone after the tribal attorneys sent their letter to the grandparents, ordering them to stop bothering us or they could be charged and fined, it would appear the truce was now over. Everyone would have to be on their guard again—especially when I was at work and not with the children. So reluctantly, over the evening meal I told the family what the neighbor had said.

Putting her elbows on the table Gahji buried her face in her hands. Through her fingers, she said, "Why can't those horrible people just leave us alone?"

"I don't know, my heart, I wish they would, too." And, without her needing to ask I told her Aqwissa would stay with the children as much as possible when they were away at school or with other relatives.

Fortunately, the next time the same vehicle showed up, the neighbor called. One look at my angry expression when I got off the far speak and Tuunac's face turned ashy and Bijah's thumb went into her mouth for the first time since school had started in the fall.

"Appi, I don't want'a live with those mean old people," Tuunac said, in a shaky voice.

Kneeling down I pulled both of them into my arms. "I know, and I don't want you to, and I am going to do everything I can to try and stop that from happening, but sometimes in spite of all we do, terrible things can happen. When I wasn't much older than you Tuunac, some of Djoven's mean priests captured me and took me away from my people and killed some of my family.

"Though it hurt me greatly I had to be strong for my war brothers, who were captured with me, so you will have to be strong, too—for all our sakes, just like you were when those alien creatures came to attack us.

"You are a young hunter and warrior, my son, and I am proud of you. If the worst should happen and they kidnap you, remember that and don't let your fears rob you of your Qwakaiva, whatever happens. Protect your sister, try to stay together, and I will come for you—as soon as I can."

Bijah took her thumb out of her mouth to say, "I won't let those bad people hurt my brother, Appi Tas; I will protect him with my Gift and kill them if they try to steal us away."

And by the determined gleam in her eyes I knew she meant it. <<Could she actually do that?>> I asked Aqwissa, horrified.

<<Maybe. I *have* been teaching her how to use her Gift, you know.>>

<<I know, but maybe a few lessons on when and where to use her Gift properly, and the possible consequences are in order if she has progressed that far under your tutelage,>> I cautioned.

Suddenly I realized that Bijah as well as Mathrom needed my magical attention. "Mm, try not to do that, my girl. That would cause many more problems than it would solve. I might have to hide you somewhere away from the family so the goldys wouldn't take you to their jail for children if you did that."

I hoped she would consider my warning and curb her protective dragon nature. But right now I needed to do something about these intruders, because we couldn't live always like prisoners in our home, afraid to leave the children with relatives, or take them somewhere like the beach or the park to have fun.

Turning to Angika, sitting on the couch with the other children, I said, "Watch your baby brother for me, my girl. I'm going to go talk to those people. Lock both the doors and don't let anyone in but your mother, me or uncle Ky, understand?"

She nodded, looking as scared as the others. As I headed for the kitchen door she called to me "Appi, has Amima showed you how to use her picta-snap?"

"Yes. I think I remember, why?"

"Because if they aren't supposed to be here spying or bothering us, then to prove that they are doing those things you need to take their picture to show the chief."

I smiled and headed for our bedroom to find it. "That is a very clever idea, my girl. Thank you for telling me. I don't want to use my Gift unless I have to, but I also want to prove what we say is true."

Sneaking out the back door I crept around to conceal myself in the tangle of bushes and tall grass of the unoccupied house on the other side of the street. As I crept closer shielding myself from notice, Aqwissa murmured into my mind,<<I want to hunt, I have a taste for juicy demon Qwakaiva.>>

<<There are four of them; you can't catch them all before they alert their hosts to our presence, and who knows what nasty tricks that old priest might know to use against us,>> I warned.

<<I will be quick and kill only the young ones with the woman while you distract them with talk and the picta-snap,>> she promised.

Easing closer I reached out a ghostly hand and unhooked something inside the motor of their vehicle. They weren't going anywhere for a while. <<Be careful.>> I said as I stepped to the vehicle and knocked on the side window.

As they turned at the sound I snapped a picture. There was a bright flash of light that I'm sure momentarily blinded them. I took another, and then stepped back so that our house across the street was in the next frame and took a few more. The priest cursed and tried to start the vehicle, but it made only a knocking sound and stayed dead.

"I believe our tribal Attorneys told your agency not to come around us anymore," I said as I let the picta-snap fall back to my chest on its strap. "When I show the defenders and our attorneys these" I tapped the black box around my neck, "your patrons aren't going to be pleased when they have to pay the fine that comes from disobeying Judge's orders."

"That is if they ever see them, you filthy zaunk," he snarled.

I was expecting either a verbal or physical attack from him, but what I wasn't expecting was a magical one. I thought this man demon-ridden but ignorant of the true nature of his ghostly advisors, like old chief Eagan back in the convert settlement I knew as a child. But I was wrong. Like Hoyt, this man knew what power he held and how to control it.

What he didn't realize was that I had power, too, and I also knew how to use it. Still, I had but a moment's warning before his little pests were flying straight for my face with claws extended. Throwing up a hasty shield I formed a knife with etheric matter and slashed at the closest of the little pests as it came for my eyes, slicing off a limb. Dripping smelly ichor it screeched and disappeared back into the Void.

The second howled and charged me. I jumped back and widened my protective shield. Elongating my knife I stabbed upward through my barrier at its belly when it flew over me. I jumped back again, suddenly afraid of what the priest might try while I was distracted fending off his pet.

I needn't have worried. Swooping down from the dead tree's branch like a bird of prey, Aqwissa grabbed the other and disappeared to enjoy her enemy feast.

Before the priest could conjure his own attack, the woman beside him made a gasping sound and slumped forward, moaning. The priest cursed and turned to her. While he was distracted tending to her I faded into the undergrowth and slipped into the house.

Peeking through cracks in the curtains we watched the priest try to start the vehicle again, then he got out lifted the hood and fixed whatever I had dislodged in its insides. In another moment he was back inside, the motor woke up and he drove away.

When they were gone I breathed a sigh of relief and went in the kitchen to pour myself a cup of kaf-tea and calm down. This confrontation was a warning, letting me know that my enemies weren't only from the Beyond. There were humans, like my little Bijah who had power enough to be dangerous if their Gifts were channeled to commit evil.

This priest had just changed the nature of the enemy's assault with his conjure. I had better be ready, because sooner or later these evil men would be back—I was sure of that. Deciding I needed to talk to someone about my concerns, I called elder Samul and asked him to come by later that evening if he had time.

As I put down the far-speak two brown faces peeked around the doorframe. "Appi, we are hungry. Can we have a snack?"

I glanced up at the time-tell on the wall. It was getting late; Gahji would be home soon and hungry, too. "No, but you all can come in here and help me cook dinner for your amima who will be home soon."

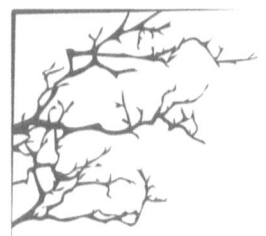

Chapter Four

Elder Samul stopped by after the older children were asleep. They still had school the next day, so they went to bed early. After greeting him Gahji too went to bed, taking O'siyan with her for his bed-time suckle, and they were probably asleep already.

Not wishing to disturb anyone I built up a fire in the yard and set the tea pot over the iron grate to make more kaf-tea. While we sat on the log rounds waiting I tossed some herbs I'd brought back from the Preserve into the flames and we bathed ourselves in the sacred smoke. When I sat back I picked up a pouch of more desert herbs and handed it to the elder.

Samul's eyebrows rose at that and he chuckled. "Isn't it usually me coming to you for prayers and counseling, not the other way around?"

I laughed and poured him a cup of the dark brew. "Maybe so, but this time it is me needing *your* help and advice."

I began by telling him about our immediate problem with the temple's private child "protection" agency actively wanting to steal our children, and the gray-haired priest who used demons to enforce his will.

"For a long time we have suspected this, even though priests like the reverend Cal say the temple no longer condones child abductions, demon enslavement, or witch killings."

"The priest I encountered today gives proof to that lie. If I hadn't had power to match his own he might have killed me, his creatures certainly tried hard enough. If I hadn't been quick to create a shield they could have blinded me, making it impossible for me to identify my assailant if I managed to survive their attack."

"Sounds like you've had some experience with his kind," Samul said, taking a sip of his cooling kaf-tea and watching me over the rim of his cup.

I barked an ironic laugh. "All too much experience. You asked me once to tell you about my stay at Saint Yon's and what happened the night it burned."

I took a deep breath. "Now maybe the time, so I will tell you what happened to me there, and about Grand Intercessor Hoyt and his demons."

And so I told him about the abuse and torture I'd suffered at the hands of the intercessor when I was accused of being a witch. I spoke of Kutima's bravery in contacting Preceptor Rushton's uncle Collin and how my father came and rescued me when Hoyt killed the director and set the school on fire. Though he tried, Samul couldn't hide the horror and the anger that I saw on his face and swirling in his spirit fire.

"The priest I met today wasn't an otherworldly half-breed like Hoyt. I'm positive he is completely human, but he has had otherworldly teachers to enhance his natural gifts—I'm sure of that, too. So for that reason he would be a formidable enemy for me to confront on my own."

"Then we shall have to see that never happens," he said.

After a long pause as he studied the flames in the dying fire at last he continued as if thinking out loud. "This man and his demons are a threat not only to your children, but to all our children. A circle of those with power was how we fought such a malicer in the past. I guess it's time we gather together to do it again."

He stood and picked up the pouch I had given him. "Have those pictures developed and then take them to Rickson. He can show them to the attorneys. Knowing we have them might make the grandparents and the devil priest back off for a while, but you will have to be on guard always, and that is very difficult, stressful and draining. I will help you as best I can."

I felt my temper and my frustration bubbling up ready to explode. "And it's no way for children to live and grow up," I growled.

He snorted a laugh. "Well from one zaunk to another, we don't often get what we want, eh? Your life and your story are proof of that, younger brother, but don't give up hope." He patted me on the back and walked to his mecho-cart.

I left out of my story the part about the priest's demonic pets when I brought the pictures to Chief Rickson. I would leave that part up to Samul to share if he thought the man needed to know. It didn't matter he was furious with what I showed him anyway.

"I will take these to our attorneys today. They will demand that Judge Fredderoth enforce his ruling and prosecute those arrogant people to the full extent of the law. Just because they are rich they think they can get away with anything! Well they can't—not anymore! Don't worry about the children, Tas. We will take care of this from now on."

I nodded to please him; he meant well. But in spite of his effort to reassure me I knew this wasn't over. I sensed that there were other forces gathering in the Beyond, hoping to crush me. The grandparents desire to raise their son's children was like the broad leaves of a water lily floating on the surface of a dark pond. Below their green leafy cover lurked a tracery of unknown roots and stems, waiting to ensnare me if I wasn't careful.

For the rest of that spring we heard no more from Djoven's minions, and as the chief predicted the grandparents were ordered to pay a heavy fine—which their attorneys were still fighting, so no money had changed hands as of yet. They were, however, for the time being leaving us alone.

And then summer was upon us, school was ending, and so was my job at ZFH. To my surprise Friendship House held a big party for Kutima and me, with good food, speeches and lots of people there to thank us for our teachings and to wish us a happy summer. Gahji and the children had also been invited and showed up a bit late in Mathrom's mecho-cart to join in the celebration.

I knew the credit belonged mostly to Kutima for his insistence on keeping the program going, but I was humbled and honored to receive my share of the praise. Kutima had tears in his eyes before it was over and my own eyes were moist as well.

Just before we left Rabbitson pulled me aside with a job offer. "Jamey wants to go back to the Preserve to stay with his elderly parents over the summer. It's only a part-time cleaning job, but if you want it it's yours."

Knowing that Rickson had already hired me to work at his bush camp program and to work at the wachidai dances I guess he figured I would say no, but he could tell Kutima or anyone else who asked that he had tried to give me something and it was my fault for refusing the offer.

So he was surprised when I said, "If you allow me to choose my own times when I do the tasks you assign me I will take you up on your offer."

His eyes opened wide at my agreement and he stammered, "B-but aren't you going to work for Rickson this summer up in the mountains?"

"Yes, I am, and that's why I said I need to choose when I do the work assigned to me, so I can do both. As long as I do my job are you content with me choosing when I do it?"

"Y-yes, but how will you travel back and forth in time to—"

I smiled, showing lots of teeth. "Let me worry about that, director, do I have the job or not?"

He scowled then nodded. "Yes you have it, if you think you can manage. Jamey goes in ten days. See him before he leaves and he will get you sorted out."

Traveling to and from the mountains using my Qwakaiva was going to be very draining, and I wasn't going to be getting much sleep for a while, but we would need the money if I couldn't find anything more permanent by the fall, so I felt I had no choice. With some help from Aqwissa and the forest, sharing its Qwakaiva with me I would manage, I told myself—and hoped it was true.

Rickson's bush-skills program wasn't going to start until the beginning of the next month, so I had plenty of time to work with Jamey and learn his cleaning duties. I had seen him around Friendship House on occasion, he was often at the free lunches, but I didn't know him well. He, of course, knew of me. There was plenty of talk going around about how I had helped get rid of the troublesome drug dealer Jakko and his family last summer.

Fortunately for me his work was done in the evening after the child care and the offices upstairs were empty and the center closed for the day.

Coming in on my own I worked with him a couple times before he left, just to be sure I understood what was expected of me. Jamey was an older man with a big belly and a good-natured laugh. The first night I worked with him, he joked, "When you do this job it's just like being back at school, eh? Lots of sweepin' and moppin' to do."

He let out one of his booming laughs. "Well, at least there won't be a mean old celibress looking over your shoulder to whack your hands if you missed a spot in the corner, eh?"

I laughed along with him. "That's good to know I was worried Rabbitson might have one of those rods somewhere in his desk," I joked and he laughed again.

Jamey was right about the work being all too similar to the tasks assigned to the older girls and some of the smaller boys like me at the live-away schools, so I had no trouble doing his assigned work.

"Have a safe journey and enjoy the time you have with your elders this summer," I told him on the last night before he left. "I will keep the place clean for you while you are gone, so don't worry."

When Rickson's bush camp program started I decided to take Bijah and Tuunac with me. Angika would have liked to go as well, but Gahji would need her to help with baby O'siyan and I had to refuse her. I told her that I was sorry for that.

"The only reason those two are going is because with Mathrom and I both gone they will be in more danger and it would be easier for me to protect them if they were with me. but you and the rest of the family canbring baby and come out to visit at the end of the course for the feast and celebration, and we can stay a couple extra days on our own after everyone leaves," I offered."

She nodded, seeing the wisdom in my argument—or so I thought until she surprised me by saying, "You know, Appi, if you are taking Tuunac and Bijah for their protection you really should bring me and baby, too."

Thinking she was just trying to convince me to bring her, I laughed and said, "And why is that, my girl?"

"Because if those bad people really wanted to get back at you or make you give them Tuunac and Bijah they might take me or baby and bargain with you for a trade."

With her words I felt a shiver slither down my spine and my blood run cold. The thoughts of my beautiful daughter, or my baby son being held and hurt by that evil man and his otherworldly handlers, just to force me to give in to their demands was frightening and definitely a possibility.

And if the enemy thought of this idea like Angika had then I would be completely at their mercy, because I would do anything to prevent them harming my family.

I hugged her and kissed the top of her head before I released her. "Not only are you becoming a beautiful young woman, you are smart, too. Smarter than your old Appi for thinking of that possibility, that's for sure."

She giggled, then with a hopeful expression on her upturned face she pressed, "Then can I come? Amima has been talking about weaning O'siyan so I could bring him and I promise I will watch him, so he doesn't get into trouble—please!"

"Let me talk it over with your mother and see what she thinks. Then I will let you know," I hedged.

Gahji and I talked over Angika's concerns and decided that at least for part of the time I would be away, she Angika and the baby would stay with Uncle Samul and Auntie Megara. She still had a few days of holiday time left, so she would use it and come up with the children. Then if she thought Angika could handle the responsibility she would leave O'siyan with her at our camp when she went back to work.

Mathrom and four other people who took my training course the year before returned to teach. There were also two Smotahlik elders hired who took turns staying at the camp to help out and tell stories of an evening. We ended up with forty children from ages ten to fifteen. There were mostly boys, but we had about six girls, so I was glad that at least one of our return instructors was a young woman.

This was the first year of the program with actual young students there to receive the teachings, so it had its rough patches, probably made rougher by me constantly wanting to make things harder for these young city-born children than they were used to.

Tobey and Carlton, the two Smotahlik elders, kept after me to ease up and not be so hard on the young ones or I would lose them all together. Growing up as I did, and knowing what might be our possible future, that was hard for me, but I did try to heed their counsel.

On more than one occasion I was grateful for Mathrom being there to take over when he could see I was growing impatient and having a hard time of it. He was good with young people and I praised him for his patience with them.

Because, though I hated to admit it even to myself, holding down two jobs, and making the night transfer several times in a seven-day, I was feeling the strain. And though he never complained to me about it he too must have felt the lack of sleep and the stress. For the time I was gone from camp cleaning ZFH I knew he and Cougar would be awake and prowling the nearby woods alert for danger.

Knowing already how to set rabbit snares and choose edible plants and berries Tuunac and Bijah were also turning out to be helpful teachers. When we broke the children up into groups to forage every group wanted one or both of them to be on their team.

I was a bit nervous about letting them go off with the campers, but had to swallow down my own anxiety, because I didn't need to worry them with my fears. Tuunac especially was enjoying the praise he was receiving for his growing bush skills.

When Gahji and the rest of the family came up to join me she told me that while she was staying with uncle and auntie our friendly neighbor called to tell her that she had seen another strange vehicle patrolling our street and paying special attention to our house. For that reason Gahji decided to let Angika and the little one stay at the camp.

I also told her to tell old Yannan that if anyone asked her, we had gone back to the Preserve for the summer. I kissed Gahji and then held the door for her as she climbed into the Elder's cart. "Maybe it will keep them guessing for a while. And you should continue to stay at Samul's when you aren't working until we come home. It won't be too long now."

"Mm, I will think about it." Frowning, she eased her way into the vehicle and closed the door. Rolling down the window, she said, "I really hate this, you know. Why must we live in fear when we haven't done anything wrong? Maybe we should move back to the Preserve, or back up north like you want. Maybe then they would leave us alone."

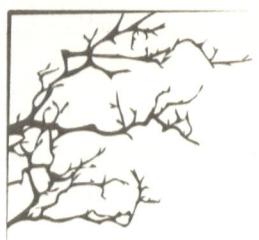

Chapter Five

Once back in Seatown we tried to enjoy the rest of our summer as best we could, in spite of the looming cloud of anxiety hanging over our heads. When Gahji was at work I often took our children out in our canoe to fish and play on the beaches located on tribal land like we had done the summer before. We all felt safer there, because even if the agency's minions came looking for us the children could hide among the trees until I dealt with the enemy.

In spite of my dim job prospects and the looming threat Tuunac and Bijah's Luuchoiyan grandparents posed, I had one pleasant surprise to keep up my spirits during that summer.

One afternoon Saskina showed up with a full-breasted, curly-haired island woman. She introduced herself as Deillah and her face lit up like a sunny day when she smiled.

To give me a break from babysitting Gahji had taken our two youngest with her to Auntie Megara's. Angika hearing Saskina's voice came out of her bedroom to greet our visitors. The two cousins, in spite of their difference in age seemed to enjoy each other's company and often spoke on the far-speak.

Stakaya was home for a change, bringing Denny with him. Those two, along with Mathrom and Tuunac, trying to be so grown up, were watching a ball game of some sort on the picta-view, so I ushered the girls into the kitchen to talk.

While I put on the kettle to make tea Angika peeked around the corner. When she saw that the boys were totally engrossed in their game she retrieved the hidden tin of chocolate cookies she had made and set them on the table to share with the girls.

I chuckled, reached over her shoulder and took one for myself. The tea now ready, I placed cups and teapot on the table next to the cookies.

"I wondered where those were. I thought maybe one of the boys had found your stash and eaten them," I said as I reached for another one.

Angika playfully slapped at my hand. "Appi, you're as bad as the boys. I have to hide my baking from you as well as them, or there'd never be any for guests who drop by."

I laughed and took a bite of my stolen cookie. "That's probably true, my girl—and thank you for reminding me of my manners." I poured each of the girls a cup of my steaming brew, while they helped themselves to Angika's treats as well.

Addressing our island visitor, I said, "You are a long way from the islands where your accent tells me you call home. What brings you to Seatown of all places in the Empire?"

"I'm studyin' ocean sciences," Deillah said. "I wanta learn how ta protect our wota back home and da Seatown Lect is one of de best in de Empire."

Giving me a teasing smile Angika said, "That sounds very exciting. Are you studying about seals? Appi knows lots about seals."

"Really?" turning to me Deillah asked, "How cum a nortern man know 'bout seals?"

Giving my daughter a toothy smile, letting her know I was aware of her joke, I said, "There are seals in some of the larger northern lakes. They are a bit different from the ones here on the coast, but I do know about those seals."

"Well I no be studying seals right now, but if I take a class about them sumtime ma'bee I cum talk ta you."

"We should go fishing with him—or swimming instead," Angika said, still not ready to let me off her hook.

After sampling the tea and a cookie Saskina changed the subject and said, "My new friend Deillah thinks we might be related, so we came to ask you about our family history."

With my spirit sight I studied our guest. Though her deep brown coloring was typical for one born in those far away islands in the southern ocean there was possibly something about her spirit fire that stirred a vague memory.

Not sure how much my niece had told her pretty friend about who I actually was I hedged, "Hmm, there was a woman in our lineage who married a soldier from the islands. When his tour of duty ended, she went back to his island home with him and never came to the Preserve with the rest of the family, so that is a possibility, true enough."

Saskina gasped and the girls exchanged excited glances. "What was her name, uncle?" Saskina prompted when I didn't add more information.

"Hmm, let me see now... was it Kati? No, no that's not it. Maybe it was Jeania, or maybe Tamina."

"Appi, stop teasing them, or no more chocolate cookies or cake for you," Angika warned.

"Oh, my girl, you are so mean to your old Appi," I whined. "Us old ones have memory troubles sometimes, you know. Please just one more cookie." As I reached for the tin Angika snatched it out of reach.

Holding it over her head she said, trying to speak around her giggling, "Appi, stop teasing, what was her ancestor's name?"

"Alright, my girl, alright." Returning my attention to Deillah, I sobered and said, "If you are truly related to the one I am thinking of, then her name was Tuulah and the island man she married was named Ma'leubwey, but I can't recall if that was a family or personal name."

"It a family name, but he die when he boat tip ova in a big storm when me granny still a girl. Great granny she marry he younger brother and dey hav tre more chillens after that."

"We always wondered what had happened to her," I said. "I hope Tuulah was happy in your islands. She lost her oldest daughter Esuli when the soldiers gathered the village up to march south, and then along the way she lost her younger girl to a sickness that spread through the camps and killed many people."

"I tink she happy, ma'bee, she have tre girl and only da one boy. But she not have good luck with men. De brotha was a drunk he."

I chuckled, but there was little mirth in the sound. "So was her first husband Ko. But as Qwani'Ya people we trace our lineage through our mothers, so I'm glad she was able to have the daughters she wanted to carry on her line."

"Dat's wha me granny say, so I guess I am Qwani'Ya too den."

"Yes, niece I guess you are. We are a pretty strange bunch, but you are welcome to join us while you remain here in Seatown."

"But I'm still not sure I understand, how exactly is she related to us, uncle?" Saskina next asked.

"Tuulah was your great grandmother Qwadalah's older sister."

"The one mother was named after?"

"Yes, but she wasn't anything like your mother, believe me."

We attended the wachidai dances, but it wasn't the same without my sister. Her death was still a half-healed scar in everybody's hearts and we missed her. We did try to enjoy ourselves, however, and I think we managed pretty well, because we invited Deillah and Saskina to join us.

Gahji found some old regalia to offer our new niece and Deillah's face lit up with that sunny smile that totally transformed her. The girls took pleasure in dressing her as they told this new relative about the wachidai and taught her to dance.

Because I would need to keep Aqwissa with me while I patrolled, Gahji agreed to sleep at Auntie Megara's with the children when they weren't at the wachidai.

Mathrom and I worked security again, but Danyo was in charge and I just did the tasks he assigned me. We had only the usual attempted break-ins and drunken fights to contend with, and no otherworldly visitors for which I was grateful in part, but it also disturbed me.

I had hoped Dathna would have showed up to let me know what ze had discovered about our missing relatives. But that kind of thoughtfulness wasn't in my paternal relative's nature—so I wasn't surprised when ze made no effort to communicate with me, or answer my own increasingly frantic attempts to contact zer.

Now that I was back in Seatown it made it much easier to do my cleaning job at ZFH, and I was very grateful for that, but Jamey would be returning soon and I needed to start looking for another job. In spite of the risk I was contemplating taking up smuggling with the chief's cousin, when Rushton called to give me some news.

"I just heard that there is an opening on the cleaning staff here at the Lectorium. If you are interested in applying I will be happy to give you a reference letter."

I laughed. "And I will be all the closer to your office if I change my mind about taking you up on your offer to record my story, eh?"

He chuckled. "Well that, too, but do consider it, Tas. The job will be a bit more, uh, 'confining' than what you are used to, but it pays very well, considering what you've been getting at ZFH.It comes with medical benefits and paid vacation time, too. Please at least apply."

"Well, alright, but they may not want to hire a zaunk if it is such a good job as you describe, friend."

He sighed, and after a long pause he said, "Tas, please don't use that derogatory word when referring to yourself. It's demeaning and you have every right to expect a good paying job and to be treated with respect. Uncle Collin and his friend Lord Bronworthy worked very hard to see that all Zacatik peoples have the same rights as everyone else in the empire, so please stop thinking of yourself as unworthy of the good things the Empire can give to you and your people."

"I will try. I know your uncle and his friend did their best to change things." *Too bad the goldys and a whole lot of other imperial minions haven't gotten the message yet.* "And I guess I won't know if I can get the nice job if I don't come and see, eh?"

"Yes, that's right, so please come."

Since I had no other offers pending and the rent and other modern necessities still needed to be obtained, I agreed to meet him the next day after his class and he would walk me over and introduce me and I could fill out the application.

To my surprise Gahji was excited when I told her what I'd done. "Oh, Tas, that would be so good for us if they hire you," she said that night when we were alone and the baby asleep at last.

I was also humbled when I learned that both Chief Rickson and Director Rabbitson sent in reference letters as well. And then it was just a waiting game while the staff finished taking applications from as many interested people as they could before the deadline.

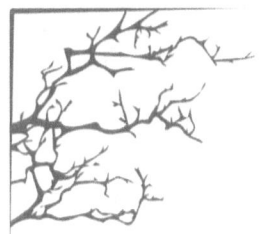

Chapter Six

Our children's school had started and I still hadn't heard about the cleaning job. Mathrom's tribal allowance was late, so he hadn't moved out, and Neko had arrived a few days before. For the moment Tuunac and O'siyan were sleeping in our bedroom, so the older cousins could share Tuunac's room. They needed a space with a closeable door to keep the ever curious and tricky O'siyan out of their things.

We needed our privacy, too, and Gahji was thinking about giving Tuunac Ky's tiny room off the kitchen, because Stakaya was spending more and more time away from our house either with his girlfriend or staying with Denny. Stakaya could sleep on the couch when he did show up at home. We were running out of space and either the whole family or the young warriors would have to move out soon.

It was probably good that for most of the day we were all out of the house and busy elsewhere or more arguments than the usual childish bickering might become a real issue. But after my fearsome mama bear roared her displeasure a couple times when things got too heated and loud, everybody decided it would be best not to annoy her further with their petty squabbles.

The children's classes had started, the Lectorium soon to follow, and we were sitting down to the evening meal when a shiver ran down my spine. Someone had opened a portal from the Beyond and my weak and wounded father was calling to me.

With trembling hands I put down my cup the kaf-tea sloshing onto the table. I don't know what she saw on my face but Gahji turned ashy with fear and quickly put down the bowl of rice she was placing on the table.

Mathrom and maybe Bijah must have felt something too, because they both were staring at me intently. "What is it, Uncle? Has one of your otherworldly cousins returned?" Mathrom hesitantly said.

Ignoring his question for the moment, I sent out my answer to the one summoning me. <<I hear you, father. I'm coming. Show me where you are.>> He sent me an image of tall trees surrounding a bubbling fountain with benches nearby and grass littered with discarded trash.

Nordstrom Park, it was nearby and I knew it. Stakaya used to sell his dealer's product there, but it was also a place the goldys patrolled regularly for that reason. If they thought he was a drunk—or had been in a fight...

"I have to go—right now, my father is here, but he is wounded." I explained without looking at anyone, my attention still focused on the park readying myself for the transfer.

I heard Gahji gasp and laid a hand on her arm to reassure her. Mathrom too stood and to my surprise Neko rose as well. "What can I do to help, uncle?"

"Bring your mecho-cart and meet me at the east side of Nordstrom Park as quickly as you can, nephew." I said as I walked out of the kitchen.

As I stepped out of the trees I saw him on the other side of the fountain standing and talking to someone still lingering in the Beyond. Was it Zeiva, or Dathna? As I looked closer I realized with a shock that the shadowy figure barely visible through the veils of time was my grandfather.

And then the forgotten knowledge hit me like a hammer blow. I had seen this before. My first teacher Chumco had taught me how to enter another's dreams and had encouraged me to spy on my mother's if I wanted to know more about my mysterious father.

To my eternal embarrassment I had witnessed my own conception and followed grandfather when he helped Star Swimmer create a portal into this place and time so he could escape the sabiyan hunters trailing him. I told Chumco at the time that I thought it was me he called to help him, and now I realized it was so.

As the portal closed on the past, I hurried over to him and threw his arm over my shoulder. He sagged into me gratefully. Neko raced up to support him on the other side. Together we hurried him towards Mathrom and the waiting vehicle.

He wheezed a laugh as he sagged against us. "I guess even with help the opening and transfer took more Qwakaiva than I imagined," he said in a weak voice. "Now I also understand why the Great One was so insistent that I not follow my natural instinct to rescue you earlier in your childhood and to let you just stumble on without my interfering until Hoyt made it impossible to wait any longer. If I had, you might not have been here—"

"It's alright father, save your strength. I know I just remembered the dream. We will be to my home soon." I told him as we eased him into the front seat of Mathrom's vehicle and Neko and I quickly hopped in to the back.

"Good thing you came when you did, uncle, a goldy patrol is just around the corner. I saw them turn onto South Street a moment ago."

"Mm, be creative in avoiding them, but don't attract their attention, eh. I don't want to try to carry Star Swimmer and transfer out of a moving vehicle if I don't have to."

Placing my hands at the back of my father's neck I began channeling my Qwakaiva into him to ease his pain and begin the healing. He let out a long sigh and rested his head in my cupped hands.

We were nearing the house when Bijah spoke into my mind. <<Amima says not to park in front of the house. Angika just saw a strange black mecho-cart drive by our house.>>

It could be anyone, a ganger, or someone lost, but I was in no mood to take any chances. I told Mathrom what I had just learned from Bijah and he made a sharp turn and headed across the railroad tracks to come into our yard from the brushy field behind our house.

"I'm sorry, Elder, this may get a bit rough for a short while, but it is safer than going down our street to the front door," Mathrom said to Star Swimmer. "We're less likely to be noticed entering from this direction."

Star Swimmer grimaced. "Do what you need to, young cougar warrior. I'll manage."

As my nephew warned it was rough and bumpy Neko and I both smacking our heads against the roof of the cart once or twice as we drove along the tracks for a short ways and then climbed up the rocky bank to the backyard.

The kitchen door opened before Mathrom had shut off the engine and Gahji was motioning us to hurry. As I helped my father out of the front seat I saw that blood oozed out of a long slash on his side, dripping onto the ground as Mathrom and I helped him up the steps and into the kitchen.

"Bring him into Ky's room, and lay him on the bed. I've already changed the sheets," Gahji said, taking charge. "Angika, bring me my medical kit from the top shelf in my closet. Neko, go with her and lift it down for her if it's too high for her to reach."

Mathrom and I guided Star Swimmer to Stakaya's bed and helped ease him down onto the clean sheet. It didn't take long for it to darken with his blood. Gahji clicked her tongue when she realized he was only wearing a breechcloth and no shirt. "Well, at least I don't have to ask you two to undress him so I can see to his wounds."

She waved a dismissive hand in our direction. "You two get out of here so I can work. Tas make yourself useful and bring me a bowl of warm water. ANGIKA WHERE'S THAT KIT?"

My amused parent caught my eye as I backed out of the tiny room. <<This Qwani'Ya woman is my wife Gahji. Mathrom and Neko, who were in the cart with us are my nephews, Kitahtla's grandchildren,>> I explained as I searched for a bowl and began filling it with warm water in the kitchen.

<<You found her then, I am glad for you; how is she?>>

<<She died in the spring, but I did manage to be with her for a while before her passing and I was able to open the portal and sing her to the ancestors.>>

<<That was a true blessing that I know eased your mind. I knew you fretted about her when you lived with me, even though you never said. The young man looks very much like Nachoga and I see he has also inherited his Cougar. But your wife seems familiar as well. Who is she?>>

Coming back into the room I set the bowl down on the wooden box beside the bed. Angika had arrived with the kit so I took it from her and handed it to her mother.

<<She seems familiar because she is Matoqwa's granddaughter. Maybe you recognized her Bear. She inherited the family guardian spirit from him.>>

<<Mm. That is probably it.>>

With efficient movements and a healer's gentle hands Gahji dressed the wound in his side and the other minor cuts on his chest and arms. Star Swimmer breathed a long sigh and closed his eyes. "Thank you, daughter-in-law, that feels much better."

Gahji acknowledged his gratitude, but her eyes and the Bear in her spirit fire told me that she wasn't fooled by his smile. Wary of this otherworldly stranger that had unexpectedly invaded our home I knew that she wasn't sure she could trust him.

"If you feel well enough to eat a little and drink some healing tea let Tas help you into the kitchen so I can change this sheet. It's bloody and wet and I don't want you sleeping on it."

"Yes, thank you, I can get up and a meal would be good."

With a little help from me Star Swimmer managed to return to the kitchen. I sat him at the table and began heating up the leftovers for all of us. Mathrom Neko and I had all had our meal interrupted and the good smells brought the young men creeping back into the kitchen.

They filled plates then went back to the ball game they were watching on the picta-view. Still too shy to come in and meet their new grandpa, Tuunac and Bijah kept peaking around the kitchen doorframe then retreating to giggle in the living room.

Suddenly there was a loud crash in another part of the house and then we heard O'siyan's wail. "Amima, baby knocked over the toy shelf again," Tuunac called in the next moment.

From the laundry room Gahji shouted. "Then deal with it, Tuunac. I'm busy." There was a long pause then more crying..., "Amima, he won't let me. He wants you!"

"I'M BUSY!"

Then from the living room Neko groaned, "No-o-o!"

Mathrom cursed. "What are you doing? DOG HUMPER!"

"No-o, dog fart, kick it; don't run. KICK IT!" Neko yelled.

"Amima!"

"ANGIKA GO GET BABY!"

From her bedroom Angika answered, exasperated, "I'M TRYING TO DO MY HOMEWORK. CAN'T ONE OF THE COUSINS GET HIM? THEY'RE JUST WATCHING A STUPID BALL GAME."

I took one look at my father's horrified expression and I burst out laughing. "Welcome to my new life. It's not always this chaotic, don't worry."

He grimaced, and then in the next moment he smiled. "Your life... And you love every moment of it, don't you?"

I paused halfway out of the kitchen, thinking. "Yes, I guess I do." Still laughing I went to get my son.

While I was getting O'siyan and taking him to the indoor privy Bijah had mastered her shyness and crept into the kitchen to stare at the new relative. As I came near I heard Star Swimmer say, "My that's a pretty necklace you are wearing."

Bijah giggled. "This is Aqwissa. She is only a necklace—sometimes. She can change and bite people if they are bad. She almost bit Mathrom one time when he hit Appi Tas with a stick, but Appi told her no cause he is a relative, so Appi glued Mathrom to a chair for a while instead."

"My that's quite a story. I can sense that your Aqwissa is a very powerful being. Where did you get her?"

"From Appi. She belongs to him. But he is letting me wear her because some bad people want to kidnap me and Tuunac and we are going to kill them if they try to hurt me or my brother."

"I see, that's very interesting."

"And you two aren't going to kill anyone, my girl, remember?" I said as I returned to the kitchen with baby on my hip. "Your mother is making your bath. Go on now, you have school tomorrow. There will be plenty of time later to visit with your new grandpa."

Untwining herself from around Bijah's neck Aqwissa reformed herself around my arm. I sat baby in his highchair. From the cupboard I pulled out a metal tin and gave him a piece of dry meat to suck on while I finished my own cold meal.

"Is this little one your son?"

"They are all my children in our Qwani'Ya way but O'siyan is a true grandson of your lineage."

Aware of the Otter peering at us from my son's spirit fire Star Swimmer smiled. "I think Qwa'osi and your grandfather are laughing at us."

I chuckled and agreed. "And the little one is already full of mischief and tricks that keep this poor seal man swimming fast to keep ahead of his playful otter nature."

Star Swimmer grunted his agreement. "The being on your arm resembles the qwissa dragon-lizards of Tokay, but I also sense she is more. It would appear we have a lot to talk about."

"Yes we do, but not tonight. You are tiring and need your rest as well as the children. Hopefully Utreal and our other enemies will give us the time to tell each other our stories and make a plan to combat him and the Crokno adversary controlling him in the coming days."

I already had realized that my father's injuries were of an etheric nature even more than a physical one. Someone had drained him nearly to the point of his fragmentation.

My mother, maybe unknowingly, had given him a great portion of her own life's essence while he had been in her care, which explained my grandfather's hatred of my father and the vague dreaminess that affected her for much of my early childhood as she recovered. She had saved him, but the transfer through both space and time to arrive here with me had sapped his power once again.

"I will come to share my Qwakaiva with you in a while but first Aqwissa and I need to ensure our guarding shield is strong for the night."

"Not tonight, son. I can reach out to the earth below us to gather Qwakaiva I have no need to call upon you. In case of an attack while I am here you will need all your strength, because until I can heal I won't be of much use to you. I don't wish to bring any trouble down on you and your family, so I will leave as soon as it is possible for me."

"Trouble?" I snorted a laugh. "Oh, that has already happened. Utreal has tried three times to have me killed and now he seeks to attack me through my children. Your presence here is just one more stone to add to the pile."

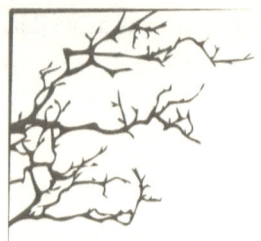

Chapter Seven

By the time I was certain our home was safe for the night. The house was quiet. The younger children and my father were asleep, Mathrom and Neko in their room talking quietly and listening to some modern music on their far-sounder.

It was dark in our bedroom, Tuunac hopefully asleep on the cot by the closet, the little one tucked up against his mother, making suckling noises in his sleep. Gahji had her back to me cradling O'siyan on the bed in front of her, protected from falling by the wall on the other. I undressed quickly and eased myself down beside her, scooting up against her back and enfolding her in my arms.

I kissed her neck and murmured next to her ear, "I won't insult you by telling you not to worry. I know you are afraid—for all of us. But I promise you I'm not going to do anything reckless and foolish, but I *will* do everything I can to ensure—" I murmured a laugh as my twig harden, and I kissed her again, "everyone, including me, remains safe."

Stifling a sob she turned to face me and returned my kiss.

I didn't know what had happened to either Zeiva or Dathna, but I knew at least for a while I couldn't count on much help from Star Swimmer while he healed. I needed both counsel and advice. I would have to risk going deep into the Dream to search for my Benefactor the great dragon Kunai.

In spite of my wanting Aqwissa to stay with the family she insisted that she was coming with me. <<The shield around our family is strong. The Cougar warrior or your father will know if it is breached. But you will be the one most vulnerable as you swim the dark and treacherous currents of the Dream. I am coming with you. Don't argue; I won't listen.>>

I hadn't had many occasions while living with my father in the Beyond to seek the Great One, and since my return to the world of my birth I hadn't bothered him with my troubles either. I was a man grown and I had reasoned

50

that he would probably just tell me to figure things out for myself—which I did, eventually.

But this time I felt I had to risk his ire and seek him out. Utreal's betrayal of my entire paternal clan—and my world, there was much more at risk than a desire for vengeance against a half-breed siyatli. I felt overwhelmed by the problem to which I had no solution. I needed guidance from someone and Kunai was the logical one, my choice.

Swimming the black currents with Aqwissa beside me we came at last to the flat ledge above the dark pool where I had often met him in the past. I climbed out upon the rock to wait and see if he would answer my call. In her natural form the dragon-lizard curled herself at my side, resting her head on her silver coils.

It felt like a long time, but that was only my worry and impatience giving that context to this timeless realm. When he did appear he had chosen to assume the form of my first mentor Chumco, a stern-faced gray haired Qwani'Ya elder, rather than coming in his true dragon form.

Climbing out of the dark water with a blue phosphorescence clinging to his human-looking body, he sat cross-legged on the stone in front of me and waited. His expression gave me no indication of his mood. Dread twisting a knot in my spirit fire, I bowed to him and began my story.

I told him everything that had happened to me since Zeiva and zer hunting pack left me stranded in Seatown, paying special attention to Utreal's three attempts to kill me, my foretelling of Star Swimmer's imprisonment, his wounding and escape.

When I finished and glanced at him expectantly, he remained silent just studying me for a long time, before saying, <<So, what do you and your father plan to do about Utreal's betrayal now that you know?>>

I'm sure my mouth must have dropped open in surprise. <<Me?>>

I was only a siyatli—what could I do against my more experienced cousin with the might of the Crokno behind him? <<I-I don't know. I thought once I told you, and you knew, you would—>>

<<Take care of your little problem for you?>> Kunai rumbled a dragon laugh. <<Ah, but I had foreseen Utreal's treachery before the Crokno captured their lost child and 'induced' zer to change zer allegiance. I know ze has been feeding them tidbits of information about the clans for a very long

time and I was amazed that Co'yeh and the elders of your paternal clan never suspected him.>> He rumbled another laugh.

<<Too bad they didn't believe you, my young Siyatli, when you tried to tell them. It was only after you and your father killed Sabisa's favored half-breed son that Utreal was instructed to discover a way to kill you both and further the destruction of the human world while doing so.>>

Shocked, I blurted without considering the consequences if I angered him, <<But if you already knew, then why didn't you stop zer?>>

Kunai growled his displeasure, his green eyes flashing with menace. <<Have a care, young one, and don't dare to question *my* actions. You may have my favor, but I won't tolerate your insolence, either.>>

When I bowed my head in submission and apologized, he decided to answer me in part. <<I knew, but it would not be wise for me to interfere in the Pattern so openly. It is your world, and your problem. And now that Star Swimmer has chosen to be free with his seed once again, when he created another siyatli—you—it is his problem, too. So I ask again, what do you and your father plan to do about Utreal and zer treachery?>>

What did I plan to do? Fear rippling in my spirit fire a picture of my sweet Gahji, my son—all my children and my newly found relatives and friends came unbidden into my mind. I didn't want this fight; I was tired and after all I had experienced as a child I wanted some peace and happiness in my life—not another war.

Knowing my unspoken thought the dragon said, <<Consider well, before you refuse this task. Long before you gained this new family you prize, you pledged your life and your service to me. Soon behalf of your people—your world—I hold you to that oath.>>

As he should, I thought grimly. Because if Utreal and zer Crokno masters achieved the destruction they craved I would lose them for certain. My family and my world would surely perish in fire and blood. I couldn't just hide myself away and do nothing. I had to act. Even if I lost I would know I died trying.

<<I don't know—yet. Star Swimmer still hasn't recovered from his injuries. I will discuss the problem with him and some human Elders. Then together we will decide what to do next.>>

Kunai chuckled, and reached out a hand to stroke the qwissa dragon lizard crouched beside me. <<Since you have acquired the love and loyalty of the little cousin here use her. She will hunt the enemy for you. Go back to your sleeping body and leave her with me for a while. I will teach her and enhance her power so that she can serve you better in the future.>>

When I woke, Sun was a ribbon of red peering through the bedroom drapes. The little one was now cuddled in my arms and Tuunac lay with his blankets tangled half on the floor, still asleep. Down the hall in the indoor privy I heard the roar of the shower. Saying a silent prayer of gratitude to the Unseen Ones who guarded and blessed us I yawned. I was still tired but it was time to get ready for the new day and all its challenges.

When the water shut off I eased out of bed and touched Tuunac on the shoulder. "Time to get up for school, my son." He grumbled and tried to pull away and turn over, but I tickled him until he was fully awake.

By this time Gahji was back her robe tied loosely around her lovely rounded womanly figure. "Come on we need to go and let your mother dress for work."

By then O'siyan was awake, too, sitting up and watching us from the bed. Knowing he might pee our bed if I waited much longer I scooped him up and the three of us headed for the privy to do our male things. "I'll make the kaf-tea and check on my father," I said and kissed her on my way out.

I heard the girls talking in their room, so there was no need to wake them. I wasn't sure what the cousins had planned for the day, all was still dark and quiet in there, but probably not for long. The smell of cooking bacon would bring them sniffing for food soon enough.

In the kitchen I sat O'siyan in his highchair and gave him another piece of dry meat and a carrot to gnaw on while I made the kaf-tea and began breakfast. With the bacon in the oven and the kaf-tea burbling away as it cooked I peeked in to see how my father was doing.

He was awake and watching me. "Did you sleep well? Are you in pain? Do I need to help you—"

"I am fine and I slept reasonably well—at least until just before dawn when a young man crept up the back stairs and snuck into this room. I figured he must be either a good friend or family because your shield let him pass with only the mildest of warnings." Star Swimmer chuckled then grimaced as he felt his ribs protest. "He was startled to see me lying in this bed, though."

Of all the times for Ky to come home late, I thought. I laughed. "It was probably Stakaya, Gahji's younger brother. this is normally his room, but he's been keeping company with a girl and spending more time with her than here, so that's why Gahji gave you his bed. I guess he's on the couch. I didn't even look when I passed through the living room."

Star Swimmer frowned in thought. "No, that wasn't the name he gave me when I asked. He said Denny, I think. You won't find him on your couch, either. He just collected some clothes and other things and then apologized for disturbing me and went out the same way he'd come in."

"Hmm, Denny is Stakaya's paternal cousin. They are good friends and have been so since childhood. Not sure why he came instead of the cub, or why he snuck in late at night. Those two are probably up to something, but I don't want to try and figure it out at the moment. They have other relatives that will sort them out if need be."

The kaf-tea pot had stopped burbling and I could smell the bacon. I had to go. "It's going to get noisy again for a little while but everybody will be leaving for work or school after that, so you can rest and I can help you more once they are gone. Would you like me to bring you a plate in here, or do you want to come out and eat with us?"

"I will eat in here." He smiled. "Where it's quieter." I chuckled and closed the door.

Mathrom and Neko agreed to escort the younger ones to and from their school, which took one task off my list for the day. Aqwissa had returned to me by dawn, a new golden glitter accenting her silver scales the only noticeable change apparent after the Great One's enhancement. I sent her with Bijah as usual.

When Gahji was about to leave, the far-speak on the wall in the kitchen unexpectedly rang its insistent bell. She was making up her midday meal so she was closest and thinking it was someone looking for the cub I let her get it while I took baby to the privy. We were in the process of teaching him how to use his own little pot we kept under the sink when not needed, so it took a while.

I expected her to have already left by the time we were finished, but instead she was waiting for me.

"That was someone in administration at the Lectorium, about the cleaning job. They want you to come in and talk to them. Your appointment is at one today."

The cleaning job, I had almost totally forgotten about that. What incredibly bad timing to call me now! How could I think about taking the job with everything else happening?

She must have seen the dismay on my face, because she added, "I already called Auntie, she will be expecting you to bring baby by their place around eleven. That will give you plenty of time to take mecho-transit to the Lectorium. Uncle Samul will be home, so don't worry about baby and I'm sure your father can survive for a while on his own."

I took a deep breath and let it out in a long sigh. "Alright. It sounds like you've thought of everything."

She must have heard the resignation in my voice, though I'd tried to hide it. "I know you aren't excited about working there, Tas, but we need the money, so please... I don't want you doing something criminal just so we can pay our rent. It's bad enough I have to worry about Stakaya all the time trying to make money that way, I couldn't stand it if you did that too."

"Alright, my sweet bear woman, I'm going."

When everyone was gone I packed up a bag to take with me to Auntie Megara and Elder Samul's then I took O'siyan and a few of his toys back into the living room to play with him till it was time to leave. Now that it was safe, Star Swimmer came out of Ky's room and joined me.

"I will have to leave in a while to take my son to a relative's while I go to the Lectorium to see about a job Gahji wants me to take."

"You don't sound enthusiastic about the prospect."

I grimaced. "The work will be hard and confining, but I'm used to hard work—that's not the problem—and we need the money. I can't just hunt and fish in these modern times to support my family. No, I'm not enthused as you put it. I can't describe why, but it just doesn't 'feel' right for me to be confined to the regular times of an imperial job no matter the pay, and I can't explain why."

He smiled. "Well if things don't work out as you want and you need money I can help you there." At my open-mouthed stare he laughed. "Think about it, my dear son, how does the clan get the funds we need to buy things when we travel from world to world?"

"...Otherworldly jewels."

"Yes, and when I am able I will provide for you and your family, never worry about that. Think of it as your inheritance from me. To make up in part for my neglect during your childhood."

It didn't—not really, but I chuckled as I'm sure he hoped I would. "That does ease my mind, but I will only take the offered plunder when I need it. I like providing for my loved ones with my work and my skill."

He nodded. "I thought you might say something like that, and I honor you for it. Now while my grandson plays at our feet tell me what has happened to you since coming to this place and time."

And so for the second time in less than a circle of Sun's travel I told my story, only this time I also included my contacting Kunai about our situation.

Star Swimmer grimaced. "I'm not surprised the Great One denied you his aid. In the past I have earned his displeasure and he has a long memory."

"Yes, I assumed that. I'm not sure what you did, but he did make a comment about you making another siyatli—me—and he didn't seem pleased with either of us. Is that what you mean?"

"That's true, but only in part, Tas, so don't be hurt by that. You have proven to be an unexpected surprise and a blessing. Your cunning, your bravery, your strength in battling the traumatic obstacles you've encountered that would have destroyed most humans both pleased and delighted Kunai and all your elders—even if they weren't able to express it to you. I—we are proud of you, never doubt that."

"Thank you for telling me. That means a lot to me." Dropping my gaze I rolled a ball to O'siyan who laughed and threw it back to me. Deciding to voice another question that chafed like an itch I couldn't scratch, I tossed the ball again and said, "Both Kunai and Zeiva have alluded to you having other siyatli children. That would certainly explain many of your long absences when you left me alone in the Beyond."

I looked up to see his face when he answered me. "What I don't understand is why. I would have welcomed having other siblings. Why didn't you tell me about your other children or bring me to be with them?"

He sighed and he took so long to answer I thought he wasn't going to explain, but at last he said, "Living among the traditions of your human, tribal ancestors you would have happily welcomed them, but the others, coming from different worlds and different traditions, they wouldn't. For that reason Co'yeh, the clan elders and I felt it was better not to risk your death by mingling my children. But now that both you and they are grown and matured, future meetings might be possible."

He thought about it further then said, "In fact, it may be to our advantage in this situation with that fish slime Utreal. Yes, my daughter Sichahntri and my son Kotahi might be of great help if Sabisa seeks to bring more of her kindred against us."

Sichahntri, Kotahi? "Ah, father, how many siblings do I have?"

He closed his eyes thinking for a moment, then, "Seven as best as I can remember. Five are siyatli—including you, and the other two are clan-born children, the Sichahntri and Kotahi I just mentioned."

"Wow, I feel a bit overwhelmed at the moment. You have given me a lot to think about."

"We should have a council and talk about all this and if you think it won't be too disruptive for your family I'd like to call those two to join us. They also can offer me Qwakaiva, so I won't have to feed from you."

I let out a nervous chuckle and nodded. "As long as you are sure they won't kill me or renew themselves with members of my family I guess it will be alright. Though this is Gahji's house and she will have to give her approval. It isn't totally up to me."

"No, they aren't like Zeiva or Dathna and that clan of the alliance. They don't need to feed off a human's life essence for a renewal, and they are curious as well, because I recently told them about you."

Trying to plan out sleeping arrangements, I added, "I don't know where everyone will sleep, however."

"They don't need to stay here, just come while we discuss what to do about the threat."

"Ah, that might be best; we can see when they get here. We can talk to Gahji later tonight about this planning council. As my wife I would like to include her, maybe Mathrom, too. He is young, but he has already killed a sabiyan tracker looking for me as I mentioned."

"Whatever you want. I bow to your counsel in this."

As another thought came to me, I said, "Speaking of Zeiva and Dathna, on different occasions I told each of them about my sending. Dathna came here looking for you and Zeiva. Ze told me that both of you were missing. Did Zeiva or Dathna ever find you?"

"Zeiva did find me and ze is the reason I escaped my captivity. Though I wish ze had heeded your warning. Zeiva was lured into Utreal's trap—as was I. We both were Crokno captives for a time. I fear Zeiva may have sacrificed zerself and may have suffered fragmentation, but zer gift allowed me the chance I needed to escape. Dathna I haven't seen. I only hope ze hasn't suffered the same fate."

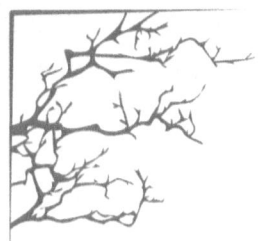

Chapter Eight

I arrived at the Lectorium in plenty of time for my appointment, so I decided to stop by Rushton's office and tell him my news. As usual the chamuqwani woman named Madeline guarding the front scowled when she saw me, but made no objection when I walked in and knocked on the preceptor's office door.

Rushton smiled when he looked up from grading student papers and saw me. "Tas, come in. what a delight to see you."

I stepped in but didn't sit. "I can't stay—and you look busy. I just stopped by to tell you I finally got a call back from the head of maintenance about the cleaning job. I have an appointment in a few minutes to talk to a Supervisor Delton about my hire."

Rushton beamed. "That's wonderful, Tas. I'm happy for you and the family. Do stop by and tell me how things go." He waved at the stacks of papers on the desk. "I plan to be here this afternoon getting caught up with these, and would welcome the distraction in an hour or so."

When I arrived at the maintenance building I was ushered into a bare-walled room with a large table planted in its center. Two men were sitting on the side by the window, their faces half hidden by the outside glare. I was waved to a seat on the other side facing them.

The chamuqwani, a small thin man with a red nose, closely cropped graying hair and watery blue eyes introduced himself as Supervisor Delton. The younger, dark-skinned island man next to him was a large man with strong muscled arms and a hard expression, his face surrounded by a cap of tightly curled black hair. He was introduced to me as Foreman Jefferth. He would be my new boss if they hired me.

Though the men had cups of kaf-tea in front of them no one offered me any from the pot I saw warming on the counter by the sink. When I was seated, Delton cleared his throat and shuffled through the papers in front of him before looking up. Clearing his throat one more time, he said, "Citizen Cougarson, you come to us with excellent references from your former employer and the chief of your band here in Seatown.

"We would like to offer you this position. Before we do, however, we have certain concerns and would like to know a little more about you before confirming your hire."

Wary now, I nodded. Their expressions were veiled, but they didn't know I could read their auras plain enough. They didn't like my people but they were also reluctant to refuse me in case I made a fuss to my chief, a politically unwise move right then. But I could sense they were looking for an excuse to do just that—not hire me.

"What would you like to know? Within reason, I am willing to answer your questions," I said.

"Well to begin with, though Director Rabbitson gave you an excellent referral that is but one job on your resume and it lasted only about a year and a half before the funding was withdrawn. Where did you work before then? We would like to speak to other employers who have hired you."

With a sinking feeling in my gut, I said, "I have only worked at ZFH. There are no other employers."

"I see," Delton said, but he didn't see—not at all. "So what did you do to support yourself before then?"

I shrugged. "Mostly I just hunted and fished and traded my catch for anything else I needed, before coming to Seatown and getting married."

"You were living on the Preserve?"

"Yes, mostly."

Giving me a toothy hard eyed smile, Foreman Jefferth said in a gravelly smoker's voice. "The Preserve, huh? How long were you in prison and for what crime?"

I jerked back as if he had hit me. I felt the flush of anger reddening my face and I swallowed before answering, trying to control my fury. "You will find no record of me being in either the empire's jails or their prisons."

I snorted a laugh. "Unless you want to call the live-away school I attended as a child, a prison. My fellow captives and I certainly did. How about you, island man? What did you call the one you were sentenced to attend?"

He sat back scowling. Like Praiser Simms back at Saint Yon's I suspected this man was a bully who kept his crews in line with fear and intimidation. I would take his orders where the job was concerned, but I wasn't going to let him bully me either. If he tried...

"Maybe you were in jail under another name," Jefferth persisted. "We also couldn't find many references to a Tassele Cougarson, either. Better tell us now; we will find out eventually. What other name did you have—when you were in jail?"

This was certainly an unexpected interpretation of my lack of identification and history that Rickson and I hadn't foreseen. A spark of fear fueling my anger, I said, "I haven't used any other name. I am Tas and have always been Tas."

Before we could get into an argument Delton shuffled his papers again then said, "Yes, you are right, I did check. And I found no record of you being incarcerated for even drunkenness—"

"And, you won't because I don't drink, and never have."

"My that's amazing for one of your, uh, people and very commendable." Not sure if he believed me, Delton glanced at Jefferth, who shrugged then returned his hard eyed stare to me. "As it happens your references and your work history was the best we received. We do have a need for such a fine worker as you appear to be. I'm sure we can welcome you onto our staff as long as you are willing to make a couple of minor changes to accommodate our regulations."

Minor changes? I promised Gahji I would do all I could to secure this job and take the burden of our finances off her shoulders, but I didn't like the sound of that. I took a deep breath. "What are we talking about here, supervisor?"

Delton glanced nervously at Jefferth, cleared his throat again, and then said, "Well, you see even though we are just the maintenance department at this distinguished Imperial Lectorium there are certain standards of appearance that must be maintained so that we set a good example for the students and uphold the school's excellent reputation."

Appearance? What was he talking about? Though I knew they were watching for my reaction I couldn't help glancing down at myself. I had taken a shower before coming here; my long hair was washed and neatly braided.

My clothes were old and a bit faded from repeated washings but they were also clean. I was going to be sweeping and mopping what did they expect me to wear? "I don't understand; what are you talking about?"

"Uh, you will need to cut your hair, citizen Cougarson. Such an old fashioned style presents the wrong image to everyone and we can't have that, now can we? You can understand what I am trying to tell you, right?"

Jefferth smirked, making no effort to hide his enjoyment of my dilemma—the dog humper.

"Yes, I understand—perfectly. What you are really saying behind your fancy words is that you don't want to hire a zaunk like me. I might remind the rich pinker, dog-humping donors who come to give you money, too much of what they did to my people when they stole our land. And we couldn't have that, now could we?"

I stood and held up my hunter's braid to show them, and then I swiped a finger across my facial tattoos. "I am a Qwani'Ya Tsa'adi man. And I am proud of it. My people and I have survived the Empire taking our land and our children, but no more I am not cutting my hair to satisfy a pinker official who is afraid a zaunk cleaning out the shit bowl will scare away a big donation to the school," I snarled. I needed to get out of this office before I did something very, very stupid.

"Now, now, citizen, there's no need to be abusive in your language."

"Oh, my language? Now that is the problem, eh? Make up your mind; which is it my language or my hair?" I snapped.

"Calm down. I can see you are growing upset and there's no reason to take this personal it is just school policy," Delton pleaded.

"Is it? Or is it just something you thought of on the spot to get out of hiring a zaunk?"

"That's not true at all. We have other Zacatik men and women working here," Delton protested.

"But none with long hair, I'll bet."

"Well," he hedged, "there are a few Zacatik women in our offices—"

"What about men?"

"Well, no, but that's different. On a man long hair isn't—seemly."

"To who? My Qwani'Ya people have always worn our hair long and braided. It is a part of our culture and traditions. But like everything else forced upon us by our conquerors you are making us destroy our past, our very spirits if we want to survive. My answer is no. I'm not cutting my hair. I'm not letting go of the little I have left of my heritage—not for you—and especially not for any dog-humping job cleaning up your shit."

"Then I guess we are done here," Jefferth growled also rising.

"I guess we are."

As he came around the table to put a hand on me and usher me out I could see in his eyes that he planned a bruising grip just to show me who was boss. I blocked his hand with my power, making both his arms from his shoulders down unmovable, glued to his side. Eyes wide, he gritted his teeth, trying harder to free himself from my conjure.

Loud enough for only him to hear I said through clenched teeth. "Don't! When I free you, if you try to hit me, you aren't going to like what happens next. I'm leaving and I don't need your help."

As I opened the door I couldn't resist a parting dart. "How much of your soul did you have to sacrifice for this comfortable job, island man? Can you still go home and look your parents in the eye, or be at peace with your ancestors, knowing they see what you have become?"

By the time I slammed out of the front door at the maintenance building my fury had worked up into a raging boil. Without giving myself time to think I transported myself to the hallway just outside the history department's door. I opened the outer door with a bang and stomped over to Rushton's office, flinging open his door, too. Whatever he saw on my face made him roll back his chair and let out a frightened yelp.

"I was a fool to listen to you! I told you they didn't want any zaunk for that job," I shouted, my whole body by this time quivering with my rage. "But you said it would be good—said it would be alright. So I went against my own inner knowing, listened to you, and applied hoping..." I choked on my emotions and couldn't speak. So I just stood in his office doorway rigid, just clenching and unclenching my fists.

We remained like that for a long moment, no one moving. Finally Rushton rose and came around his desk and pulled out the chair he kept for students and motioned me into it. His voice calm and soothing, he said, "Come in, Tas, sit down and tell me what's happened."

After a moment's hesitation I came in and did what he suggested. I sat and buried my face in my hands as I reached for some control.

Squeezing past me, Rushton stepped out of his office shielding me from the view of the woman in the outer office with his half-closed door. In a low voice I heard her say, "Preceptor, shall I call security and have them remove that crazy man?"

"No, no, Madelyn, that won't be necessary. My friend has obviously suffered a terrible shock, but we will be fine now." He paused, then said, "I know it's not part of your duties but I would be very grateful if you would bring us some tea and cookies from the staff room."

There was some more murmured talk, but I didn't listen, wrapped up in my own misery. I was furious with myself for nearly losing control, something I was always cautioning the younger ones like Mathrom not to do, and yet I had fallen into the same iron-toothed trap myself. And above all, I was sorry that by my refusal I would be disappointing my Gahji.

Maybe I should have agreed to cut my hair... No, I couldn't do that, not even for my sweet bear woman—I just couldn't.

When Rushton returned he carried a small tray with two steaming cups and a small plate of golden cookies. Pushing a stack of papers onto the floor he sat the tray down and handed me a cup. Taking his seat again he picked up the other and looked at me over its rim. "It sounds like they didn't offer you the cleaning job."

I let out a bitter laugh> "Oh they offered it to me—could have had it, too—if I agreed to chop off my hair."

In the process of drinking Rushton choked and put down his cup coughing. When he could speak again "They wanted you to do what?"

Reaching for a cookie, I said, "Cut off my braid. They said it was a school policy—and unseemly for a man to have long hair."

"That's preposterous! I've never heard of such a policy."

"They also wanted to know why I had only one job reference—and how long had I been out of prison—and for what crime was I jailed."

Forgetting all about his tea, Rushton leaned back in his chair red spots appearing on his pale cheeks as his own anger simmered. "You had better tell me all about it."

When I finished he was quiet for a long time, finally he said, "How badly do you want that cleaning job? I will help you fight for it if you do."

I brushed a hand across my face and sighed. "Right now I don't know. It would be hard working for Jefferth; he's a bully, but I could deal with that—I've taught bullies the error of their ways before, I can do it again, if I have to. I don't want the job so much as I don't want to worry or disappoint my Gahji.

"O'siyan is still too young for her to go back to work full-time, so that means I need to be bringing in my share of the money the household needs. My hunting and fishing skills help, but they aren't enough."

"Mm, if money is the real issue here then I will pay you to be my informant and you can relate your story to me instead of mopping floors."

Catching the stubborn look in my eye, he continued, "I know it will be hard to trust a chamuqwani, as you call us, even me, but Tas, I truly feel that it is important for you to tell your story for the future of both our peoples. Maybe Delton didn't hire you because you need to work with me on this project instead."

"Aqwissa said I should record my story as well, so maybe I should," I said, putting my thoughts into words. "But how will you afford me? A preceptor's pay isn't that grand is it?"

He laughed. "No it's not, but you see I also have an inheritance from Uncle Collin that I can tap, and I know he would want me to help you."

"I didn't think Collin was that rich either, his friend lord Bronworthy seemed to be the wealthy one."

"You are right there, His family is very rich, most of their favored sons ranking high in the Emperor's government even today. But what you probably didn't know as a child was that my uncle and Yon Bronworthy were more than just friends."

"You mean they were lovers, right?"

"Yes. Oh they were very discreet about their love, and eventually Yon's family forced him to marry a suitable lady, to ensure the succession, but they still managed to see each other, especially when they went on long research trips to the Tribal Preserve. In his will, Yon provided very handsomely for Uncle Collin, who in turn passed on his wealth to me. I being the only one of the nephews interested in history and the one he entrusted with your necklace and amazing story.

"So you see, I am able to provide for you and your family for a while until something better presents itself for you, my friend, so please don't refuse my offer."

I thought about it for a while as I chomped down the cookies and finished the last of my tea. At last I said, "If I do this for you, I want to tell my story in my own way. I will speak of my Gift, of Kunai, my true father and the otherworldly beings who are also a part of my life, not just the parts of my tale that will be suitable for your future history projects."

"It is your life story; you may tell it in any way you like."

I snorted a laugh. "You will be wasting my time and your money if you plan to use what I might tell you for your academic research. No one will believe you if you tell them about otherworldly beings and Qwakaiva."

He chuckled. "That's true, so I will pick and choose what I include in my books and papers, but I think your people and your descendants in particular will appreciate what you and I gift them."

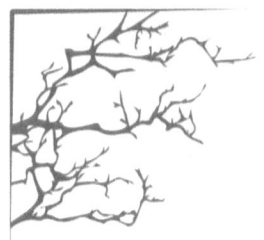

Chapter Nine

When I left Rushton it was growing late, but we had worked out a schedule when I would come in to record my story and he had agreed to put my first payment in my bank account the next day so we could pay our rent on time.

I also invited him over next evening to meet Star Swimmer. His eyes popped wide at that, and he excitedly agreed to come. "As you may recall, he knew your Uncle Collin. I'm sure he will want to meet you as well."

Though I was badly provoked by Delton and Jefferth, it had been a while since I had allowed myself to become so enraged. I would have to take a good look at my thoughts and actions, so I could better understand why I had let that happen. I needed to restore my nahawa, my inner harmony before I went home to my family. So, for that reason, I decided to walk home rather than taking mecho-transit.

It was nearly full dark when I crossed over the railroad tracks and walked up the back steps and into the kitchen. Everyone was still sitting around the table, having just finished a meal, and to my surprise Star Swimmer was with them. He rose saying he was getting tired and offered me his chair. Nodding to everyone he went back to Ky's room for a rest.

Aqwissa had already told them that I was fine, and just taking some time to sort through the events of my day, so no one looked overly worried by my late arrival.

When he saw me, baby let out a happy cry and held out his arms for me to pick him up. Cooing to him I sat down in my father's vacant chair and put him on my lap. As Gahji handed me a cup of kaf-tea and removed my warming plate from the oven Elder Samul, who was also visiting, said, "I take it you didn't get the cleaning job at the Lectorium you hoped for."

I snorted a laugh and took a bite of my fish. When my mouth was clear again, I said to the Elder, "After today I have a better appreciation of the difficulties the cub always complains about when he looks for work."

Baby wanted some of my fish, too, opening his mouth and making impatient grunting sounds. "Alright greedy little otter, wait a moment and I will share." After a couple more bites for myself the next bite I took, I only chewed then put it on my finger for him to take. O'siyan now occupied I hastily grabbed some more for myself.

At my partial explanation Samul grimaced and sipped at his own drink. "What happened?"

"Oh, they offered, but I refused it." When I saw the dismay on Gahji's face I put down my fork and said, "I'm sorry, my heart, I couldn't take the job under their conditions—I just couldn't."

"What did they want you to do that was so terrible, Tas?" she grumped. "The rent is due in ten days; surely you could have suffered with it till something better came along—"

"No, I couldn't—even for you, my sweet bear woman."

"But why? We need—"

"I already have another way to pay the rent; I agreed to record my story for Rushton. He will put money in our account tomorrow that will cover the upcoming rent."

"But you didn't want to do that. What made you change—"

'What were their conditions, younger brother?" Elder Samul asked in a quiet voice, hoping to avoid Gahji's further displeasure with me.

I sighed and resumed eating. I was hungry; a lunch of cookies was hardly a meal. "First they wanted to know why I had only one job reference, and then they asked how long I was out of prison—and what crime I was jailed for. When I protested that I had never been in prison, they said the job was mine if I agreed to shave my head.

"Supervisor Delton said it was a school policy and 'unseemly' for a man to have long hair. It would give the wrong impression to their rich donors if they saw me looking like some tattooed, heathen savage just off the Zerve." I snorted my disgust and took another bite of my food. As I gave baby his next bite, I said, "I told Rushton that in spite of all his uncle's hard work on our behalf, it's still the same old shit if you are a zaunk."

On his way to the living room to turn on another ball game, Mathrom swore and stepped back into the kitchen to hear more. Samul sat back, stroking his chin in thought. "Under the circumstances I would have done the same. You should tell the chief, though. The tribe will fight for you, if you want. That kind of discrimination affects all of us."

"And if I tell the Kukiya Action League, KAL will organize some protests on campus, too," Mathrom growled. "The dog-humpers shouldn't be allowed to get away with this—even that shit Rody would support that!"

Glancing at my father who had come back out of Ky's room to join us after he heard my tale. Our eyes met and he shook his head.

"I can tell Rickson, but I don't want the fuss—or the job." I sighed. "With the children's grandparents looking for any excuse to renew their claim for custody of Tuunac and Bijah, the timing is wrong for me to be so visible in a protest that would involve both the imperial newspapers and the imperial courts."

"Tas is right," Star Swimmer said resuming his seat at the table, and thanking Gahji for the cup of herbal tea she handed him. "Beyond the threat looming in the physical world from Djoven's demon-ridden priest and angry grandparents, there are the Crokno guiding and manipulating events on your world from the Beyond. Never forget about that.

"Right now they are most likely enhancing this demon-ridden priest's power to encourage the children's paternal grandparents in hope of a big donation to his agency, as Tas thinks. Launching a public outcry involving members of this family will only add more fuel to their stuttering fire."

"But, Elder, we can't just let them get away with such open discrimination," Mathrom protested, holding up his own long braids. "We have a right to express our culture and our heritage as we want."

"Yes, in principle that is true, but there will come another time, and another place to challenge your warrior skills, young cougar. It would not be wise to do so now. Have a little patience. You and your spirit ally may be needed for other combats soon enough."

Glancing at the time-tell on the wall Gahji rose and announced, "I have to get the younger ones ready for bed and then I'll come back for baby. Tas, there's berries in the ice box and yellow cake in the tin on the top shelf. See if our guests would like some while I'm gone."

They would, so I got down the cake and grabbed the berries from the ice box while Mathrom fixed another pot of kaf-tea and put it on the cooker. As I handed out bowls of berries and cake I sensed there was a reason Samul had stopped by this evening, which had gotten buried under my own concerns. With that in mind I said as I filled his cup, "It's always good to see you, Elder, but was there another reason behind your visit tonight?"

Samul glanced at my father and his lip curled in a lop-sided grin. "He keeps calling me his elder and though I appreciate the veneration implied it should be me calling him that, eh?"

Star Swimmer smiled in return. "He is only honoring your wisdom, Elder, as am I. His grandparents taught him well, so accept what is due you with good grace, because he is also stubborn and unlikely to change."

Samul chuckled and took a bite of his cake. "There was another reason or two behind my visit, true enough. I didn't know about your father being here, Tas, though Denny had some garbled tale about some strange guy now moved in to Ky's room, but it was about Stakaya that I came to talk to you and Gahji about."

"Stakaya?" with a sinking feeling I realized that the cub was another young man searching for guidance from an elder and maybe I had failed to understand that he might need me, too, in spite of his stubbornness to take my advice about many things.

"With everything else going on, and the house full to bursting with Mathrom and Neko, baby, and my worry over the threat to my other children, I must admit that I haven't given his frequent absences much thought. What has happened?"

"I learned about this only after it occurred, but it seems that the goldy he was dealing drugs for has been pressuring him to come back and work for him. About three nights ago some of the goldy's men beat him up bad."

"Why would Benton do that? Was Ky working for somebody else?"

"He says no, but I'm not sure I believe him. I think he's serious about wanting to marry Jula, though. He's been trying to find a steady job for that reason, so he may be telling me true."

"After today I can sympathize a little better with his search. How badly was he hurt?"

"Pretty bad, but he managed to make it to Denny's and Denny called me. Megara and I went and brought him to our house, where she has been taking care of him. Because of the threat to Gahji's children he didn't want to come here, or tell his sister and worry her further, but I think you and she should know, because I need your approval and your help with what I intend for him."

Gahji had come in and heard the last of what was said. Picking up baby she sank into a chair, holding him on her lap. "What do you want to do, Uncle?"

Samul took another couple bites of cake before answering. "The winter ceremonies will start in about a month, or sooner if the winter rains come early and the storms touch our coast with their power before that. With your permission, Gahji, Tas, I want to sponsor a drubbing for him.

"It's time he enters the ceremonial house for his initiation and gets to know the true meaning of our ancient ways and becomes one with the Spirit who will be his guide and teacher for the rest of his life."

He chuckled and drank more of his kaf-tea. "It will also have the advantage of keeping him away from the goldy and his gangers for a few months, and by spring... Who knows what might have happened to that evil man, eh?"

Gahji and I glanced at one another; she gave me a slight nod and I returned my attention to the Elder. "A drubbing. Not being from the coast I'm not sure what that is or what will be required of us, but we will do what you think is best, Elder Samul."

"If I remember correctly a drubbing is when masked men with weapons, take an unwilling initiate, by force if need be, into the ceremonial house for his or her teaching and keep him there for the winter," Star Swimmer said as everyone turned to stare at him.

"Basically that is it, Honored Elder," Samul said.

At my expression Star Swimmer chuckled. "Close your mouth, Tas, I have visited all parts of your world for several hundreds of your human years, remember? I *have* managed to learn a few things in that time."

I felt my face heat and I laughed, embarrassed. "True enough. So what will you need from us Elder Samul?"

"I have already spoken to some people who will act as his minders and see to his teachings and discipline while inside. What I need most from you, Tas, is your hunting and fishing skills to make sure that the people helping him are fed."

"I will do that for certain," I said.

"I believe there is a financial cost to these things as well," Star Swimmer added. "To pay for the wood that will need to be chopped and for the food for the feasts that will be needed to be bought and cooked, for example. If you allow me I would like to help with that. I've already told my son that he has an inheritance coming from me if he chooses to remain on the world of his birth. He is stubborn, as I said before, wishing to take care of his family himself. But I don't think he will object if I offer on his behalf. That is customary isn't it, Elder?"

Samul nodded. "It is, but I wasn't going to ask, knowing how tight their money is right now. Your contribution would be appreciated."

"Thank you, father." Then, "What else can we do as his family?"

Samul chuckled. "Well, don't tell him what's going to happen, of course. We don't want him taking off to avoid his initiation like he's done in the past." Turning to me, he said, "When he feels better, I was planning on returning him to you to keep an eye on him for me—so he won't suspect what's coming, but you have a house full at the moment, so I guess he can stay where he is for now.

"But maybe on the planned day you could bring him here for a meal, or something. We wil take him here; too many nosy neighbors by my place, who might call the goldys if he puts up a fuss."

"Yes, that will be good," Gahji agreed.

"I will be feeling better myself soon, so I can return to my own realm and the young man can have his bed back." Star Swimmer said.

Samul must have seen my dismayed expression, because he added, "That may not be necessary, Elder. There might be another solution here, if we think creatively."

Samul glanced to Mathrom and Neko standing in the doorway. "It's getting pretty crowded in this house and since you two haven't moved out yet there's that empty house across the street just rotting away, tempting the gangers to come back, trying to hang out there. Why don't you guys go down to city records and find out who owns it?"

"Why would we want to do that, Elder?" Neko asked.

"Oh, because you could offer to buy it with your tribal money instead of paying rent. It might take some work, but you would have your own place and still be nearby for Tas's teachings or if you are needed to protect the children if those demon-ridden priests come back, so think about it, eh?"

"Hmm, that's an interesting thought, and one I never even considered." I glanced at Star Swimmer, who nodded.

Gahji couldn't resist going over to Auntie Megara's next day after work to check on her brother, make sure he was doing alright, and I suspect giving her own version of a verbal "drubbing" for being so stupid as to get himself ambushed by the gangers.

To my surprise the cousins took a look at the abandoned house across the street and decided it was *fixable*. They didn't need to go to records at the city offices, though, because when our friendly neighbor saw them looking at the property she told them she knew the people who owned it and had their contact information somewhere at her home.

Later that afternoon when I was home with O'siyan and Gahji was at work she knocked at our door, holding out a slip of paper to me.

"I found the address and far-speak number those nice nephews of yours wanted," she explained.

I smiled and held the door open wider for her. "Come in elder, and I will make you some tea. Have you eaten? We have some rabbit stew left over from the midday meal would you like some?"

She hesitated, blushing. I knew she had a hard time living on her meager pension, so I coaxed, "Come in, it's no trouble, really, elder. I was just heating up some for my father who is staying with us at the moment."

Yannan followed me into the kitchen and sat at the table. I introduced her to Star Swimmer who was sharing a piece of scau-bread with his ever hungry grandson.

She handed me the paper when I put a bowl in front of her. "Betty was my dear friend for more than thirty years. She died about three years ago and I still miss her. Her daughter Molly lives back east and hasn't really known what to do with the place.

"She tried to sell, I think, but no one wanted to buy in this neighborhood because of the gangs and those who were willing to live here didn't have the money to buy."

Sitting down with my own cup I said, "We might not have enough money, either if she wants too much for it. My nephews say it will take a lot of work to make it livable after the gangers stayed there."

"I will talk to her. It's been a true blessing to have you and your family here, young Tas. I don't know how you did it but everyone feels much safer since you came and made those horrible ganger boys stop coming around. Gahji told me you might have to move, because your family is growing too big for this house. I hope if you can get Betty's place you will stay."

The next day was my first session with Rushton and I was a bit nervous, not sure how it was going to turn out. "When you begin, allow your Qwakaiva to guide you. And stay within the Dream as you speak into his machine," Star Swimmer advised. "Your Gift will decide what our descendants need to know. I know it will be hard as you relive the past, but your sacrifice gives you honor among all beings of the alliance. Consider this work as a part of your service to the Great One as well, my son."

Taking Gahji's advice on my way to his office I stopped by a corner store and bought a flowering plant for Madelyn. I would be coming to Rushton's office regularly now so I would try to make peace with her. In spite of her prejudice I owed her an apology.

When I entered at the appointed time I approached her desk and handed her my offering. "I want to apologize for scaring you when I was here before. I hope you like yellow flowers. I thought they would look pretty on your desk."

She seemed flustered by the gift and the apology. "I am a good hunter and fisherman. If you like fish or meat I can bring you some next time I come," I offered. Rushton came out of his office then and we went to a little room down the hall where he had set up his recording machine.

Taking my father's advice I allowed myself to go into a light trance and swam into the Dream. I began to relive my life, starting with my childhood and the day I had the sending that foretold our removal from our northern home. By the time Rushton came to collect me I was exhausted, but at peace. I had begun my work for my people and for the Great One.

Deciding to strengthen my Qwakaiva by fishing for the family in my sealskin I transferred to our favorite beach and swam for a time just enjoying the feel of the cool sensual water against my sleek fur. When evening shadows turned into nightfall I caught my fish and then returned to the thicket of trees at the back of our house.

Entering the kitchen I laid the fish in the sink and looked around. I could hear the picta-view talking in the living room, but no good smells of kaf-tea or baking scau-bread greeted my arrival. I was hungry. Gahji was at work, but I thought Angika and Mathrom would have at least have started our meal. Feeling a bit grumpy I poked my head around the doorframe to find nephews and children sitting on a brand new couch, watching a favorite program on a new and larger picta-view. It was no wonder everyone was entranced the pictures behind the glass were in color, not just black and white like our old one.

Refusing to become ensnared by the shimmering images I went back into the kitchen and began preparing the fish. Gahji would be home soon after picking up baby from auntie Megara's. They would be hungry, too. Hearing me in the kitchen Star Swimmer came out of Ky's room yawning.

"I take it you are responsible for the new additions to our home," I said as I breaded the fillets and laid them on a tray for frying.

He laughed at my sour expression. "Your Gahji is a very practical woman, who doesn't mind presents from a grandfather who can afford expensive gifts. So set aside your injured male pride, the family desperately needed the new couch. And this one opens up into a bed, which was what Gahji wanted so she could bring her brother here.

"She thinks the gangers might find him over at his uncles or his cousin Denny's and he would be safer here with you and your otherworldly kin around to protect him. So I offered."

"Did you go shopping with her, too?"

He laughed and sat down at the table. "No, I'm not that crazy. And I'm trying to hide my presence in this time and place. Sichahntri went with her and paid for everything then paid extra to have it delivered today. Evidently they had a great time shopping together. You might find other new things in your room later."

I turned round with flour-coated hands to stare at him. "My sister was here? Why didn't she wait so I could meet her, too?"

"She will be back, possibly tomorrow, but for certain when we call our war council. And she will bring your brother Kotahi, if she can pry him out of his favorite tree, and maybe the eldest and most powerful of my siyatli children Wahtzuul will show up for the council, as well."

"All these new relatives, are you sure it will be safe for my human family with so many otherworldly beings here? I know from personal experience your part of my family can be—unpredictable." I said, my voice revealing my concerns.

"Yes, Tas, your family will be perfectly safe. Not only because they belong to you, but because there is a great debt owing to all Matoqwa's descendants when he killed Hoyt that will continue throughout time. We both could have fragmented that night, and I honor my debts, and so does our clan. Your family will be safe and protected now and in the future, no matter what happens to us when we battle our enemy."

Sichahntri, when she next came by to share her Qwakaiva with father had chosen the form of a tall regal-looking dark-skinned island woman dressed in a brightly colored silk dress her arms and breast covered in gold and jewels.

Gahji beamed when she saw her and reached for the teapot to pour her a cup. "Oh, Sichahntri you look lovely today."

Sichahntri laughed, twirling in a circle, making her dress flow with color. "I'm glad you like it. When I finish giving father what he needs, want to go shopping with me again? I plan to exchange these with our friendly broker, and then we can have lots of fun."

Gahji's expression saddened. "I'm sorry; I would love to, but I have to work until the late afternoon today, then I will have to get baby from my auntie's, because I think Tas also has work." She handed the little one another piece of apple, since he had just dropped the last one on the floor.

"Ah, that is too bad, sister-in-law. You work too much and too hard." She held out her arms to Gahji. "Before I trade them let's go in your bedroom and you can choose a necklace and a couple bracelets for your own private horde. I guess I will just have to stay here with father and my grumpy brother—hello, Tas, do you remember me?"

I had to laugh in spite of myself. "No, not really, not in that human form anyway, though your spirit fire is somewhat familiar."

"It should be; I was the old woman who took care of you when Star Swimmer brought you as a badly wounded youth to live with us. Do you remember old Nimua? That was me. I didn't know of our sibling relationship until later, however."

Sichahntri reached up a graceful hand and plucked a tiny hairy creature from the crown of curls atop her head and plunked him down on the table. "And this is your brother Kotahi, though he is being difficult at the moment, insisting on his wood sprite form." The green eyed little creature blinked up at me.

"Asiya brother," I said hesitantly. I couldn't help but wonder who this new brother's mother might have been, but glancing at Star Swimmer's blank expression gave me no clue.

Suddenly Baby gave a delighted coo and reached for him. Not sure what Kotahi might do if O'siyan grabbed him I hastily snatched my son away. "No, Baby, that's not a new toy." When O'siyan began to wail I soothed him with a cookie from the jar on the top of the ice box and he quieted before I sat him back in his chair.

"Oh Kotahi, please change," Star Swimmer said in a bored voice. "My grandson might try to eat you again otherwise."

The being hopped from the table and grew in size, but still kept his hairy rounded body. "Alright, Father, if you insist. Hello, brother Tas."

Not sure if she could trust this new relative, either, Gahji, picked up our son, and they headed for the bedroom.

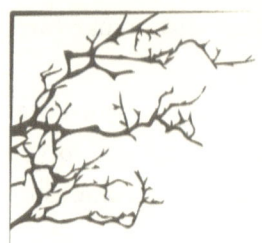

Chapter Ten

About four days after our new furniture arrived Denny's battered old mecho-cart drove up to our house and a bandaged and limping Stakaya got out. He hobbled up the steps and into the living room. His eyes popped wide when he saw our new couch and the new picta-view.

"Welcome to your new bedroom—at least for the time being," I said.

"Wow! This is--amazing." He sat and picked up the little box that turned it on, and began pressing its buttons. Still focused on the picta-view, he said without looking at me, "When did you guys buy this—and who's the new guy you have in my room?"

"The new guy is my father, and he's the one who bought the furniture. And you better keep the noise down. Gahji is sleeping. She has to work tonight. And you know what might happen if you wake her early, eh?"

"Yeah, yeah, I'll keep it down." Then what I said about my parent finally registered and he put down the box and stared at me. "Your Father—your real father, the Qwa'Nayhi Seal?"

"Yes, Ky, that one. He's been injured, and he's trying to sleep, too." I put on my jacket and headed for the front door. "Try not to make a mess in the kitchen if you get hungry."

"I won't. Sounds like Gahji is in one of her moods. Is it her time of the month or something?"

I snorted a laugh. "She better not hear you saying that. And no, it's not her time of the month, as you put it. You just happen not to be one of her favorite people right now."

"Oh." Something on the screen caught his eye and I headed for the door, but before I got there he asked another question, "Where are the desert cousins?"

"Mathrom maybe at the Lectorium today, Neko and my brother Kotahi are probably at the house across the street beginning the cleanup."

"Cleanup? Why do they want to do that? And you have a brother?"

"Because the 'desert cousins' are buying the place—with a little otherworldly help, this house is getting too crowded for everybody. And yes, I have a brother—and a sister, too."

"Wow, is your sister pretty, like Mathrom's sister?"

"Sometimes. Now I have to go. We can talk later."

The truce continued with the Crokno and the children's grandparents so we settled in to a sort of routine after that. Mathrom and the children attended their schools. Gahji and I traded off babysitting and went to our part-time work and my father and Stakaya stayed home and watched the picta-view, or slept, visited at times by clan members from the Beyond or Smotahlik Elders like Samul who were curious about my relatives and wanted to learn more about the Crokno threat.

My brother Kotahi was a gentle creature who spent most of his time in the forests of the Beyond or on worlds similar to my own where he could channel his power into healing.

He was attracted to Neko, a quiet lonely youth who also loved animals and growing things. Neko hadn't yet decided if he wanted to go back to school, but he desperately needed an escape from his troubled home life. I was happy to have him remain with us and even happier when Kotahi chose to linger and wanted to help Neko with the cleanup project across the street. At night he changed into his wood sprite form and stayed in the big dead tree in the yard.

He told me he could sense the seed of life deep within its roots and he was trying to coax its spirit back into its trunk and branches. During the day he became human and the two worked quietly side-by-side, content in each other's company but rarely speaking.

Then the winter storms arrived with power and fury. Mighty waves crashed against the rocky shoreline and the big log drum inside the house of ceremony beat out its insistent cadence, calling the coastal people to honor their ancestors and renew their power for another year.

Though Samul never told even us when the "Bugatzi" were coming, I knew it wouldn't be long. So, one evening when everyone was eating the evening meal—including Elder Samul—who just *happened* to have stopped by, I wasn't surprised when a loud pounding sounded at our front door.

"That sounds like the goldys," Mathrom said and gave Stakaya a murderous look. "Anything you forgot to mention to us about your clash with the gangers?"

"Me? I've been here at the house for the past month. What about you, school boy? You piss off the wrong preceptor at the lect with another stupid, useless protest for Kukiya rights?"

"All right you two, stop! It may not have anything to do with either of your past brushes with the imperials," I said. Like cats and dogs sometimes, it didn't take much to have those two snarling and nipping at each other.

Chastened, Mathrom's mouth hardened and he said, "Do you mean the noise might be that damned agency priest again?"

Both Tuunac and Bijah turned ashy and a frightened whimper escaped from one of them as the pounding came again.

"Angika, take baby and your brother and sister and go in my bedroom and close the door," Gahji said in her firmest no nonsense voice.

<<Aqwissa, go with them and don't let Bijah use her Qwakaiva and try to interfere.>> I told her. <<What is about to happen is Smotahlik tribal business, no affair of ours.>>

Her face as ashy as the others Angika picked up O'siyan and hastily ushered the other children from the kitchen. When they were safely down the hall, well on their way to our bedroom the knocking came again, this time even louder. We all looked at one another, wondering who should go answer it. Finally Star Swimmer rose.

"In case it is the enemy I will go. Tas," he motioned for me to follow, but to stay back.

When Star Swimmer opened the front door a truly frightening sight greeted us. Three tall muscular men carrying heavy wooden weapons and dressed in black with their Entire heads and faces covered with a helmet mask woven of peeled willow branches were on the porch. The weave was loose enough so they could breathe and just wide enough for their hard black eyes to peer out at us.

These masks were also painted black and from the crowns of their masks hung long ragged streamers of cedar bark fiber like snaky hair. Their human forms totally engulfed within the otherworldly power they had called to them for the occasion they were an awesome and terrifying sight.

Showing no surprise or fear my father bowed to them and said in the Smotahlik language, "Welcome, Bugatzi. The one you seek awaits you within the next room." With another bow he stepped aside, as did I and let them pass.

When the fearsome trio entered the kitchen another Bugatzi opened the back door without knocking and came in, blocking off any escape from that direction.

Mathrom and Neko's eyes popped wide and Mathrom started to call his Cougar to him, but when he saw Gahji and the Elder continue calmly eating their meal as if the visitors weren't there, he blinked and picked up his fork and did the same. In another moment Neko followed.

Stakaya, on the other hand knew exactly what was about to happen. Shaking his head he rose quickly, hoping to run, then he saw the ominous figure just inside the back door and turned back to us trembling and ashy. "No, no Gahji, Uncle, I can't do this now—I can't—maybe next year."

Then as two of the three grabbed him and he began to struggle, "Samul took a drink of his kaf-tea and said without expression, "Better go with them quietly, nephew, or they will hurt you and 'make' you."

Stakaya didn't listen and in between his futile attempts to free himself, he gasped. "I can't go—not now. Y-you don't understand! Jula's pregnant with my baby and I have to help her, because her parents will kick her out when they find out. I was getting money together so we could rent a place—"

Gahji put down her fork with a clang. "You stupid ass! And just where were you planning to get this money, eh? By dealing for Benton's rival? How stupid can you truly be, Ky?"

"I was just gonna do it a couple times for her uncle. One of his guys is in jail, but will be out soon. He promised to pay three month's rent on a place for us if I did. I didn't think Benton would find out. And, I figured I could get a real job by then and we would be all right. Please Sis, I have to help her!"

"Help her? Should have thought of that earlier and kept your trousers buttoned," she snarled and picked up her fork and began eating again, ignoring him.

By this time in spite of his frantic struggles the Bugatzi had managed to drag the now bleeding and desperate cub to the living room. I opened the front door for them. As he passed me he pleaded "Please, Tas, help me! I know you have the power to do it, PLEASE!"

The last of the three Bugatzi stared at me his hard black eyes assessing me and my potential threat.

I bowed. <<Be at peace, Bugatzi. I honor your sacred task.>>

"I'm sorry, Stakaya, this is Smotahlik tribal business and neither me nor my father will interfere. Go with them and save yourself a lot of pain."

"Alright, alright, I'm going. But please see what you can do for Jula!" he said as they placed a hood over his head and shoved him roughly into the back seat of a large mecho-wagon.

After they drove away I opened our bedroom door and picked up the whimpering O'siyan and told the others they could come back and finish their meal. They had heard the struggle, maybe even peeked through a cracked open door and seen some of it. Angika was old enough to have heard the stories about Bugatzi and already knew what had just happened. But the younger two were frightened in spite of Aqwissa appearing in her silver dragon form to guard them.

So I spent a moment assuring them that no, it wasn't that mean priest again, and Ky would be alright and we would probably see him later when we attended the winter ceremonies.

Back in the kitchen Gahji had finished her meal and took our son from me, so I could do the same. "I wish he had told us about Jula."

"The young woman's condition doesn't change the fact that this was long overdue," Samul said. "He might not have been so careless if his Siiqwah had been there to guide him."

Gahji sighed. "I don't know much about her, or her family, but I guess if it comes to it Jula can join our bunch. We will just toss a few more potatoes in the pot," she smiled at me, "and it will keep my Seal busy and out of trouble fishing for all of us."

"You don't know much about her family, my girl, because they belong to the faction on our Zerve that are very devoted to the blue-robed priests of Djoven's temple, so Stakaya might be right about them kicking the girl out when she starts to show," the Elder said. Finishing his kaf-tea he rose. "I should go and report to my 'boss.' Megara will want to know it is done."

Continuing the conversation after Samul left, I said to Gahji as I helped her clean up the kitchen. "We can have her come here if her own family abandons her, and we can surely let her know we are here if she needs us, but let's wait and see what happens for now."

My mouth hardened as I thought of these tribal converts who would abandon their own child because of an alien god's teachings.

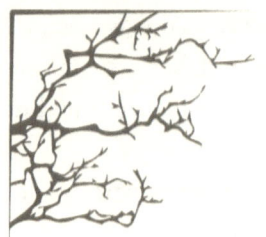

Chapter Eleven

The news that we were fixing up the house across the street must have spread around the neighborhood and the homeless camp beyond the railroad tracks, because several carts of gangers drove by making their vehicles roar like hungry beasts as they slowed down to take a look at our progress over the next few days.

On the day they finally stopped and challenged us I was grateful that Gahji had taken O'siyan and the other children over to Auntie Megara's for the afternoon. The cousins and my brother and I were focusing on finishing up the painting and putting down the last of the tiles in the kitchen so the cousins could move in soon.

The bare skeleton of the plumbing and electric had been already resting between the walls, but in places the pipes were rusted and the wires had been chewed on by mice and other little creatures, looking to nest out of the cold and the weather, so we had had to fix them with some "creative" otherworldly power.

Kotahi and I were in the kitchen laying down the new tiles while Mathrom and Neko were finishing up painting the living room a bright buttery yellow that they said would remind them of their desert home on gloomy winter days.

Suddenly we heard the rumble of one of the ganger vehicles roar down our street. At first I thought it was just another drive through, hoping to scare us, but then we heard it come back and park right in front.

Mathrom peeked out the side of the sheet they had hung over the big living room window and swore as three tough-looking men got out of the vehicle while the fourth stayed in the cart with the motor awake and rumbling. Two of them were chamuqwani with spiked short hair and tattoos of skulls and bloody knives on their arms. The third man was Smotahlik just as big and just as tattooed, and I thought I'd seen him selling tishwa outside the ceremonial house last year. Talking loud so they would be sure we heard them they headed up the side walk towards our front door.

"Looks like they're tired of just looking," Mathrom growled and I saw his spirit fire change as he called Cougar to come to him. "You ready for this?" he asked turning to Neko. Neko swallowed hard, and then nodded.

As I started for the front room Kotahi spoke into my mind, <<I cannot help you, brother. I am sorry the warrior's way isn't the path for one such as me,>> and then he faded away.

<<It's alright, older brother, I understand. Maybe stay with father and try to keep him hidden. These men will expect to see me, no need to alert them to other visitors from the Beyond in case they have a demon companion or two with them.>>

<<Father doesn't need me. I will stay with my tree and the little ones.>> he called and then he was gone.

The cousins hadn't asked for my help, so curious to see how Mathrom would handle this threat I held back, standing just inside the living room, I let him answer the door and watched the gangers through a side window. Neko picked up a heavy metal rod I hadn't noticed, and moved up beside his cousin, keeping his weapon out of sight. Neko already having a weapon to hand made me wonder if they had been threatened before when I was hunting or at work.

Just as the gangers were about to step onto the porch Mathrom appeared and block the doorway. The biggest, and probably their leader hailed him. "Hey, school boy, it's lookin' pretty good. Real nice of you desert brats to fix up our new pad for us. Ain't that right, Waldo?"

The man wearing a red shirt on his left, laughed and nodded.

"It isn't yours or your gang's property, so leave."

"Ain't yours, either, zaunk and the old woman it belonged to is dead, so we say it's ours now," Waldo said.

"City records might not agree with you," Mathrom said, "because we just bought it from Betty's daughter. So, I repeat, leave. You're trespassing."

Harris snorted his disbelieve. "Where'd you get the money? Was it from what Ky owes the goldy?"

"We got our own money," Neko said. "We get a tribal stipend from the pinker mining companies that stole our land. We don't need to sell drugs that kill our people."

"Ah, such righteous words, you a little temple altar boy?" Harris said. "I ain't no priest, but com'ere I got somethin' for ya." He made a rude gesture that made Neko turn red.

"Leave him alone dog humper," Mathrom said taking a step out onto the porch. "He does have money and we did buy this place."

"Oh, yeah? And what about you, Zacahwish'ta'bii with your braids and pretty cougar tattoo, think those make you a real fuckin' zaunk? You got tribal money, too?" The Smotahlik ganger taunted with a sneer.

I tensed expecting Mathrom to explode, but he surprised me by just laughing. "Yeah, actually I *do* get money from the Kukiya allotment, and there's no wish to be about it. I'm an enrolled tribal member and related to one of their great war leaders, Nachoga, he was my great grandfather. You know, he was one of the warriors who used to take some of your people as our slaves."

"Fuck off, fancy boy. We kicked your ass."

Deciding he had had enough of their threatening bluster Mathrom said in a hard voice, "What do you really want this time, Harris?"

"Same as before, we want that stupid shit Ky. Benton says he wants his money that Ky owes us."

Mathrom snorted. "Ky says he doesn't owe the goldy anything. Benton just wants him to work for him again. And that ain't gonna happen."

"Why? 'Cause he's workin' for Dixson now? How'd that work out for him last time he tried cheatin' the boss?"

Mathrom shrugged. "You guys made your point, but Ky isn't here, like I told you before, and he's not dealin' for anybody no more."

Harris laughed. "Sure, the stupid zaunk has said that before, but next time he gets in a jam, he'll be back dealin' only this time he better not try workin' for the wrong guy."

"Where is he?" the chamuqwani named Waldo said, impatient with Mathrom's evasions. "He can go with us and explain himself to Benton. See if he believes that shit."

"He's gone where even Benton can't touch him, dog humper. Go back and tell your goldy boss that."

Harris snorted and stepped a bit closer to the cousins balling up his fists. "Benton can get to him anywhere he tries to hide. You tell him that, school boy. He can't escape. He broke the rules and there's still more owing, so where is he?

"Not here, like I keep telling you."

"Yeah, you keep saying that, but we got our orders. So, it's either him, or maybe someone else in the family will end up paying for what he done," the one named Waldo growled.

Harris pointed across the street to our house. "There's a pretty little girl over there maybe we take her instead, we show her what a real man can do for such a sweet young thing. Then we put her on a corner and she can pay Ki's debt, if he's too much of a coward to make amends himself."

The air around us sizzled with otherworldly power and a low rumble began in Mathrom's throat. "If you, or any of your piss-drinkin' dog-humping gangers ever touch her—or any of my kin, you are a dead man," he snarled. Whatever Harris saw in Mathrom's green cougar eyes made him pause and step back.

Before he could regain his courage and start a physical fight, Neko looked at the Smotahlik ganger with them and taunted, "The Bugatzi came and took him away when the storms came back and the ceremonies began. He isn't here, and won't be coming back, so go away and leave us alone."

"Buga-whatza? What the fuck you talkin' about?" Harris snapped, turning to him.

Neko pointed to the Smotahlik ganger. "Ask him; he knows."

The two chamuqwani turned to their Smotahlik companion for some clarification. The man spat on the ground and swore. "He's talking about some heathen superstitious crap. Which if it's true it means that Ky is going to be tucked away in the ceremonial house on the Zerve for the winter," he said with disgust.

"So, you go there all the time to deal product. You can give him Benton's message even if he's hiding in some fuckin' house," Harris said.

The man shook his head, trying to explain. "It's not that simple."

"No, it's not," I said as I stepped out from behind the big tree Kotahi was trying to coax back into life. "And if I see you over there this winter interfering with the sacred work, well, I'm sure the Bugatzi know how to deal with even a tough guy like you, eh?" At my jab I had the small satisfaction of seeing him pale.

"Stakaya is fine where he is, and no one, not even Benton is going to be bothering him. Understand that well, piss drinker." Rudely staring at Harris I allowed him to feel a bit of my Qwakaiva, as my ghostly hands clamped hard upon his shoulders, pinning his arms at his sides.

"As my nephew says, it's time for you to leave." Tightening my grip I said, "You are a slow learner, gang leader. I warned you what might happen if you came back again. I heard you threaten my daughter—my family. The cougar warrior is right all of you are dead men if I see you here again. Don't come back."

"Maybe next time you won't see us," Harris growled, his struggle increasing. "Boss has new and powerful allies now, so maybe it will be you who is the dead man, witch!"

My lips curled into a mirthless smile. "Maybe so. But you won't live to rejoice in my death if you hurt my daughter, because as the witch you name me, even as a ghost I will come for you. Now get out of here, before I change my mind."

I turned him around with my Qwakaiva and gave him a shove in the direction of the rumbling cart. Knowing that I hadn't come near enough to physically touch his leader, Waldo stared openmouthed at the purple bruises beginning to show on Harris's upper arms. The Smotahlik ganger met my eye for just a moment. Still ashy he bowed then followed his friends back to the vehicle and climbed in. They took off with a loud roar, trailing a cloud of choking black smoke in their wake.

The cousins came down to stand beside me as they drove away. "I hope we've seen the last of them," Neko said.

I shook my head and sighed. "Unfortunately that's not likely, nephew."

"What did Harris mean, uncle, when he said that Benton had a new ally?" Mathrom asked as we went back inside to continue our work.

"I'm not sure, but it means we will have to be extra vigilant for a while, I suspect." I didn't want to worry my family over much, but I feared I knew. I shuddered, suddenly aware of Utreal's traitorous hand reaching out to cut a thread in the weave of my life. When I could catch him alone I would have to talk to my father, and maybe Sichahntri about Harris's taunt.

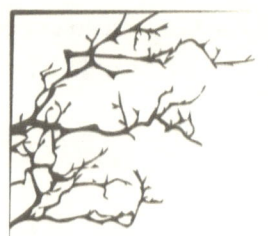

Chapter Twelve

Three nights later the first skirmish in the war that would change all our lives began. In the darkness just before dawn Aqwissa hissed a warning into my mind that had me instantly awake and reaching for my clothes. I had barely pulled up my trousers when I heard the rumble of a mecho-cart motor coming fast onto our street. Moving swiftly into the living room I heard my father come out of his room at my back. The sound was growing in volume as the vehicle came closer.

Peering out the living room window we saw two sleek black vehicles with their cloth hoods lowered roaring down our street. As they passed, a man in the first cart rose up and threw a fiery object at the cousin's house across the street. The missile shattered the big living room window and then exploded into a tower of flames. Seeing that both Star Swimmer and I were now on our front porch the man who threw the fiery missile shouted a taunt, but his words were lost in the mecho-cart's noise as it raced away.

Picking up speed the second cart raced towards us, and another figure rose, and aimed a similar fiery projectile, this time at our house. As he threw his lethal weapon, however, Star Swimmer invoked a powerful conjure that caused his missile to reverse direction and spill its contents over the ganger and the others with him in the back seat of the vehicle.

Instead of my home, the ganger himself burst into flames, screaming. In another moment the entire back portion of the cart was engulfed in flames. Panicked, the driver glanced behind him and then raced away, his speed only making Fire sing all the louder as it feasted.

Trembling with my own fear and rage I watched them go and made no effort to help them. They had just tried to kill me and my family. Then from somewhere in the darkness on the other side of the tracks we heard a loud boom and saw a cloud of smoke and flames rise above the trees in that direction.

By this time, of course the family and half the street were awake and staring. Gahji clutching O'siyan to her was now beside me. I put a comforting arm around her and tried to sooth her trembling. I wasn't sure if she had seen the man aiming at our house. "It's alright, my heart. They've gone. We are safe now."

"For tonight maybe, but will they stay gone?" she said, her eyes flashing with anger. "Oh, Tas, what are we going to do if they come back?"

I kissed her forehead and hugged her. "We will do whatever we can to fight them and all those who want to hurt us. We can do nothing else." Giving her one last hug I encouraged her to take the children and go back in the house.

"I'll make some kaf-tea and start breakfast." She glanced at the lightening sky. "No point going back to sleep now."

Joining Star Swimmer and me on the porch Mathrom swore when he saw the unnatural glow in the living room of their new home.

"Guess those fuckers figured we were asleep in there and they'd be rid of all of us after tonight," he said over his shoulder as he and Neko started across the street.

"Good thing you weren't," I called after him, my heart still pounding in my chest.

"What I would like to know is, were they ordered to do this, or did these stupid gangers decide to seek revenge on their own," Star Swimmer mused loud enough for me to hear.

My mouth dropped open at that chilling thought. "That's a prospect I hadn't counted on," I said grimly. "Let's go see how bad the damage is."

"You go. That conjure has tired me again. And I think Kotahi has already nearly extinguished the flames," Star Swimmer said as he yawned and turned back to the house. "I'm going back to bed."

I stared after him, suddenly worried that he was far more drained of life force than he was letting us see.

Catching up to Mathrom and Neko, together we walked across the street our footsteps slowing as we grew closer, reluctant to see how bad the damage was when we had all worked so hard to restore the old house.

By this time the flames were indeed out, the room inside as dark as a cave. "We will need a new window," Mathrom said, stating the obvious. I snorted a laugh and opened the front door.

Hoping the indoor light still worked I flipped the switch on the wall by the entrance. The light flickered and then glowed bright. It illuminated a golden room with sooty black smoke streaked on the ceiling and the wall where the big window once had been. The floor glittered with shards of glass. Where the missile struck a large charred patch marred the surface of the wooden floor.

Kotahi blinked up at us as the light came on. He knelt at the edge of the damage with his twig-like hands flat upon the charred wood. With my spirit sight I saw him channeling his Qwakaiva into the injury. The damaged wood broke away from the floor, leaving a shiny new surface underneath.

"Go back to our house and get the broom and the other things needed to clean up this mess," I quietly said to the cousins. "I will stay here and help my brother with his restoring work. Tell Gahji I will be here for a while." When they were gone I crossed and knelt behind my brother and placed my hands gently on his shoulders.

I closed my eyes and reached down into the ground below us to draw up the Earth's Qwakaiva to channel to Kotahi. I lack the skill to weave the healing patterns as Kotahi, or even my grandfather could do in a more limited way, but I could offer them the raw power they needed to complete the task.

When we finished sun light was streaming through the gaping hole where the window had been. The walls would need more paint, but the mark, though a bit darker than the wood around it was hard and solid. All traces of the damage no more than a heap of black ash ready to be swept away now.

I got stiffly to my feet and helped my brother to rise. "Thank you, brother," he said, suddenly shy. "Tree was very frightened when it sensed the fire those bad men threw. I had to stop Fire before it hurt Tree."

"It is me who should thank you, brother. The cousins have worked so hard it would have been a true shame to see the house lost. And all the living beings that call this yard their home might freeze or starve if they had to go elsewhere. I was glad you were here to help."

Then his mention of the tree being frightened cut through the fog in my mind. "You have managed to save the ancient then? Will it come back to shade and guard this yard in the spring?"

"Perhaps. As long as no more fires come to frighten its spirit away."

An exploding mecho-cart in our neighborhood was bound to attract the wrong attention, so I wasn't surprised when a cart of goldys drove through, saw the broken window, and began asking everyone questions. The cousins were across the street, trying to nail a couple pieces of old flat-wood over the damage until they could replace the glass.

Just about to walk the children to school I was still in the kitchen finishing my meal when Tuunac alerted me to the goldys coming down our street. Lunch bags on the table by the door Tuunac and Bijah were peering out our window, watching as the mecho-cart parked, the two men inside got out, and then walked over to confront Mathrom and Neko.

Not all the goldys on the city force were thieves and drug sellers like Stakaya's former boss, so it was hard to know what to expect from this pair. By that time Gahji had joined us. "I can take these two to school if you think you need to stay here in case of trouble," Gahji offered.

"I think I should for a while, but I don't plan on interfering unless I have to. Mathrom needs to learn how to handle himself when trouble threatens, so I'd like to just hold back and observe for now."

I put my arm around her and gave her a hug. "If you take them this morning I will get them this afternoon."

She blinked and looked up at me. "I thought you had a session with Rushton then?"

"I do, but I can put it off. You start back on a day shift tomorrow, right?" when she hesitated then nodded, I said, "Well, until your time changes again I can start taking them in the mornings and you or Mathrom can pick them up in the afternoons on your way home." She frowned at this change in our schedule, but at last agreed.

Angika had already left with a group of friends. She was attending a different school this fall for older children, so to avoid the goldys Gahji and the younger two left out the kitchen door and would take the back way to their school. Aqwissa would alert me if there was any problem, I was certain of that, so I kissed them all and wished them a happy day, and went back to my vigil by the living room window.

When the two finished talking to the cousins they split up. One headed down the block to talk to other neighbors, the other man, noticing me come out onto our porch walked over to talk. "Good morning, defender, can I help you?" The goldy was a tall dark-skinned island man with only one badge of rank on his shoulder, and he wasn't very happy to be questioning people he knew weren't going to tell him much of importance.

When he asked me about the broken window I explained, "Gangers used to stay at the abandoned house across the street, but then I guess they decided that it was too rundown for even them so they left. When my nephews bought the house and started fixing it up they changed their minds and wanted it back. My nephews disagreed with that idea, so they figured they come back and destroy it, so nobody would have it."

"Where doze two get da money ta buy da house? Dey dealin'?"

"No, they aren't dealing drugs. Mathrom is attending the lectorium and Neko plans to start next term. They get a tribal stipend while in school, so instead of renting for a high price nearer the Lectorium they decided to buy the abandoned house from the daughter of the old woman who died and fix it up instead."

He nodded his agreement. "Dat smart of dem—if you tell me true. So, what happen last night?"

I shrugged. "I was asleep when it started. By the time I got to our living room the house had a broken window and two dark colored mecho-carts were racing away. I could see flames inside my nephew's new house."

"And where were da boys when dis happen?"

"They are still staying here, but were going to move in soon when they finished and got some furniture." I failed to mention the attempt on my own home, and if he didn't ask, I wasn't going to tell him.

After they'd gone I walked over to check on the cousins. They basically had told the goldys the same story and no one had mentioned the attempt on our house. To the neighbors who might have seen anything at all, the second vehicle starting on fire would have appeared to be nothing more than a failed attack on the house across the street.

But both the gangers and we knew that wasn't true. The little war they had started wasn't over and by the next day when the signs scrawled in red paint, threatening "Death to all loozer wichez, and lect fansee-boyz," began appearing on walls and wooden fences, everyone else in the neighborhood knew it, too.

No attempt to bother Tuunac and Bijah had occurred in a while and this new front of attack was focusing our attention and our Qwakaiva in the wrong direction, Utreal and the Crokno's true plan hidden behind a powerful shield that nearly cost me everything—including my life, and the lives of many I held so dear.

I had forgotten a part of Kunai's instructions to me when he had kept Aqwissa with him for a time to enhance her power. Sending me back to my sleeping body, he instructed me to let her hunt the enemy for me when he next returned her. My failure to use the knowledge gifted me until it was nearly too late, will haunt me for the rest of my life, and unfortunately my gentle nephew Neko paid dearly for my laps.

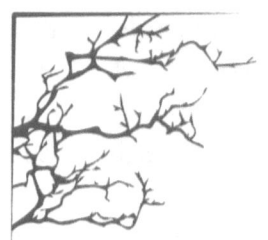

Chapter Thirteen

We had just finished a session and I was having tea with Rushton in his office and trying to restore my inner nahawa from reliving a part of our time on the Preserve, when a cougar's angry scream reverberated in my mind. My hand trembling I hastily put down my cup and rose.

Whatever Rushton saw on my face made him set down his own cup and stare at me, his skin turning a lighter shade in color. "What is it, Tas; what's wrong?"

Focusing on the vision Mathrom was sending me of the brushy trail by the tracks behind our house that passed by the homeless encampment and some old warehouses, I barely heard him as he repeated his question.

"I have to go—no time explain—trouble!" Then not caring if I frightened him when he saw me disappear, I made the transfer.

I projected myself to an alder thicket near a small clearing just out of sight from where men hired to guard Train's road usually patrolled. Stakaya had shown me this hidden spot once, telling me it was a place where people often came to use or sell their drugs and drink their booze.

The first thing I noticed were the two tipped over cans of yellow paint their contents splashed here and there, staining the tall grasses and brush a cheerful warm sun color. But there was nothing warm and cheerful about what I saw next.

Mathrom was surrounded by three gangers with knives drawn. Just as when he had fought the sabiyan hunters he had called Cougar to him, the etheric body of the big cat totally engulfing its human host. Snarling and moving with a cougar's speed and grace he was managing to evade their lethal thrusts. A couple of the gangers had long bloody gashes on their faces and arms and I wasn't sure if it was from the jagged branch he had grabbed for a weapon or from an enraged Cougar's etheric claws.

On the other side of the clearing in the trash and broken plants a bloody Neko lay face down with his trousers around his ankles, exposing his slim brown rear. A large hairy chamuqwani ganger was kneeling between his spread thighs pumping the sap from his twig into my struggling and cursing nephew while another ganger held him down.

Around the smirking gangers danced several little red-eyed demons. The little monsters were chortling and encouraging the men to inflict more cruelties as they gobbled up the pain, fear and malice, wafting in a heavy gray cloud about the struggling trio.

In the middle of the clearing, surveying the whole scene with a cruel smile curving his lips stood Harris. When he saw me push aside the last of the scrub alders and enter the clearing, too, his smile widened. "They told me you would come, witch, and here you are." Harris raised a small gun, aimed it at my chest and fired.

With no time to form a shield I dropped to the ground and rolled back into the brush. The missile skimmed across my upper arm and went to ground in the trash behind me. The gun fired again, before I could get to my feet and I flung myself away in the other direction.

Unfortunately for me that was the wrong direction. I had trapped myself in low brush away from the alders by the path and any hope of escape. Not that I was looking for an escape; I wasn't going to leave my nephews to fight this enemy on their own...

In the clearing beyond a man laughed and a sobbing Neko begged him to stop. Another man cursed and claimed it was his turn. The big cat snarled and screamed its defiance.

Slithering on my belly like my old ally Rattlesnake I tried to move into a more favorable position to make my own attack. I conjured a hasty shield, hoping it would stop one of the weapon's lethal projectiles. Harris couldn't see me among the plants, but if I tried to stand, I would become a big target, he couldn't miss.

He must have seen the bushes move, however, because in the next moment a bullet slammed into the ground right in front of me, kicking up dirt into my face. I jerked back, then leapt to my feet and jumped to cover on the other side of the path where the alders were growing in a thick cluster.

Harris laughed again and fired twice more, keeping me on the move."Not such a bad-ass now eh, witch? I told you we had powerful friends. You and your fancy boys and your whole damned family are going down. Nobody messes with me and my crew and gets away with it."

He backed up his words by firing into the alders again. It would have been a killing blow, either by luck or with magical help, if his bosting hadn't given me time to create a stronger barrier. The missile flared white-hot as it struck my shield and disintegrated.

Then to my surprise and relief Aqwissa appeared. In the form of a large silver dragon she spat out a stream of fiery Qwakaiva that caught Harris full in the chest. With a startled scream he burst into flames.Then, finished with Harris, Aqwissa began happily gobbling up the little demons that after gorging themselves on Neko's pain were too slow to evade her.

Harris's death cries alerted the other gangers to the new threat and as the trio attacking Mathrom turned, Cougar pounced on the nearest man, bringing him to the ground, his throat a bloody gash, torn wide by etheric teeth and claws. Not staying to feast on his kill, Mathrom leapt for another of his adversaries, also bringing him down.

Though the second man had had a moment to prepare for the enraged creature that was now my nephew it didn't matter his fate was the same. He got in a nasty slash with his knife across Mathrom's chest, but then he too fell to Cougar's claws.

His third adversary, a small wiry man dropped his weapon in panic and raced out of the clearing, Cougar's triumphant scream encouraging him to run faster.

I was only partially aware of what Cougar and Mathrom were doing on the other side of the clearing, because my attention was focused on Neko and the two men who were hurting him. The large chamuqwani who had been molesting him when I arrived had finished and was putting his wilted twig back into his dirty trousers. Glancing from my grim face to what had happened to his companions he swore and pulled Neko roughly to his feet. Holding him like a bloody shield in front of him he started backing out of the clearing.

His partner, a Kukiya with a shaved head and cruel mouth pulled a gun from a carrier at his waste and pointed it at me. "Stay back or we will kill the boy," he warned as the pair pushed through the scrub, dragging Neko with them.

I let out a mirthless laugh and followed. "Do you think that puny weapon you are holding will stop what is going to happen to either of you now?" I shouted and kept coming.

Looking back over his shoulder he fired more shots in my direction. Sensing this new threat Aqwissa broke off her demon feasting and leapt for the fleeing Kukiya. Pouncing like a big cat she flattened him to the rocky ground, her claws digging into his back and shoulders.

Coming up to them I laughed, wrenched the weapon from his hand with my power and hurled it into the bushes out of sight. My next blow flipped him over to face me, then pinned him to the dirt. Terrified he struggled for a time as I watched, then he collapsed, begging for my mercy. "Please, Puhani, don't kill me. I was only following my orders—and—and I never touched your relative. Please!"

Holding him with my Gift I pulled him to his knees and lifted his chin, so he could look me in the eye. "Whose orders?"

"I-I don't know. Boss said a guy hired us. We could have our fun as long as we killed you, too."

"You're lying. Who hired you?" And I enforced my question with pain.

He cursed, gritted his teeth and growled "I don't know!"

Ripping the images I needed from his thoughts as Dathna had once done to me, I spat into his face and called him the most insulting name I knew in the Kukiya language when I got what I wanted. He didn't know the man's name but the image of the blue-robed priest I tore from his thoughts was that of my traitor of a cousin, Utreal.

Unfortunately for him I took other knowledge as well. "You were the first one. And you enjoyed giving that gentle young man all the pain you knew he would feel when you tore him wide open. You are a coward and a lire, but I will let his powerful relatives waiting in the Beyond see to your further punishment."

And without another word I placed my hand on his chest and a fiery spear of Qwakaiva shot from my fingertips into his heart. He let out a terrified cry then lay dead at my feet.

When it was done I glanced around looking for Neko and the other big ganger. No one was left alive that I could see but Mathrom, still ensnared within Cougar's power. He was crouched over one of the corpses savagely tearing at the bloody meat.

I let him be for the moment. Mathrom would need some help when he gained control of his human form and he realized what he was doing, but I had no time to spare for him right then. Mathrom's problems could wait. I needed to find Neko and the other ganger who had taken him hostage, so I headed back into the brush following their bloody trail.

I called Aqwissa to my side, her snaky body rounded in the middle by her demon feast. <<Where are they?>>

<<Not far ahead. Though weak the young warrior fights the evil one who has captured him.>>

My own rage nearing the boil I commanded her, <<Find them and kill the evil one in a very painful way.>>

I trailed after her and when I heard a terrified scream and smelled scorched meat I quickened my pace and found Neko in a crumpled heap among the broken bottles and trash in the gulley below Train's metal road. A little further down the shallow ravine a charred mound of still smoking ash was already scattering in the breeze wafting down the ditch.

Slowing my pace I approached him carefully, so as not to frighten him further. His face bruised, his clothes covered in blotches of yellow paint and blood, he was curled in upon himself sobbing quietly and trying without success to cover himself with his torn and bloody trousers.

A trickle of red blood was still trailing down his inner thighs from his injury and I wondered how bad the damage was inside him. I crouched where he could see me, but I made no move to touch him or help—not yet. I remembered how I felt after a few intense sessions with my own torturer Hoyt. I didn't want anyone to see me; I didn't want to be touched. The shame that others would know about my humiliation was as bad as the physical pain of my injuries.

When he had at last covered himself as best he could and was quieter, I spoke his name in a soft voice. "Neko, we can't stay here. Someone will have called the goldys by now. They will find us if we stay much longer; we have to go. You don't want to try and explain to them what has happened."

When he made no move to rise or answer me after a long moment, I said more sternly, "Get up, nephew; it's time to go." I rose and held out my hand. "If it hurts too much to walk then I will have to help you, but we need to leave—now."

He wouldn't look at me and finally mumbled, "Go away, uncle, I just want—let me be."

"I'm sorry I can't do that. I know right now you are hurting and you wish you could die. That's how I felt when I was captured and tortured by one of Djoven's cursed priests. I would have killed myself if my father hadn't come and taken me away from that torment. But as a younger relative in my care I'm not going to let you die over this humiliation and pain. Like me, you will survive and be the stronger for this, because if you give into despair these evil men will have won."

Helping Neko to his feet I took off my jacket and tied it around his waist to conceal the blood and his ripped trousers. Our progress was slow, but we were moving at least. I needed to collect Mathrom and bring both of these young men to our home or another safe place.

As we passed the dead Kukiya Neko stopped to gaze down at his fallen enemy. There was a large charred hole in his shirt the smell of burnt meat thick and pungent in the cool air. I gazed down at the man's face contorted in a rictus of horror and pain. I had no sympathy for him and what awaited him in the Beyond.

Sensing Aqwissa at my side again, I said, <<We don't need the goldys or his friends searching for these bad men here so close to our home. Feed if you wish, but then make their remains disappear for me, my brave little hunter.>>

<<I will do that for you, siyatli brother,>> she said. Tilting her silver head to one side she listened, then added, <<Your brother comes.>>

As she predicted in the next moment Kotahi pushed aside some alder branches and came over to us. Cloaked mostly in his otherworldly form Kotahi seemed as much tree as human. He was only somewhat taller than I was myself but the covering of his thin human-looking body at the moment looked more like tree bark than brown human skin. His hair was long and like many of the fall trees around us golden in color. His face was human in feature, but his eyes were the green of the forest in summer.

<<Asiya, brother, I'm glad you've come to help me. Your healing skills I think are what my young relative needs more than what I can offer with my own Gift>> I said, and I'm sure he could see the relief in my spirit fire.

<<Yes, the young cougar warrior I passed on my way here needs you now. I will take care of this young relative.>>

"Asiya, Neko," Kotahi said to the young man who was just staring down at the grass now that we had stopped walking.

Ignoring Kotahi's greeting Neko stared at the yellow paint spilled on the grass and his mouth twisted as he stifled a sob. Speaking to no one, he said, "We thought it would be so pretty in our new home. It would remind us of the desert—and like Saskina said, of new beginnings."

He let out a mirthless laugh that ended in a sob and turned to me. "But now—I hate yellow—and... Uncle I can't stay here."

"Do you want me to call your mother? I can borrow some money from Rushton and we can send you home, if you want," I said, feeling the knife of guilt twist a little deeper in my heart.

Neko shook his head violently. "No, no, that's the last thing I want to do right now. Mam would cry and carry on and papa would—" he shook his head again. "No, not that. I don't know what I want to do..." he sighed and stared down at his blood-crusted hands anxiously twisting them together.

"I think right now it hurts too much to be a human man," Kotahi said in his gentle quiet voice. "I remember how it was for my brother when he came to us as a wounded bleeding youth.

"If you can trust me completely, Neko, and truly believe that I would never do anything to hurt you I can help you."

My brother's soft words caught his attention and he looked up, the naked pleading and hope plain in his eyes and his spirit fire. "How, Elder?"

"I will take you away with me and you can live and grow in a special place where you can forget the pain of your human existence and not be a man for a while."

I stared at my brother trying to read in his spirit fire what he was planning. But like all my otherworldly relatives when he wished to, his thoughts were veiled from me. At last I said, <<As far as I know Neko has no otherworldly blood in his lineage. You know, brother, if you try to take him

with you back into the Beyond his spirit will separate from his human body and he will die in this world.>>

Kotahi gave me an amused smile. <<I know this brother, so we will stay here in this world, but in a different place—a place of the young man's choosing. Will that ease your mind? Maybe it is you, too, who must have trust in me and what my healing Gift says is right for this young man.>>

When I nodded, but he could still see the unease floating just below the surface of my spirit fire he said, <<I know being left in the care of Zeiva and that bunch has taught you to be wary—which I might add was our Elders' purpose—but I swear to you on our father's blood that I would never do anything to harm this gentle and vulnerable young human.>>

<<Alright, I will honor your Gift and trust you.>>

Kotahi smiled and bowed to me. <<Go see to your young cougar. If your Neko accepts my offer then I will take him with me. If he chooses otherwise I will heal what I can of his physical injuries and bring him to your home later. Then it will be up to you and him what happens next.>>

<<And if he accepts your offer and goes with you will you let me come see him at some point to insure Gahji and his mother that he is doing well?>>

<<Yes, I will take you to him in his new place of healing for a brief visit so you can assure the rest of the family that he is well.>>

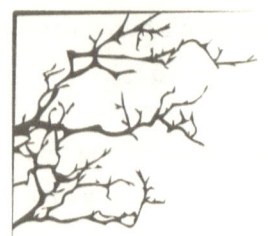

Chapter Fourteen

When I returned to the clearing Aqwissa had managed to whisk away and destroy all but the corpse of the man Mathrom and Cougar were crouched over eating. When I squatted down, far enough away to not seem a threat, but near enough that he could see me, the Cougar still occupying its host's body growled and placed a possessive human hand on their kill.

I remained perfectly still, giving no sign of aggression. Still watching me with inhuman green eyes, the man-cougar growled at me, bent and ripped another piece of bloody meat off the arm he'd been eating before I arrived. I watched in silence making no move to stop him, and wishing, not for the first time, that my sister or Nachoga was still here to advise me.

My own experience with my otherworldly Gift was so different, so a part of me that it always amazed me the amount of trust and courage it took for the humans who inherited the ability, to surrender and allow a creature from the Beyond to enter and possess their physical selves so completely.

But along with the surrender must also come wisdom and control, I mused, something this young one was finding it hard to master on his own with only a bumbling mentor, such as myself for a guide.

When threatened by alien hunters Mathrom had allowed Cougar to enter our world and inhabit his physical body. His survival depended on that—like it had now, but also like before, he lacked the wisdom to hold back enough of his core essence to reclaim his body once the danger had ended.

The wisdom and control would come with time—if incidents like this didn't drive him insane first, I thought. I hoped I could always be there to help him until he mastered his power. I sighed; Cougar had to go and I might have to hurt him this time if he couldn't do it on his own.

We had to get out of here before we were discovered. Putting a conjure into my voice I said, "Mathrom, come back. The threat is over; your enemies are dead. You have let Cougar feast long enough. Control your partner, or I will have to do it for you."

<<Cougar, you will hunt with him again, I promise, leave him now!>>

Mathrom's whole body began to tremble and shake, but at last he mastered his guide and protector and became once more completely human. He wiped a hand across his mouth and contemplated the blood staining his fingers with dismay. Shuddering, he regarded me with frightened eyes. "It happened again didn't it? Cougar came and I—"

Suddenly we could hear the sounds of men talking to one another down by the tracks. Rising swiftly to my feet I pulled Mathrom up with me. Pushing him a head of me I moved back up the trail towards our home and hopefully safety—of a sort.

"Yes, but we can talk about this later, right now we have to get out of here," I said as I threw his arm over my shoulder and urged him to move faster. He had also heard the shouting men, too, and gave me no argument.

<<Aqwissa!>> Looking back I saw that she had known what I wanted and had changed into a winged dragon form and was carrying the mutilated corpse away to dispose of it.

My father was waiting with the back door open when we stumbled into the backyard a few moments later. In the kitchen I motioned Mathrom to the indoor privy down the hall. "Go take off those bloody clothes so I can get rid of them in case Benton sends a cart of his goldys here. Take a shower and let me see how deep that cut on your chest really is."

Mathrom nodded. Safe, he was now able to think about more than his own situation, so he turned his frightened expression back to me again. "Uncle, where is Neko? We can't just leave him—I have to—"

"Neko is with Kotahi right now; he is safe and being cared for, so don't worry about him for the moment," I assured him with more confidence than what I actually felt, in spite of Kotahi's promise.

Reassured he left and Star Swimmer waved for me to sit down at the table while he made us both cups of kaf-tea. "Tell me what happened."

I told him what I knew and when Mathrom joined us he was able to fill in the rest. Handing me his filthy clothes he said, "The cut wasn't too bad so I bandaged it myself. I can ask auntie to look at it later." Then he noticed a splotch of the yellow paint mixed in with the red staining his shirt and added, "We were coming back from the paint store when they jumped us." He grimaced. "Guess I'll have to go back and get some more paint. Though I don't think it will be yellow again."

"Probably a good idea. Neko said much the same thing."

His voice cracking on a sob, he choked out, "Uncle how is he? I wanted to help—stop what I knew they were doing to him, but—"

"But you had your own enemy to fight, nephew. You did the best you could by keeping the rest of them so occupied. They might have hurt Neko worse otherwise and done the same to you if you hadn't called Cougar to you. They weren't expecting that kind of resistance."

"Will he be coming back soon?" his next words caught on a sob. He swallowed and then said, "If he isn't coming back right away maybe I should rent a room up by the Lect for the rest of the term. I don't think I can live over there by myself."

"Nor should you, young cougar," Star Swimmer said. "But I doubt if your cousin will be returning for a while yet, and when he does return he may find his life path will take him elsewhere." Star Swimmer drank more of his kaf-tea, allowing his meaning to penetrate Mathrom's shock and misery. At last he said, "However, there are several options open to you that you haven't had time to consider just yet."

"What have you seen, father? What are you thinking?" I asked him.

"Well the young warrior could always stay here—like now. Or he could rent the house out to someone else, perhaps Jula, Stakaya when he returns and their new baby, for example." He gave us a mischievous smile, "Or you could stop paying the high rent here and everybody move across the street." Turning to Mathrom his grin grew wider. "How would you like to become your uncle's new landlord, eh?"

At his stunned expression I laughed. "That is a possibility nobody has ever considered, father. Maybe we should think about it, though. The house is a bit smaller, no room off the kitchen like here, but it does have a bigger yard. And if my brother will let us, we could build an extra room on the back for some of us to sleep in. That is, of course if our new landlord agrees and his rent isn't too steep," I joked.

Mathrom's mouth dropped open in shock. "Uncle, I wouldn't charge you rent after everything you and the family did for me!"

"Of course we would pay you rent, nephew, if we move in. There arestill taxes and other things to pay for and buy, but I can see you are tiring, so that's a discussion for another day after..."

I left the rest of my thought unvoiced. There was no need to speak out loud what we all were thinking. After the war with the gangers had ended, after Utreal and Djoven's evil minions had been fragmented and eliminated—after all that, if we survived.

His eyes now heavy Mathrom yawned, took my suggestion, and went to his room down the hall. I hoped he would sleep and regain some of his nahawa. I wanted to talk to Star Swimmer and I'd prefer to do it while we were alone.

The house now quiet I sipped my drink and glanced at the time-tell on the kitchen wall. Gahji and the children would be home soon. Knowing I hadn't much time I got straight to the important questions I needed answered. Leaning my elbows on the table I looked him rudely in the eye and asked, "How badly were you injured while confined by the Crokno?

"Though I haven't been gifted with a foretelling I sense the confrontation with the enemy is coming soon. And I also sense that we aren't ready to face them. So, my next question must be, have you healed enough to be of use to us?"

He sighed and dropped his eyes not willing to let me probe any deeper than he chose to share with me. "When I came back to our home beach that last time before you left for this world I had been wounded by the enemy, as you knew. Utreal and two other cousins were with me on that raid. I thought I was among relatives and allies. In fact it was Utreal who helped me escape. By doing so, another warrior was fragmented during that combat in my place.

"The young suka had little Qwakaiva and I now believe ze sacrificed him, hoping by doing so I would be willing to trust zer later when ze had a better opportunity to betray me to his Crokno masters."

He sighed and drank more kaf-tea. "And I did trust zer. Utreal had fought beside us for thousands of your human years—why wouldn't I? So, I was ensnared like an innocent child."

Leaning forward he took my hand. "They nearly fragmented me, Tas. I would have been lost to the clans and to the alliance if it hadn't been for Zeiva's sacrifice and your mother's gift. I know I took far more from her than she thought she was offering, but I had to, my son. I hope you can understand that."

I nodded and released my hand from his. "I can understand in a way. When you came to me in this place and time I remembered mother's dream I knew why Grandfather hated you, because he saw it too. And I also saw with fear and wonder how the strands of time can twist and mingle with the patterns of our lives in so many unpredictable and wonderful—yet terrifying ways."

I allowed our words to be digested for a time then repeated my earlier question. "Your imprisonment and near death explains many things, like why my siblings—that I never knew existed before—have been hovering about you so much since you arrived at our home, but it doesn't answer my earlier question.

"If a simple conjure like you used upon that cart of gangers the other night tired you enough that you went back to bed afterward, are you going to be able to help when the enemy truly comes for us?"

Star Swimmer considered my question for a long time, then as he opened his mouth to answer the front door banged open and Angika shouted a greeting.

Walking into the kitchen, she set down her bag of groceries on the kitchen counter and shrugged out of her back pack. Smiling, she came over and gave me a warm hug. "Asiya, Appi, we stopped by the store and Amima got your favorite to make for dinner."

Knowing it was going to get noisy for a while Star Swimmer gave me a crooked smile, greeted his granddaughter and headed for his room. Our talk was over; my questions left unanswered. Not wishing to share my worries with the family just yet, I joked, "Oh, my girl, what did you buy for me? Seaweed and grease, stink eggs, roots and berry jam, or maybe moose nose?"

"Stink eggs, moose nose? Oo yuk, no! And you can't buy those traditional foods at a chamuqwani market." Then realizing I was teasing she laughed, and began emptying her bag onto the counter. "No, silly Appi, we are making you chocolate cake to go with the red-fish patties and potatoes we are also cooking for you."

"Mm, sounds yummy I can hardly wait." But I never did get that chocolate cake—not that night nor for many nights after.

As Angika was putting away the contents of her bag the front door opened again and soon after Gahji entered the kitchen with my son on one ample hip and another bag of groceries on the other. Setting her bag next to Angika's she put O'siyan in his chair and got him a carrot stick and some sliced apple from the ice box to keep him occupied while she unpacked and started cooking.

Following her in, Elder Samul put his two bags down as well for my oldest daughter to unpack. He sat down at the table and Gahji went to the cupboard for cups. Pouring the Elder a cup of kaf-tea she smiled at me and poured herself one as well.

"It was awfully quiet in here when we came in. Where are Bijah and Tuunac? Are they across the street helping the cousins paint? The boys told me they were off to the paint store today."

She scowled, recalling something she thought I'd done. "And Tas, next time call the infirmarium and let me know that you are getting the kids early, so I don't make the trip over there for no reason."

I stared open mouthed. Before I could craft an answer, a sleepy Mathrom reappeared and leaned against the kitchen doorframe. His clean shirt was now streaked with a crimson ribbon of fresh blood. His voice slightly slurred with pain and sleep, he said, "Hi, Auntie, I thought I heard you come in. Can you help me? I tried to bandage the knife slash on my own, but I guess I didn't do a very good job of it."

Gahji stared at the blood and then turned to me, her eyes demanding answers. "I didn't pick up the children from their school, my heart," I said in a quiet voice.

"Mathrom and Neko were attacked by gangers while I was with Rushton today. When my nephew called to me I made the transfer to help them. Both young warriors were wounded and Neko was repeatedly raped and badly injured before I got there to stop it. I have been dealing with that problem for most of the afternoon."

Standing like a statue Gahji stared unseeing at the far wall the cup of hot kaf-tea slipping from her numb hand to crash unnoticed onto the floor. I rose and guided her around the mess and sat her down in another chair on the other side of the table. I brought her a glass of water. She took it without thinking, drank some and then sat it down on the table.

Taking a shuddering breath, she looked deep into my eyes. "They told me at the school that it was you who came with another man in a cart to pick them up. Bijah's teacher said she didn't want to go, but when you put an arm around the children's shoulders and promised them ice cream they went to the mecho-cart and got in with no more fuss."

Fear, and mama bear rage swirled in a chaotic maelstrom in her spirit fire. Blinking back tears, she demanded, "Tas, if you didn't pick them up from school, then who did? And where are my children?"

"It was probably Utreal mimicking Tas to fool the children's teachers who took them," Star Swimmer said as he returned to the kitchen to join us.

"Your children are, or will be, with their paternal grandparents sometime soon. Djoven's priests may keep them and hide them away for a while, in case the tribe proceeds with legal action to have them returned to you, but they won't be harmed, Gahji, in the meantime, I assure you. It would defeat the enemy's greater purpose if they were."

My father's calm words did nothing to reassure her.

<<If the priests have them, they may give Tuunac to the grandparents but they will want to keep Bijah if they discover her Gift. Which they might, because she has too much of a fiery nature to hide and keep silent when she should,>> I warned. <<She has already told me that she would 'kill those mean old people' to protect her brother if they are taken.>>

<<Hmm, then it will be up to you and your new warband to see that doesn't happen, my son.>>

<<My warband?>>

"And what greater purpose is that, Honored Spirit Warrior?" Elder Samul asked, interrupting our mind communication.

"The children are but a trap to ensnare me and my son, so our Crokno enemies can finally kill us. Aiding the grandparent's obsession with ensuring a descendant to care for their ancestral graves after their passing was only a convenient ploy to hide their true purpose."

"Hmm," Samul said, stroking his chin in thought.

There seemed nothing else to say as we all considered what had occurred. I knew more than perhaps anyone sitting around our table, what could happen to a gifted child captured by Djoven's priests and their demons. But now wasn't the time to surrender to the fear writhing and coiling itself in black knots of guilt and despair within my gut.

As I rose to find the broom and dust pan to clean up the broken cup Gahji lifted her face from her sheltering hands and happened to notice that Aqwissa had returned to me and was once more a silver bracelet upon my arm. "I see your pet is with you and not protecting my children," she accused, her voice dripping with her contempt. "With all your power, couldn't you take care of a few stupid gangers on your own, without abandoning my children to the threat we knew was waiting for just such an opportunity to happen?"

Each word my frightened bear woman spoke was like a spear thrust entering my heart. I glanced down at my wrist. My attention had been so focused elsewhere I hadn't even realized she had returned to me. "I'm sorry, my heart, but I didn't summon her she just—came. I...."

<<Aqwissa, why?>> Sensing my displeasure she blinked up at me, confused.

"Don't be angry with her, Tas, or you either, daughter-in-law," my father said. "She could do nothing else when faced with such a choice and Tas would have no say in the matter—thus is the nature of her bond."

Tearing my attention away from my arm I narrowed my eyes and glared at him. "What do you mean? I know we are bonded, but I should be able to tell her—"

"Only to a point, son. When the Great One foresaw, that if you survived the otherworldly challenges he placed along your path and then you chose to return to your birth-world as a man, then he knew you would need a powerful guide and protector to help you fend off the Crokno.

"So to aid you if you chose one of the many possibilities available in which you would need one such as her, he captured and enhanced the abilities of one of Tokay's little dragon-lizards especially with you in mind. When faced with a choice, as long as you need her, she will always choose you over another you may love and want to protect."

<<I did come to help you as I was instructed, siyatli brother,>> Aqwissa said when I gazed down at her with a new understanding, <<but I didn't abandon the little human who holds a dragon's blood in her lineage, either. When you no longer need me, perhaps I will bond with *her*.>>

Aqwissa raised her head and drew my attention to some dark spots on her silvery hide. <<Before I left her I placed four of my scales into the wings of the butterfly barrettes penning back her braids. In a small way I am still linked to her. And I will be as long as Utreal or the Crokno with zer doesn't detect my presence, or separate the siblings I can find them for you,>> she offered.

<<That was very clever of you, little one,>> Star Swimmer said.

"Tas, what's going on?" Gahji complained. "I know you three are talking but you are sharing too fast for me to follow. Stop and explain to the rest of us lowly humans, eh?"

Feeling my face heat, I apologized and hastily explained what Aqwissa had just told us.

"That's good to know when we are ready we will need that kind of information," the Elder said. "Does she know where the children are?"

When I posed that question to her, she told me and I repeated her answer for him, "She says the two are still together and it is dark and cold, and somewhere outside the room where the enemy is keeping them at the moment there are people talking and others singing—temple songs."

"They are keeping my babies at their damned agency as you thought, Tas," Gahji growled her expression murderous.

Samul laid a hand on her arm to sooth her and asked me, "Can she talk to Bijah as well?"

I looked down at Aqwissa who had heard him. "She says maybe," I translated, "but she doesn't want to try right now. The traitor or the Crokno emissary might detect their communication and destroy Bijah's barrettes."

Samul nodded and rose. "Yes, I can understand that. It will be good to wait till we are ready. And to *be* ready, we have a lot to do."

Turning to his niece, he said, "My girl, you and Angika go pack for you and the baby. You are coming home with me till this is settled."

Gahji folded her arms across her chest and set her mouth in a stubborn line. "They are my kids and I am staying right here."

"Yes, they are your children, but do I have to remind you that you also have two other children who will need you right now," the Elder argued. "I know it is a part of your nature to want to protect and defend your babies, but this time you are going to have to let your man and the other men of your family help you.

"Tas, I will expect you and your father at our ceremonial house with suitable offerings as soon as it can be arranged," the Elder instructed. "And bring our Kukiya cousin with you. He shouldn't be left here alone. He can pack a bag and stay there as well."

When I glanced at my wife she was still angry and wearing her obstinate expression. I knew that look all too well and braced myself for a battle. She wasn't going to be happy with me if I had to use my Gift to make her leave, but the Elder was right she needed to go with him to a place I already knew was guarded by powerful Smotahlik ancestral spirits.

But her objections died when Star Swimmer reached across the table and held out to her one of his opalescent shell pendants. Recalling that as a child he had gifted me one and gave me two others for Nachoga and my mother to wear I sighed with relief.

"Take this and wear it, daughter, we can keep you linked with us that way so you will be with us whatever happens. Now go with your uncle and take care of your remaining children as he suggests, and you know in your heart is the right thing to do. My grandson is still too young for his mother to abandon him and join his father's warband."

As she nodded and held out her hand for his gift Angika stifled a cry and pointed to Mathrom sliding down the doorframe a growing pool of red on the floor around him. Gahji swore and snarled at me to catch him before he fell on his face. "Guess I'd better stitch up this one before I leave. Angika, bring me my med kit and then start packing for you and baby."

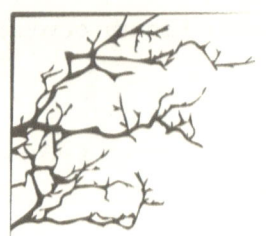

Chapter Fifteen

Another winter storm was building on the western horizon as Mathrom, Star Swimmer and I loaded my canoe with gifts and ourselves, to cross to the ceremonial house to meet with the Elders summoned for our war council. Iron gray clouds roiled in a heavy mass as the storm approached, a howling wind and sheets of rain preceding it. Unlike most winter storms I had grown to know while living on the coast, this one came with bright flashes of purple lightning shooting from its belly.

It was a rough crossing and we were all soaked to the skin in spite of wearing heavy woolen ceremonial cloaks trimmed with embroidery and white yarn fringe that Sichahntri produced for us just before leaving.

Though she said, as emissaries from the Beyond, it was necessary for us to make a good impression on the human Elders and the ancestral guardians of this land with our appearance, by the time we arrived with the weather hurling us across the inlet ahead of it, I feared we looked more pitiful than the impressive delegation that she'd hoped for.

She, of course, along with another siyatli brother Wahtzuul, a truly magnificent and scary-looking being, with his long hair twisted into thin braids down his back and a sleek black fur covering his somewhat humanoid face and four muscular arms, had shown up with Sichahntri at my house last night unannounced along with his two equally impressive guards as escort. All were dressed in metallic studded armor and carrying lethal-looking, but unknown weaponry.

There hadn't been room for all of us in my canoe with the other gifts from the Beyond Sichahntri had also brought, so they had made the transfer across the inlet and were only damp not soaked.

Giving me a toothy grin that showed his long fangs Wahtzuul plucked two bundles from the canoe. He motioned to the on-coming tempest with a jerk of his head. Unable to speak my human language he said in the mind talk, <<I didn't expect to see such a mighty display of raw magic on your tame little world, brother.

<<We have such weather in my land as well and we have the skill to channel and use its gifts. The deluge brings with it much power. It is a good omen for our coming fight.>>

I returned his smile, and picked up another bundle. Still a little in awe of this new sibling, I said, <<I hope you are right, elder brother. I think we will need all the help we can get if the Crokno come in force to back up the traitor who almost killed our father.>>

Up the hill in front of us loomed the long wooden plank structure of the ceremonial house. Gray smoke plumed from the two smoke holes in its moss-covered roof and the sound of the log drum and deep throated singing welcomed both us and the storm.

I had taken only a few steps with my bundle when Midaz, the younger of Wahtzuul's guards, took it from me and bowed. <<You honor us and this land with your humbleness, Tigring, (war chief) but it isn't proper for you to enter burdened like a lowly battle-claimed slave. I will carry this for you.>>

Feeling my face heat and wishing there had been more time for father—or someone to instruct me better about the customs of my relatives from this distant world, I bowed. <<Thank you. I am honored by your concern for me.>>

Catching Star Swimmer's amused smile I hurried to join him and Sichahntri, now wearing the form of a large, middle-aged brown-skinned woman with her long black hair woven into a dark crown atop her head. Behind her walked Wahtzuul and his two guards burdened with our plunder and then came a shy and over-awed Mathrom carrying only his bed roll and a bag of warm clothes.

The Elder was waiting by the entrance to usher us in. His expression never changed as he noticed the four otherworldly beings accompanying us, but I detected the surprise ripple through his spirit fire as we came near enough for him to actually *see* Wahtzuul and his escort.

"Welcome to you, younger brother, our visitors from the Beyond—and our young Kukiya cousin," he said as we stepped into the firelight.

He motioned to a low bench along one wall that I knew from past visits here was reserved for honored guests. "Please come in and warm yourselves.

We will begin shortly." He gave Star Swimmer an inquiring looked. "Some of the initiates have prepared hot spruce tea for you." His eyes focused on the unknown newcomers. "Would that be appropriate to serve to all our 'guests'?"

"Yes, it will be fine," Star Swimmer said. "Though my son Wahtzuul will be too proud to admit it even he can feel the west coast chill. Unfortunately, he and his escort cannot speak a human tongue, so either Tas or I will have to translate for you." He grinned. "Unless you would like to try your mind speech skills and directly speak to him yourself, of course."

Samul nodded. "I just might do that—as long as someone is near to help out in case I can't make myself understood."

Suddenly shy, Mathrom held back, not sure what to do next. He wasn't officially part of the delegation, but as Elder Samul had said, we couldn't leave him behind.

Aware of his dilemma the Elder pointed to the rows of seats climbing up the side walls of the long house. "Find an empty bench up there where you can leave your things and later spread out your bedroll. You will be joining the initiates for now."

Then Samul pointed across the dirt floor to a lighted doorway on the other side of the house. "The kitchen is in there. After that, get yourself some tea and some food if you are hungry."

As the young man nodded and turned away, Samul called him back for one last word. "Your Uncle has told me about the problems you have experienced when you have had to call your Siiqwah, your Cougar guardian to you when your life has been threatened.

"The initiates, like Stakaya, are here to learn about their own guardians—which you have already accomplished, but we may be able to teach you how to control it when you invite your Siiqwah to come to you."

Mathrom let out a long sigh. "Thank you, Elder. I know uncle wants to help me—and is trying, but as he says his relationship with his Gift isn't the same, and since my granny Kitah died—there is no one to help me, really."

Samul smiled and put a hand on his shoulder. "We will see what can be done. Go now put down your bags and get warm in the kitchen. Stakaya may already be in there helping prepare a meal for our guests."

When Samul turned back to us and saw me still standing near, I said, "Thank you, Elder. It would truly be a good thing if you or one of the other Elders can help him with that. I hope the other Smotahlik people here can be so welcoming."

He grimaced, then ushered me towards the bench where the rest of my family were already sitting. "It may not be easy for him at first, true, but he has a strong spirit and it's time we stop all this ancient feuding and work together. If what your father says is true we will need to if we want our world to survive."

On this particular night there were no ceremonies taking place. The only ones here were the Elders Samul had called for this council, and the initiates and their minders. All but the Elders were either in the kitchen or observing quietly sitting on the tiered benches in the shadows.

As Stakaya served me a cup of hot spruce tea, he murmured from under his own basket mask when he thought no one would hear but me, "I saw Mathrom in the kitchen. Why is he here?"

"Gangers have attacked us twice since you left. We couldn't leave him alone there, and he will be staying here to learn as well."

"What? Where is everybody else then?"

The cub maybe thought he was unobserved and unheard, but he wasn't. Before I could explain further a tall muscular man carrying a willow switch came up behind him and whacked him sharply on his bare legs twice. Ky flinched and quickly backed away. Speaking in the Smotahlik language his minder ordered him back to the kitchen in a gruff voice.

"Ask Mathrom for more details—if you are allowed to," I called after him. Beside me Wahtzuul chuckled and said something to his escort in their language that had them grinning.

<<That slave was very impudent to speak to you without permission. If he belonged to me I would punish him with a whipping for his insolence.>>

I snorted a laugh. <<There's been many times I've wanted to do something just like that, but he's no slave. No one keeps slaves on this world now. That one is my wife's younger brother. When he kept getting himself into trouble, his elders and I decided to confine him here for the winter to teach him the secrets of his heritage and also to teach him discipline—since he wasn't listening to us any other way.>>

Wahtzuul nodded. <<I have a son like that, always rebellious and uncooperative. But I, like you, Tigring-Brother, cannot make the transfer from world to world without help, otherwise I might send him to you and these human elders for a season in this big house, as well.>>

One of Wahtzuul's fearsome children in the ceremonial house watched over by the Bugatzi? My mind shuddered at that image, but I bowed and thanked him for his trust.

I had barely begun drinking my tea when an Elder on the bench facing us rose and stepped to the center between the two fires. Raising a hand drum up to the sooty roof, he began to sing in a deep booming voice a prayer song. He sang to welcome the Ancestors and other guiding spirits to come, witness and protect us. An answering peel of thunder echoed in response to his call and we rose to honor the ones who had joined us. Feeling the spirits gathering, I lifted up my voice with the others to welcome the Unseen Ones to our council.

When the song ended Elder Samul stepped to the center and introduced the Elders, sitting on the bench across from us. He concluded by announcing my father as an emissary of Kunai's great alliance, here from the Beyond to speak to them about matters of importance for all our peoples.

When he finished my father, wearing the ceremonial cape Sichahntri provided, walked to the center and spoke in the Smotahlik language. "Can everyone understand me if I speak your beautiful language? I am aware of the hardship forced upon your people when the children were compelled to attend the live-away schools, so if not, I will speak what I have to say in the imperial tongue."

"Our young people will have a hard time of it," Samul said. "But I think the old ones, like me, would appreciate hearing you speak our language. When I have listened to you before you speak in the ways our parents and grandparents taught us and that is a rare pleasure these days." Samul glanced at the others who gave him confirming nods.

Star Swimmer bowed. Going to a pouch of sacred smoke by one of the fires he tossed some of its contents into the flames. "So be it then. My daughter Sichahntri or my son Tasimu can translate for the younger ones who have been robbed of their heritage."

He began by introducing himself, me and my two older siblings. Then he gave them an account of his clan lineage back for several generations as was the custom among my human tribal people. When he finished he motioned for me to bring our gifts forward and open them in front of the bench of Elders facing us. To my surprise Midaz, from Wahtzuul's escort picked up what I couldn't carry with his four arms and followed me over.

I saw a few eyebrows lift when they finally realized that the beings with us weren't just men in funny costumes. As we untied the bindings mounds of brightly colored blankets were unveiled as well as coils of bark for weaving, and bags of opalescent shells. There were also two small but heavy bags of imperial gold coins that father explained to Samul were for the care of our relatives, staying with them for their teachings that winter.

"I believe these are suitable. My daughter traveled into your past and bargained for these things at one of the old trading posts along this coast. It would be hard to find them here in your time now, so I hope you will treasure them. I offer these to the ancestral spirits and the Elders of this house with all respect and honor," Star Swimmer said.

"The problem I bring to you tonight, like many evils, has several layers to unwrap as we discover the rot hidden at its core. The first layer is that two of my son Tasimu's children—your children—have been stolen away by a priest of Djoven's temple. A priest who is guided by demons and otherworldly beings who work for your destruction.

"The boy, who has no Gift, they will eventually give over to his paternal grandparents after they pay a large money gift to the temple. These people are imperial immigrants to this coast and want him to carry on their own flawed family line.

"The young girl the grandparents don't care about, so they will be happy to let the priest keep her and torture her until they can break her to their will if they discover her secret. Why? Because *she* is the one with the Gift, and the sect the priest belongs to still wants to harvest the power they can suck from your children.

"Most of Djoven's priests today are either ignorant themselves, or are lying to you if they say this evil isn't still happening in secret. All of the children among you who may have a spirit gift that will guide future generations of your people are in danger, if these evil priests aren't discovered and fragmented."

Going to one of the fires, he knelt and tossed into the flames some of the sacred herb lying there for that purpose, and brushed the smoke over himself again. "The second layer to uncover is that, though this priest and his demons are a formidable enemy my son is strong enough to handle him if he were alone, but he is not. The priest has powerful allies—otherworldly allies, allies who wish all life on this world destroyed....

After my father finished telling the Elders about the Crokno threat and I added a bit of my own story everyone decided to take a break to talk and consider the problem. For quite some time delicious smells had been wafting from the kitchen where the initiates and their minders were cooking for us. Now was a good time to eat and relax for a bit. It was going to be a long night, I figured.

As the storm continued to roar and boom overhead, making the rafters tremble with its power, I sensed a restlessness growing among Wahtzuul and his companions. While Star Swimmer was still speaking one of the escorts, the older man with gray starting to show around his mouth and among his braids quietly left. When I was able to look around I saw him standing just outside with his two upper arms raised to the storm. I felt that he was chanting, but from where I was standing next to father by one of the fires I couldn't hear him.

Fortunately the council broke up soon after that. I knew many of the people were anxious to talk with father during the break, but Wahtzuul and Sichahntri had other ideas for him.

Taking him firmly by his arm Wahtzuul grinned, showing his fangs. <<Come along peaceful now, Old One. Don't make me carry you; it would be so undignified. Duuzra is holding the storm for us.>>

When he saw my mouth drop open, his grin widened. <<Give my apologies to these elders for me, but we want to take advantage of the storm's power and do a healing on this ancient while the tempest is still strong.>>

Star Swimmer laughed <<So that was why Sichahntri hasn't been here to offer me her Qwakaiva. She went to get you on her own. I wondered why she was so secretive.>>

<<I was secretive because I had to make three crossings and rest in between. That's why I haven't been around to help you. I had hoped Kotahi would be there to do what I couldn't—but I now know he has been *occupied* with other matters.>>

As they hustled Star Swimmer out into the rain she turned and said,<<"Come join us if you want, brother, and tell the humans they can witness, but not to interfere.>>

Turning to Elder Samul who had come over when he saw my brother hauling my father out into the rain, I asked, "Did you understand what they were saying?"

"Not much," he admitted. "They want him to come because they want to do something. He isn't sure about what they plan, but he didn't put up much resistance either."

I chuckled and started for the entrance. "I think you got the idea of it pretty good. Father was badly injured before coming to my home and because his injuries were so severe he hasn't been able to heal himself, even with help. On Wahtzuul's world he says they use the power of storms in their conjuring, so they want to try and help him.

"That's really all I know at this point, so I'm going to join them and get wet too. They said you and the others could watch if you want," I called as I stepped out into the storm.

By the time I pushed my way through the wind and the rain they had taken off Star Swimmer's fine ceremonial cloak and Sichahntri had whisked it inside to stay dry. He was squatting on a blanket with Wahtzuul, Sichahntri and his guards forming a diamond shape around him. The three men with four limbs held each other's lower set of arms while raising their upper set to the cloudy sky.

Sichahntri held Wahtzuul and Duuzra's lower arms, but when she saw me she called me over. "Good, your courage hasn't failed you. Come over here and between us we can complete the healing jewel."

Not sure what she meant, I walked slowly over to them. "I've never done anything like this before what must I do?" I said hesitantly.

Motioning me to stand directly in front of her she placed my hands in those of my brother and Duuzra, who formed the top and bottom of the diamond. Together me and Sichahntri, and Midazacross from us completed the design.

Standing close enough to mold herself to my back she raised her arms like the others. Aqwissa who had been quiet ever since we'd left my house suddenly unwound herself from my wrist and wrapped her snaky silver body around my sister and me to insure the magical connection stayed strong.

Wahtzuul smiled when he saw how we had adapted ourselves. <<Very clever Tigring Brother to use your protector so.>>

I laughed. <<She is a very independent guardian who thinks of such things on her own without any help from me.>>

He laughed, too, and shared an affectionate smile with the oldest of his escort. <<My guards can be willful creatures as well at times.>>

The older one named Duuzra snorted and said something in their language that had them all laughing until a peal of thunder over the inlet sobered everyone and reminded them of our purpose.

In a deep throated voice, similar to those I often heard coming from the house behind us Duuzra began to chant. I was vaguely aware of Samul and several others crowding the entrance just out of the rain as we began. And then I had no more time to wonder about them as I was caught up by the power the Hathuuri generated with their conjure.

I had seen Iyantsha call down the lightning and channel the power of a storm into a healing but what the Hathuuri, under my brother and Duuzra's direction channeled for us was raw and chaotic, as easily directed into war and destruction as healing and creativity. This force needed a master's hand to control it.

As we chanted the first clap of thunder boomed over us and lightning struck the diamond made by their upraised hands. Our hands and arms turned silvery blue and I smelled the stink of scorched hair and wool. I knew Aqwissa was absorbing much of the power and shielding my weaker human body from the full force of the Hathuuri's conjure, yet what I did absorb was both painful and exhilarating.

My hands held tight to help stabilize our working I felt the current called down from the storm coursing through me nearly taking my breath away. I had barely caught my breath after one bolt when Wahtzuul called down another bolt and then another. A glowing white tower was gradually building in the circle between their hands. His braids twisting and writhing in the wind, his violet eyes glowing with an inner fire, his mouth wide and smiling as he sucked in the power of the storm and chanted the lightning to come to him, my brother was an awesome and terrifying sight.

I suddenly realized that what I had thought were just metallic ornamentation on the Hathuuri's armor were actually crystals capable of catching and storing the power in a wild storm like this one.

When Duuzra judged the circle of light and power they were building was strong enough he changed the cadence of his chant and they directed the full force of their conjure downward and into Star Swimmer's form.

The power hit him in a blinding halo of blue-white fire. He screamed and I saw his shape fragmenting and reforming into several configurations, some human or Hathuuri, some otherworldly creatures like his seal, some unrecognizable at all. I screamed right along with him I was so frightened for him—for me. I wanted to break the diamond, I wanted to help him, but I dared not do anything, but maintain my hold on my brother's and Duuzra's lower hands and allow the power to flow through me, into my father, and eventually to ground itself in the earth below us.

When we at last finished and the storm had rolled on to dump the rest of its rain against the side of a mountain farther up the Seatown valley, a Qwa'Nayhi Seal lay on the blanket between us.

Sichahntri laughed at my dismayed expression. <<Don't worry about him, Tas. He will be able to change into a human form once he has had time to rest and absorb what we have gifted him.>>

I glanced back at the ceremonial house where an awestruck Elder Samul still waited with Mathrom and one or two others by the entrance. <<We should bring him in out of the wet and the cold. And maybe they will let us borrow back a few of those new blankets to lay him on by the fire.>>

<<And after we get the Ancient settled, I want to eat. I need some good bloody meat—and plenty of it,>>Wahtzuul said as he effortlessly picked up our seal father and started for the ceremonial house.

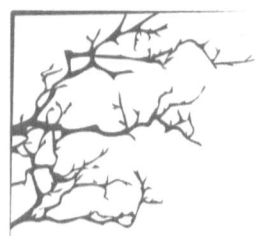

Chapter Sixteen

When we reached the entrance and I told the Elders that after such a powerful working Star Swimmer needed to sleep and stay warm, they told us to bring him to the ceremonial fires and produced a straw-filled mattress and several warm blankets to cover him.

Mathrom asked if he could sit by my father while the rest of us went to the kitchen to eat. No one had had time to assign him a minder yet, so he had been one of the ones witnessing from the entrance during the healing. As family members, he and Stakaya were posted at father's head and feet to watch over him and see to his needs if he woke while the rest of us ate and then slept.

To my dismay the Hathuuri managed to deplete much of the deer meat and red fish stored in the ice box as well as several flat pans of scau-bread, before they were replete and crawled up into the high benches to sleep for a time. When I offered to go hunting to make up the loss, Samul shook his head and touched the pouch of gold at his waist.

"This is more than payment for the food, Tas. I sense we all will be busy in the coming days, so the initiates can eat hamburger soup for a while, in exchange for the honor of telling their children one day when this story is retold during ceremony that they were here.

"We are proud to host such distinguished visitors. The account of what we witnessed last night will be told and honored for many generations to come. I am humbled that I was here to see it."

Much improved in health father awoke later that day and easily shifted back into his human form. Following me into the kitchen he sat at the table and I served him some red fish, eggs and fried scau-bread. There was a ceremony planned for that evening and though it was still only just after midday people were starting to arrive. Sichahntri had transferred along with

124

my brother and his escort back to my house as other tribal members showed up.

We would be leaving soon as well. and taking my canoe back with us. I hoped to do a bit of fishing in my sealskin along the way; otherwise my own ice box might become an empty shell like the one here.

When we arrived home with our catch I found Midaz sitting on the new couch watching the picta-view with a rapt attention. My brother and Duuzra were sleeping in Tuunac's old room where the cousins had been staying until the trouble changed things.

Star Swimmer chuckled when he saw Midaz. <<Aren't you supposed to be guarding this dwelling?>>

Midaz jumped to his feet and bowed. <<I am sorry Ancient I—>> He glanced at the picta again. <<Your daughter showed me how to use it when I asked...This device is so amazing—>> He broke off speaking as his attention was captured once more by the tiny figures inside the box.

<<Well don't be so quick to covet one of these toys for your own world, young guardian,>> father chided. <<It is because of machines like this and the other technologies these humans have created that the Crokno enemy so badly wishes to destroy them.>>

Muttering another apology Midaz tapped a button on the little black box and the glass went black.

<<And just where is my daughter?>>

<<She told your son she was—going shopping?>>

At father's pained expression as he headed to his room I laughed and went into the kitchen to start cleaning the fish and cooking. <<Turn the picta-view back on if you want, Midaz. We are here now and it will be safe enough.>> I heard the picta talking to him as I began filleting my catch at the sink and put on the kaf-tea.

I was engrossed in the task of cooking when the front door opened and then Angika let out a startled scream. By the time I made it to the living room Gahji had thrust a whimpering baby into Angika's arms and had pulled a lethal little hand gun out of her purse and was pointing it at our guest. Bear snarling in her spirit fire she gave our visitor a murderous glare, not at all intimidated by his size and alienness as he rose to meet her threat. "Who are you, dog humper and what are you doing in my house?"

"Gahji, it's alright he is a friend. Please put away that gun!" I shouted. "Where did you get a gun anyway—and what are you doing here?"

Glaring at both of us Gahji put away her weapon and folded her arms across her ample breast. "I live here, Tas, or have you forgotten that? And auntie lent me her gun when she knew I was coming back here to get some things. Angika forgot her homework assignment and baby needs some warmer clothes now that the weather has changed."

She glanced at the tall imposing alien standing in our living room. "And maybe she sent me with her gun for a good reason, I might add. Because nobody bothered to inform me we might have otherworldly guests. How was I to know he is a friend and not a damned Crokno agent, eh?" she added and I couldn't miss the sarcasm in her voice.

"I'm sorry, my heart. So much has happened—in a good way—we did a healing for father—and Wahtzuul channeled the lightning—and it was so—wonderful—and,"

"Oh stop babbling," she growled. "You always do that when you are nervous and you know I'm going to be cross and scold you—usually because you deserve it, I might add."

<<I'm sorry—I forgot—I didn't think you would be coming—"

"Oh stop! You're doing it again, damn it."

Midaz hadn't understood our words, but he knew whatever was going on was somehow his fault. <<I am sorry, Tigring. Perhaps what your father says about the box with images inside is true. I wasn't paying attention like I should or this mere female couldn't have surprised me as she did.>>

<<This mere female, as you put it is my wife,>>I said, getting annoyed in spite of myself. <<So I am glad neither of you hurt the other. I'm not sure what weaponry you have on your world, but the little weapon she pulled from her bag can kill very effectively. And believe me she would have used it, too, if I hadn't stopped her.>>

<<So remember that, stupid dung-eating insect, when you next allow yourself to be distracted from your duty,>> Duuzra growled as he preceded my brother into the living room.

"Uh, Gahji this is my brother Wahtzuul and his escort," I said as the two joined us. They can't speak a human language so father Sichahntri or

I will have to translate for you," I explained as I told my relatives who the newcomers were.

Smelling something burning in the kitchen Gahji swore and took charge. "Angika take baby to the privy and change him if he's had an accident. Tas, what are you doing still standing here, see what's burning and get your brother and his escort cups of kaf-tea, or whatever, while I take over cooking. Where is Sichahntri by the way?"

"Shopping, so I was told."

We were drinking kaf-tea and sitting at the table waiting as Gahji finish frying the fish. She had just pulled the second pan of scau-bread from the oven, when I heard a cart park out front. Someone was coming.

As a punishment no doubt, Midaz was left in the living room where, last time I checked, he was dividing his attention between rolling a ball to O'siyan and glancing out the window for enemy scum, who might be creeping up on us. To add to his torture, Angika, as usual, was sitting on the couch doing her homework while she watched one of her favorite programs on the picta-view.

<<Tigring, someone is coming to your dwelling,>> the young guard announced in my mind.

<<I know, I heard the cart stop. Be wary, but don't attack until we know more.>>

"Angika, put down your book and see who is coming. Midaz is there to protect you if it is an enemy," I said.

In the next moment she called out, "It's only uncle Rushton, Appi. Shall I let him in?"

I glanced at my father, silently asking for his opinion. He shrugged. "Why are you asking me? It's Gahji's house ask her."

"I wasn't sure..." I glanced at my alien brother and his escort.

Gahji made a disgusted noise in her throat, and yelled, "Let him in, Angika. He already knows a lot of Tas's story anyway. He might as well find out more of the craziness going on around here," she grumbled half to herself.

She flipped a piece of fish and then pointed her turner at Wahtzuul. "And you, tell your man in my living room to behave."

My father must have been translating, because with an amused twinkle in his eye, Wahtzuul bowed his head in agreement, to hide a smile.

<<The man who is coming is a scholar and one of our esteemed lore keepers,>> I explained. <<He has been encouraging me to tell him my life's story so that he can transcribe it for my descendants and others to read.>>

Wahtzuul grunted his approval. <<You are a great man among your people. It is only proper that a scribe collect your stories and wisdom.>>

Great man, me? I felt my face heat and caught the amusement in my father's eye. <<Thank you, Elder Brother, I'm not sure I deserve your praise, but I am honored by your regard.>>

Then I heard Angika greet Rushton. As he entered he must have noticed Midaz. I heard him take a deep breath and ask Angika a question, too low for me to hear. Before she could answer, I called, "Don't worry about Midaz; he won't bother you. Come into the kitchen Rushton. You are just in time for a meal."

In the next moment a cautious preceptor stepped into the kitchen. I got up from my chair and offered it to him. "Sit down. I'll get one of the extra chairs off the porch."

Gahji handed him a cup of kaf-tea as he studied the others at our table. At last he turned to my father and hesitantly asked, "More—uh—family come to visit?"

Star Swimmer laughed and was introducing him to my brother and Duuzra as I returned with the extra chair. "They are here for a visit, true enough," I said as I poured myself more kaf-tea, "but unfortunately it isn't for a happy occasion."

"I wondered what had happened after you left so—abruptly the other day. And then when I couldn't reach anyone on the far-speak, and you missed your session today... I was worried and decided to stop by, hoping Mathrom or someone would be here to explain what was going on."

"I'm sorry friend I didn't think to let you know what has happened. That day when I left you..."

As we sat over a meal I related in brief about the gangers' attack and about Tuunac and Bijah being taken.

When I finished he sat in a stunned silence for a long moment. At last he swallowed hard and said, "That's horrible, Tas, have you contacted the imperial authorities about this?"

"No, we have not, preceptor," father said in a firm voice. "And we don't plan to. This is our Clan's affair. The gangers who attacked my son's nephews have already been 'eliminated.'"

Understanding his meaning Rushton shivered. "And as for the traitor, who is one of us, and the demon-ridden priest who has been used to abduct my grandchildren—their fragmentation is coming," father stated motioning to the Hathuuri. "This isn't something the imperial authorities are equipped to handle, believe me."

Rushton nodded, swallowed hard again and looked down at his empty plate. Looking up when he'd collected his thoughts, he said, "This is certainly a lot to absorb for an academic like me."

He took in a deep breath and let it out slowly. "And I guess, Tas, I will hear the entire tale when you get around to it in our sessions together."

"Unfortunately, that may not be for a while yet. I can return the money you sent me in advance if you like."

Rushton waved his hand in a dismissive gesture. "Don't even think about that. I am happy to be here to help you in that small way." Glancing around the table he took another sip of his drink and then asked, "What do you plan to do next?"

I raised my own cup in salute to him. "That is the main topic to discuss this evening, and you are welcome to stay and offer your suggestions."

Before he could answer the front door banged open and a call from the living room let us know that Sichahntri was back. As she came in the kitchen and shrugged out of the backpack bulging with groceries we all saw that she wasn't alone. Dressed in filthy ragged men's clothes and stinking of booze, came a smirking Dathna.

When Dathna saw both Gahji and Rushton sitting at the table ze growled an oath in an alien language, zer human features twisting into a fearsome snarl. "What are these humans doing here?"

Feeling the threat from this intruder, Wahtzuul and Duuzra bristled, the gems on their armor suddenly flaring with menace.

As aware of the potential for violence as the rest of us, Rushton shrank away, his eyes going to my face pleading. Gahji on the other hand wasn't at all intimidated and glared right back with her lips curled back in her own threat display, her Bear in her spirit fire, echoing her snarl.

Slapping a hand down upon the table hard enough to get everyone's attention, Star Swimmer rose. Calling Dathna a vile name used only rarely among the clans, he snarled, his voice quivering with his rage, "Don't you dare come in my son's house and tell him or anyone else who can be a part of his war council. It is his world, and he is the war leader here, not you. You and the fragmented Zeiva forfeited that right when you allowed your prejudice for a siyatli's gifts to blind you to the truth in his sending and that ignorance has cost the alliance a valued combatant.

"You swore an oath to me and to the Great One that you would protect and guide my siyatli son. But you broke that promise when you injured his human body and took from his mind the information he had already willingly supplied. Now sit down if you have something meaningful to contribute, and my daughter-in-law may be willing to feed you if you are hungry—otherwise, get out of my sight," he growled, calling zer the forbidden name again.

I hadn't told father about Dathna's attack. I hadn't wanted to foster more bad feelings among my relatives, but one look at Gahji's grim expression when she figured out who the drunken zaunk really was, told me that she had had no such reservations.

Dathna trembled, glancing from one hostile otherworldly face to another as ze mastered zer own emotions. At last ze bowed zer submission and sat in the chair Duuzra offered zer. "I do have something important to contribute, and, maybe you are right. " Ze turned to me zer eyes flicking to Gahji and then briefly Rushton as ze bowed.

"And maybe I do owe you an apology, little siyatli cousin. Both Zeiva and I should have paid more attention." Turning to Star Swimmer, ze also said, hoping to placate his anger, perhaps. "I arrived too late to prevent my Zeiva's sacrifice, Elder, but I did manage to salvage a great many parts of my dear one's essence to bring back to the healers for a remaking, so all isn't totally lost. Ze will in time be able to join us again."

Though it won't be the same, never the same, were zer hidden thoughts that I happened to capture before ze tightened zer mind shield.

Star Swimmer bowed in agreement, deciding to drop the matter for now. Instead he repeated his earlier question. "I have already 'eaten' but I will eat some of the human's food," ze said, glancing at me.

Not so willing to drop the matter entirely, Gahji plunked down a cup of kaf-tea in front of zer and then served my unwelcome cousin a cold plate of the fish I'd burnt. Dathna glanced up sensing Gahji's unforgiving anger. Ze smiled to taunt her and began to eat anyway.

When ze finished, father said, "Now that the niceties are done, proceed with your report. I take it the reason you stink and are wearing those disgusting clothes are because you have been spying on the enemy."

Dathna grinned. "I have—and it was a good ploy, too—"

Before ze could go further, Rushton finished his kaf-tea and rose. "I'm sorry, Tas, but I think I really should go. Your offer is tempting and most—intriguing, but as much as I would like to, I can't stay."

"Surely remaining with us will be more 'interesting' than grading papers this evening," I teased. "Please, you are welcome to join us."

Rushton glanced warily at a fuming Dathna and shook his head. "Truly I would like to, but the other reason I had for hoping to find you home this evening was to tell you that Martin called me this afternoon. Keveneth—uh—Kutima, as you call him, is in the infirmarium and Martin doesn't think his grandfather's going to recover from the bad case of pneumonia he caught this time.

"I was on my way to visit him when I stopped by. Keveneth wants to see you, Martin says, but he hasn't been able to reach you either." Rushton studied my stricken face for a long moment, sensing my inner turmoil.

At last he sighed, glancing once more at all the alien faces around my table, he said, "I can understand why that won't be possible at the moment. I will tell him what has happened and that you will come see him as soon as you possibly can."

Reading my agitation, as father translated our words for him Wahtzuul held up a large four-fingered hand to stop Rushton as he turned to leave. <<This elder the lore keeper speaks of he is a relative?>>

<<A distant one by blood, yes. But more importantly he is my oldest and dearest friend. We were boys together in my home village, before the imperials came and forced us to leave our sacred home. When father rescued me from the Crokno's child who wanted to steal my power, we were separated. When I returned to the world of my birth as a man I was fortunate

to find him again, but now he is a very old man who my friend here says is dying.>>

<<Mm, tell the lore keeper to wait a moment. I will give him something to help prolong your friend's life until we have rescued the children and you are able to go to him.>>

Speaking to Duuzra as I translated for Rushton the older guard left the kitchen. He returned shortly with a small pouch in which a tiny crystal lay. As he handed it to me I could feel its pulsating Qwakaiva.

I passed it to Rushton. "Give this to Kutima when you see him. It contains a very powerful conjure. My brother says it will help, so tell Martin not to let the doctors take it away. Tell him to wait for me; father and I will come as soon as we can."

"I'll go see him when I am at work tomorrow, Tas," Gahji promised, "so don't fret about him. I will see that he is taken care of properly." Turning to Rushton she asked as she stood. "It's getting late can you give me and the kids a ride back to Elder Samul's? I don't want to have to walk to the nearest mecho-transit stop in the dark. I noticed somebody shot out the street lamps again when Denny dropped us off."

Seeing my disappointment plain on my face, she laughed, and then relented and kissed me. "No, I am not staying to keep you warm tonight. Your job is to bring our children home and I'm not letting you get distracted from that."

As I helped her gather up the children and the bags Angika had packed for them, she let me see, for just a moment as I held her close in my arms, the fear and worry that she'd been keeping hidden in her heart. "Good night, my sweet seal love—and keep yourself safe," she whispered and kissed me. Her tears damp on my cheeks, she walked into the night.

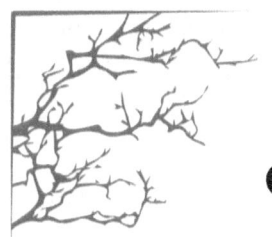

Chapter Seventeen

I had just waved farewell to Gahji and the children when Denny drove up in his mecho-cart with Elder Samul inside. Greeting me, he went around to the back of the vehicle and sat a heavy box on the vehicle's hood, then reached for another. He didn't need to tell me what was inside them. I could smell the lingering scent of blood on the frozen meat right away.

He grinned when he saw my relief. I had been wondering how I was going to feed everyone. "I thought you might need the extra meat to fortify our allies before they begin their work."

"You are right about that, but won't this clean out your entire winter supply as well?"

He snorted a laugh. "It does put a big dent in my cache, true enough, but the tribe is more than happy to contribute as well. We have a long tradition of being good hosts. And though I doubt if any of us will be attending a feast on your brother's world it is also a matter of pride to make sure our esteemed visitors are well taken care of while among us. We will hold an event with suitable gifts to send back with him when all this is over."

I couldn't argue with that and reached to pick up the other box from inside the cart. As I turned Midaz took it from me and then took Samul's as well before heading back into the house.

Pulling a bag of red fish off the back seat of his cart Denny happened to look around and caught sight of the four armed alien carrying the boxes into the house. His eyes popped wide. "Not a word to your friends about what you might see here tonight, grandson," Samul barked. "This is Ceremonial Society business and you are not to speak of it to anyone outside the family. Do I make myself clear?"

"Yes, grandfather, you do."

"Good. Then take what you are carrying to the kitchen and then go on home. I will call you when I want to be picked up."

Curious about my visitors, Denny suggested, "I could just wait for you in the living room. Ky said they have a new picta-view that is in color—and there is a game tonight—and I won't bother anybody."

I laughed. "Midaz has had enough torture for one day. He has been ordered to guard the house and that means no more picta-view. It's too much of a tempting distraction for my otherworldly relatives, I'm afraid. So if you were to stay you would just be staring at a black box. Better go home to watch the game. Another time maybe," I offered.

Entering the kitchen I noticed the talk had continued in my brief absence. As Samul greeted everyone and sat at the table I reached to bring down the nearly empty jar of kaf-tea from the cupboard to make another pot. While I was busy with the chores of making kaf-tea and storing the meat, Wahtzuul said to me, <<Your wife is a formidable woman. She is a fitting partner for a great mage such as you.>>

I chuckled <<I agree, my sweet bear woman is imposing. She manages to keep our household running smoothly. She helps me ground in this place and time and reminds me often who is truly in charge here. I don't know what I would do without her.>>

Duuzra smiled and said to my brother. <<See, not only is your siyatli brother powerful, when he praises his female he displays his humbleness, too. You could learn from him and your first wife would thank you for it.>>

Wahtzuul snorted and his crystals flared again. Privately I wondered if this brother was at least one of the siblings my father was talking about when he said that a jealous sibling might have killed me as a vulnerable child—Wahtzuul might even still try if he felt threatened.

To ease the growing tension, I laughed again and said, <<I don't know if I am worthy of being called a 'great mage' as you put it, honored Duuzra. I could never have channeled the storm as my Hathuuri brother and his escort did. That was a wonder to me and far beyond my puny capabilities.>>

<<But your brother is right to praise you, Tas,>> my father said. <<You might not be rich or famous, which are the qualities most valued in the Empire today, but you are a powerful Qwakaihi. Few among the humans gifted with power in the past, or now, could have withstood the storm's might summoned and channeled into a Hathuuri healing jewel.>>

Deciding the talk was drifting into dangerous territory Sichahntri asked Dathna to retell what ze had discovered while lying about near the temple's child protection agency.

<<I had to shift my appearance several times, but I now know that the human children are being held in a lower level room of the building I was watching,>> ze began. <<I became a cleaning man at one point over the course of the last couple days and while mopping, cleaning and emptying slop buckets I learned that there are others being held down there as well. Tas's is children are still together, but may not stay that way much longer.

<<The grandparents are anxious to reclaim the boy. The girl... they have been told that she is possessed by a devil and must be exorcised before she can be claimed.>>

My heart sank at that revelation and I tried not to let my fear cloud my reason. I knew exactly what could happen to a Gifted child left in Djoven's priest's care. And Utreal would know I knew, and might be setting a trap for me and using my wild and fearless daughter as bait.

Not wanting to think about that possibility, I asked another question, <<Are the other prisoners being held down there tribal children, children with a Gift?>> I asked when ze stopped for a moment to take a drink.

Dathna shrugged. <<They are human—and children. I dared not probe any deeper>>

Ze smirked, continuing zer account. <<I returned later to sit on the front steps as a woman, asking for money. A scowling priest gave me a couple coins and told me to go somewhere else to sober up, so I left.

<<Then I watched as a raven from a nearby tree for a while, then I wandered back as the one you see now. It was growing late when you summoned me and things were changing at the priests' temple building.>>

<<How so, cousin?>> Sichahntri asked.

<<The people who are there during the day to handle the work assigned them by the imperial government or the temple went home for the day and then more people began to arrive. Some were wearing regular clothing, others in blue robes, but most had little pesky demons clinging to their shoulders. The little I heard of their talk made me think that they are planning something—maybe a ritual for later tonight.>>

<<Hmm, it sounds like they are going to conduct their own ceremony in preparation for our battle,>> father mused, and then directed his next comment to me. <<Utreal would know that you wouldn't let him take two of your children without striking back. And he may also suspect that you would gather other allies to help you.>>

<<So the next question to ask is, does he know who has answered your summons, my brother.>>Wahtzuul mused.

Sichahntri nodded. <<That would depend on if zer and the Crokno guiding zer have as many good spies as I do.>>

<<A storm is building off the coast,>> Elder Samul said. <<It will be here later tonight, by my reckoning.>>

<<Yes, Elder, I can feel it, too,>>Wahtzuul grinned, showing his fangs. He glanced at Duuzra who was also grinning. <<And it will be a mighty one, just like before. Do these puny priests know how to tame and use such a magnificent being?>> he asked Samul. <<It will be a most glorious combat if they do.>>

<<I have never known Djoven's priests to use such power in the past,>> Samul said as he stroked his chin in thought.

<<Don't forget that Iyantsha could call down the lightning, so the skill isn't unknown on this world,>> I reminded him. <<I watched the Prophet do it several times while my family stayed with him.>>

<<And with Crokno guidance these demon-ridden creatures might be capable of far more than we suspect of them,>> Star Swimmer added. <<So we can't afford to underestimate them.>>

Wahtzuul bowed, accepting my father's warning, but I could sense the excitement of the Hathuuri building like the coming storm as the night progressed. Born to a world of volcanic eruptions, quakes and intertribal combats they were eager to test themselves against our human and Crokno adversaries.

Just after that Aqwissa announced that Utreal and a priest had come to take Tuunac to his grandparents. While in contact with her, however, Aqwissa had managed to tell her to give Tuunac one of her barrettes. Tuunac had taken her gift and put it in his pocket.

Bijah put the other in her own pocket, just before the priests came for her brother. Unfortunately for us, she was now being magically and physically restrained after she tried attacking the priests who came for Tuunac.

<<I can no longer talk to her>> Aqwissa said. <<Your cousin or the true Crokno with him is now shielding her, but she still has my token.>>

The council decided that since the children were no longer together we would have to split up our force. <<Utreal or another Crokno agent may be waiting to entrap us whichever child we try to reclaim,>> Star Swimmer said. <<But I think my granddaughter is the one in most danger. She is the one with the Gift and the one the priests and their Crokno masters will want to torture until she is broken to their will and becomes another weapon to use against us.>>

<<I agree,>> Dathna said. <<The boy has no importance and can be taken back from these stupid grandparents at any time once the Crokno are dealt with. So we need to focus our attention on the temple agency.>>

Banishing images of my own torture at the hands of such evil and misguided people I took a deep breath and said, <<I agree that we need to go after the priests especially since other vulnerable children seem to also be caught up in their net.>>

Then as the memory of a very frightened boy's face peering out at me from the nurse log where I had stashed him during my fight with the sabiyan hunters came into my mind, I knew I could never abandon him. He might not have a powerful Gift, but he was mine and Gahji's son—and I loved him.

<<However, I am not willing to abandon my son, either. Utreal may anticipate our focus on the temple, so ze may not be there. Ze may be waiting to pounce when we think we have won and go after my son, thinking he is now unprotected.>>

<<That is a very cunning idea, Tigring. You are clever to think of it. It is what I might do if I were this traitorous enemy, who wishes you and my chieftain's father dead,>> Duuzra said to me.

Once again I felt my brother's irritation as his older advisor praised me. I was sure the man must be aware of what he was doing, if a stranger like me could sense the growing storm, and I wasn't sure why he was courting this danger. Refusing to be a part of his game, however, I said to Wahtzuul, <<I

have little experience in matters of war, elder brother. I would welcome your advice and that of your noble escort.>>

After a bit more talk it was decided that the Hathuuri and I would go to the temple for Bijah. Star Swimmer, and Dathna would hold back until we determined if ze was there. If ze wasn't, then they would hunt for zer and my son at the grandparents' mansion.

<<Utreal has never paid much attention to any of my children, so ze and the Crokno with him won't expect me recovered enough to be of much danger to zer and zer plans,>> Star Swimmer said, <<so that will be to our advantage.>>

<<Nor will ze expect to see me among your warband, either, siyatli cousin,>> Dathna said, zer human face grim with determination.

<<That is probably true, cousin,>> Sichahntri agreed. <<Ze would expect you to be deep in our territory grieving the loss you received.>>

Elder Samul left not long after that. <<I will gather my people and we will begin our own preparations for this battle with the priests later tonight when the storm arrives. We will be ready when you have need of the power we can conjure from our land to help save our children,>> he promised.

"It might be wise for you to bring Gahji, her children, and your own wife and family to the ceremonial house while we conjure," Star Swimmer advised in our human language.

I chuckled. "She isn't going to like it, because Angika is going to miss more school and she may not make it to work tomorrow, but tell her that the ceremonial house will be where we bring the children and that may stop her protests," I suggested.

He nodded. Hearing Denny beep the horn on his cart he rose and bowed to the rest of us. Sichahntri went with him. She would act as the channel directing the power raised to where it would be most useful.

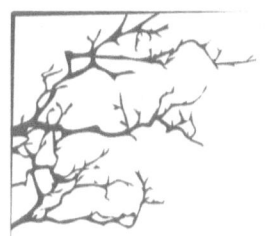

Chapter Eighteen

With the storm fast approaching, we left my house near midnight through the door leading into the yard, dressed in dark hooded capes that my sister provided. Lightning flashed on the horizon as I raised my face to the storm and felt the bite of its cold wind. I paused and held out my hands palms upward, drinking in the power of the land around me.

In the darkness I could feel the spirits gathering. In this heartless city, in this discarded place filled with trash and human misery trees and grasses still struggled to grow and nurture the little ones who sheltered among the foliage. Life was forever renewing itself—and hopeful, and I should never forget that.

My heart swelled with the love of this land—my world. I had sworn to protect it and I prayed to the Unseen Ones who hovered near to witness that they also bless our working and give us the strength needed to overcome this alien threat.

With my etheric roots sinking deep into the soil beneath me I heard the big log drum in the ceremonial house beat out an answering cadence to the gathering of Smotahlik elders as they began to sing. The wind and the rain flattening my hair and streaming down my face, I too sang, echoing their song as I drew to me the power the spirits of my land had to offer. Knowing what I was doing, my brother and his escort joined me.

Like me, the Hathuuri could make a transfer between different places on a world, but we couldn't transfer to a past or future in time or to another world without the help of our relatives from the Beyond. With Dathna to guide us we managed to transfer to an alley across from the agency as the storm increased in power.

Because it was late and raining no one was about to see us appear. From inside the agency's chapel we could hear people raising their voices in a hymn, praising the Thunderer and asking for his blessing. I also sensed the strong magical shield that had been erected around the building to protect them as well as contain their own conjure until they were ready to attack us.

Grinning, Wahtzuul stepped up beside me studying their shield. <<What are they singing about?>>

<<Their god is an alien being our conquerors brought with them from their land across the big ocean. They call him the Thunderer and his symbol is the lightning.>> I pointed to the sigil painted on the outside wall of the building. <<He is supposed to bring down his lightning bolts when he wants to punish a 'sinner', someone the priests think is a bad person.>>

Wahtzuul and his men laughed, the crystals on their armor flaring as the rumble of thunder came ever closer. <<If it is thunder and lightning that they are praying for, then we should give these foolish priests what they want, my brother,>> he said and slapped me hard upon my back.

I grinned, caught up in their excitement. <<Their shield appears quite strong.But they may have other tricks prepared for us inside once we break through,>> I cautioned.

Wahtzuul's grin became even wider. <<Not to worry, younger brother. this enemy has never felt the thrust of a Hathuuri war spear.>>

Guessing what was about to happen I said hesitantly, <<Without our sister hear to complete the figure I doubt if I will be of much use to you in this conjure.>>

He laughed and slapped my back again. <<You were a part of a healing jewel, a restorative conjure. That does need four mages, but what we plan now is for war, and we only need three mages for that.>>

He formed a triangle with his upper set of hands to demonstrate.<<You need only be ready to lead us once we have opened the way for you.>>

As Duuzra called the storm to us I asked Wahtzuul, <<If you can link with me I will show you some of what these Crokno slaves have done, and it would appear, are still doing to my people's Gifted children.>>

He agreed and took my outstretched hands. And so while we waited for the storm to be fully over us I fueled my anger by reliving in part once again my capture and imprisonment and torture by the Crokno's half-breed child. I also relived for him Hoyt's death and explained that Gahji was the granddaughter of the brave young warrior who had saved our father by stabbing Hoyt while he was focused on subduing Star Swimmer.

His respect for her growing he bowed. <<As I said she is a formidable woman and her lineage is impeccable. Thank you for telling me.>>

Knowing now what the Hathuuri planned I feared for my daughter and the other children. <<Aqwissa, can you sense where Bijah is?>>

<<Though I can't speak to her, I know she is inside. All the children the priests' have been holding are along the far wall.>>

Still concealed by the darkness Duuzra's chant grew as he called the storm to us. I stepped back as they stood side-by-side forming a triangle with Wahtzuul standing slightly in front at its point. Their crystals blazed as the first bolt of lightning struck their upraised hands. Glowing with a blue-white phosphorescence Wahtzuul cried out and called to him another bolt, and then another.

Inside the temple they could hear the thunder and see the nearby flashes of lightning through the colored glass window above the Thunderer's altar and rejoiced, thinking Djoven had come to answer their prayers.

How wrong they were... Storm had come to answer mine.

When the Hathuuri judged they had collected enough from the storm, they directed the force of Lightning's Qwakaiva at the colored window over the altar. With a deafening peal of thunder booming overhead a beam of blinding white light hit the glass and that entire portion of the wall exploded in a shower of glass and flaming debris.

From inside the chapel I could hear people screaming, as I leapt through the opening, the Hathuuri right behind me. Pointing metallic rods alive with snaking currents of fire the Hathuuri shouted their battle cries and aimed their weapons at demon-ridden priest, or anyone else foolish enough to challenge them. Thinking their worst nightmare was coming true Djoven's worshipers shouted and pushed and jumped over each other in a total panic to reach the front door and escape.

But there was no escape. We had magically barred the door from the outside before making our dramatic entrance. Nobody was leaving until we gave them permission—if we gave them permission.

The children were clustered in a terrified huddle along the far wall as Aqwissa had told me, guarded by a blue-robed priest that was only in outward appearance human.

Bijah was among them and saw me, but made no move to call out to me, her eyes unable to focus on my face for more than a moment. I became aware of the conjure binding her and I wondered if she had also been drugged. Leaping high over the milling people I landed on the floor beside her. Midaz who saw me jump followed and landed close by.

"Don't be afraid," I shouted to the children over the din. "We are here to take you away from these evil people."

Along with the others Bijah heard and recognized me at last. She held out her arms and called to me. Before she could escape her minder, however, the Crokno priest snatched her up to hold like a shield in front of him. "Your cousin said you would come for the girl, but he didn't say you would come with the Hathuuri at your back."

I laughed. "I guess he forgot that Star Swimmer has more than one siyatli child, eh?"

"Yes, quite, and ze will pay for that lack when next I see zer."

"You won't see zer soon, because you and ze aren't going to be alive much longer. Let go of my daughter, Crokno scum."

The priest laughed. "Maybe after I am safely out of here, but she is my insurance that I won't be fragmented in the meantime."

"You sure about that?"

"Yes, I am. Utreal has told us how sentimental humans can be—and you in particular. You care too much for one of your own to risk me killing her," he taunted and began to slide towards a small side door.

<<That is not our Bijah he is holding,>> Aqwissa, shielding her thought, whispered into my mind. <<This is a trap. The conjured doll assassin has been made to look like her and imprinted with your scent. She will try to kill you if you touch her.>>

"Appi," Bijah cried and held out her arms to me, her eyes pleading. "Don't let the bad man take me away again!"

Trying not to let my spirit fire or my expression reveal my inner turmoil, I asked, <<How can you be so sure? Maybe it is my Bijah and they have just drugged her, or something?>>

<<You will have to trust me, siyatli brother. I know because Bijah has the blood of dragons flowing in her veins and this creature does not. Plus she has no butterfly barrette in her pocket.>>

Tears streaming down her face she cried out again as the Crokno priest slowly crept towards the door. "Appi, help me!"

They could have taken the barrette away and this was my Bijah...

"Appi!"

But this Bijah wasn't sucking her thumb—and hadn't been when we burst into the chapel. She still resorted to that soothing action when she was frightened in spite of her age. And now, was definitely a frightening time for anyone, even a child with an otherworldly Gift. Gahji was going to kill me if I chose wrong—if I didn't kill myself first...

Trust. This was all about trust, and having faith in another's abilities... I wouldn't be like Zeiva and make a fatal mistake. <<Then if this is not our Bijah, hunt and find her.>> Slipping off my wrist in the darkness under my cape, she changed and disappeared.

Still keeping my eye focused on the priest I said, <<Midaz, kill them both.>> Not questioning my order, Midaz raised his weapon and loosed a stream of lightning's essence into the Crokno and the one he was holding.

An expression of shock coming onto his face the Crokno screamed and burst into flame, dropping the bundle of rags, sticks and claw-like hands tipped with their tiny lethal blades that were hidden behind the illusion of his conjure.

When I looked away I caught the eye of a tough-looking Kukiya youth who had been fearlessly watching me. "I don't know who you are, but you did us all a favor when you got rid of that dog-humping turd. Sorry about the girl, though. She was always telling us her papa was coming to save us. Guess that was you, eh?"

"Yes that was me, but that thing wasn't my daughter and I need to find her. Got any idea where they might be hiding her?"

He shrugged. "She could be in any of the locked offices on this floor or in the rooms down in the basement where they've been keeping us."

I glanced around us the building was on fire and people were trying to force the front door. The Hathuuri were methodically wading through them and killing demons and their hosts alike as they sang a deep rumbling war chant.

"I need to find my daughter. How do I get to the basement and these offices you spoke of?"

The youth pointed to the door in the wall the priest had been aiming for. "The offices are on the other side and the stairs down are at the end of the hall. You can't get out from down there which is probably why nobody has tried to escape that way."

"Thank you for telling me. I'll worry about getting out once I find her. Can you help these other children to safety, young warrior?" I pointed to the shattered window. "You can go out that way and Midaz here can clear a way for you, or if you know of a more conventional way out besides the blocked front door there, he will release our shield for you."

He glanced at the window and grinned then coughed as a plume of smoke made its way to us. "If that big guy will help the little ones we'll go out the quickest way—over there."

"Goldys and firemen may already be out front and I think the emergency team from ZFH is coming. I'm not sure who has arrived yet, but try to stay together."

"I'll help the others get out, but after that I'm gone. I'll take my chances in the streets," he growled. "So don't tell me what to do."

"And how well did that work out for you last time, eh? Stay together!" I ordered him. "You need the teachings we can give you before your untrained Gift destroys you. Nobody is going to let a damned priest lock you up for being who you are again. I will see to that." *If I'm still alive after I find my children,* of course, I thought to myself.

Telling my brother I had to search for my daughter, who was being held in another part of the building, I directed Midaz to help get the children out then report to his chieftain for more orders.

<<He will want me to find you. I already know what he will say.>>

<<Fine, get the children out and then come back to me,>> I said as I lurched open the little door and stepped through.

The hallway was quiet only dimly lighted by a few weak overhead lights in the ceiling. The office doors I passed were locked when I tried opening them. Not taking the time to pick the locks open with my Qwakaiva I wrenched the doors wide with the power gifted me by the storm.

My Bijah wasn't in any of them. Knowing how these records had been used to enslave and torture tribal children I decided to fire them if there was time when I left. Slipping through the door at the end of the hall I headed down the stairs, my feet making no sound as I went.

It was cold down here the walls and floor of stone bricks painted a dull gray. Somewhere ahead I could hear the rumble of the old furnace grumbling to itself. I passed several closed doors. Most were unlocked and when I looked inside I saw a windowless cell, furnished only with a cot, wash basin and pee bucket in the corner. This was where they had been keeping the children, no doubt.

And if these cruel priests turned off the lights... These cold dirty cells would become like a modern day Perdition Box, I thought, my anger fueled as the echoes of my own imprisonment rose up from the past to haunt me.

<<Aqwissa, where are you?>>

<<I am here, siyatli brother. The little one is further along this hall, but have a care the priest who came to our house is with her. Though he thinks he is hiding behind the shield the Crokno priest taught him, I can see him clearly. He has a tether binding him to Bijah and he's waiting for you.>>

A little further down the corridor an open door and light invited me to enter. I did not walk into his trap. Instead I stepped silently into the room next door and called Midaz to me.

He came as silently as Mathrom's Cougar, crouching by my side in the next moment. <<My daughter is being held captive in the next room by a human priest trained by the Crokno. Can one of your weapons create an opening here that will distract him but not hurt my daughter? If so, I wil enter by the doorway, while you go in from here.>>

Midaz signed yes and pulled a smaller rod from the collection at his waist. I moved into the hall and when he gave me the signal I leaped for the open doorway. At the same moment there was a loud boom and a glowing hole began enlarging in the wall in front of him.

Bijah was huddled on a dirty cot a blanket folded around her shoulders. Beside the cot was the priest, his wavering form behind a shield he had clumsily erected for concealment and protection.

As I walked through the door Midaz stepped through the hole he had created at the same moment. The priest took one look at the Hathuuri and his eyes grew wide with fear. I shattered his badly-formed conjure as I moved further into the room in the next moment.

He let out a strangled cry and moved back closer to Bijah. "Tell your creature to get back, witch, or, or your daughter will die, you heathen devil from the abyss," he shouted holding up Djoven's sigil around his neck.

"Appi, is it really you?" Bijah cried taking her thumb from her mouth.

"Yes, my girl. It's really me."

Raising Djoven's sign a little higher he thrust it towards me, his voice quivering as he shouted, "Get back, devil, before I call down Djoven's mighty lightning to destroy you!"

I laughed. "Really? You think that useless talisman is going to save you?" When I translated for Midaz the priest's threat he joined me in my laughter.

"But Appi, if it is really you, you look all—blurry—and I'm scared. Can you tell Aqwissa I need her?"

Bijah sounded like she was speaking to me under water. And Aqwissa was plainly visible curled around my arm. Why couldn't she see her. The priest obviously could, which added to his terror.

<<It is the Crokno's conjure binding her senses. Tell Midaz not to attack until I can free her from the tether linking her to the priest.>>

My lips curled into a snarl, showing my canines. "Me, die? If you hurt my daughter it is *you* who will die in the most painful way I can imagine."

He swore an unpriestly oath and grabbed for Bijah. She scooted further back on the cot out of his reach unless he took his eyes off me to find her. When he couldn't physically touch her he pointed to the etheric tether binding them. "If you hurt me she will feel it, too." He motioned for my daughter to come to him. When she refused he sent a bolt of pain down their link to "make" her. She screamed. "Do you see now?"

"I see that you are a dead man."

He laughed. "We will see about that." Risking my ire, he turned and snatched up Bijah by her shirt and jerked her to him, then stood with her in front of him. "Now we are leaving to find my colleague and you won't dare to stop us, will you?"

I folded my arms across my chest, still blocking the exit. "If you are thinking to find the Crokno agent posing as one of Djoven's priests, he has already preceded you to the fiery abyss you priests are always talking about. But—not to worry, you will be joining him soon enough."

Startled he stepped back. "You're lying; he couldn't be?"

Now it was my turn to laugh. "Because he told you he was one of Djoven's emissaries sent by your god to help you uncover heathen evil?"

My word struck like a well-aimed spear thrust and I laughed again. "Stupid human. He is no more sent from your god than I am, or the Hathuuri warrior over there. You and the rest of Djoven's deluded followers imprisoning our children are but expendable victims of a war being waged on many worlds across time. It is a war far beyond the narrow limits of your reason to comprehend.

"Why would I bother to lie to you? You and your puny god are of no importance to those who wield power enough to change the course of entire worlds within the Starry River. Release my daughter and go upstairs and see for yourself the chaos you stupid priests have conjured. When you summoned the lightning you got what you prayed for—us."

I motioned to Midaz standing by the hole he had created. Reading my thoughts as I spoke to the priest, he had remained alert and ready for whatever I needed. "His people are masters of the art of taming and wielding a storm's power. Can't you hear the screaming, smell the smoke?"

He shook his head stepping back again. When his attack came I was expecting a magical assault, not a physical one. I wasn't prepared for the little black gun he pulled from a pocket in his robe. He got off a shot, which my quick-thinking daughter spoiled when she rammed her head into his stomach, causing him to miss the vital part of me he had been aiming for.

I had seen the gun at the last moment and was leaping away, which is why the bullet only cut a deep furrow across my right hip and bum-cheek instead. Before I could tell him otherwise, Midaz saw the threat to me, aimed his weapon and a fountain of lightning-fed power hit the priest.

As it raced down the tether to engulf my girl Aqwissa leapt from my arm and bravely severed the etheric cord with her teeth. In a sudden burst of luminescence the dragon-lizard disappeared in a sizzling flash, as the tether, too, disintegrated.

Ignoring the blood dripping down my leg I snatched her up and enfolded Bijah in my arms. I hugged her close. "Oh my sweet baby girl, I love you so much." In spite of the Crokno's conjure giving out a stinging sensation, I hugged her even tighter.

"Appi, I was so frightened. What is happening to me?" she wailed still sounding like she was underwater.

"I know. Don't be afraid. We will take you to Ati Star he can break the mean priest's conjure. He did for me when a mean priest did something similar to me. You will be fine soon."

<<Tigring, we need to get out of here or we may be trapped. The fire is getting worse above us. Can you transfer the child out of this place?>>

I stepped over the smoldering corpse and headed for the doorway, looking round for Aqwissa. <<I don't know. Her Gift is still blocked so she can't help me and I've never tried to transfer someone who isn't able to make the shift.>>

<<Then if she will permit it give her to me. The storm has shared enough of its power that I can help her. We need to go soon.>>

Midaz was right, so I explained to Bijah that this new relative was taking her to her mother, and I would be coming soon. Relieved I handed her over, because I had another problem to deal with, before I could leave.

In the far corner I had just caught sight of my Aqwissa and she was injured. When I hurried over to her and scooped her up I saw that her mouth was only ragged silver where her teeth should have been. She couldn't reform into the bracelet by clasping her tail around my wrist. <<Oh my brave little sister, I am so sorry you were injured, too.>> Cradling her in my arms I made the transfer.

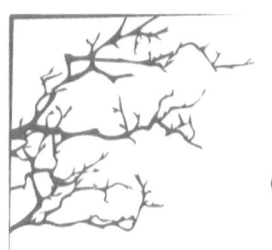

Chapter Nineteen

We had agreed to meet at the ceremonial house ahead of the attack, so that was where I projected us. When I arrived Midaz had handed a crying Bijah over to Gahji, who was sitting on a low bench near one of the two sacred fires. Sichahntri had sensed my arrival and looked up. She was already sitting beside Gahji as Midaz told her about the fight and the conjure confining our daughter.

From the kitchen came the smells of kaf-tea and frying meat. My empty stomach rumbled in answer. I could also hear my brother's booming laughter and Star Swimmer translating for some of the Smotahlik Elders I could see sitting around the long table. Good they were safe and here as well. Only Dathna seemed missing.

Sichahntri looked up from her examination of my daughter as I approached, a quivering Aqwissa, about the size of a cat, held tight against my chest under the concealing folds of my cape. In the darkness above some of the initiates and their minders either slept or talked quietly among themselves where they sprawled upon the benches.

"Ah, good, there you are," Sichahntri said. "We were starting to worry when our brother showed up and said they had to leave because the building was collapsing around them. And then when Midaz came with only the little girl..."

So as not to worry my bear woman, who didn't seem to feel the sting radiating from the conjure confining her daughter, I said in the mind talk, <<"Are you able to release her from the Crokno's conjure like Star Swimmer did for me?>>

She studied the weave a moment longer before answering, <<In time, perhaps, but what was done to you, was done in haste and by a Crokno half-breed, lacking the knowledge to make a truly powerful working. This, on

the other hand, was made by a master who had time and skill to weave a truly strong conjure.>>

<<I don't understand; why would they bother? She is but a child.>>

<<A child with dragon blood, brother, even though it is quite diluted, it is there and links her to all dragon-kind—including Kunai—never forget that, Tas.>>

And that meant if they could break her and mold her to their purpose... I shuddered, not wanting to imagine that.

Gahji looked around then and gave me a worried look. "Asiya, my heart, is Tuunac with you?"

It was hot so close to the fire, so I had taken off my cape and laid it on the bench near her. I placed Aqwissa on it and put a fold of the thick cloth over her. Wincing, I eased myself down to sit beside them.

"No, my heart. Tuunac wasn't at the temple. Utreal split the children up before we got there. I assume he is with his paternal grandparents by now—along with my cousin and more enemy fish slime waiting for us."

Suddenly feeling the past night's events catching up with me I felt the total weight of my exhaustion settle upon my shoulders. I needed to eat—and then sleep. "Where is Dathna?" I asked my sister.

"Hunting."

"Hunting for Utreal and my son, or just 'hunting'?"

Sichahntri shrugged. "Who can say with that one."

"Tas, we need to find Tuunac," Gahji said, interrupting, an urgent note coming into her voice. "If he wasn't at the temple then have you sent Aqwissa to find him?"

I sighed. I really needed to eat and—sleep. "No, my heart, I haven't."

"Why, damn it, why? Tas, who knows what those horrible people might do to our boy, after what they've done to our daughter!"

"Why? Because she was badly wounded saving Bijah." I motioned to the silver form on my cape. "She needs a healing like Bijah, before I can send her hunting again."

The full meaning of what I said finally coming to her, Gahji looked away while she mastered her fear. "Then he is truly lost to us," she choked out, silent tears streaming unnoticed down her cheeks.

I scooted closer and put an arm around her and our daughter who was sucking her thumb again. "Don't even think that, my love. We will find him—I promise."

"Don't tease me with a promise you won't be able to keep. You can't know that for certain," she growled, her eyes flashing with anger.

I barked out an ironic laugh. "Oh yes I can. My cousin and the Crokno will be happy to let me find him when they have their trap ready to ensnare me and Star Swimmer. I am totally sure of that. Tuunac will be the new bait—since we didn't die at the temple, as they hoped."

"Then Aqwissa needs to find them, before their plans are set.'

"I can't argue with that." Turning to Sichahntri I said, "She tore up her mouth when she bit through the Crokno's magical tether to save Bijah. Unfortunately, I am too exhausted to help with her renewal and healing right now. Can you help her for me?"

"And you are also bleeding all over your boots and the ground under the bench," Star Swimmer said as he and my brother came over to us.

Startled Gahji saw the blood and swore. Handing her daughter over to my sister she stood arms folded glaring down at me. "What did you do to yourself this time? Tas, I swear... Stand up and let me see."

"It's nothing, Gahji—really," I protested.

"I'll be the judge of that. Stand up."

"The bad priest tried to shoot Appi with his little gun, but Appi jumped and I hit him with my head and he missed—almost," Bijah took her thumb out of her mouth and said.

Noticing where the blood was coming from, my brother laughed.

"He shot you in the bum?" Denny said, coming over to us.

In spite of her fear and the uncertainty about what might happen next, Gahji was finding it hard to keep the smile off her face, too. Glaring at my still laughing brother, she scowled and motioned. "Well, don't just stand there. Bring him into the better light in the kitchen and Denny, stop hanging around gaping with your mouth open. Tell somebody to get whatever this house has for healing supplies and bring them to me."

Wahtzuul didn't need my sister to translate. Still chuckling, he picked me up and carried me into the kitchen where he placed me face down upon one of the long hastily emptied tables.

I was the focus of more good-natured teasing while I ate a long overdue meal after Gahji finished with me and went back to her daughter. While I was eating, Elder Samul came and sat down beside me. "When it was decided that everybody was coming back here I sent Denny back to your house to get a box of the meat I brought over." He glanced at the Hathuuri filling their plates again. "We are sending out a hunting party this morning for more food."

I chuckled and took another drink of my kaf-tea. "They do have formidable appetites. Father says it is only after a great conjure that their need is so great, though, so don't worry. And ask father or my sister for money to buy a couple cai if you need to."

"I just might do that, depending on how successful the hunt is today."

As another thought came to me, I said, "If it's permitted, send Mathrom and his minder along with the hunters. I have been with him when he has called his Siiqwah, his Cougar to him while hunting. My sister taught him how to do that successfully. We got two nice bucks that day. It might help the ones teaching him see what he needs. He seems to only lose control when his life is threatened and he gives into his fear and allows the big cat too much freedom to enter our world."

"Hmm, that's a good idea. We paired him with Tobey, one of our Elders you worked with last summer. I will speak to him about that," he said as he rose and let me finish my meal.

Feeling full myself at last, I limped back into the main hall to roll into my cape to sleep. Somewhere in the tiers of benches above me the Hathuuri also slept bundled in their shadowy cloaks.

At first I was vaguely aware of the life of the ceremonial house going on around me. An Elder chanted a morning prayer and the minders woke the initiates for a run along the beach and a swim in the cold water of the inlet. But in time the activity around me became just another blurred part of my dreams. I let my body relax and spirit renew itself by touching the Qwakaiva of the land around me.

I awoke to an ominous feeling of storm clouds massing on the horizon and Bijah crying. It was night again when I opened my eyes. Rumbling sounds told me that my brother and his men still slept in the darkness above. As I tried to sit up I was painfully reminded of the stitches sewing up my bum. Stifling a groan I stumbled off to the privy and then went to the kitchen for water and kaf-tea.

The hunt had been successful. Mathrom and several minders and initiates were finishing the butchering and cooking liver in a large frying pan. Snatching a hot piece from the mounting pile set to cool I took my drink and wandered back into the main hall.

In the clear space between the two fires my sister sat cross-legged on the ground with Bijah on her lap. On either side of her crouched a grim-faced Star Swimmer and Kotahi. They were studying the magical weave confining her and occasionally pulling on one of the weave's luminous strands. As I approached, sipping my drink Kotahi did something and Bijah cried out, Sichahntri soothing her gently in the next moment.

I crouched down in front of her so she could see me. "It will be all right in a while, baby girl, Ati Star and Uncle are just trying to take away the mean priest's conjure," I soothed.

"Appi, I want Aqwissa. Can I hold Aqwissa so I won't be so scared?"

I glanced around for the little dragon-lizard and got another surprise. Gahji was sitting on a blanket holding Aqwissa on her lap, the injured little one under her shirt drawing substance from her human body. She had her feet planted firmly on the ground and someone had shown her how to open a channel down into the earth, so as not to drain herself of Qwakaiva.

"Not right now, my girl. Aqwissa is hurt, too. She can come later."

"Where is Tuunac? Can he come sit by me?"

My heart gave a lurch and I shook my head. "No, baby girl, your brother isn't here. You will just have to be the brave warrior girl I know you are. Amima and I are close by, so don't be afraid." Turning to my father I asked, "Can I do anything to help?"

Switching to the mind talk, which at the moment Bijah was unable to hear, he said, <<Not right now. This is going to be a slow process, so maybe later you can channel Qwakaiva to one of us. The fiend who did this was cunning, zer work filled with knots and tangles that will kill her if done improperly. Even so we have only managed to clear away enough so that she can resume eating and drinking to keep her human body alive. Otherwise she might have died soon. She hasn't been able to eat or drink in several days.

Her purpose was to ensnare us; they would have let her die too once we were fragmented.

Oh, Bijah! I hated that she had had to suffer because of me. <<Is she going to survive now?>>

<<Maybe. We called Kotahi back from his garden, because of his healing skills are far more powerful than mine or your other siblings, but even he isn't sure he will be able to totally cure her. She may live he tells me, but she may never get her Gift fully restored.>>

His prediction sent the rage bubbling up like a volcano in my chest. What was done to Bijah and other gifted children—even Hoyt himself by the Crokno was so unbelievably cruel. How could they so self-righteously claim to be "protecting the universe from the potential evil inherit in children fostered by Kunai and the clans of our lineage when they could justify such insidious harm inflicted upon innocent children—even those—like Hoyt, who were of their own making?

I went over to sit by my wife next. She glanced up a grim expression on her face, then she returned her focus to the task of channeling Earth's Qwakaiva to the dragon-lizard. "I can take over if you are tiring," I offered.

She glanced down at the silver scaled body next to her breast, half concealed under the blanket tossed over one shoulder like she used to do when feeding O'siyan. "In a bit, we are fine for now."

"Where is O'siyan? He might get jealous if he sees you feeding somebody else."

She snorted a laugh. "Auntie Megara took the children back to town with her. Angika has school today you Know. And Terry Red Bird will watch baby while auntie is at work."

"Didn't you have to work today, too?"

"I did, but I called in sick. I will go back tomorrow—if I'm better."

"Mm, who taught you to channel like that?"

"Your father. He says I could do much more with my Bear and my Qwakaiva if I can get over my fears. Right now my fear for my son was stronger than my fear of my Gift so I could let him show me what I needed to do. We need to find my son, and we need Aqwissa for that."

"Kunai has enhanced her abilities so she can hunt for me, so she would be my first choice, true enough, but there are other means at our disposal, so don't risk your own health to speed up her recovery," I chided.

She gave me a disgusted glare and told me to go bring her some water and tea. I brought her what she asked for and a plate of scau-bread and fried liver to munch on as well. Then with no one needing me for the moment I went back into the kitchen to help with any tasks needing a willing hand to do them.

While I was washing some big stew pots with Mathrom, Ky and two other initiates, I noticed Chief Rickson come in with a few of the children we had rescued from the temple, and the young Kukiya warrior I had ordered to stay with the others was with them.

With my back to the group who were just sitting down at a far table and being served some stew and bread, I asked Mathrom, "Do you know that Kukiya youth that just came in with the chief?"

Overhearing me, Ky also glanced in their direction and it was he who answered, "I don't know his name, but I've seen him. I think he was working for Jakko and his family at one point. He hasn't been around lately, though." Ky smirked and set the pot he'd just finished washing on the counter upside down to dry. "Guess that was because the temple social workers got him—maybe after a tip from Benton's boys."

"His name is Jerriton, I think," Mathrom supplied. "I knew his older brother and a sister better. They were part of a bunch that was always picking on me and sis once they moved to town with their parents. At one point they were all drinking buddies with mom, but they had a big fight—and it was after that me and sis started having trouble with his older siblings. Why is *he* here?"

"Because, like you he has a Gift and those dog-humping priests were keeping him and the others over there confined in dark cells below the agency offices we destroyed last night."

Mathrom thought about what I'd said for a moment while he scrubbed at a spot of burnt on grease, when he understood the meaning of what I'd left unvoiced he stopped and turned to me, his mouth set in a hard line. "You mean like what happened to you?"

I nodded. "I'm not sure if these modern children were starved and tortured like I once was, but they were being kept in cold windowless cells in that temple agency's basement, so the potential was certainly there to inflict such cruelties. We shall see what the children are willing to tell us once they feel safe enough to speak openly about what happened to them."

"Is there anything you want me to do to help him?" Mathrom surprised me by asking next.

I smiled and touched his shoulder, letting him know I was proud of him for overcoming childhood resentments enough to think of another's need. "Nothing for the moment. Your big task while here is to learn how to control Cougar, and that task must always be your priority this winter. If Tobey agrees you can speak to him, but leave his instruction to others."

Catching sight of me at that moment, Rickson waved me over to his table where Elder Samul and two other Smotahlik Elders had joined him. Grabbing a clean cup and the smaller kaf-teapot, I went over.

When I had refilled the chief and the Elder's cups and sat down with my own drink, Rickson plunked down a copy of an imperial news-sheet on the table in front of me. In large black writing it read, Temple Agency Destroyed by Massive Lightning Strike. Below the words was a picture of a building in flames with dark silhouettes of people clustered around the outside watching it burn.

"The fire wagons sent to the alarm called in by a citizen, said the building is completely destroyed. Several burnt bodies have been found in the smoldering wreckage," he summarized for me.

Hoping neither my face nor my voice hinted at the part I played in the agencies demise, I said. "How unfortunate—for the temple—and the priests lost to the flames."

He snorted and put down the paper. I doubted if he believed me, but he also wasn't willing to pursue the matter further at that moment. But he did study my face carefully before continuing, "These children say they were being held captive in dirty cells in the lower level of that building. If we can verify that, our attorneys will begin legal proceedings against the temple for this violation of their imperial charter.

"I'm sure a few of the staff who worked there during the day and weren't a part of the agency's 'other' activities will be willing to testify when they understand that they, too, might face prison for their part in the matter," he mused. "That kind of abuse was outlawed hundreds of years ago by the Imperials. To now realize that it is still continuing..."

"I know it is hard for you modern tribal people to believe, but it is as I warned you, Chief Rickson. The war against our people still continues on all fronts, not just the physical."

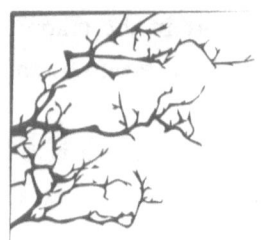

Chapter Twenty

It was the end of everyone's work cycle for the seven-day and people would soon arrive for ceremonies. The tribal Elders decided it would be better to keep the identity of our otherworldly guests a secret. So, with that in mind my family transferred, or took more conventional means, back to my house. No one knew where Dathna had gone since the night the temple burned, but Star Swimmer figured ze would turn up eventually—if the Crokno didn't fragment zer first.

It was good to sleep in my own bed with my wife and baby beside me and the girls back in their own room with Sichahntri nearby. Her mouth still not fully healed, Aqwissa curled up next to my daughter. And even though Bijah couldn't speak to her mind-to-mind the little dragon-lizard's presence seemed to comfort her, so I left her there. My brother was in Tuunac's room with his escort taking turns resting or being on guard.

All this should have meant that I would sleep well, but unlike the peaceful snoring I could hear coming from the room down the hall where my brother lay, I did not. My dreams were tortured with uncertainties that kept me at the edge of wakefulness most of the night.

As the sky began to lighten I gave up trying to sleep and quietly rose and went to the kitchen to make a pot of kaf-tea. Drawn by the chill at her back perhaps, or the smell of the perking kaf-tea Gahji soon joined me. When she appeared she had her work uniform on. She poured herself a cup of kaf-tea and pulled out a chair across from me at the table.

"Looks like you plan to go into work today," I said stating the obvious.

She sipped her drink and then said, "No sense staying home and just worrying. At the infirmarium I will have other people's problems to think about for a while instead of my own. And, I want to check on Kutima for you," she reminded me.

Ah, Kutima, another stone to add to my worry basket. "If I can, maybe I can come by to see him today."

I fixed her some breakfast and was making her a lunch to take with her when Kotahi opened the back door and came in. He shook his head, no, to a drink and a meal, and he also said no when I asked if he wanted me to wake Bijah for more conjure work.

"Not just yet, brother." Including Gahji in his next comment, he added, "I know you would wish your daughter restored to health as soon as possible, but in order to remove the Crokno's shield completely both Star Swimmer and I feel she needs to eat and be cared for as best that can be managed under the circumstances, until her human body has had a bit of time to recover from the starvation imposed on her by the binding."

Gahji muttered a curse under her breath and her Bear snarled within her spirit fire. I knew what she wanted to do to such evil creatures. It mirrored my own thoughts. Kotahi was aware of the potential for violence swirling in the etheric currents about us and I saw him try to mask his revulsion. To distract us from our vengeful imaginings, he said to me, "I came here this morning to see if you wanted to come away with me. "

He was being evasive, but I was curious. "Right now?"

"Now is as good a time as any."

Still being evasive. "Where? Into the Beyond?"

A troubled expression coming onto her face, Gahji warned, "Tas, I don't think you should go with him. With everything else going on if he takes you back into the Beyond I may not see you again—for a long time—or, or maybe never! And, and I couldn't cope with that, too!" though she tried to hide her feelings, her voice broke when she uttered those last words.

"No, Gahji, I'm not taking him away from you and his family. I know how much he means to you and you and his family mean to him. I don't want to take him to our clan territory in the Beyond."

"Where then?" I asked.

"You asked me to take you to see Neko, so you could assure the family he was well," he said. "I am here to fulfill that promise."

"Where is he?" Gahji wanted to know. "Can we all go see him?"

"Not at the moment, he is too far away. Tas and I will have to make a transfer to come to him. Maybe in the summer when travel is easier in the mountains, perhaps," he offered to sooth her.

"Mountains, eh? Alright I'll get my coat."

When I was ready and about to leave out the back door Gahji stood blocking our path. Giving Kotahi her stern, 'give me no nonsense glare," she said, "Promise me on whatever you hold sacred and dear, that you will bring him back to me safe and well—and no later than tomorrow!"

He placed his hands together over his heart and bowed. "I so promise, honored Bear Woman, wife to my siyatli brother. I will bring your mate back to you safe and well." His thin lips curving upward into a faint smile, he added, "In fact I promise that he will be here to welcome you home when you come from your job today."

Tears gleaming in the corners of her eyes, she nodded and stepped aside to let us pass.

In the backyard Kotahi stepped behind me and hugged me close to his tall, branch thin body, engulfing us both in his long blanket cape. I closed my eyes, and when I next opened them again we stood amongst a grove of willow and cottonwood trees bright with the last of their autumn colors. Further down the slope was a stream of shallow green water, its rocky bottom revealed after the heat of a long summer had shallowed its flow.

On the north and western horizon was a ridge of high purple mountains with patches of snow here and there near their crests and tree covered slopes of juniper and pine lower down. To the south and east the land flattened out to rolling hills of sage and rabbit brush, with thickets of aspen and willow defining the river's channel.

I took in several deep breaths of the cool resinous desert air and felt the desert's tranquility soothing my soul.

"When I asked your nephew where he felt most at peace and where he would like to go while he healed, he showed me an image of this place" Kotahi said. Standing beside me in the dry winter grass he too gazed over the land spread out below us.

"He said when family trouble got too bad for him to stand, he would take his pony and camp out near here, until the hurt eased and he felt strong enough to go back home."

I crouched and sank my fingers deep into the sandy soil at my feet. Yes, I could feel it, too, the puwa, the ancient power sleeping deep in this desert land—and so akin to my ancient northern home.

"I can understand why my fearful and angry young nephew might want to begin his healing journey in such a place," I said to my brother. "It has an allure for me, too. It is very much like my northern home. Only where here in this high desert the puwa of earth and fire are most powerful, in my northern home it is earth and water that help us when we conjure."

Kotahi chuckled. "And whether it is in the dry hot deserts or the waters of Big Ice Lake, there is always the wind to add its power to any working, eh?"

I chuckled along with him "Yes, that is very true, my brother, very true." Glancing around us again I didn't see a house or any other kind of human shelter—so where was Neko staying? No smoke rose from a hole in the hillside to tell me of a nearby pit house, either.

"Brother, I don't understand. You said you were bringing me to visit my nephew, but where is he?"

Kotahi gave me a puzzled look. "Can you not sense him? He is very close to you, brother."

When I still looked confused, he said, a tone of exasperation coming into his voice. "Close your eyes and use your Gift. Neko is right here with us. Truly he is."

When I did as he suggested and closed my eyes I did sense the spirit fire of a young human—that must obviously be Neko. When I opened my eyes again, however, all I saw about us were the trees of the thicket, settling in for their winter sleep.

Kotahi saw my puzzled expression and chuckling he took my hand and placed it on the smooth bark of a slender cottonwood poplar growing near the ancient mother tree of this grove.

Neko... Though he chose not to speak to me, even with the mind talk, I could sense the spirit fire of my nephew within the wood and bark of the young tree.

Arms and hands now become slender branches reaching up for their golden leaves to taste Sun's light, body and legs firm and straight, swaying gently in the wind, feet reaching down into the cool sandy earth to suck up Streams life-giving water, and then to mingle with the others of its kind in a silent sharing beyond the understanding of one such as me. This being was now my nephew.

My voice thick with emotion, I said, "You transformed him into a tree? Why? Why change him into another life form so different from his human essence? Was there no other way to heal him?"

"There was, but this was what he wanted, Tas," Kotahi said.

I snorted, shaking my head, not sure I believed him. "But surely you could have healed him without taking such drastic measures," I accused.

"Yes, I could have helped his physical injuries to heal and then returned him to you. I gave him that option, but he realized—as did I—that the specter of what had been done to him would be there to haunt him, making him easy prey for the sweet escape available in drink or the o'piyo that so many of your human kind choose to dull the pain of their suffering.

"He wanted to forget about all the pain that had been so much a part of his young human life—not just the rape. I told him that as tree he could forget and learn a new way to understand what it means to be an aspect of the great blessing that is all life.

"To taste Sun's light, to drink up water flowing beneath the rocks and sand and to be nurtured and enfolded within the love of the others sharing this peaceful grove with him, that is what he wanted when I showed it to him, Tas. He chose of his own will to be bound here by my conjure. I would never have forced him to do this, believe me."

I barked out an ironic laugh. "Oh, my dear otherworldly brother, how am I going to explain to his human family what you've done? Nobody will believe me, or be happy if I try to tell them about this."

Giving me an uncomprehending look, he repeated, "I don't understand. It was his choice, brother. He is well and healing. I only did what he wanted of me. Surely they will understand and be happy for him."

I let out a mirthless laugh. How could I explain to him? Taking a shuddering breath I leaned my head against his bark, tears coming to my eyes. <<Oh, Neko, I hope you did the right thing by choosing this.>>

Gently, but firmly Kotahi after a long moment, guided me away from the tree that was now my nephew. We began walking along the river's bank. "Come away, brother, you will upset him with your grieving if you cling to him. He can sense you, truly. There is still a human youth within—and he will remain human for as long as he wishes to be so."

Wiping my nose on my sleeve, I gave him a bewildered look and asked, "But isn't he a prisoner in that form and lost to us—his human family—forever?"

"No, he isn't lost to his human relatives forever at all. I have told him that I foresee for him the path of a great Puhani among your people someday, if he chooses to learn what I can teach him. I have also advised him to remain as tree for at least four years or maybe more, but when he feels it is time I will come and release him and he will become human again and take up the tasks he is destined to fulfill."

Giving me a gentle smile he added, "This is a terrible shock perhaps, and maybe you think me cruel to have done this, but I assure you I am not. And there may come a time when you, too, siyatli brother will seek me out for a similar transformation."

We had been walking along the stream bank as we talked, but now I halted and turned to face him, my mouth set in a hard line. "I would never ask that of you—never!"

Unfazed by my growing anger he only smiled. "Never? I think my siyatli brother, you haven't had time to give your own life's cycle much thought."

"I don't understand; what do you mean?"

"I mean that as a siyatli, if the Crokno don't kill you first, you are going to live much longer than the full humans of your family—even those with a powerful Gift. You will survive your bear woman, her children, and maybe even your son O'siyan and his children. None of us can predict for certain, because for each siyatli, carrying our life's essence it is different.

"Oh, you will age, but much more slowly and there will come a time when you will have to leave this first family and begin your life anew elsewhere."

"I could never leave my Gahji," I objected, feeling anger heat my face. "If I have to I will become her son or grandson, but I won't willingly abandon her, before it is the time for me to entrust her spirit into the care of our ancestors."

He nodded, agreeing with me. "I know; you are a very loyal being and I admire you for that. And it is because of such a quality in your nature that you will feel her passing most keenly and at that time, you may want to call upon me for such a conjuring to take away your pain. And becoming Tree in my otherworldly garden will ease your transition—after a suitable time has passed—into the new life and purpose you will be willing to take up to fulfill your oath to the Great Kunai."

My brother was right. I hadn't as yet given much thought to my future. I was too busy trying to cope with the spectres haunting me from my past and combatting the dangers of my present, to give any thought to a vague future that I wasn't sure I would survive to inherit. Even so, I didn't think I would want to be confined within an unmoving life-form like a tree. It seemed too dangerous—both for me in the future and for Neko now.

I glanced around at this isolated spot that seemed so far away from humans and their destructive weapons and machines, but was it really? "Will he be safe here while he learns and grows?"

"Yes, as safe as I can make it. And I will check on him often—I promise you that. And when I am not here the little ones will watch over this grove for me and warn me if danger threatens. He will be cared for and nurtured until he is ready to decide whether to become human and a healer, or remain a tree until he falls and his spirit passes into the beyond."

It was only afternoon when Kotahi brought me home as he promised Gahji. He didn't stay, however, when I offered to fix him a meal.

"I will be back, brother, but I have to return to clan territory first. I know Star Swimmer speaks highly of my healing skills, but I want to speak to our Elders and maybe the Great One about Bijah. I fear you and your wife and Bijah herself may have to make choices that will affect all of us."

Kotahi refused to say more until he had had his consult, so I had no choice but to wish him a speedy return. As often happened to me when dealing with my otherworldly relations I was left feeling resentful and uncertain, because of their lack of understanding for my human world.

They viewed the life around them from a different perspective and were often uncaring or unsympathetic to our human problems and feelings even beings like Kotahi who meant me only good, failed to comprehend, or appreciate the dilemma I was now faced with, concerning Neko.

He was a young man his mother had entrusted into my care. A young man who had family, family who wouldn't accept that he would go off and disappear without a trace, they would miss him and wonder what happened to him. I might be even accused of a crime, if my niece or her husband decided I was guilty of doing him harm and got the goldys involved.

Unknowing and unsympathetic Kotahi, like the rest of them, had left me alone to figure things out for myself—again. This was a human problem—and being half-human, it was my problem, they reasoned.

What was I going to tell Janata when next she called to talk to him, or wanted her son to come home for a visit? What was I going to tell Mathrom and Gahji for that matter?

Chapter Twenty-One

All was quiet in the house when I walked in the back door. Putting away my heavy coat I peeked in the girls' bedroom and saw Bijah asleep on her bed, Aqwissa curled at her side. As I poked my head around the door frame Aqwissa rose up and blinked at me. <<I see your mouth is healing nicely. If you come with me I can feed you while I begin cooking for the family,>> I offered.

<<Maybe later. Right now I will stay with the little one. She is afraid when I am not here, though she is often angry when she thinks I won't talk to her. I try, but she can't hear me.>>

<<I know. I will explain to her again when she wakes about the Crokno binding.>>

Returning to the kitchen I put on a pot of kaf-tea and opened the ice box to see what I might be able to cook for my hungry family. Wonder of wonders, there were several red fish lying on a bed of fresh ice. Fish not being one of the Hathuuri's favorites, I wasn't surprised. I was putting the two largest into the oven to bake and filleting the rest to fry, when Star Swimmer came out of his room yawning. "Where is everyone?" I asked as I poured him some kaf-tea.

"Your sister took your brother and his escort over to the ceremonial house. Wahtzuul was getting restless, so she thought a hunting trip might keep him and his men occupied." He chuckled. "And, I think the tribe and your family would appreciate some of their winter food supply being replaced, as well."

I smiled and when back to filleting the red fish. He watched me for a while then asked, "Gahji told me before she left that Kotahi took you to see Neko. How was he?"

I put down my knife and glared. A note of accusation coming into my voice, I said, "Did you know that my brother planned to transform Neko into a tree?"

"I suspected, but I wasn't certain. I can see that you are angry about this, but I'm not sure why. Truly, son, if Kotahi chose to transform him so, it was the young man's choice."

I sighed letting go of my irritation. What was done, was done—and it was his choice—or so my relatives kept telling me. "I know, but what am I going to tell his mother and other relatives who will ask about him—and they will, father—they will, believe me. I could be arrested by the goldys if his parents think I've done something to harm him."

"Hmm, that's a consequence I doubt anyone has thought of, but it is a possibility, true enough."

He thought about it for a long moment while he drank his kaf-tea and I went back to frying the fish. "I think perhaps your nephew has become a sailor," he finally said, speaking his thoughts out loud. "And, after what happened to him he needed to get away, so he signed on to the first vessel leaving Seatown.

"He will be traveling for several years and will send his mother the occasional posted letter and suitable gifts from very faraway places in the Empire. Maybe he will even decide to stay and marry in one of those faraway places, eh? Or maybe he will die in some bad shipwreck. Who can say? It is so dangerous to travel these days."

I snorted, and began peeling and chopping onions. "If you or my sister can arrange that, it would ease my mind, but I think Mathrom, and maybe Gahji should be told the truth."

Star Swimmer frowned and took another drink before answering. "That will be up to you to decide. I know you won't like to keep things from your partner, but also remember that she is also very friendly with your niece, and the knowledge of what has truly happened may be a difficult secret for her to keep. Think about whether it is fair to burden her with that knowledge before you make your final decision."

Recalling that she had told me about my sister's fatal illness, even though Kitahtla had asked her not to tell me, I realized my father had a point. "What should I tell her then, she already knows Kotahi was taking me to see Neko somewhere in the mountains—not along the coast."

We were working that out when I heard people coming up the back steps and a moment later, my brother and his escort came in loaded down with haunches of bloody meat. Star Swimmer smiled. <<It would appear your hunt was successful.>>

Wahtzuul grinned and set his burden down on the counter by the sink.<<We went into the tribe's mountain forests with a human Elder and your nephew. At first I thought he came along with us just to drive one of the machines that move without beasts to pull them. Then we realized he came with us for another reason, too.>>

<<The spirit of the large hunting animal that comes when he calls it to him is a magnificent hunter and a wonder to us. It is a magic unknown on our world,>> Duuzra said to me as he set down his own meat. <<It was fascinating to watch him hunt, the creature seemed to engulf its weaker human partner. But together they formed a mighty pair.>>

I nodded. <<A mighty pair, I agree. Mathrom and his Cougar have already killed a sabiyan tracker sent to hunt and kill me.>>

The Hathuuri murmured their praise, which I accepted on his behalf. <<Did he bring down a deer or other prey for the ceremonial house as well?>> I asked.

<<Yes, he and the Elder with him got three beasts with the weapons they called 'guns'.>>

<<They sound like thunder,>>Midaz added, <<but they have only a puny magics compared to what we can draw from our own weapons.>>

<<That is very true,>> I agreed. <<But the weapons they were using for hunting are small and not as powerful as the ones used by the empire when they war against their enemies. And they aren't using magic, as you call it, at all, only technology.>>

I might have explained more to my interested audience but at that moment the front door opened and Gahji came in, calling for me. She had baby on her hip and Angika was trailing in her wake.

When she saw me in the kitchen doorway she breathed a sigh of relief. "Tas! Good, you're back. Angika, turn on the Imperial Seatown news."

Angika hurried over to the picta-view and turned it on, then plunked down on the couch, Gahji joining her as soon as she put down baby and hung up her coat.

Curious, I came into the room, but remained standing, conscious of my boiling noodles on the cooker. "What's going on, my heart? You aren't usually this excited about the Empire's news,"

"I'm not, but if what I heard while riding home on the mecho-transit is true, what's in the news might affect us."

Hearing the noise out in the living room, Bijah woke up. Thumb in her mouth, she crawled into her mother's lap. Aqwissa came to me and for the first time in days was able to clasp her tail and form the familiar silver bracelet around my wrist. The tinny sounds coming from the picta-view brought my father and the Hathuuri in to see what had stirred our interest.

It took a few moments for the chamuqwani man speaking to get to the story that Gahji wanted to know about. But soon enough pictures of a large house engulfed in flames appeared behind the talking man.

Gahji pointed with the little black box she was still holding. ""That's Win's family home where his parents still live." We listened for a while longer as the announcer stated that it was unclear at that time how the fire had started, or if anyone was in the house at the time.

Pointing the black box like a gun at my father and brother she demanded, "Did you cause this?" Her voice cracking on a sob, she pleaded, "And if you did, damn it, where's my boy?"

Father and I exchanged meaningful glances. Dathna was the unspoken thought shared between us. "Gahji, my dear, this is the first any of us has heard of this," Star Swimmer said in a soothing voice, and I detected the slightest nudge of Qwakaiva in his words as he spoke.

"I was here caring for my granddaughter and the Hathuuri have been hunting on tribal land in the mountains all day. Sichahntri was also with them for much of that time. And Tas, well you already know he went with his brother to see Neko earlier this morning. We know nothing of this fire."

"Then if no one here caused this, who did, and where is my son?" Gahji said and buried her face in her cupped hands as she tried to control her emotions.

Turning to hug her mother Bijah took her thumb out of her mouth and said, "Don't cry, Amima. My friend Aqwissa is all better now. She can go hunting and find Tuunac for us."

Gahji put down her hands and hugged her daughter close. She looked at me with such a pleading in her eyes it broke my heart to see it. Considering the dragon-lizard coiled around my wrist, I asked her in a private communication, <<Are you well enough to hunt for the boy and my traitor of a cousin?>>

<<If the Hathuuri will allow me to feed on their crystals I will be healed enough to hunt. Tell his mother that the child was not in the house when it burnt. Tuunac still has the barrette his sister gave him. He is somewhere dark again, but he can hear the ocean waves on a beach nearby. He has plenty of food and a warm bed. Tell your mate that now that I am nearly healed it will be much easier for me to find him.>>

<<Utreal or his Crokno companions may know about the barrette and are letting him keep it to lure us into a trap,>> I warned. <<So, be careful. We can't afford to lose you, too.>>

I relayed our private communication to the rest of the family and Wahtzuul willingly agreed to share his lightning fed power with the little hunter. Aqwissa left my wrist and reformed on one of his lower arms. Several of his crystals flared in the next moment as she began to absorb the Qwakaiva she would need to hunt.

She left us as soon as she had absorbed enough Qwakaiva to give her the strength she would need for the task I assigned her. Then there was nothing more we could do but wait for her news. Gahji and I finished cooking the evening meal. We left the picta-view talking so we could check for updates, but little more of importance was revealed before the last report came on at bedtime.

And it was also no surprise when Rushton stopped by again after his visit to Kutima earlier that evening. Two major fires so close together in time, and both somehow connected to the people we believed were responsible for our missing children, of course he was curious to know whether we had had anything to do with this latest event. I wasn't sure he totally believed us when we said, no, however.

"We were occupied with other matters all day," Star Swimmer told him. "We know about as much as you do right now, Preceptor. But since they are the same people who have been pressuring the imperials to give them the children sired by their son—and one of the children is still missing, we are definitely trying to find out more."

"Ah, has one of the children been returned to you then?"

Leaning forward to look the man in the eye, my father's voice hardened. "No, Preceptor, we 'took' my grandchild back from the enemy."

"Unfortunately," I continued, "knowing we would come for them the enemy separated them before we arrived at the temple to free them and the other children being held captive there."

Rushton didn't say it but he now understood that we had been responsible for the destruction at the temple agency. After a long pause while he digested our words, and the unvoiced menace lingering behind it, he ventured to ask, "I see, is the one you rescued well?"

"No, she is here with us, but she was starved and would have been left to die if we hadn't found her," I answered. "Her injuries are of a magical nature as well and we can't cure them with just food and drink."

"That's terrible; I hope she gets better soon. Who is still missing?"

"My son, Tuunac," Gahji said. "The house that burned earlier belonged to his paternal grandparents."

"And I take it he wasn't there when the blaze started."

"No, we are searching for him now." I held up my empty wrist. "Aqwissa is hunting." Then to change the subject I asked him how Kutima was doing.

Rushton glanced at Gahji standing at the sink, running water for the dishes. When she continued with her task he turned back to me and said, "I guess Gahji hasn't told you yet. The family has taken their grandfather out of the infirmarium. They are gathering at Martin's house where they have taken him to die. Tas, he is trying to wait for you, but it's becoming more difficult. Even with your brother's talisman he is struggling."

When all was quiet at my house and Gahji and our children were asleep, I made the transfer to a shadowy corner of Kutima's family's backyard. I climbed the front steps where Martin was waiting to let me in. Several people were sitting in their tiny living room, keeping the vigil—including Rushton. They were talking amongst themselves or quietly sobbing with faces covered by their hands or a shawl. I nodded a greeting to the group, most of whom I knew, but didn't stay to talk.

I followed Martin into a dimly lit bedroom near the kitchen. The shrunken body of my oldest friend lay nestled among pillows and brightly colored blankets on a narrow bed. Martin's wife was with him, holding Kutima's gnarled hand.

When she saw me she breathed a sigh of relief and got up to give me her chair. Sitting down I took his hand. Kutima's breathing was shallow and ragged, the congestion filling his lungs making it hard for him to take in enough life-giving air. He didn't look at me but kept staring at the far wall where I saw his mother's spirit watching us.

In our Qwani'Yan language, I said, "Thank you for waiting for me; I know she has come for you."

At the sound of my voice he turned and smiled at me. "I'm glad you could come, old friend. I would have hated to leave without saying farewell. Rushton told me why you were unable to come earlier. Are the children back with the family and safe?"

"We are still working on that problem," I admitted, "but that's nothing for you to be concerned about now. This is our time together and I don't want to spoil it by worrying you with my troubles. Father and I, and the rest of my otherworldly relatives will handle what is needed."

It took him several breaths before he found the strength to continue. "That's good. I know you will bring them home safe. It is in your nature to always care for those of us who needed you. Even when we were children you stood up for me—and, tried to protect me when Matoqwa and the others teased me—and not just because I snuck you sweet treats when father wasn't looking."

I chuckled. "And got beaten for your generosity, too, as I recall."

He started to laugh with me, but his effort ended in a coughing fit that left him weaker than before. "Don't try to speak in the time we have left together," I said. "Save your breath; I will hear you if you talk to me in your mind. Just think what you want to say to me, old friend."

Kutima nodded then coughed and I raised him up and handed him a cloth to spit up the phlegm choking him. When it was over he fell back even more exhausted. Much closer now, his mother stood on the other side of the bed. He hadn't much time. <<I'm sorry that I had to leave you behind when we were children. I'm glad you were spared our long march south to the Preserve, but it would have been a comfort to have you in my little warband back then if you had been sent south with us.>>

<<I would have followed you, you know, but my father wouldn't allow it. And later at the live-away school when we found each other again, it was *your* father that time who separated us. But if I could have gone with you into that other world I would have, Tas, because I have always loved you. But once again I was denied your companionship—and now it is much too late for us.>>

The images his untrained mind projected weren't those of friendship shared, but were far more intimate in nature. I sat back stunned, not knowing what—to think—or say. At last I squeezed his hand gently and said, <<I'm sorry, old friend. I didn't know.>>

He tried to grip my hand but was too weak. <<Old friend,>> he repeated. <<That was all there was, or could be between us, because I knew you didn't think of me like that, so I was content with what parts of your life I could share—and there was much you had to give me, truly.>>

I chuckled. <<And I learned so much from you. I might never have learned to read and write the enemy's language if not for you. I would be lost without such skills in these modern times without them—something for which I will be forever grateful.>>

<<I'm glad you appreciated my efforts.>> His breath was starting to make a rattling sound in his throat and chest. <<Sing to me old friend, sing to me of the old days back home. Let me see our village and feel the cold winds blowing off the lake as you sing my spirit away to join my mother and the others waiting for me.>>

Still holding his cooling hand, I sang. I sang of the high snow covered mountains and deep blue waters of Big Ice Lake and the dark green forests of pine and fir covering our ancient land. And I sang of the good times we had as children, before the miners and the soldiers came to spoil it all.

The people keeping vigil in other parts of the house heard my singing and knew what it meant. They gathered just outside the open bedroom door to listen. When I finished, I rose, and laid his folded hands atop the blankets.

His spirit was gone. I left soon after, but promised to be available to hunt for the funeral feast and anything else the family might need in the meantime.

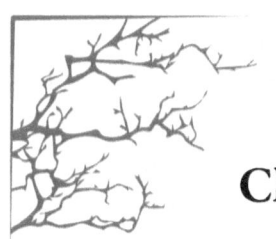

Chapter Twenty-Two

When I arrived home, feeling raw and drained, the sky was paling in the east. Everyone was up and sitting around the kitchen table. Gahji took one look at my face and handed me a cup of an herbal tea that I knew would help me sleep. I didn't want it—there was too much to do—but her stern glare told me I had better drink it.

Suspecting he understood our silent communication, Star Swimmer chuckled. "You better drink it and go get some rest, son. We will wake you if there is news, and I know his death is a heavy blow."

"It is," I admitted. "He was the last of my old human friends and family still alive." *And my last link to my past is now severed*, I thought, but didn't say. He knew anyway and gave me a sad smile.

Recalling Kotahi's prediction for me I knew Kutima and Kitahtla's passing were only the first of many others to come in my future—if the Crokno didn't get to me first.

Gahji followed me to our bedroom and after comforting me with her womanly charms I fell soundly asleep in her arms.

When next I woke the light in our room was gray as before and my first thought was that I had been asleep for only a few moments, but the time-tell by the bed told me that I had slept through the day and it was now evening. I wanted to sleep more, but decided I'd better get up and see if there was food in the ice box I could cook for our evening meal. Gahji would be home from work soon.

Hearing the noise of children laughing and women talking I finished in the indoor privy and walked into the living room. To my surprise Saskina and the new niece from the islands, Deillah were sitting on the couch with Bijah, baby O'siyan playing with a few of Tuunac's old toys on the floor nearby.

When they saw me baby gave me a happy cry and Bijah hurried over for me to pick her up too. Deciding it would be easier I sank down into a nearby chair and pulled them both onto my lap, ignoring the tingling I still felt whenever my Gift encountered the half dismantled Crokno conjure. "You got stuck with babysitting, while Gahji is at work, I see. but there was no need for you to miss school; I could have gotten up to watch them."

"E wa no trouble, Unca Tas," Deillah said and gave me one of her delightful smiles. "Me field trip wa canceled because da wotta in da inlet was too rough fa da work we planned fa today." She shrugged and motioned to Saskina. "So I come wit me cousin here."

"And, when Gahji called me I was free and I did need to talk to you about Mathrom," Saskina said. "As usual he hasn't let anybody know what is going on with him—and he's missing a lot of classes again. A friend who works in admin said they might expel him soon if he doesn't contact them or start back up with his studies again. He might lose his tribal stipend, too, if he doesn't smarten up."

I groaned and mentally kicked myself for another laps. It was so complicated living in this "modern" world. I sighed and sat baby back on the floor to play. "This time your brother isn't being irresponsible, but he won't be coming back to the Lectorium for at least this winter. You two have been so busy with your own classes this term, and I haven't wanted to involve you, or worry you with our troubles—something you couldn't help or solve, but being family, I guess you have a right to know...."

Though I had no idea what Gahji, or Bijah herself had told them before I woke, I didn't tell the girls everything; I mostly focused on the gangers and their attack on Mathrom and Neko. The fewer people who knew about the Hathuuri and our part in the temple agency's destruction the better, I reasoned.

Saskina burst into tears and covered her face with her hands when I finished. "Does, Auntie Janata know about Neko?" she finally asked when she could speak again.

I sighed. "No. We haven't told her yet. Neko has told me that he definitely doesn't want to go home—I don't think he even wants them to know—so please don't say what I told you to anyone.

"Right now he is in a safe place and healing from his injuries, until he decides what he wants to do I don't plan on telling his mother anything.as for

Mathrom's situation... I guess I should call Preceptor Rushton and see what he suggests."

Giving one last sniff she next asked, "Do you think Neko will be coming back to attend school next term—even if Mathrom is still at the ceremonial house?"

"Last I spoke with him he was looking into signing up on a merchant ship as a seaman. He said he wanted to see new places in the empire or elsewhere, until he had time to forget about what happened here."

"Hmm, da ma'bee a good ting. I have a cousin who got inta trouble and did dat," Deillah said. "It tun out be good ting fa he. Now he olda wit family and nice job."

Saskina didn't seem totally convinced, but let the matter drop for the moment. To change the subject I next asked, "Where is everybody?"

"Angika is studying at a friend's place and your father went across the street to the new house with another man he said was your brother Kotahi. I guess they had things to discuss without the children interrupting."

"Hmm, well if you two don't mind continuing to babysit I guess I'll go talk to them." The girls didn't mind, so I slipped out the front door and crossed to the new house.

When I arrived I found that someone had moved our old saggy couch from the back porch across the street to the new place. Star Swimmer and my brother were sitting on it steaming cups of tea setting on a wooden box in front of them on the floor. There were still black stains of soot on the wall by the boarded up front window, giving the room the gloomy air of a cave in spite of its golden color.

Deep in a silent mind communication they looked up when I came in. "Good you are awake now; we wanted to talk to you before Gahji got home from work." Father motioned to the kitchen. "There's more hot tea in the pot if you want some."

I wanted kaf-tea to help me finish waking up, not one of my brothers herbal brews, but I went to the kitchen to get a cup anyway. Then I returned to sit on the floor facing them.

After taking a sip of my tea, I said, "I assume sense Kotahi has returned from clan territory, and that you are over here talking instead of in my own kitchen that I'm probably not going to like what you have to tell me about Bijah's condition."

"You may not," father agreed, "but like it or not, it is the right thing to do at this point, son."

"And that is? Tell me."

"When I left you after showing you Neko I went back to our territory," Kotahi began. "I spoke with some of our elders, some who knew you as a youth wounded by the enemy, and some more ancients, who didn't know you personally, but had long memories of the Crokno. I even took my concerns to the Great One himself. They all gave me the same advice."

"You are being vague again, brother, so I know I'm definitely not going to like what you need to tell me. Spit it out!"

He made a face at my bluntness, then said, "The Great One and our elders want me to bring Bijah to them."

I stared open-mouthed as his words sank in. "To the Beyond? But she's human; how could she survive there?"

"She isn't completely human," Kotahi corrected. "I don't think you have been aware, but Aqwissa has been bringing forward her dragon nature as she has been teaching her."

Then he drew from a pouch around his neck a tiny shining crystal that gave off its radiant power even in the dimness of the dark room. "Kunai gave me this for her, which will give her the power she will need to live among us in the Beyond so we can protect and teach her."

"Right now the way she is, still with the Crokno's net clinging to her she is a danger to both herself and to everyone around her, son," my father added interpreting my horrified expression correctly. "Still linked to the Crokno as she is now, they could use her to spy or even as a weapon against us."

Recalling my own experiences as a siyatli half-breed while living in the Beyond I had no wish to inflict that experience on any child—especially one I loved."

"it won't be like it was for you while living among us, Tas," Star Swimmer added. "Sichahntri, whom she already knows and likes has agreed to stay with her until her maturity. She will have no other children or responsibilities to take her away." Unlike me, was his unspoken admission.

"And to ease her transition she can also bring Aqwissa with her," Kotahi added.

Lose Aqwissa, too? I had grown quite fond of the little one. My heart saddened at the prospect. "But she's bonded to me," I said.

<<*I am yours for only as long as you need me*>>I heard once again Aqwissa's words echoing in my mind.

"Aqwissa is very young—and inexperienced, Tas." Kotahi said, sensing perhaps my confusion. "The great one feels that those two young beings are a better match for the future. They can both grow and learn together among our clans in the Beyond.

"But he has agreed that if you stay among your human relatives you will definitely need another teacher and protector, a more mature being or beings who can also teach you as well as help you combat any future Crokno threat, should you and the child agree to the changes he and the elders recommend."

Kutima's death and now this—all within the span of only a few hours—it was, too much. How could I decide such important matters when my nahawa was so unbalanced?

"But she is still so young," I protested. "Such a decision will affect her, affect all of us who know and love her. Isn't there another way to keep her safe while she remains with us?"

"She is seven, Tas. Even among your human relatives in the past a child that age was old enough to make such a life changing decision," Star Swimmer reminded me.

"Maybe we should let her decide," Kotahi said quietly. "It is her life we are talking about, after all. Shouldn't it be her choice?"

"You weren't much older than Bijah when you were faced with a similar choice as I recall," Star Swimmer said into the silence that followed. "With your grandfather's urging you chose your family over the future Kunai had planned for you.

"Have you ever wondered how different your life might have been if you had stayed in your northern home—how you could have helped your land and your people if you had studied with the Qwakaihi the Great One had chosen for you? Be careful that, for your own personal reasons you and Gahji don't make the same mistake for your daughter."

Yes, I could understand that, too. How much suffering could I have avoided if my life had taken a different path? "Is there no other way? Can't we shield her till she is older? And then we can let her decide."

"No. such a shielding would cost too much in time and Qwakaiva and it would act like a beacon on a foggy night to the ever searching enemy," Star Swimmer explained. "And cut off from her Gift for so many years, after knowing and being taught the joy of using what is so a part of her nature—as it is of yours—would you, or could you live like that without sinking into a black despair that would in the end be life threatening?"

Well, he had a point; I couldn't—and maybe she couldn't either, but I wasn't willing to give up yet. "Is there no other way?"

"There is only one other course of action, brother, and it is a drastic one that if she survives it she may not thank you for," Kotahi said.

Feeling a tremor run down my spine I said, "What, tell me?"

""With the Hathuuri's help we can strip her of her Gift completely. You will also be a part of the conjure with us—and Bijah will know."

And maybe hate you and blame you for it later, were his unspoken words that I heard loud and clear. It echoed my own resentment towards my grandfather that I had carried in my heart till his death claimed him.

"Wahtzuul won't agree with or like to do it. But if you ask him, and she survives your daughter will become completely human and nothing more."

What to do, what to do. I buried my face in my hands, my thoughts in a turmoil. Grandfather with his hatred of my father to guide him was so damned certain that he was doing the right thing, both when he forced me to choose the family over Kunai's teacher, and later when he used his own Gift to convince Nachoga not to take me with him on that last raid that got my beloved adopted father captured and hanged.

I, unfortunately had no such luxury. I couldn't make such a decision for anybody. "I can't decide this for Bijah," I told them. "In keeping with our Qwani'Ya traditions Bijah belongs to Gahji and her clan. We will have to talk to her mother before anything is decided." I stood up and headed for the front door, "Gahji will be home soon and if the girls haven't started cooking yet I will need to make the evening meal now."

"We can't leave this for too much longer, son, or the Crokno might decide for us," Star Swimmer warned.

Gahji arrived home with news of more fires to property owned by Tuunac's grandparents, the Luuchoiyan family. "I was working in the Urgent Care Department when they brought in three badly burned people from those fires," she told me as we set the meal the girls and I had prepared on the table.

Giving me a troubled look, she murmured, so only I could hear, "Do you know what's going on—and where are the rest of your crazy relatives? Are you sure they aren't behind these fires?"

"I don't know where Sichahntri has taken the Hathuuri. They were gone when I woke up, but I'm sure they aren't behind the fires. But you are right to suspect otherworldly involvement, my love."

She thought about it for a long moment as she got the scau-bread from the oven. Straightening she slammed the pan down on the top of the cooker. "It's that bitch Dathna, isn't it?"

"Probably. That's who father and I think is doing it."

"But why? Ze might get my son killed if ze keeps this up much longer, damn it!"

"Dathna and Zeiva were very close, my heart," I said as I gently guided her into a chair at the head of the table. "Right now, after Zeiva's near fragmentation ze feels ze does have that right. Dathna is hurting angry, and wanting revenge on Utreal and the Crokno and probably feels that making it difficult for their human minions is the best way to force Utreal out of hiding, so ze can be killed."

"That's all well and good as long as it doesn't get my son killed, too," she grumped.

After the meal we watched the pictures of the Luuchoiyan burning buildings on the picta-view as the announcer read us the latest news stories. When he turned his attention to other topics that didn't interest us, father and I exchanged troubled glances.

"Somebody sure don like dose peoples," Deillah said, shaking her head in wonder. "Dis be da fourt or fift fire dis seben-day I tink, and all the places but da temple be owned by dose peoples. Wonder what dey do ta deserve all dat?"

Well for a start, stealing my children, I thought. And being guided by Crokno enslaved priests would be another reason.

"They aren't our favorite people at the moment, either," I admitted when Saskina gave me a questioning look. "But no one in this household has had anything to do with these latest fires."

"But Appi and some of the new uncles did rescue me from the temple where those mean priests were keeping me and Tuunac before it burned," Bijah added much to my dismay.

At the mention of Tuunac Saskina was reminded about our missing son. "Where *is* Tuunac by the way? Is he with Elder Samul's family?"

"No, he is still missing," I finally said after a long silence, and I put enough of a conjure in my words that she understood the subject was now closed to further discussion. Claiming they had early classes the next day the girls left soon after that.

When we were finishing up cleaning the kitchen and our three remaining children were in bed and hopefully asleep my father and Kotahi came back into the kitchen. I dreaded what they wanted to talk about, but it wasn't going to get any easier by waiting.

When they explained to Gahji what they had told me earlier she reacted with fear and anger as I expected. "No, absolutely not. Bijah is definitely too young to leave her family. No!"

"Is that the right decision for her, daughter-in-law," Star Swimmer said quietly, "or for you?"

Her eyes flashing with fire she said through gritted teeth, "There's nothing wrong with her just being a little human girl and living a normal human life."

"I think it's too late for that now, my dear," Star Swimmer said. "The dragon's blood is part of her lineage even if you hadn't met Tas. And after your marriage to him his protector has been helping to enhance what was already her Gift to develop and use. Your daughter could never be what you call a 'normal' human."

He chuckled. "Even you yourself, though you try to deny it, aren't a 'normal' human. And you could do much more with your own Gift if you could let go of the fear you cling to. Drawing up Earth's Qwakaiva for Aqwissa so she could heal proves that, my dear. Bijahgwi has more of a Gift because she has inherited her power from both her parents."

Burying her face in her hands, I heard her quietly sobbing, her whole body trembling. I started to go to her, wanting to put my arms around her and comfort her, but Star Swimmer shook his head, warning me not to. He was probably right. It was in her nature to lash out when troubled or hurting. Like her ancestor Matoqwa. I had learned to leave her alone to sort things out for herself for a time before I offered my sympathy and comfort.

"Try to understand, sister-in-law," Kotahi said. "Having a Gift, is like having eyes and being able to see all the beauty of this world. Taking away Bijah's Gift would be like someone blinding you. Yes, you could survive, and maybe in time have a good life, once you learned to cope with your disability. But you would always remember what it was like to see, and deep inside you would always carry the memory of your loss. Is that the legacy you want to give your child?"

Nothing was decided before we went to bed, and I'm sure like me Gahji's sleep was troubled. When we were alone she asked me what I thought of this plan. "The little you told me about the time you spent among your father's relatives didn't sound like it was very pleasant."

"No, it wasn't; I won't lie to you about that. But like Bijah, Crokno malice drove my father to bring me into that dimension, we had no choice. And I did learn, Gahji, I did learn, and I am grateful for all that, truly. And father and Kotahi have sworn to me that it won't be so bad for Bijah."

Before we tried to sleep I left her with one further thought. "When Grandfather forced me to quit my studies with a teacher he thought unsuitable he hoped I would just become a 'normal' human. But that was impossible for me; I deeply felt my loss. When I thought I would never touch my Gift again I hated him for making me choose.

"Though my anger lessened with time as I learned to regain my power, my relationship with him was never the same. Until his death claimed him at the Gold Creek massacre there was always that wall between us that neither of us could totally break down or climb."

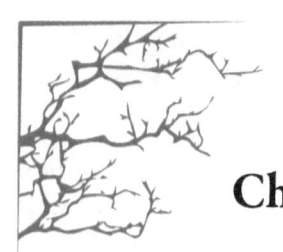

Chapter Twenty-Three

We hadn't heard from Aqwissa in a while, but that night she swam into my chaotic dreams, urging me to follow her. She led me to a darkened little room where Tuunac lay sleeping on a narrow bed. <<Where is this place?>> I asked her.

<<In a big house near the ocean,>> she said. <<He can hear the waves crashing against a pebble beach when the wind comes bringing another winter storm.>>

<<Can you bring us there to rescue him?>>

<<I can, but the house is owned by his paternal grandfather and well-guarded both by human guards paid by the Luuchoiyan family and also it is guarded by Utreal and the Crokno. They are waiting for you to attack. If you go inside their fortress to get your son, you or anyone else will be ensnared in a magical net, as Bijah was.

<<If you try to use your Gift while within their conjure you will be cut off from your power—and easily killed or enslaved after that. This is why I have only come to the young bear warrior in his dreams like now, so they won't capture me, too.>>

Enslaved by the Crokno again? Well that was a sobering thought and one I didn't want to experience. As I was pondering her words she drew my attention to my son's dream. As best I could tell he was reliving what had happened to him earlier that day or sometime in the near past...

In his dream a large guard with his hand on his shoulder marched Tuunac from his cell to stand in front of a seated elder in a large room richly decorated with expensive furniture of an old fashioned type like I had seen in the priest's parlor at Saint Yon's. Heavy dark drapes partially hid the large window and over on the far wall sat a small table with candles and offering bowls surrounding a blurred picture of another ancient.

As I listened Tuunac was saying, the note of desperation and fear plain even in his dreaming voice. <<I keep telling you, grandfather, I am no dragon. Why won't you believe me. I am a bear. My people are the Qwani'Ya Tsa'adi—my power comes from Bear, my sister is the dragon.>>

<<Don't be ridiculous, no woman can inherit the power of the dragons linked to our lineage,>> the old man snapped. <<You will learn to know your true purpose and the spirit of our family will make itself known to you in time under my tutelage.>>

Tuunac snorted a laugh.<<Your tutelage—you mean your beatings, eh? It doesn't matter how many times you hit me. I will still be of the Bear People and I will always be of the Bear People and nothing you can do to me can change that. I want to go home—to my real family. I don't belong to you, you mean old man.>>

Rising, the old man slapped him hard enough for my son to bite his lip, making it bleed.Within the dream I felt the slap, too. In the next moment Tuunac surprised me when he spat the blood pooling in his mouth back into his grandfather's face, which earned him another slap.

<<He has obviously not learned his lesson yet,>> a new voice said. <<Shall I have the guard take him back to his room now, Elder Luuchoiyan? He will submit to your will in time. Enough hunger and pain can make even a stubborn child agreeable.>>

When my son turned to face the newcomer I saw that the other man was my traitor of a cousin Utreal. <<I helped bury the sabiyan hunter's slaves you sent into our world and when my Appi comes I will help him bury you, too,>> Tuunac said and wiped his bleeding mouth with his sleeve. <<I'm not afraid of you, traitor.>>

<<What is he talking about? How does he know you, intercessor?>>

For just a brief moment Utreal's human face paled. He hadn't expected my son to know him. He waved a dismissive hand and said, <<He doesn't know me. The child is speaking gibberish.>>Then to Tuunac's guard, he said, <<Take him back to his cell, now that his grandfather has seen him. It is obvious he is still unwilling to comply with our patron's wishes.>>

I saw no more after that, because Tuunac turned over in his bed and dreamt no more. What I had seen tore at my heart. He was being so brave, but I hated to see him suffer. Like all parents I wanted to protect my children. I wanted only the best for them.

<<Can you tell him that we are coming to rescue him—we won't leave him among the enemy for much longer?>>

<<I have told him, and now I have showed you, but I can't stay over long to watch or guard him. I must return to Bijah soon. She is also frightened and needs me.>>

<<Father has told me that you wish to go with her back to our clan's territory in the Beyond. I will miss you and her, but I understand why it is necessary. I just wish it could be otherwise.>>

<<As do I, Siyatli Brother.>>

Martin called next morning to tell us about the funeral arrangements and the gather preceding it, so no more was said about Bijah leaving us for the time being. To my surprise one of the places that Sichahntri had been showing the Hathuuri on my world while keeping them occupied was hunting caribou on the icy plains north of my mountain home by Big Ice Lake. So when they returned the evening before the funeral they had a real northern treat, roast caribou hind quarter, I could share with the people coming to my old friend's feast.

Reverend Cal was asked to officiate at the funeral and his little temple was packed with family and friends who had known and loved my old war brother. Gahji and I went to the funeral, but for safety reasons we decided to leave the children home with our otherworldly relatives.

When we arrived we were ushered to the front to sit alongside Martin and his family. Rushton too had an honored seat in the row just behind us. Most of the staff from Zacatik Friendship House were also present, as were many more grieving people I didn't know. Kutima had lived a long and productive life as a teacher of our language and culture and was well loved because of it.

As was the old custom, the graveyard where he would rest was next to the Mother of Mercy's Temple. I had already sang his spirit away to join our ancestors, but Gahji and I, holding hands, went with the family to the graveside, where I added a shovel of dirt to his grave with the others who had been close to him.

Gahji had already gone back to the temple hall to help lay out the funeral feast, but I had stayed to talk to friends by the grave, when I noticed a long black mecho-cart pull up on the road just outside the cemetery. Two big, grim-faced men, wearing expensive clothes that nearly hid the weapons they were also carrying, got out of the cart. A third person, along with a driver remained behind in the still rumbling vehicle, concealed behind darkened windows.

When the two men spotted me they began slowly walking in my direction. Sensing trouble I said good bye to the people I was talking with and went to meet them. I stopped near a cluster of flowering bushes that partially hid us from anyone still lingering by the grave side.

When they were close enough for them to hear me without shouting, I said, "What do you want?" They came a little closer then stopped, spreading out to flank me should I try to run. There was no chance of that.

Moving a hand under their jackets to demonstrate their intent, the one with the dead eyes, nearest to me said, "Don't give us any trouble; you are coming for a ride with us. Our employer wants to talk to you."

I laughed. "So you can hold me captive, too, like you are holding my son? I don't think so." I motioned to a nearby bench under a shade tree. "If elder Luuchoiyan has something to say to me we can talk over there—where everyone can see us. Otherwise I am expected inside the temple for the meal. Ask your employer if he would like to join us."

"Don't make a fuss about this," the other man said. The two of them stepped even closer, their hands on the weapons inside their jackets now. "No one is going to come help you, nor will the defenders come if anyone calls them. Our employer has seen to that."

I laughed again and remained where I was. "I don't care what your employer thinks he has arranged with the city's corrupt peace defenders. And you can tell him that, and the dog-humping pretend priest advising him too. It's not going to be that easy to entrap or kill me."

When they reached to show me their guns, I used a conjure to make them too hot to hold, the now glowing redmetal burning through the leather carriers and the cloth of their trousers underneath. Cursing they dropped the guns to the grass, where they sizzled and steamed in the cool air.

They might have physically tried to harm me at that point, but Midaz stepped out of the flowering bushes at my back and came up behind me. The young Hathuuri was still as tall and imposing as always, but his alien face and extra pair of hands and arms were concealed behind a well-crafted illusion, making him appear human.

I motioned to the bench again. "We can talk over there—or not at all—his choice."

When the two walked back to the cart I said, without turning to look at him, <<I assume my brother or my father sent you. How long have you been here watching?>>

<<They both sent me,>> he admitted. <<But it was also a lesson for me. Duuzra is testing my concealing powers, so I wasn't to let you know I was here unless I was needed, Tigring.>>

I chuckled. <<Well, you did quite well. I wasn't aware of your presence until I walked to meet those men.>>

It took them a bit of time to discuss my proposal, but eventually the person in the back of the cart got out and came slowly over to join us. His guards once more armed walked to either side of him, fading back to a discrete distance when he came near enough for us to talk without being overheard. I sent a thought to Midaz to do the same.

Except for that brief encounter in Tuunac's dream this was the first time I'd seen one of the Luuchoiyan family in person. This elder was of medium height thinly built with short gray hair and a drooping white mustache. His black eyes were similar in shape to his grandchildren's but more hidden by an extra fold of skin because of his age. He was dressed expensively according to the modern fashion, and his spirit fire was still alive with his need to dominate and master.

To offer him the respect his age was due—if not his actions, I bowed and motioned to the bench again. "Shall we sit? I understand you wish to talk to me."

"I wil stand, because what I have to say won't take long," he growled.

"Very well. What do you want to say?"

"I came to warn you that I will make it very difficult for you and your whore of a wife if you don't stop."

"Stop what?"

He growled a curse. "You know exactly what I am talking about. Why do I have to tell you—the destruction of my property. It stops now or I will see that she is fired at the infirmarium and your preceptor friend, too will be looking for a new position. Do you want that?"

"No, of course not, but I'm not the one burning down your property. I haven't done anything to you or your family. In fact it is quite the opposite. It is you who has harmed us. You have my son—and I want him back."

The grandfather snorted a disgusted laugh and his guards shifted restlessly. "Your son—bah! He is my grandson and belongs to my lineage—not your savage heathen tradition. Be glad you got the girl back unharmed when your devilish minions destroyed Mighty Djoven's temple."

"Ah, but according to my way of thinking, Tuunac is my son. I have sworn to love and protect him when I married his mother—and that is our 'Qwani'Ya' tradition—heathen though it may be. As for his sister, are you sure we reclaimed her unharmed? Is that what the pretend priest told you?"

Startled the grandfather stepped back. "What are you saying? And how dare you call one of Djoven's holy men a pretender."

"Because that's what he is. He is no more a priest than I am. What he truly is, is a traitor and a murderer who is too cowardly to do his own killing so he is hiding and wanting misguided fools like you to do his work for him."

"You're lying. He and the other intercessor with him are holy Djoven's servants."

"Does Utreal or whatever he is calling himself, know that you are here talking to me?"

"What does that matter? I don't need to tell the intercessor what I do."

"Your pretend priest isn't going to be happy with you when he learns that you are here. And, you won't like it if he becomes angry with you—believe me," I taunted.

He growled and swore. "I don't take orders from any priest. I give them money for their good works, but they don't own me. It is you who lie, trying to make me give you my grandson. Well, I won't. He is born to our house of the dragon, and he stays with me."

"I should let him stay with you? So you can mess up his life like you did your own son's?" I shook my head in a sad reproof of his words. I knew I was being rude to an elder, something I had been taught never to do, but I was finding it hard to respect this rigid, small-minded man.

"You have no idea of the true forces gathered around us at this moment or what is their real purpose. Your desire for an heir has blinded you to the truth and also cost you and your house a dragon's favor."

"What are you talking about, you ignorant heathen? My family back in our ancient land have been allied with, and received the blessings of our dragon benefactors for hundreds of years."

"Yes, that's true, back in your own land. But as for you personally, you forfeited that favor when you chose the conqueror's religion for your own gain, over the traditions handed down to you from your ancient beginnings."

He had no quick response to my jab; a part of him knew I spoke true. Then before he could respond to that, I hit him with another angry accusation. "And then, once again you failed to see what is right in front of you and what I believe the children themselves have told you. Tuunac is not a dragon. It was Bijah who inherited the dragon's blood and its Gift that had been handed down to your family through the generations."

"Impossible!"

"Why do you think that?"

He was a bit flustered by my question and gave me a glare that so plainly said that I was too stupid to understand the obvious. "Why? Because a woman is too weak-natured to handle such a responsibility. Only a man is strong enough to wield such a gift of power."

I laughed. "Who told you that? It certainly wasn't any dragon." Still chuckling I added, "You've met my Gahji. You may not like her, but you certainly can't say she is 'weak-natured'.

"Bijah is the one who inherited your family's dragon Gift, not Tuunac. He is his mother's son and claims his mother's Bear Qwakaiva. He can never be the one you want him to be—no matter how much you beat or punish him. And the pretend priests you are listening to, know that. They hate all dragon-kind and have fooled you into throwing away what might have saved you."

"I don't believe you. This is all a heathen lie!"

"What reason would I bother to lie to you—you aren't worth my trouble." I brushed a hand across my face, revealing for a brief time the hidden dragon tattoo drawn into my skin just above my jaw. He saw my dragon glyph and understood what it meant, he gasped and stepped back. "What I tell you may be heathen, but it isn't a lie. Since my childhood I have been sworn to the Great Dragon Kunai. Oh, he isn't the same powerful being aligned with your people, but he is a being of the same kindred, unlike the traitor who now advises you."

In the stunned silence that followed my revelation, I said, "Believe me or not—I don't really care, but believe this. I am not to blame for the fires destroying your property. Utreal has angered other powerful beings who are taking out their vengeance on you, hoping, no doubt, to flush him out where he can be killed or captured. Tuunac can never be the one you hope him to be, so show some kindness and give him back to his grieving mother."

He spat on the ground. "Never, I will have him killed first, before I let the whore who tempted my son into evil have him!"

"Then this is truly war. Tell my traitor of a cousin and his Crokno master that with Co'yeh's clan and the Hathuuri at my back we are coming for—all of you."

Chapter Twenty-Four

When he returned to the Luuchoiyan compound the elder must have told his otherworldly advisers about confronting me, and my declaration of war. Because later that evening my father's prediction about the Crokno taking Bijah's fate out of our hands came true when Bijah found Gahji's little gun and tried to kill us.

Another building owned by that family went up in flames that afternoon and we were all in the livingroom watching the imperial news when a blank-eyed Bijah, that we all thought was asleep, came from down the hall to join us. With our attention focused on the news no one saw her raise the weapon until it was nearly too late.

Midaz who was on guard duty, and who had learned his lesson well about not being distracted by our picta-view, saw her first and lunged to grab the weapon from her. He jerked back as his power came into contact with the strengthened Crokno conjure, but he did manage to deflect her aim enough so that she didn't hurt anyone. When the gun fired its projectile it smashed the glass of the picta-view's screen instead, and the box exploded in a bright flash and flames.

Ignoring his scorched flesh in the next moment Midaz wrenched the gun from her hand and tossed it to the other side of the room, while holding her in his lower set of arms, so she couldn't try to retrieve it. Bijah screamed curses at him and fought him with the Crokno controlling her adding to her strength.

At the first signs of trouble, Angika grabbed up her baby brother and raced for the safety of her bedroom, slamming the door behind her. Terrified both for me, and her daughter, who was now fighting with a more than human strengthGahji had backed up against the far wall uncertain what to do. The rest of us were using our Qwakaiva to try and drive out the Crokno possessing my daughter.

We were making progress and the Crokno had realized that he had lost the advantage of surprise and was giving way when Aqwissa appeared and curled herself around my struggling daughter. Raising her silver head she looked Bijahgwi in the eye and told her to stop. I don't know if Bijah heard her, but in the next moment she went limp in Midaz's arms.

I breathed a sigh of relief; the fiend had left her. Bijah stared at everyone clustered around her, now seeming confused, but not aggressive or frightened. "Appi, what's going on? I don't understand—and I feel..." Bijah broke off and then started to cry.

<<I think you can let her go, Midaz,>> I said. <<Thank you for being so gentle with her. I know you could have killed her to protect us just now from the Crokno threat. I will be forever grateful that you didn't, however.>>

<<She is just a child. That evil one is to blame and it is that one who I want to kill,>> he said.

<<I share that desire with you. Bijah won't be bothered again for now and you need the burns on your hands tended to, so you can let her down to go to her mother.>>

Midaz set her down and Gahji opened her arms to embrace her, tears streaming down her face as she gathered her daughter to her breast.

<<My injury is nothing, Tigring. I am still able to perform my duty.>>

<<I'm sure that is true, nonetheless you need those burns bandaged,>> I said as I walked down the hall to find Gahji's med-kit.

A while later when the destroyed picta-view had been removed and things had calmed down we sat in the kitchen over cups of one of Kotahi's soothing brews. Still unwilling to let her go, Gahji sat with her daughter on her lap, with a now quiescent Aqwissa a silver choker around Bijah's neck.

Into the silence as we drank our tea, Star Swimmer said in a soothing voice with just a hint of a conjure in its tambour, "I'm sorry daughter-in-law, it is as I warned you. The enemy has taken the decision out of your hands. For everyone's safety she must go with Sichahntri now."

Resisting his attempt to sooth her, Gahji clutched her daughter tighter. "She is so young—please—is there no other way?"

"No, I am sorry; there is not. The enemy will overpower her again, using the conjure still clinging to her, and next time..." He left the rest of his thought unvoiced, but we all knew someone might die next time.

"Bijah," Kotahi said. "Do you understand what has just happened?"

Bijah nodded and took her thumb out of her mouth to answer. "Somebody blew up the picta-view." Turning to Star Swimmer she asked, "Ati, can you buy us another picta-view tomorrow? Angika likes watching Dance Party, and Tuunac will miss the next episode of Mighty Martiin when he comes home, if we have no picta-view."

"Yes, granddaughter I can do that. Do you know how the picta-view we had was destroyed?"

At first Bijah shook her head, "no," then a memory must have broken free of the Crokno conjure and her face contorted into a terrified mask. In a tiny voice, barely above a whisper, she said, "I did that... I listened to the voice inside my head, telling me I had to kill Appi Tas—and you."

Her frightened eyes flicked to me and then back to Star Swimmer's solemn face. She started to put her thumb back in her mouth, but resisted the temptation. Shifting so she could see her mother's face, her voice trembled when she pleaded, "Amima, I'm sorry! I don't want to hurt Appi or Ati Star, but my head hurt so bad and the voice said I had to get your gun and—if I wanted the pain to go away, I had to..."

Gahji hugged her daughter close, silent tears streaming down her own face, the Bear in her spirit fire roaring its anger and grief. "I know, my girl, we all know you didn't want to hurt anyone. It was that damned evil priest and his magic still clinging to you who wanted to hurt everybody—not you, my sweet, baby girl."

Bijah burst into tears again and hugged her back. When she was quieter Bijah sniffed and with her face still next to her mother's breast said, "Amima, I don't want to hurt anybody."

"I know, my girl." Gahji looked up and met Sichahntri's eye. Her voice thick with her emotions she continued, "And that's why you are going to have to go with Auntie Sichahntri to the Beyond—just like your Appi had to do when another mean priest wanted him to do bad things."

Bijah raised her head and looked at her mother the questions plain in her eyes. "Will you come with me?"

"No, baby girl. I can't go into the Beyond, my Qwakaiva isn't powerful like yours and your Appi's."

Turning to me she next asked, "Will you come with me and auntie?"

"Not right now, dear one, but I may come to visit you in time," I said.

"When we have removed the last of the Crokno's conjure I will teach you how to come visit your Amima and your Appi in their dreams," Sichahntri offered. "That way you can visit them sometimes and you won't forget them or miss them so much."

" But I wil miss them—I don't want to go."

Gahji looked at my father, her eyes pleading. He shook his head. "No, my girl, you have to go—for a while, so the bad priest can't find you and make you do anymore bad things.

"How about we let Aqwissa come with you," Star Swimmer coaxed. "In the Beyond among others who share a Dragon's blood you will learn many new things and you will be able to talk to Aqwissa again. I bet you miss talking to her, eh?"

"She is my best friend, but she belongs to Appi," Bijah protested.

"Aqwissa will belong to you now," Kotahi said. "I have a new protector that the Great One has instructed me to give him, so that Aqwissa can stay with you, little one."

Bijah smiled at that, deciding with Aqwissa coming this new adventure might not be so terrible.

Coming around the table Sichahntri motioned for Gahji to put Bijah down. Sichahntri placed the pendant around my daughter's neck, its power radiating throughout the room. The Hathuuri bowed in respect for such a powerful talisman and the child with the dragon's blood who now wore it.

"Now go and say good bye to your family my dear, because we must go soon," my sister urged. Bijahgwi did, giving me and her mother extra-long hugs. She cried a bit when she realized that she wouldn't be able to say farewell to her brother Tuunac, but Sichahntri cheered her with a promise that she could visit him in his dreams when she had learned how to use her Gift well enough.

Then holding hands with Sichahntri and my brother Kotahi my brave daughter walked out of our back door and into a new life.

After offering us their sympathy, my brother and his escort retired to their room to talk among themselves and plan our next combat.

No one in my little family felt like sleeping alone that night. We had lost two of our four children and everyone was upset. So, as we used to do in the "old days", my childhood, I put our mattress on the floor of our bedroom and brought Angika's mattress to lay beside ours. We would all sleep together in one big bed until the pain of our grieving had lessened.

Chapter Twenty-Five

I t took a long time for our dear ones to settle, but at last they drifted into a fretful rest. With the children so near my Gahji couldn't express her grief as openly as she wanted, for fear of waking them. For the rest of that awful night I held her trembling body in my arms and murmured soothing words to her in our language. Sometime near dawn she finally drifted off. Using a small conjure I deepened her sleep as I crept out of bed, a half-awake Angika taking my place beside her mother as she fell back into her dreams.

I crept through the house and out into the back yard. A morning fog blanketed the world in its cottony folds, masking the ugliness beyond. The air smelled of salt, fir trees and leaf mold. From somewhere in the mists a raven called and a mecho-cart rumbled as it moved further into the city.

Singing a prayer to the new day in a low voice I built a small fire and tossed in a handful of cedar, and pulled its healing smoke towards me.

<<Unseen Ones, give me the strength I will need to meet the challenges this day will bring. And give me the wisdom I will need to help those in my care who will look to me for their guidance and protection,>> I prayed as I sank to the damp ground to draw up Earth's Qwakaiva into myself.

I lost track of time as I lay in my silent communication with the land around me, but at last I became aware of another person nearby. Star Swimmer had come out and was now building up my fire. He tossed on a couple cedar branches and the hiss and crackle of their burning brought me back to my body and that place and time. I sat up and breathed in deep lungfuls of the sacred smoke.

"Come inside, son," he said in a soothing voice. "Your clothes are wet and I have made kaf-tea for you."

"Thank you." Having no will to do much else, I rose and followed him into the kitchen, where he sat me at the table and set a steaming cup in front of me. I took a couple sips then asked, "When I passed by their room I noticed the Hathuuri were gone. Do you know where they are?"

"Wahtzuul told me that Sichahntri has been showing them places on your world where they can tap reservoirs of power to use when they battle the enemy. Your brother said something about a fire mountain in the southern ocean where there were often great thunderstorms as well. They will be back later, no doubt."

I snorted a laugh and took another drink of my kaf-tea."I guess one of us better go hunt, or to a city butcher to buy some meat then."

Baby, of course was the first to wake and I snatched him up before he could undo my efforts and wake his mother. I let both Gahji and Angika sleep and called school and work to say they were ill. Later when everyone woke I made breakfast but only my always hungry little otter ate much of the meal I cooked.

Star Swimmer called the furniture store as he'd promised Bijah, and bought another picta-view, so we could keep track of the local news. I wasn't surprised when the news announced another unexplained fire at a building owned by the Luuchoiyan family.

And as father predicted the Hathuuri returned at nightfall the crystals on their armor glowing with renewed power, and ravenous for the meat we had purchased to feed them. But what was a surprise was that Dathna and three other Seal-Clan cousins from the Beyond arrived soon after.

Our kitchen was too small for so many, so we moved the living room furniture against the wall and we sat in a circle on the floor after everyone had grabbed some food, to have our war council.

"The enemy is no longer hiding in Seatown," Dathna began. "They are afraid, because in spite of their conjures to protect their human host's property we have managed to pass their barriers and destroy them.

"And from what we can tell from our spying," one of the cousins said, "the old human is very angry with his Crokno advisers."

One of the others laughed. "The traitor dare not leave zer conjured fortress because ze knows we are waiting. Ze and the Crokno cower behind their shield and pray we won't find their secret hide away on the Luuchoiyan estate up the coast."

"Be careful that you aren't too over confident," Star Swimmer warned. "They may be aware of your spying and are just waiting to lure you into their trap before springingit to catch you."

Agreeing with father, I told them what Aqwissa had told me about not being able to use their Qwakaiva once inside the estate, or they would trigger a nulling net like had been placed on my daughter.

My mention of Bijah prompted Dathna to ask, "Where is the little human and your pet? We could use the dragon-lizard to spy for us if she has a link to your human son."

"They are both gone, and Aqwissa is no longer bound to me. She is now linked to my daughter. Neither Sichahntri nor Kotahi could free Bijah of that damned Crokno net so my sister took them back into clan territory as Kunai wanted. So we won't be able to call upon her for any aid," I explained.

"A pity, it would be good to know where Utreal is before we begin our attack," Dathna said.

A worried Gahji squeezed my hand hard to get my attention. "Tas, if I'm understanding what they are saying correctly this means that with Aqwissa gone no one will know where our son is when they attack. Tuunac could be killed, by the enemy as revenge, or by your family by mistake. Tas, we need Aqwissa back so we can rescue our son."

A cold chill running down my spine I realized she was right. Aqwissa could warn Tuunac or protect him... "I'm sorry, my heart, it would be impossible to bring Aqwissa back now."

"Then what are we going to do?"

"I don't know, my heart, I don't know." Gahji covered her face with her hands her body shaking with her silent weeping.

Noticing her, Star Swimmer asked, "What's wrong, daughter?"

When I explained, he gave me an exasperated look and chuckled.

Annoyed, I growled, "Father, what's so funny our son could die."

"You are the one that is so funny, my son, think!"

When I continued to glare he relented and said, "Tas, what was your first lesson from your old mentor Chumco?'

It took me a moment but then I figured it out and laughed, too. Removing the cord braided from my mother and father's hair that I always wore around my neck, ever since Rushton had returned it to me, I looped it over my hands and began to weave the diamond-shaped pattern of the Seer's Pool.

The patterns created in long loops of string were simple figures like diamonds and triangles that most tribal children in my youth knew. Collin, Rushton's great uncle had even known a few, that as a chamuqwani child, he had learned, a relic of their own tribal past, no doubt.

Back home in my village we had used them to tell simple stories to younger relatives or to amuse ourselves while doing boring tasks like watching the small fires set under drying fish or meat. But under the tutelage of those from the Beyond those among my people with the right kind of Gift had created new patterns that could be put to a different magical purpose.

As I formed a picture of Tuunac in my mind, father said, "I doubt if the enemy has warded against such a simple conjure, so it's probably safe for you to use the string to find your son—and your traitor of a cousin."

It had been a long time since I had worked with the string patterns, but I eventually was able to bring an image of my son into the center diamond. Though she couldn't see him, I was able to tell Gahji that he was fine—considering. He was in a small bedroom and was eating a meal from a tray placed on a table by the bed.

My success caught the interest of both Dathna and Wahtzuul who wanted me to search for Utreal. My traitor of a cousin was harder to imagine in the Pool, because being able to change zer shape my Gift had no solid point to hook onto. "I have a vague idea of where ze is, but I wouldn't want to base an attack on what I can spy out in this manner."

<<Can you find the old man who threatened you within the string's pattern, Tigring,>>Midaz asked.

I smiled as an idea came to me. <<That is an excellent idea. But I will use a different pattern for him.>>Allowing the pattern to slip from my hands I quickly reformed it into the pattern kunai himself had taught me called the Aseutl's Gift.

In the center diamond elder Luuchoiyan appeared almost immediately. He was sitting at a large desk and seemed to be yelling at a servant. Over in one corner a blue-robed priest stood with arms folded across his chest, his expression telling me that he was enjoying the other man's discomfort.

On the other side of the room a large, elaborately painted pottery vase stood on a small table. My lips curving into a mischievous smile, I plucked one of the cords in the surrounding pattern of the central image. Suddenly the big vase wobbled then crashed to the floor, splintering into hundreds of tiny pieces.

Looking into the central diamond with me, a smile curving his own lips, father said, "That was a Wuuton dynasty vase, my son, a very valuable collector's item, so I'm told."

Wahtzuul laughed. I laughed with him and knocked a picture off the wall, breaking the glass and allowing the also valuable no doubt, silk painting of pretty flowers to fall into the puddle of water caused by the broken vase. But then I allowed the pattern to unravel before the priest, if he was Utreal, discovered my medaling.

<<That was very clever of you, younger brother,>>Wahtzuul said thoughtfully. <<With this new way of seeing we will be careful not to injure your son.>>

<<If you don't use such patterns on your own world, brother, maybe father or the Great One could show you how to weave them. With four hands, not two to conjure with, I would think the workings you could create would be most amazing.>>

Wahtzuul and Duuzra exchanged looks and a broad smile appeared on my brother's face. <<That is a most clever idea, which we will have to explore further once we return home.>> Then glancing once more at Gahji's worried face, he added, <<Tell your admirable wife to be at peace. This puny enemy has never tasted the bite of a Hathuuri war spear. It can break through any conjured barrier.>>

They talked for a long time that night about war strategies and how to use the resources available to us, but I let most of it pass over me, like water poured over a seal's oily fur. I would bow to their wisdom in such matters and do whatever they assigned to me.

Later that night when I eventually did fall asleep, Kunai ensnared me in his own conjure, and deposited me on the flat rock ledge by the dark pool where we usually met. This time he appeared to me in his true dragon form, rather than the human image he usually wore when we spoke.

Leaning his great horned head on the ledge in front of me, he said, <<You didn't listen to me when I enhanced your qwissa dragon-lizard and now you have lost her.>>

Bringing up my laps, also brought an image of a bloody and hurting Neko into my mind and I felt the grief of allowing him to be injured and then transformed nearly overwhelm me once again. <<No, I didn't listen and a younger relative paid dearly for my inattention—to my shame—and I will be forever sorry for that,>> I admitted.

He snorted, unimpressed with my admission. <<So, how do you plan to survive in your human world without her added protection now that the Crokno have your scent again?>>

<<I don't know... Do the best I can with my Gift, and use the lessons I learned while among my father's relatives.>>

He snorted again. <<Do you think you have learned enough to face your enemy and carry out the tasks I have given you on your own?>>

<<I don't know; I hope so.>>

<<You don't know. You hope so,>> he echoed, a mocking tone coming into his deep voice. <<Shall I return you to Co'yeh's territory like the little human with our ancient blood so you, too, can learn how to open your ears and listen better?>>

I shuddered, my spirit body trembling with his threat. <<Please don't take me back to the Beyond—my wife, Star Swimmer's grandson, my other human children—they and others of my family and friends are depending on me to guide and teach them in our troubled world. I don't want to leave them.>>

Not again, I thought privately, but didn't dare to project that.

He probably heard me anyway, and studied me thoughtfully, his thoughts veiled from me. at last he said, <<You don't want to leave your new human family. You are a creature of the light and of the dark, as are most of your kin. And because of that your attachment to others of your species is both your strength and your weakness, young siyatli.

<<Very well then, I will leave you to muddle through your life among your new relatives for now.... I will even grant you other guides and protectors to aid you.>> He rumbled a laugh. <<And this time try not to be so willful and lose them.>>

With Aqwissa gone I would definitely need otherworldly help to carry out my tasks for the Great One, but Kunai's "Gifts" in the past had always been a mixed blessing.I bowed my head in thanks, hiding my concerns.<<I am honored by your regard, Mentor. I hope always to be worthy of your favor.>>

Reading my mind, no doubt, he chuckled. <<By surrendering to me my hatchling sister's child you have earned my leniency. The crystal resting on my forehead you may take without having me test you further. It will help you in your coming battle with your enemy and in your future should you survive what awaits you in your present.>>

<<How is my daughter doing, Mentor? I would like to assure my wife that she is well.>>

<<She is well enough and making her transition without too much difficulty. You would be wise to give your human mate another child to care for as soon as possible, however,>> he advised. <<And this time make sure the child is female—and only human, so she won't have to lose another in her lineage, should the Crokno want to use another of your children against us.>>

I must have had a surprised look on my etheric face, because he rumbled a laugh again. <<Of course you can decide those things. I see that there are aspects of your education that your father has sadly neglected to inform you about. Ask him later when there is time. Now it grows late, so take your Gift, because there are others who wait to help you, which you will discover when you wake.>>

When he rested his head atop the ledge, I removed the glowing crystal being from his forehead. The crystal I retrieved was a many faceted stone with points on both ends about the size of my thumb that radiated a blue-white radiance. Unlike the crystal I had taken from him with my cleverness earlier in my life, and my father had returned to him to keep my torturer Hoyt from obtaining it, this crystal had more than one shadowy form swirling within its depths.

<<Feed the crystal well and often and it will reward you with its wisdom and protection as the beings enclosed within make themselves known to you,>> Kunai said.

When I awoke in the gray light of a new day my left arm ached and a gleaming crystal lay nestled in my bloody palm. On the pillow beside my head lay a long knife crafted from ivory or a fearsome being's tooth. The blade was held fast in the claw of a large bird of prey that had turned to stone. The handle was wrapped tight with leather to form its grip, a blood-red ruby at its pommel.

Gathering up my plunder I crept out of the bedroom still half asleep, my arm throbbing, heading for the kitchen. My father and the Hathuuri were waiting for me. I sat down at the table and gave them an inquiring look, wondering why they were up so early.

<<We sensed Kunai's Gifts pass through our barrier and have been waiting impatiently for the Great One to finish with you so we could see what you were gifted,>> he explained.

I chuckled and sat down at the table. <<Pour me some kaf-tea and I will show you then.>> Making them wait while I took several mouthfuls of the invigorating brew I at last had mercy on them and laid out the crystal and the knife on a folded dishtowel on the table in front of me.

The Hathuuri having several powerful crystals of their own paid my new acquisition only a passing glance. It was the knife that drew a hiss of awe and wonder from each of them.

With my permission Star Swimmer picked up the knife and held it reverently in his hands and closed his eyes. When he opened them again he gave me a long searching look. "Tas, do you know what the Great One has Gifted you?"

"No, not really, but I sense that like the crystal the knife is powerful, but I haven't had time to get to know it yet, or the beings within the crystal either."

He tapped lightly on its ivory blade. "This was crafted from the tooth of one of the ancient dragon creatures who lived on your world in the long ago past. A powerful ancient spirit was melded into its bone as it was shaped and sharpened. It will tell you its name as you get to know each other better."

"Can you sense what creature holds the tooth in its grasp, father? I know it is a bird of prey, but I don't recognize it."

Star Swimmer chuckled. "Look at your arm, my son."

Startled, I glanced down at the arm that I had just raised to take another drink of my kaf-tea. There tattooed into my forearm was the image of the night hunter, the great Owl, the silent one, who hunted his prey in the darkest of nights, Owl, the one I called to help me when I opened the portal and sang a dead person's spirit intothe realm of the ancestors.

While I had slept the image had been carved into my flesh, never to leave me till the Night Hunter carried my own spirit home to rest with my ancestors.

Staring at the being, I couldn't help but laugh. "Kunai said something about not wanting me to keep losing my guardians, so I guess he was making sure I don't lose this one."

My family joined me in my laughter. When we quieted, not wanting to wake the others asleep down the hall, father said, "Though you will feel her release, the Owl you can summon to fly from your arm when you have need of her.

"But since most people in these times don't wear such weapons on their person I would suggest hanging the knife as a guard of your home unless you are going into battle."

<<As we will be soon enough, Elder,>>Wahtzuul reminded us.

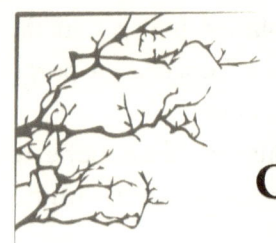

Chapter Twenty-Six

Another storm was gathering off the coast by early afternoon. As aware of the coming weather as the Hathuuri, Elder Samul arrived while we were eating a midday meal.

"I stopped by to tell you that our circle can be ready if you plan to take advantage of its power," he said. "And to bring the children and Gahji with me to the Ceremonial House as before, if you want."

"We do plan to use its power and it would be a great worry taken out of my basket if the family went with you," I agreed.

Without voicing any complaints this time Gahji rose and left the kitchen, calling for Angika to help her. When they were ready and waiting by the front door Samul finally noticed that Bijah wasn't with them.

Before he could voice his question, I relayed how we had had to send Bijah away, using the mind talk. For Gahji's sake he quickly mastered his emotions so as not to upset her further, but I could see the flares of anger in his spirit fire that told me he was as angry and upset as the rest of us.

Taking my wife and children into my arms I hugged them close but my mind was already half focused on the combat to come.

"Keep yourself safe, my love," Gahji murmured as I held her close. "Bring yourself and our son back to me—and in one piece this time."

I chuckled and gave her a long and deep-felt kiss. "I will try very hard to do that for you, my heart," I said when we came up for air.

With the storm fast approaching I hadn't had much time to attune myself with my new gifts. Going into our room after the family left I cradled each one in my hands, offered them my spit and my blood and explained to them as best I could in the little time I had about my situation, and how I might soon need their help.

Before leaving I tucked my new crystal helper into a soft leather pouch I had made to hold other sacred items. I had made the bag to wear around my neck or secure to my waist. The knife was a more difficult problem, however. Fortunately Wahtzuul had among the items he was able to bring with him into my world a leather sheath studded with several tiny crystals that fit the blade perfectly.When he gave it to me I detected that faint glimmer of envy glowing just below the surface in his spirit fire again.

In truth I had wondered why Kunai had gifted me with such a weapon. I was no warrior, and didn't really want to be. I would defend those I loved and my home and world till my death claimed me, but I had no wish to constantly seek out the glory to be gained in victory over an enemy as I sensed my brother and his older advisor did.

Kunai must have had his reasons, seeing something in my future that prompted his bestowal, so I didn't question the gift. But I did try to ease Wahtzuul's jealousy, by saying that I guessed that because of my weaker powers the Great One had felt it necessary to provide me with some extra help and protection.

Later I wondered if the enemy was also drawing power from the turbulent weather. They were waiting for us when we transferred ourselves to the place Dathna showed us with zer strong mind image, just outside the Crokno's magical shield.

We had barely time to erect our own barrier before they began pounding us with spears of blinding white fire. The storm was still only a grumbling black mass on the horizon. We had planned to wait and launch our own attack under the cover of its fury. But all that changed as soon as we materialized among the trees.

When their first spear crashed into a nearby tree, setting it aflame Wahtzuul laughed, his crystal studded armor flaring bright with power as he absorbed some of its impact. In his own language he roared, "Want to challenge me, Crokno insect puke? Come then, and taste the might of the Hathuuri war spear! Meet the fiery death I have waiting for you!"

Behind him I heard Duuzra begin a deep-throated chant as he joined lower hands with Midaz, and then Wahtzuul with a demonic smile joined them to launch their own counter attack.

Over the din my father said into my mind, <<I don't think Utreal and his Crokno mentor knew the Hathuuri were tapping into other sources of

Qwakaiva on your world. They most likely hope to catch them weakened and vulnerable if they sprang their attack before the storm reached us.>>

I laughed. <<Then the more fool them, eh?>>

<<Maybe,>> Star Swimmer hedged. Moving away into the trees we headed for the rocky shore. <<But we shouldn't underestimate them. I have learned that lesson in a very hard manner.>>

Our task was to rescue my son, and to do that we needed to see if we could enter from the ocean cloaked in our sealskins. Deciding that Utreal and his watchers would be looking for beings hidden by magical shields of some sort, we headed deeper into the trees unshielded, hoping not to be detected.

It had started to rain by then Wind whipping Water into a froth where it crashed against the rocky shore. It was going to be a rough swim even for us in our sealskins. As much a seal as I was human my father and I reasoned that we weren't using our Qwakaiva to make the change because the seal in our nature was always there and a part of us. We hoped we were right and we wouldn't set off any warded alarms if the enemy had even bothered to cast their shields out this far.

We were slammed into the rocks as we entered the surf, and I would have the bruises to prove it later, but once we swam out into deeper water we were able to ride the waves without much trouble. It was a hard swim, nonetheless. Water kept trying to carry us back onto the beach, before we had reached our goal.

At last I saw the roof tops of the Luuchoiyan compound. Though drenched in rain and pounded with flashes of etheric fire it looked much as Dathna, and the news announcers on the picta-view had shown us. Painted white with many glowing windows I had no idea where in that sprawling maze my son's tiny room would be located—or if he would even be in it. For all I knew he might be held captive elsewhere by now.

Below the big house and its cluster of smaller buildings was a narrow winding stairway leading down to a long dock, a boathouse for storing added equipment, and a large rich man's boat I had heard was called a yacht. There seemed to be some activity going on by the boat. People in bright yellow raincoats were bringing several boxes and bundles aboard it. If I ducked my head below the water's surface I could hear the rumble of the boat's motor ready to move away from the dock when the ropes were released.

Surfacing beside me in his sealskin my father watched the activity for a time then said, <<I think elder Luuchoiyan is planning to take a trip.>>

I snorted water out of my nose and barked a laugh. <<Perhaps he has finally figured out that his priestly advisors are more than they seem and aren't interested in his welfare.>>

<<Hmm, maybe. But I want to know who he is planning to bring along with him. It would be just like our cowardly traitor to run while he thinks we are occupied with his Crokno masters,>> Star Swimmer mused.

Suddenly there was a deafening blast of thunder, and a streak of lightning slammed into the top of the central house. That roof burst into flames. Over the din we could hear humans screaming. Then several dark figures fled the chaos heading for the shoreline and the boat moored to its dock. <<Let's swim a bit closer and see if we can climb aboard. I think they will be leaving soon,>> he suggested.

<<But what if Tuunac isn't with them? I can't use my string while I am in my sealskin,>>I cried.

<<Change one of your flippers back into a human hand,>> one of the beings within my new crystal said. <<I wil find your son for you if you show me his face.>>

Trying to balance myself in the churning maelstrom I held to my eye the crystal that hung from a cord around my neck and formed an image of Tuunac to project to it.

And there in a tiny facet of the crystal I saw my son. He was struggling between two large men who were dragging him down a smoky hall and then out of the burning house. There he joined a line of people hurrying down the stairs towards the idling boat. <<Thank you,>> I said to the one who had helped me. Then to my father I said, <<He is coming. We should definitely climb onto that boat, before it leaves. It can go much faster than we can swim.>>

<<Tuunac's grandparents and the cowardly traitor are also coming with that crowd of people,>> Star Swimmer added as we submerged and swam closer to the rumbling vessel. In the chaos of frightened people trying to scramble on board the yacht, we surfaced as humans and climbed onto the

divers' platform and from there to the main deck, where we hid amongst large metal bins and boxes that had been loaded aboard in haste.

When the grandparents, Tuunac, the traitor, and a small number of others were safely aboard, the ropes tethering the vessel were loosed and it rumbled out into the choppy water, leaving a large number of the frightened people still milling about on the dock, cursing and shouting.

Tuunac saw the retreating shoreline and screamed his defiance. As a boom of thunder and lightning exploded in the trees by the burning house, Elder Luuchoiyan cursed. "Why did you want me to bring that rebellious brat along with us, intercessor? Much of my fortune has now been destroyed because of him. I should just drop him overboard. He can't possibly be that important."

"Oh he is, truly he is, elder Luuchoiyan," Utreal soothed.

"I'm not your dragon heir, so you're right I'm not important to you, grandfather, but to him," Tuunac shouted. "He wants me with you on this boat because he wants to capture my Appi and maybe Ati Star as well. He is using me as his bait to ensnare them and he doesn't care at all if all your property is ruined as long as he can kill them."

"Be silent, little worm, or I will make you be silent," Utreal threatened.

"Why, because I might tell my grandfather the truth, traitor?" Tuunac answered back.

Utreal might have done something painful to my brave son, but at that moment there was another blinding flash of lightning on the shore. And then the sounds of a Hathuuri victory cry rang out over the crash of another peal of thunder. I saw Utreal pale, then I saw no more.

Taking advantage of the distraction Tuunac broke away from his minders and leapt overboard into the crashing waves of the storm.

"Go get your son," father shouted. "I will deal with the traitor."

<<I will come back to help you,>> I called as I shifted and dove. <<Don't let him kill you before I get back!>>

As I leapt back into the waves my father stepped out so everyone could see him and I heard him say, "Hello, traitor. Are you looking for me?"

Even though I had returned to the water in my seal form only moments after my brave son had jumped it was difficult to find him in the darkness and the noise of the motor and the churning waves.

<<Crystal beings, help me!>> I cried, knowing I had little time to find him alive. Though still unable to see him in the maelstrom, one of the beings in my crystal guided me until I bumped up against his sinking body.

Changing my upper body back into a human, I grabbed onto his now limp form and propelled myself upward. When we surfaced, he wasn't breathing. I felt the Owl on my arm stir but I commanded her to be still.

Breathing in a great lungful of air I raised Tuunac's head high out of the water and pushed my breath deep into his lungs. "Don't you dare die on me, my brave son!"

It took a few more breaths and some of my Qwakaiva, but at last coughing and choking, he began to breathe on his own. When he was calm enough to recognize me Tuunac threw his arms around me and cried, "Appi, I wasn't going to help the traitor trap and kill you. I was willing to die rather than let that happen," he said as he clung to me.

"That was a very brave thing you did, and I hope you will never be faced with such a choice again." Still aware of the battle going on at the Luuchoiyan compound and my father speeding away once more a prisoner of the traitor, I said, "Tuunac, with the help of my new crystal ally I am going to take you to be with your mother at the Ceremonial House. Close your eyes and don't be frightened. You may feel a little strange for a moment, because you are coming with me by transfer."

"Alright, I won't be scared. Are you going to stay with us?"

"No, I will have to come back and help Ati Star and Uncle Wahtzuul, now no more talk. Close your eyes." Tuunac closed his eyes as I instructed and I made the transfer.

In the next moment we were standing between the two fires at the Ceremonial House. I heard the deep-voiced chanting and someone nearby let out a happy cry. Then both Angika and Gahji were racing to embrace us. Giving over Tuunac to his mother's arms, I kissed her briefly and then was gone again.

Chapter Twenty-Seven

Deciding to return to the Luuchoiyan estate first to see how my brother and my cousins fared, I made my transfer there first. I reasoned I might need them before confronting Utreal. And, if they didn't already know that Utreal had deserted the area, I should tell them they weren't going to find the cowardly traitor in the wreckage, no matter how much they pulverized the place.

The storm was dumping a deluge of rain, and between it and the otherworldly war being fought on its grounds it was a chaotic scene that met my eye when I made the transfer. Burnt and broken trees, flaming buildings, people stumbling about, shivering and dazed, the Luuchoiyan property looked like a ravaged war zone. The estate was quite isolated, which might explain why the fire hadn't brought an army of firemen and goldys hadn't appeared to investigate.

The battle was pretty much over by the time I arrived. The big house was engulfed in flames and unsalvageable. Inside I could hear the occasional explosion as something in the mansion caught fire. Over by the gate a small group of human guards had barricaded themselves behind a couple of mecho-wagons, but no one in my family was paying them much attention in spite of the occasional gunshot directed their way. Somebody had erected a magical barrier and the projectiles flamed out when they encountered it.

Most of the Hathuuri's attention was focused on the heavily shielded Crokno pretend-priest on the porch of a smaller house that hadn't caught fire yet. Spying me, Dathna came over as I watched the Hathuuri send another piercing bolt of lightning at the Crokno.

"Can the Hathuuri break through his shield," I asked zer, "before the storm's waning lessens much of their power?"

Ze shrugged. "It won't matter. Sonda has crept around and will burn the house at the enemy's back. He and Utreal will have nowhere to run, but into our nets soon enough."

"That's what I came to tell you. Utreal isn't here. He left with the humans in the big boat that left a while ago. And I need help because he may have captured Star Swimmer again, if my father wasn't able to handle him on his own."

Dathna cursed and gave me an angry glare. "And where were you, all this time? Weren't you supposed to be helping him?"

"I *was*, until we rescued my son, and then he told me to take Tuunac back to his mother while he dealt with the traitor. Now I am back and I could use your help. So if you want Utreal..." I left the rest of my thought unvoiced. I didn't have time for an argument. "Come with me or not—it's your choice; I'm leaving."

Ze would come. Calling two of the others to join us, we left the Hathuuri and Sonda to deal with the remaining enemy. They could catch up to us later.Sending Dathna and the cousins an image of the Luuchoiyan yacht we projected ourselves to the ocean near where the boat struggled to maintain speed in the violent swells.

I shifted into my seal form and swam to overtake the vessel, so I could climb on board and find Star Swimmer. Dathna and zer cousins changed into seals as well, but it wasn't an easy form for them, being of a different clan lineage, and they wouldn't be able to maintain it for long.

<<We need a way to slow the vessel down before we are too weak to fight,>> Dathna said.

<<Too bad this ocean isn't the one in my northern home. There, a spring iceberg could stop that boat, no problem,>> I said.

<<Well, it's not, so think of something else, siyatli cousin,>> ze said.

<<Me?>>

<<Yes, you.>>

Once again, it was my world, my problem. With the Smotahlik Elders already in circle, I opened my awareness until I heard the log drum and their deep-voiced chanting. I knew they were waiting to help should I ask, and so I asked, sending Dathna's request to them.

I heard the cadence of the song change as Samul said, <<There is a powerful serpent-like being living off our coast,>> he chuckled. <<I guess someone like you might call it a dragon. The kahsietla will be hungry this time of year. We will call it to come to stop this boat for you.>>

I told my otherworldly relatives about the kahsietla and we slowed our pace to give the creature time to swim up from the depths and find us. It didn't take long before we heard its deep moan as it rose from the depths to meet us.

Unsure if it would see us as its next meal, my companions shifted into translucent forms to ride the wind. As they left me, one of them said, <<Your iceberg idea isn't without merit, little siyatli cousin. Maybe we could hide a barrier to stop the boat behind such an illusion.>>

<<Hmm, we could try,>> Dathna mused.

Leaving them to discuss the idea, I chose to stay in my seal form. I swam faster, wanting to catch up with the boat. I plunged through the boat's wake and when I was close enough I propelled myself upwards and slid onto the diver's platform that no one had thought to retract.

I must have made too much noise, or maybe it was the shift in the yacht's balance I made as I landed, but something caught the attention of a crewman on board. The next thing I knew a chamuqwani face was peering down at me. Then another man with a rifle joined him.

"Is it the zaunk the boss warned us about?" the second man asked. "If so..." he raised his weapon and sighted down the barrel.

"Put that thing down, you fool!" the first man said and pushed the barrel down below the rail. "It's just a stupid seal trying to hitch a ride."

The man made a shooing motion with his hand trying to make me jump back into the water. I blinked up at him and barked, calling him a dog-humper in Seal.

He might have come down to make me leave, but at that moment the vessel gave a violent lurch and then stopped. "What's going on?" someone shouted over the wind.

"We just hit an iceberg!" another voice called out.

"That's impossible," someone else cried.

"Oh yeah? Come see for yourself then."

Forgetting all about me, the chamuqwani who wanted me to leave and the man with the rifle hurried forward to see what his crew members were talking about. Taking advantage of their inattention, I became human again and hid myself amidst the large metal bins on the main deck.

This yacht was a large vessel. I had no idea where my enemies were keeping Star Swimmer. He could be in a cell or in one of the main rooms where I sensed more people were gathered. While everyone's attention was focused elsewhere, I needed to find him and get us off this vessel before kahsietla found the yacht.

Unfortunately when I called out to him with the mind talk he didn't answer. I had no sense that he was fragmented, or that he had been taken into the Beyond to Crokno territory, so that eased my mind somewhat. Utreal was probably waiting until he caught me, too, or he was joined by the other fake priests, before that happened.

So that probably meant that Star Swimmer was now enclosed in one of their nulling nets—damn it! Pulling my string over my head I quickly formed the pattern of the Seer's Pool, hoping I could find him in that way...

The picture that formed in the center diamond showed Star Swimmer bound to a high-backed wooden chair in a large room with thick rugs and comfortable lounging chairs placed together near low tables in several locations.On the far wall was a long polished counter with several bottles of booze and wine on the shelves above it.

There were also a number of people in the room with father, most of their faces were blurred because I was focused mainly on Star Swimmer. And to my relief, there was no glowing null-net around him, only a loose tether, a similar conjure to the one I had used to glue Mathrom to one of my own chairs after he had attacked me.

I wondered as I let the pattern dissolve whether Utreal hadn't had time to conjure the net, or he hadn't been trusted with that knowledge by his Crokno mentors.

More of the crew were heading towards the bow of the vessel so it was easy for me to slip through a doorway and down into a dim hall that at its end contained the room where they were holding Star Swimmer.

As I was nearing the door I heard elder Luuchoiyan shouting. "Captain, there is no iceberg out there blocking our passage. The good intercessor here says it is only an illusion conjured by this devil's son to delay us. Tell your crew to keep the yacht moving!"

Peering through a tiny window in the door I saw elder Luuchoiyan facing two men in sailor uniforms. The one with more colored insignia on his shoulders and sleeves looked exasperated. "I mean no disrespect, sir, but if the berg is just an illusion then how does he explain this?" He handed a bowl of ice to the elder.

Oh, clever cousins, I thought. The ice was probably gathered from the galley freezer and added to the illusion, but it had done its work well. I could hear the fear and awe in the voices of the people in the room as they saw the ice, too.

"Wintoh, what is happening?" a woman demanded. "I told you your stubbornness would destroy us. And now your refusal to listen to me is going to get us all killed. Set this creature free and stop listening to that priest! It's as my grandson tried to tell you, there is more going on here than we know."

"And I told you to be silent, woman! I am the patriarch of this family and I say who we believe and who we trust—not you!"

Ignoring his bluster the unknown woman—probably Tuunac's grandmother, shouted right back, "Then as the 'patriarch' go with your captain, see what is the trouble—take charge—and do something about it!"

Muttering curses under his breath elder Luuchoiyan banged open the room's door and he and his minions hurried past the shape shifted and hiding me, heading for the stairs to the deck above.

When they were gone, I resumed my own human form. I withdrew my blade from its sheath and walked into the silent room.

Father noticed me first and this time he spoke quickly to me in our private mind talk. <<Be careful, son. Utreal has an ally on board, a human crewman he has been teaching. I hope you haven't come alone.>>

<<No, I have not, so be at peace. Who is the human?>>

<<I'm not sure I have only heard his voice not seen his face.>>

When the people in their expensive clothing and jewelry noticed the wet and dripping tattooed savage suddenly among them they stared, openmouthed. Following their gaze, Utreal gave me a toothy smile. "There you are, little siyatli cousin," Utreal purred. "I've been looking for you. I think your father is lonely and needs some company."

I laughed. "And I've been looking for you, too, 'cousin.' You've tried to have me killed three times now and I want to return the favor."

Utreal chuckled, moving closer to me. Dressed in priestly robes, ze had assumed the form of a tall muscular chamuqwani. I threatened zer with my blade. "I'm not going to let you tether me to a chair, Utreal."

"But sitting in a nice chair will be more comfortable while we wait for the others than what is going to happen to you in the Beyond," Utreal said.

I laughed. "Nobody is coming to save you, you know. Your allies have been fragmented by now. Father and I didn't come alone. Some of your other enemies have joined us. None of the Crokno are traveling to their home in the Beyond today—especially not you, enemy slime."

As he lunged for me, I leapt aside and swiped at him with the knife Kunai had gifted me. To my surprise, the blade moved of its own will in my hand, and its sharp edge found the enemy target for which it searched. Otherworldly green blood colored its creamy surface. The blood disappeared as the spirit melded into the blade tasted its enemy—and wanted more.

Utreal hissed and stepped back snatching a cloth from a nearby table to press over the wound. "Curse you siyatli brat! Do you think with that puny blade's help you can actually fragment one of us, hmm?"

"For the sake of my people and my world, I have to try," I said.

Utreal's counter attack came in the form of a fiery missile aimed at my head. I leapt sideways, tripped over something behind me, and fell heavily to my knees. Utreal laughed and hurled another magical arrow before I could scramble to my feet.

I rolled and flung a bolt of my own, which missed zer and slammed into the far wall. There it flamed for a moment, and then extinguished, leaving a scorch mark on the wooden paneling.

As I struggled to my feet ze hit me again, numbing my right arm, holding the blade. I nearly dropped it, but tossed it into my left as my arm momentarily lost feeling. I jumped sideways as ze aimed for me again.

Blade quickly tucked into my belt I leapt atop a table and then threw an empty bottle at zer. Dodging my projectile Utreal's aim was spoiled, and the missile ze had been trying to throw missed me and hit a hanging lamp instead. It exploded in a shower of shattering glass and flames. People around us were screaming, adding to the chaos.

Utreal was now positioned between them and the way out, so they had no choice but to run in my direction, making it difficult for me to maneuver, or launch my own attack without endangering someone.

Keeping on the move, ze continued to hurl missiles in my direction. Dropping down behind an over turned padded chair, I taunted, "When I lived among father's relatives, the cousins always boasted how they could never be taken, never betray their own. And now here you are, treacherous fish slime, a traitor and a loathsome murderer of your own kin.

"Even a lowly Siyatli like me was able to resist Hoyt and his Crokno enhanced power. Oh mighty superior being, why couldn't you, eh?"

Utreal aimed another fiery bolt that set my hiding place aflame, making me hastily jump for another cluster of chairs further away.

"Because the Crokno are my kin, and I happened to agree with them. Humans are a loathsome, destructive cancer that can't be allowed to spread further to other worlds."

I threw my own magical arrow. He ducked, but it scorched a hole in his sleeve as he dodged. "You, a Crokno? If that's true then I applaud your skill in concealing that fact. But are you a true blood, or just another kind of half-breed like me?"

I threw a heavy bottle of booze in his direction. "Do your Crokno relative's torment you? Is that how you learned so well to take out your frustration and spite on me and others?"

I dropped to one knee and picked up another bottle and threw it after the first. I wished Dathna and the others would get here and help me out. Where were they, damn it? "That's how my tormentor Hoyt learned. His mother Sabisa taught him well. He told me so before we killed him, you know. Did she have a hand in your making, too?"

That taunt must have struck a sensitive spot, because he then abandoned his amusing game. Diverting my attention, he slashed at a nearby maidservant with a broken bottle. When she screamed, clutching at her bleeding arm, I looked in her direction. Then he lunged for me to make his kill. He hit me with a powerful conjure that slammed me across the room and pinned me to the far wall. Ghostly fingers closed about my throat, and I was soon choking and gasping for air.

"Siyatli brat, the Crokno can have your father, but you are mine!" Utreal snarled as ze approached.

I clawed at my throat in a vain attempt to banish his conjure. Black spots were appearing in the corners of my eyes. Was this how it was going to end for me? How could I have been so stupid? The maid had only been a distraction to ensnare my attention.

Where was Dathna? My uninjured hand dropped to my side. I couldn't banish his conjure. The world around me was growing dimmer. I had no more air.

<<Throw me!>> the deep voice of the spirit within the blade commanded.

With the last of my strength I groped for Kunai's blade, pulled it from my belt—and then dropped it.

I was a dead seal man...

<<Gahji, I'm sorry.>>

I'd been too weak to throw it; but I had done enough. The blade never touched the floor. Transforming in mid-air it became a snarling winged dragon-like creature, flying straight for my treacherous cousin's face. Utreal screamed once, tried to form a shield, and then the creature slammed into zer and ze sprawled at my feet. With a mouthful of long teeth, similar to my blade, the dragon tore into his flesh.

Still breathing heavily I stared down in shock at what I had unleashed. Did Star Swimmer know Kunai's gift could change like that? I glanced in his direction, but he only sat calmly still bound to the chair, his expression unreadable.

"Don't kill him, cousin the traitor needs to come back with us to clan territory where he can be suitably questioned," Dathna said.

Startled, I looked up from the bloody mess at my feet and saw Dathna and the other two cousins entering the room in human form.

"Where were you a few moments ago when I needed your help," I croaked.

Dathna shrugged. "We were busy." Then ze repeated, "Don't kill him."

I sighed. <<Enough, ancient one!>> I told it and to my further surprise it obeyed, transforming back into the bloody knife, which I then picked up off the floor. Still overwhelmed, I touched the now quiescent blade to my forehead in awe. <<Thank you, Ancient One.>>

Moving quickly into the room, the two cousins with Dathna enfolded Utreal in a net of glowing fibers.

My mouth dropped open, another surprise today. "A null-net? How?"

Dathna chuckled. "Close your mouth, little cousin. They learned how to construct one by taking apart the one enclosing your daughter."

I felt a great weight lifted off my shoulders at that news. "Bijah free to touch her Qwakaiva again. That is excellent news. Can she come back to her human family now?"

"No, not yet so the healers tell me. She must learn to defend herself and she will need to be taught her work for Kunai now that she, like you, has pledged her life in service to your world and the Great Ones."

As they passed me with a bound Utreal between them I couldn't resist a last taunt. "I guess I was wrong about you traveling into the Beyond today, eh?"

He cursed me and then they were gone.

I crossed to release Star Swimmer from his binding only to find him removing them himself, the conjure wrapped about his right arm dissolving into mist as I watched. When he saw my expression he smiled. "You didn't think I was stupid enough to let Utreal capture me again, did you?"

"Uh, no—I hoped not, but..."

He chuckled as he stood and stretched. "Haven't you figured out by now that this old bull seal is full of tricks. The conjure binding me was but illusion. I nulled Utreal's bindings when he was distracted arguing with the old human. I was only waiting for him to come close enough for me to use this." He held up for my inspection one of Wahtzuul's little rod weapons. "I became quite good with a kasuuri while courting his mother, long ago."

Well, that was a little more information than I wanted to know. "Uh, that's good, I guess; I'm glad," I said and felt my face heat.

He laughed again. "Oh my human son you are such an innocent about some things."

"Kunai said much the same to me when last I spoke with him."

"Did he now. Well I guess I shall have to find the time to see to your education, eh?"

I felt my face get even hotter, but I was saved answering when Tuunac's grandmother came over to us.

Dressed in one of the traditional long silken robes her people favored, she gave me an imperious glare. "Who—or what are you? Are you a devil or an angel?"

I laughed and turned to face her. Father left us to speak to some of the other people in the room, still frightened and unsure what was happening.

"I am maybe both, maybe neither, or maybe, like most people I am a mixture of the light and dark elements of the world."

She thought about my answer for a moment and then bowed to me. "A good answer perhaps, but you are something more than just a human. I sense that as the children told us, you are a powerful man, a man who can command the obedience of dragons."

I shook my head. "No, I don't command them; they command me—in a way. I swore an oath of service to them. I am charged with the protection of my world and all people of good heart, elder, as I told your husband."

She snorted a laugh. "That man never could listen—and now it has cost us everything," she said bitterly.

"I am sorry for that, but it isn't just you who has lost much. We lost our daughter to that evil pretend-priest and my nephew to the gang violence he ordered to distract me from his true purpose."

"Is she dead then—did the intercessor kill my granddaughter?"

"No, we saved her from that, but in order to heal her of the fiend's conjure we had to send her away. My dragon benefactor took her into the Beyond. She was the one who inherited your family's Gift, as the children told you, and now she is lost to all of us living in the human world."

I could have told her more, but suddenly the vessel gave another violent lurch that had many of the humans cowering on the other side of the room screaming again. Then from above came the sounds of gun fire and men shouting. Crossing to one of the little round windows on the wall star Swimmer peered out into the gloom.

"Speaking of dragons, I think there is another one attacking this ship. Does it belong to you, too, my son? If so you should tell it to stop before it sinks this craft."

I had forgotten all about the kahsietla. As it turned out we had managed without its diversion, but now what to do…? "No, it's not mine," I told him. It is an ancient being of this land and the Smotahlik Elders Circle summoned it to help us."

He chuckled. "Well then, I guess you'd better contact elder Samul and tell him to have the circle send it back."

The Circle was able to send the creature back into the depths—eventually, but not before several human lives were lost. One of those finding its way into the beings great belly was the Luuchoiyan patriarch and four other crewmen, one of which Star Swimmer thought was the Crokno human agent.

I was sorry for Tuunac's grandmother's loss—and told her so. I wasn't sure if she was just a very private person who wouldn't show her grief to strangers or she really was as relieved as she seemed.

Before father and I shifted back into our sealskins to leave I had one last piece of advice I hoped she would hear. "I am sorry that you and your family have lost so much—including your dragon's favor, who is female, by the way, according to my own Benefactor.

"Take what you have left of your fortune, hire a good attorney, and get Win out of prison, before the place destroys him. Go back to your own people and land. Find him a good wife and renew your vows with the traditions of your ancestors. And maybe in time your house's fortunes will change again."

Sensing a foretelling coming to me, my gaze looking inward, I said, "You may not live long enough to see it, but someday if you do as I suggest, Bijahgwi herself will come to bless and guard your descendants with her dragon protector and friend Aqwissa. Win will get to know his daughter and your house can regain a dragon's favor. Don't give up hope for the future."

Then to strengthen my words, father and I allowed her to see us make the transfer.

Chapter Twenty-Eight

I was able to keep my promise to Gahji, and except for a few impressive bruises I returned to her in one piece. But when father and I arrived at the Ceremonial House I saw right away that Wahtzuul and his older escort Duuzra had preceded us. Unlike their usual boisterous good humor and eating frenzy that I had learned to expect after they called upon their power I sensed that there was something amiss. Then I noticed that Midaz wasn't among them.

Drawing father's attention to the fact just before we were overrun by our relatives, I said, <<Where is Midaz?>>

<<I'll talk to Wahtzuul or Duuzra privately when I can and find out. I don't sense that the young Hathuuri was fragmented in their battle, but you are right there is definitely something wrong, and unfortunately I may know what's happened.>>

I started to ask him what he meant, but then I had no more time to consider the problem, because my sweet bear woman had reached us and flung herself into my arms, the children right behind her.

"Oh my love, I was so afraid for you," Gahji said in between her kisses. Then pushing me back to hold at arm's length, she growled, "And don't ever do that to me again, Tas, I mean it!"

I chuckled and drew her close again. "I will try very hard not to, my sweet love." But deep in my heart I knew that I couldn't promise that—not completely. When Kunai called upon me again...

Then we were caught up amongst the excited people crowding around us, everyone glad to see us and wishing us well, offering us food, and drumming and singing prayers of thanks for our victory.

I let father, who turned out to be quite a gifted storyteller, recount the battle and its significance for my world and especially the tribal people here in Seatown and elsewhere. I sat with my wife next to me, my baby son on my lap and Angika and Tuunac nestled on either side. But in a part of my mind, like an itch I couldn't reach to scratch, Midaz's absence nudged at my awareness.

Being the center of attention for the recounting of our tale and acting as translator for our otherworldly visitors I knew father hadn't found an opportunity to speak to my brother alone, so when I saw Duuzra heading for the outdoor privy I excused myself from the family to follow him.

On his way back to the house I hailed him and then drawing him back into the shadows I asked about his missing companion.

<<No, Tigring, he didn't die during our final battle with the Crokno enemy,>> he admitted when I pressed. <<His deeds of valor will be sung about by our lore keepers for many generations to come. His bravery and his sacrifice may have saved our chieftain, your brother, from a fate worse than death itself. Midazwill be known as a great warrior among us for many generations to come.>>

<<Then if that is so, honored Duuzra, and he isn't dead, where is he? We would like to honor him, too.>>

He looked at me strangely, and at last he said when I pressed him further, <<He has gone to do what is necessary.>>

That was all I could get out of him, and finally with an impatient growl he pushed past me to return to my brother still inside.

His answer both puzzled and frustrated me. still mulling over the problem I returned to my family. Gahji sensed my mood and when she drew me away from the others to a quiet bench in the shadows I told her that I had a bad feeling about the missing man.

"He's the one who brought Bijah to me and didn't kill her when he could have, isn't he?"

"Yes, that was Midaz," I admitted. "Which is why I feel obligated in part to find out what has happened to him. I can't explain it, exactly, but I feel I owe him something for that."

"Yes, I agree with you; we do. Can you find him if you use your string like you did to find Tuunac?"

"That is an excellent idea, my love." I kissed her and pulled my special string over my head and sat down on the bench to loop it over my hands to form the pattern.

An image of the missing young Hathuuri formed quite easily in the central diamond. He was sitting on a rocky ledge contemplating a stream of molten rock, pouring down a barren cliff face on the opposite side of the deep crater below him. On his lap he held with his remaining lower arm a long unsheathed blade. Blood was still draining in a sluggish stream from the half-burned gash where the other limb should have been.

Still focused on the image so as not to lose it I said to Gahji, "Please find my father and bring him to me—alone if possible, as soon as you can." She didn't waste time on asking unnecessary questions. She must have read my expression and knew Midaz was in trouble.

It didn't take long before my father sat down beside me. "Where is this place and what is he doing?" I asked him without looking up from the pattern.

"It's one of the volcanic mountains in the southern ocean. I guess that Sichahntri must have taken the Hathuuri to visit there. It is very much like many places on their own world. It would have been a good place for them to renew their power."

"Hmm, he doesn't look like he is wanting to renew his Qwakaiva, father. What is he doing?"

"Preparing to meet his death, I would imagine."

His words shocked me so much I almost lost my focus. "But why? Why would he want to do something so terrible?"

"You have to understand, Tas, the Hathuuri's world is a young world, a world that was still growing and maybe it was too young to host the life the Great Ones seeded there eons ago. I'm sure you noticed his missing limb. On his world a disabled warrior is a dead warrior to his family and tribe. Suicide is the only path for one such as him.

"He has chosen well for himself, a place to hold his bones that will always remind him of the home he has lost."

"But that's so terrible," Gahji said. "How can his people be so cruel?"

"They live on a harsh cruel world, my dear," Star Swimmer said. "It is how they have learned to survive."

"But can't we do something to help him?" she protested.

Yes maybe we can, I thought. "Father, have you been to this place?"

"Yes, I know it. What are you thinking, son?"

I stood, banishing the pattern. "Then take me there. I'm thinking that I can't let him do that. He may have only three arms now and be considered disabled on his home world, but we only have two arms here, so that's not a problem." Turning to my wife, I asked, "Is your med kit here with you?"

"Yes of course, I will get it and be ready."

When she was gone Star Swimmer said to me, "Do you truly understand what you are doing, son? I think your brother, when I tell him will be pleased, but it won't be an easy adjustment for any of you.

"Like the old chamuqwani lords I'm sure you have read about, he will want to swear an oath of allegiance to you as his new Tigring, if Wahtzuul releases him from his current one, which I believe he will. This is as much a life bond as is your marriage, so be sure you really want to do this. You won't be able to change your mind a year or five from now."

Did I really want to do this? I would be making this decision not only for myself but for Gahji and the rest of the family as well. Did I have that right? I wished there was time to talk it over with them, but there wasn't. I sensed time was running out both for me and Midaz.

"Yes, the Crokno will still be hunting me. I foresee that I may need him and his warrior's skills in the future."

Star Swimmer nodded and brought up another point. "And then there is the matter of his alien appearance to consider," father continued. "We will need help from the clan, because we will have to make some permanent 'modifications' to his appearance. Keeping up an illusion all the time would be too draining."

"Can that be done? If so, then I would like to ask him if he would want to stay here with me."

"He may not want to, so be prepared for that option as well, Tas."

"It will be his choice and I will abide by his decision, but I feel I owe him the opportunity to choose."

"So be it then." Grasping my shoulders, we made the transfer.

We came to a location just down the slope from where Midaz sat. I could see him, a hunched dark figure on the ledge above, still cradling the long bone blade across his knees.

"I will leave you now to talk to him,while I return to the ceremonial house to speak to your brother," Star Swimmer said and then disappeared.

I walked slowly up the rocky slope and sat down on the ledge not far from where he sat looking out over the fires below us. The air was hot and stank with a sulfurous odor that left a bitter taste at the back of my mouth. Midaz was aware of my approach, but didn't speak or turn his head to look at me. I didn't speak to him, or look at him directly, either. I let him be and watched the stream of molten rock cascading from a crack in the cliff.

At last he turned to me and asked, <<How did you find me?>>

I held up my special string for him to see. He grunted and turned back to watch the lava. After another long pause he said, <<I killed the Crokno that placed the conjure on your little daughter.>>

<<Thank you. That makes me glad.>>

<<Did Duuzra send you to see that I did the right thing?>>

<<No, what is the right thing?>>

He held up the blade. <<My Tigring has promised to honor my memory in our lore and songs, but as a wounded three-armed warrior I will be unable to continue my service to him. I am dead to my chieftain and my kin now, so I might as well finish it in truth.>>

He tapped the blade with an uninjured limb. <<I must do my duty... it is good you have come to witness, so you can tell your brother it is done.>>

<<I will stand witness, if that is what you want to do, but with the threat of Crokno vengeance still looming at some point in my future I have really come here to offer you another alternative.>>

This time he truly did turn to study my expression and see me with his Gift, trying to judge if I was joking with him. I let him look; I had nothing to hide from him.

<<What is this 'choice' you would offer me, a cripple, a disgraced no-good warrior?>>

<<To stay here on my world with me, as my bonded arms-man.>>

Midaz eyes opened wide at that. I think the idea had never even entered his mind. <<But why? Why would you want to take a disgraced, disabled warrior into your service, Tigring Tas?>>

I chuckled and held out my two arms for him to see and count. <<If I were to follow your own logic I too am a disabled warrior—everyone on my world, where people naturally have only two arms would be considered disgraced and disabled.

<<Having three arms on my world would be considered odd, but it would not be the hindrance here that I believe it would be for you back home. If you were willing to try and adjust, with a good conjure to make you appear more human and some concealing clothing you could manage, I think. If you wanted to, that is.>>

Midaz put the blade back onto his lap and turned back to the view. <<I don't know. It is a possibility I never considered...>>he said finally.

<<Having someone bonded to my service isn't something I ever considered, either. On my world and especially among my own Qwani'Ya people we don't keep slaves, or bind people into our service. We are people who, before our imperial conquerors forced change upon us, lived simple lives in harmony with our land.

<<Neither my father nor my brother has had time to explain very much to me about your people and your ways. I foresee that such a bond isn't going to be easy at first for all of us, but I am willing to give it a try—if you are.>>

He gave me a noncommittal grunt and after a pause asked, <<It is true I have seen little of the place your father calls a city where you live, but I don't think you have much use for a warrior in your life. Your Earth Mother is so old—and tame, compared to my home. If it is pity that has prompted you to make your offer, then don't bother.>> He tapped the blade. <<I would rather do what is the custom among us.>>

Was it pity that guided me? I would like to think not, but perhaps he was right to question my motives in part. I took a long moment before giving him an answer. <<Pity? I don't think so. When I look at you I see a man with skill and knowledge that I think I might need in the future. It is true I now live in a place where it would be rare to need a warrior's skills, so if you did come to live with me there would be lots of times where you and I will be babysitting, cooking or other chores of daily life that might become tedious and boring for you.

<<But I wouldn't expect you to stay with me all the time. As you said, this is a tame world, compared to your own. So when you learn to speak a human language and I don't need you, I would give you permission to go exploring in its wild places to get to know the land and all its living beings.

<<I also sense that many changes are coming for me soon, and as my brother has told me more than once, I am no warrior. I may need someone

with your skills to advise me and work at my side. But as I said before it is your choice and I will accept your decision.>>

Night had fallen in that place, the fires glowing brightly while he thought about his answer. I sat quietly nearby and watched the mountain in the distance belch smoke and more flames. Truly I had no idea that such places existed on my world. Though my northern home or the Kukiya's desert could be harsh, they were nothing like this. It was impressive, frightening, and fascinating.

At last Midaz rose and with a low bow handed me his blade. <<I will come with you and if my chieftain agrees I will swear my oath of service to you, Tigring Tas.>>

Chapter Twenty-Nine

As it turned out no one but Kotahi was willing to leave clan territory to help with Midaz's remaking. They were all busy questioning our prisoners or elsewhere, so it becamejust a family affair. Taking Elder Samul, Mathrom and his minder Tobey along to act as guards to keep out curious hunters, or other wandering humans, we brought Gahji, Angika and Tuunac, to witness the event. We retreated to a clearing near my new campsite in the tribe's allotted lands in the mountains.

I was to be pared with Kotahi for the healing diamond and it was quite a shock for me when Star Swimmer assumed his Hathuuri form and I got to see him as the father Wahtzuul had known growing up.

Midaz had already removed his armor and weapons for the conjure. His expression determined yet fearful, he crouched on the ground in the center of the healing diamond, his mini long braids cloaking him like a dark shawl.

As I had done before with Sichahntri Kotahi and I bound ourselves together to complete the fourth facet of the diamond. There had been no approaching storm on which to draw power so the Hathuuri and father, borrowing Midaz's armor, had gone to a fire mountain somewhere to gather as much power in their crystals as possible before beginning.

The working was both painful and exhilarating for me as before, though probably not as impressive to watch for my human family as father's healing during a violent thunderstorm had been.

When we finished a tall three-armed being with dark skin and strong human facial features sprawled on the ground between us. He was still unconscious from the conjure, so we wrapped him in blankets and laid him next to the built-up fire to rest.

Mathrom and Tobey had anticipated our need and had gone hunting for us, before we started. The roasting meat was now finished, its tempting smells whetting our appetites. They also agreed to keep watch over the still sleeping Midaz while the rest of us ate andthen slept.

As I expected, Kotahi didn't stay for the feast. Promising to come see me soon he left us to seek his own sustenance elsewhere.

Replete at last I too, sought my bed. Gahji cuddled close to me and murmured next to my ear, "Thank you for bringing us along and letting us witness Midaz's remaking. It means a lot to me that you want to include your human family as much as possible in this other part of your life."

Her words touched me deeply. To my surprise, I still had energy enough to make love to her, before I fell into a deep dreamless sleep.

It was late morning when I finally woke, the sunlight filtering through the fir branches above glistened with droplets of rain that must have fallen while I slept. Gahji and the children had left without disturbing me. I knew she had to get back to work and O'siyan would be missing her. And as soon as Midaz awakened, we would complete the ceremony that transferred his oath of allegiance from Wahtzuul to me. Then we would be leaving, too.

Father and the Hathuuri would be traveling to the power place they had found to renew themselves before they could make the transfer back to Wahtzuul's home world. And Mathrom, with a deer carcass in the back of his mecho-cart, would be driving Midaz and me back to our home in Seatown where we could get more rest, before he returned to the ceremonial house to complete his work with Tobey.

The Hathuuri were anxious to return home, so the feast the Smotahlik Ceremonial Society planned took place only a few days after the battle and the remaking. I was grateful that Wahtzuul chose to leave Midaz's armor and weapons with us, saying he might need them to protect me, and repeating his jab that I wasn't much of a warrior. Whatever his reasoning, I was glad for my new arms-man. I felt he needed that link to his past and his lost home the armor and its crystals could provide.

The entire community had been invited to the planned feast at the ceremonial house, so we masked our otherworldly visitors beneath illusions that made them appear more human. After speeches, singing and dancing witnessed by ancestral spirits as well as the community, suitable gifts were exchanged.

Most of the ones the Hathuuri were given, my brother later gave to me, because they couldn't carry them when they traveled into the Beyond. As was our custom, I would offer the plunder back to various community members during future ceremonial events.

But theHathuuri did manage to bring a few small items with them. Gifts they could display to prove their travel to another world was real, when their own stories were recounted around the winter fires back home.

Just before they were to leave my brother slapped me hard upon my back and told me that as my elder brother he would always come to save me if I was bothered by the enemy again.

<<It is good you have chosen to take Midaz into your service, brother. He is young but Duuzra is a good teacher. On your tame world he can become the protector you will need if the Crokno threaten you again.>>

I smiled. <<I am honored that he chose to stay with me. I just hope he won't get too bored on my 'tame world.'>>

He laughed. <<Well, now that he is with you, maybe in a few years if our father is willing, I will send you my rebellious son to manage. Then neither of you will get bored.>>

Was he serious? My heart skipped a beat at the idea, and I bowed my head to mask my concern. <<I would be honored,>> I said.

Father had read my worry and later privately told me, "Actually, Tas sending you Kozra at some point now that you have Midaz with you is a plan Kunai himself might approve. This 'rebellious son' is the one we have the most hope for, because he is more moderate in his thinking, and searching for other alternatives for his life than obtaining war honors. You I think, could further our plans by showing him a different way to live." I gave him a noncommittal grunt and he left it for me to think about.

Father chose to go with the Hathuuri. He had recovered completely from his injuries. He would be needed to return my brother and his remaining escort home, and I knew he planned to stay for a while among them. I had grown to enjoy having him here with me. Not knowing how many of my human years it might be before I might see him again, I told him that I would miss him.

He chuckled and hugged me, much to my surprise. "I will try to visit whenever I can, son, but until then you have Kunai's gifts and your new arms-man to keep you busy and safe." Then changing the subject, he added, "I know you want to do things for yourself, but in case there might come a time in the future when you might need it, that inheritance I spoke of will be there and waiting for you."

He gave me the man's name that secretly brokered for the clans, and how to contact him should I wish to. "Thank you that is good to know, but I hope I won't need to call upon him anytime soon." He shrugged and gave me a secretive smile.

Before I could ask him what he had seen in my future to make his offer, he changed the subject. Noticing Midaz standing silently near Gahji and the children he said, "You know your reputation as a powerful Qwakaihi has just been enhanced with you acquiring that warrior?"

"Enhanced? What do you mean?"

His smile widened. "When people see him in his armor and weapons following you and the family around and doing what you tell him, they think he is a captured being from our legends. I have already heard some people talking about the Nye 'dah you have bound to you with your powerful Qwakaiva."

"But, but Midaz isn't a bush man, a bigfoot!"

"No, maybe not, but you have to admit that he certainly looks like those legendary creatures that are talked about in almost all tribal people's stories. Not knowing his true history it will be natural for people to think of him in that way. They will call him the Nye 'dah, and you are the one who tamed him to become your new protector. In its way it's a compliment for both of you, don't you think?"

I snorted. "A compliment? Well I haven't really thought of him or myself in that way, so I will have to *think* about it."

He laughed. "You do that, my dear son, you do that."

When they were ready to leave, to my surprise Sichahntri showed up to help instead of Kotahi. That gave Gahji and I the opportunity to ask how our daughter was faring.

"She is well—considering." Sichahntri chuckled. "She misses you—even the older brother she always fought with. But soon I think she will have mastered the art of visiting her human family in your dreams, so that might be good for all of you."

"I miss her, too," Gahji said. "I hope she learns her lessons well and soonshe can visit us in our dreams at least."

"Hmm, we shall see." Turning to me she added, "Chi'ya, the Ancient who has chosen to act as a Benefactor to her father's family has taken a special interest in your daughter and plans to work with her personally, which is a great honor—rarely given to a human. She is very pleased with the care and teachings Bijah has received from you Tas—and her mother. You should be proud to have another Great Dragon's regard."

"Thank you for telling us," I said. "Give her my love, and tell Bijah we will hope to see her soon in our dreams."

I remember wondering at the time if Sichahntri's soothing words were actually true. I knew how ruthless the beings living in the Beyond could be when it suited their end goals. I didn't think my daughter was being abused, but allowing her to reopen the wounds of her leaving by contacting us would only make it harder for her to sever family ties and for us too.

Later when I had more time to think about our situation I saw how once again, history was repeating itself for me and my Qwani'Ya family. Through circumstances not of our making, we had been forced by violence and threat, to send our child away to the otherworldly equivalent of a live-away school. Like others before me we had no choice, and our grieving was terrible.

And the child we had to send away would learn a new way of thinking—of being. If she ever came back to us after her lessons were complete, she wouldn't be the same girl who left us—none of us would be the same. Like so many grieving parents in our past, I feared we had lost her—forever.

The place they chose to open a portal into the Beyond was in a deep cave in a mountain elder Samul call Vatlikahntla meaning, the place of the green healing pool, in his Smotahlik language. It had been a sacred place for the western tribes for many centuries. People traveled from up and down the coast to come there to pray, bathe and drink its healing waters, water that when brought into the sunlight was a strange luminous green and known for its magical powers.

The family and the representatives sent from the Ceremonial Society to witness, climbed to the cave on a well-worn trail and entered behind our otherworldly visitors. In the shadowy cavern by the pool father, Sichahntri and the Hathuuri gave us their last hugs and farewells and then stepped into the pool and waded out into its depths.

As the Elders chanted to draw up the Earth Mother's Qwakaiva Star Swimmer and Sichahntri opened a portal and our visitors from the Beyond swam down and out of our world.

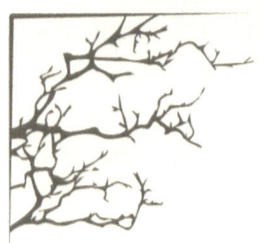

Chapter Thirty

As the winter passed we drifted into our old routines. Gahji went to work and I resumed my sessions with Rushton. No one took much joy in our being left in peace. Our victory wasn't without its casualties. We had lost both Bijahgwi and my nephew Neko to the enemy's violence and their hunger for vengeance. Mathrom, Gahji, and I, all had our internal scars, and Angika and Tuunac, were suffering from nightmares.

There were also the practical details of our modern lives that had to be dealt with. Gahji had missed a lot of work, and was being threatened with a firing. And then there was the children's school complaining about their missed attendance. And how were we going to explain about our now missing daughter to the imperial agencies who had been keeping an eye on our family for several years, thanks to the Luuchoiyan elders?

The school didn't believe that Bijah was now living with other relatives, but they and the social worker backed down, when the tribal attorneys reminded them that they had allowed a man impersonating me to take the children, even though Bijah and Tuunac both tried to tell their teachers that the man wasn't me.

Because of that error, they had been two of the children held captive at the temple agency that was under investigation. The scandal was still being discussed in the news, as legal actions were introduced into the court system, by several different Zacatik and imperial organizations.

So far we had kept our involvement out of the media, but it was a handy threat to make the school and the social worker leave us alone. Angika and Tuunac were still too upset to return to their classes, but we did compromise with the school by having assignments delivered to our home for them to complete for the next couple of moons, and that seemed to satisfy everybody.

And then there was Midaz to deal with. As father had warned me adjusting to him as a part of our blended family wasn't easy for any of us. Though he tried not to show it I knew through my bond with him that he was suffering from a lot of pain associated with his remaking.

Gahji knew it, too, and my mama bear had to roar her displeasure several times when he pretended not to understand her when she wanted him to take her medicines and go rest in Ky's old room. I often had to order him to take the pain meds Gahji brought home for him, because he thought I would see him as weak and unworthy if he gave in and took her pills—which I repeatedly assured him wasn't the case.

<<To suffer unnecessarily is the mark of a fool,>> I snapped at him one day when I too was losing my patience with him. <<No one bothered to tell me the remaking would be so hard on you. I would have asked father or Kotahi to help you more before they left if I'd known. But I assure you I won't think you weak or unworthy if you take my wife's medicine until your body has completely healed. I would do the same if I was in your place.>>

Maybe he thought me a weak fool in his private thoughts. I didn't care; I was his Tigring. He was going to do what I told him, and that was that. He bowed to my wishes, but I knew he wasn't happy about it.

Midaz was emotionally also having a hard time adjusting to his new body and human look. He had lost not only one of his lower arms, but he was no longer covered in sleek black fur and his face was not the face he knew as his own. Imprisoned in an alien body on an alien world, when even the face that stared back at him from the indoor privy mirror was a stranger's was hard for him to accept.

My heart grieved for him. In trying to be kind I wondered if once again I had made a terrible mistake. When I voiced my concerns to Gahji one night when we lay in each other's arms after making love, she thought about it for a while, then said, "It was his choice, as well, Tas. We will just have to wait and see."

What often eased the tension in our home was my ever-cheerful son, O'siyan. I learned that Midaz liked children and even when he was in pain he tolerated the little one climbing all over him. When he saw him my little otter would smile and hold out his arms to be picked up. Midaz seemed to possess endless patience with the little one and even seemed to enjoy watching and playing with him when everyone else had things to do.

O'siyan turned out to be a great help in teaching my arms-man our spoken language. Baby learning as well, they had fun laughing and practicing new words together, when they played with his toys.

During that winter I remembered my obligations to provide meat and fish for the initiates at the ceremonial house. I often took Midaz and baby with me on fishing trips or up into the mountains to hunt. As long as their school assignments were completed Tuunac and Angika were welcome to accompany us, which they often did.

Away from the noise and disruption of the city Midaz seemed to be more at peace in the wilder places of this land. Elder Samul told him he was always welcome at the ceremonial house. I encouraged him to go there often and retreat to my bush camp whenever he felt overwhelmed by his new family and city life.

Though not strictly a part of our combat with the Crokno, there was another event to trouble our heart that winter. Gahji came home from work one day fighting back tears, but it wasn't until the children had gone to bed that I was able to find out why.

Sitting around the kitchen table with soothing cups of an herbal tea Kotahi had left us I asked her what was wrong.

"Jula was brought into the Urgent Care Center today. As Ky predicted, her parents kicked her out once they found out about her condition," she explained. "Instead of coming to us, as I told her she could do if that happened, she chose to take an aunty's advice and get an illegal abortion instead."

Gahji wiped her eyes, her tears now flowing as she related the rest of her news. "Whoever she went to, messed her up pretty bad. She had lost both Ky's baby and a lot of blood by the time someone found her and called the medics."

I sat back stunned. "Why would she want to do something so terrible? I know she knew we were willing to help her out until Ky got back."

"Yes, she knew, but she told me when I went to see her that she hated Ky now and if she had his baby he would always be around bothering her, so she decided to end everything. And that was the price her family demanded she pay if she wanted to come home."

"But if she didn't want Ky or his baby we would have taken the child and raised the little one until Ky smartened up enough to become a good father. There was no reason for her to kill the life inside her," I protested.

"I know and I agree with you, but maybe she feared she might change her mind if she let it live."

Or maybe her dog-humping family had heard—and believed—the stories about me being a witch, and that frightened her even more, I thought privately, but didn't mention that to my sweet bear woman.

I sighed and finished the last of my tea. "I will go to the ceremonial house in the morning and talk to Samul about this. Ky will have to be told. As part of his task this winter, he will have to take responsibility for his part in what has happened. Do you want to come with me?"

She thought about it, then shook her head. "No, you go. I would probably get mad and start yelling at him for being so stupid, and that won't help the situation any."

"Alright I, will go and give him the sad news." I rose and pulled my dear one into my arms. "But that is a problem for another day and it would be good for me to check on Midaz anyway. Let's go to bed."

Deciding to do some fishing in my sealskin along the way I anchored my canoe near the ceremonial house and slipped into the water. When I felt I had caught enough and my thoughts were more at peace, I resumed my human form and paddled the canoe onto the shore.

Midaz was waiting on the beach to help me pull the canoe the rest of the way onto land. He picked up my heavy string of fish and followed me up the hill to the house.

Our bond meant that he could sense that I was troubled about something, and so I told him about Jula and Ky's lost baby.

He thought about it for a while as we climbed and at last, he said, <<That is sad news you bear, Tigring. Back home we lose so many children to storms, quakes and war that if a woman did that she would be killed too and her family might be exiled.>>

<<Among many tribes here, like my own, we claim our lineage through our mother's. That can mean that a woman may have more of a right to

choose whether she bears a child or not, but it isn't common even among my people to do what Jula has done. Her family's ways are strict. Jula disobeyed them and the price for her to come home was the death of her and Ky's child.>>

He was shocked by my explanation, but we had reached the ceremonial house by then. I told him I would answer more questions later if he had them.

Spying Elder Samul, Ky's minder Jacobton and Tobey sitting on a bench near one of the central fires, I said to Midaz, <<Please take my catch into the kitchen. I need to talk to the Elders over there before I find Ky.>>

Samul looked up and smiled as he saw me approach. "There you are, younger brother, we were just talking about you."

I chuckled and squatted in front of them. "So that is why my ears are burning, eh."

He laughed. "Oh, to be sure."

Before I could speak of my news Midaz returned with a cup and the small pot of kaf-tea. He poured me a cup and then asked in halting imperial standard if the others wanted some too? When everyone's cup was full he retreated to the kitchen to help clean my catch.

Watching him go I asked, "How is he doing? I hope you don't mind him spending so much time here. It seems to be easier for him on tribal land than it is in our home in the city."

Samul took another sip of his drink. "Your Nye 'dah is doing fine."

I laughed. "My Nye 'dah? Not you too. He isn't a bigfoot, you know."

Samul chuckled. "We know, but it's so much fun to threaten an unruly initiate with him taking them back into his land if they don't smarten up.

"But seriously, Tas, he is doing fine. We like having him here—and not just to scare unruly initiates. Mathrom, Tobey and I are getting much better with our mind communication, so when his words in our language fail him, he can usually make us understand that way."

Leaning forward to see me better, Tobey asked, "The frogs will be singing in the forest ponds in less than a moon, younger brother. The house will be closing till next winter. What have you planned to do with him during the spring and summer?"

"I suppose I should start thinking about that for all of us, Mathrom and Ky included. I would like to take everyone and move out of Seatown to some place more natural, when I can figure out what is my purpose now that the enemy threat has been stopped—for a while anyway."

Then changing the subject I told them the true reason for my visit. They were silent drinking their kaf-tea for a long time after I finished. At last Jacobton, a lean dark Elder with a wolf peering at me from his spirit fire said, "If it's all right with you, younger brother, I will tell him. You are right he will need to understand the part he has played in this tragedy, but perhaps this isn't the time to tell him.

"Right now he has been isolated to allow his Siiqwah to strengthen its presence within him. And when he comes back he will need to dance, and let his wolf move within him. I will tell him when my own Siiqwah says it is the right time."

I nodded. "I will bow to your wisdom in such a matter, Elder. I am here if I am needed. Midaz can always contact me." I smiled, "Or just call me on the far-speak, the imperial way."

He laughed and we left it like that.

I stayed for the meal so I could observe both my arms-man and Mathrom. And to my further surprise Jerriton and one of the older girls from the temple rescue were also here. When they realized that Midaz had been the one helping them to safety, they were able to set aside fear and accept his presence among them easier than most.

The Smotahlik initiates were wary of the Hathuuri-Nye 'dah, however, but Mathrom and Jerriton, being Kukiya outsiders in Smotahlik territory had befriended him. And Mathrom had the advantage of being able to talk to him using the mind communication I had already been teaching him.

Tobey's words still scratching at the back of my mind I asked Mathrom to accompany me back to my canoe. Switching to the mind talk, so as not to leave Midaz out I asked Mathrom, <<Tobey tells me that you are progressing well and can hold the core of your spirit separate even when you are threatened and you call Cougar.>>

He laughed and rolled up a shirtsleeve and showed me a long scorch mark down his arm that was still scabbed over. <<It took some doing on Midaz's part for me to get angry enough—or afraid enough to call Cougar to protect me from those alien weapons he can use so well, but I am learning.>>

Midaz gave him an approving smile. <<He is very fast when his Siiqwah comes. I thought it would be nothing to master this puny human.>> he aimed a playful blow in Mathrom's direction. <<But it wasn't. We had a true combat happening for a while.>>

Mathrom returned his playful punch and laughed, too. <<I didn't want to hurt him. You might get mad at me and glue me to another chair again. So I sent Cougar back, and let your poor weakly Nye 'dah live.>>

"Ha! I let live you. And I kick with big foot you, eh?>>

"Hah, never. I kick your ass!"

Feeling a weight fall off my shoulders I laughed. <<All right you two, I understand and I am happy. Just try not to take your mock fights too far and somebody gets injured or killed, because whoever survives will have to face Gahji, remember that.>>

Still grinning, they nodded.

Nearing the canoe I became serious again and asked Mathrom, "As Tobey just reminded me in there, the ceremonial house will be closing soon. Have you given any thought to what you plan to do afterwards?"

He shook his head. "No, but I suppose I should."

"Well, you are always welcome to stay with us, nephew. Rushton and I have eased things for you at the Lectorium if you want to go back there for the next term. You, Midaz, Ky and maybe that Jerriton boy—if we can convince him to go back to school, could stay in your house, so you wouldn't be alone over there, if you wanted to resume your studies."

"Thank you, but I don't know if I want to—not yet anyway." He fell silent watching the waves rolling in to lap against the gravel shore. At last he got up the courage to ask, "Neko isn't coming back, is he?"

At the thought of my gentle nephew, who had paid so dearly for my inattention to Kunai's instructions, guilt and sadness stabbed my heart once again. "No, he won't be back, not for a long while anyway."

"Is he dead?"

How to answer Mathrom's question? In a way he was dead—dead to his human kin—like our Bijah, so he might as well be. "No, he isn't dead, but in order to heal him in mind and body, at his request, Kotahi has transformed him and taken him away to recover in a sacred place—for an indefinite length of time. When and if he comes back Kotahi assures me will be up to Neko to decide."

"Transformed? What do you mean by that? Do you mean he is now a rock, a tree, a bird, or something like that?"

"Or something like that."

"But couldn't your brother just have healed whatever those gangers tore up inside him and let him come back to us?"

"Yes, he could have, and that was one of Neko's options. But Neko himself decided that even if his physical wounds healed the memories would still be raw and tempting him to find relief in booze or o'piyo. My brother assures me it was Neko's decision to take his other offer."

Giving him what I hoped was one of my sternest looks, I said, "And that information is for you alone. I haven't even told Gahji the truth, because I know it would be a hard burden for her to bear, being so friendly with your Aunty Janata.

"At my father's suggestion we are telling everyone that Neko has decided to become a sailor. He signed on a ship leaving Seatown and will stay gone until he feels he has forgotten well enough what happened to him here that he can return."

He tossed a few pebbles into the water while he digested what I'd said. "Even with Midaz and that crazy Ky as company I don't think I could stay there without Neko.... We had so many dreams..." his voice choked and he fell silent. At last he said, "But if I'm not going to live there I don't know what to do with the house. I guess I could give it to you."

"You could, but I don't know how long we want to stay here, either."

"Neko I think would want me to give his part of the ownership to his mother. I would do it and invite her and the kids to live there—if she could find the courage to leave the ass hole she's married to—and keeps taking back after he gets drunk and beats her."

"We could make Rafton not living there a condition of her coming," I offered. "With Neko away for several years—and maybe longer, the house is, for all practical purposes yours. He has signed his portion over to you, as I understand."

He gave me a look that said plainly that he wasn't sure he believed me, but didn't question me further.

"Gahji and I will help her get settled, and it would be wise to also tell her that she would have to go back to school, so she can afford your rent with a tribal stipend like you receive. Father has given me the name of a man who can set all this up for us, if you want."

He nodded. "I will think about that."

"You do that, nephew. Now help me put this craft in the water."

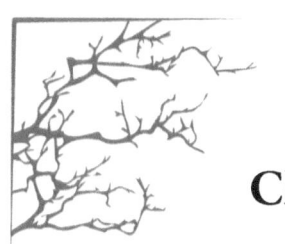

Chapter Thirty-One

The winter ceremonies and the storms that enhanced them were gone for another yearly cycle. The frogs were croaking in the forest ponds and road-side ditches and the leaves were greening on the aspen and willows. Everyone welcomed the warmer weather. With spring also came our hopes for a new beginning and an end to our grieving.

With three young men descending on us, Gahji and I decided that we would respect Mathrom's reluctance to live in his and Neko's house. We would be the ones moving across the street, but still paying the rent on the house we lived in now, so they could stay there. When they got jobs they would help us out, I was sure.

We left them most of the furniture, including the color picta-view and the living room couch-bed Star Swimmer had bought. Angika could always walk across the street if she wanted to watch some of her favorite programs, and so could we, if we needed to see the imperial news.

When Tuunac also wanted to stay with them Gahji said he could, as long as he kept up with his school work. With his growing knowledge of bush survival skills, what he had gone through during his kidnapping, and how he had handled himself when we had been attacked by sabiyan hunters, I no longer considered him a child, so his place was naturally to live with the young men of the family.

I wasn't too worried; we would be right across the street anyway. They weren't going to get into too much mischief with me so near and Midaz there to keep an eye on them.So, after we repainted the rooms a pale green, it was just me, Gahji, Angika and baby who moved in to Mathrom and Neko's house.

At least until school finished for the younger ones we would stay in Seatown. After that... Who could say. We all were feeling restless and needed a change. Like the wild geese I could hear honking as they flew north—I wanted to travel with them. I wanted to go home.

I was sitting on my new front porch one early morning, watching a dark V of the travelers flying overhead when I sensed someone standing nearby. When I turned, Kotahi was by the big tree whose spirit he had coaxed to come back into its wooden body. Little green leaves were popping out on almost all of its branches. I smiled and patted the step beside me.

He had assumed a tall thin leathery form, his eyes were their usual otherworldly green, and so was his long hair, now as green as the grass shooting up in the yard below me. It flowed down his back like the supple branches of a weeping willow. "Asiya, brother, did you come to see how your tree is doing?"

He smiled and accepted my invitation to sit. "Yes, I did come to see tree, but mostly I came to check on Neko and especially to see you."

"How is my nephew?"

"He is well. His roots are enmeshed and entwined with his siblings within the grove. His branches are bursting with new buds. He is drinking in sunlight and water from the creek below."

Not allowing me to distract him with further questions about Neko, he changed the subject and said, "I want to show you something if you will come with me for a while."

"Hmm, go with you. For how long—and where? I have a session with Rushton later today and Gahji will need me to stay with baby O'siyan while she is at work tonight."

Hearing more geese he looked up and smiled. "Like the geese you were just thinking about, brother, I want to take you north."

Had he been reading my mind, sensing my longing? I was nine or ten when I was marched to the Preserve with the rest of my people. About the age my son Tuunac was now. It had been so long; what would I find there after all this time...?

"If you want to come you will have to cancel your meeting with the lore keeper today and get your daughter and your arms-man to watch the little one," he continued. "I won't keep you over long but you will need time to digest and understand what I want to show and hopefully gift you."

"Hmm, I am curious, but you will have to give me a little time to prepare. Would you like to come in and have some tea? We still have a bit of the herbal one you left for us."

"I will have tea, then I will visit with tree while you get ready."

When he followed me into the house Gahji was sitting at the new kitchen table drinking her first cup of kaf-tea for the day. Still a bit wary of my otherworldly relatives she nodded and motioned to an empty chair.

I made fire on the cooker to heat the water for his tea, and announced, "Kotahi wants me to go with him for a while today. He has something to show me."

Instantly on her guard, she said, "Are you taking him into the Beyond?"

"No, where I want to take him is here on your world."

"Are you taking him to see Neko?"

Over her head I caught my brother's eye and shook my head.

"No, not today. I have something else I wish to show him this time."

"How is Neko doing? His mother was quite annoyed with him for not calling or coming to see her over the winter holidays."

"His ship might have been far from a port during that time, so he wouldn't have been able to keep in touch."

I breathed an inward sigh of relief. Father had told him about how to explain my nephew's long absence. As I headed out of the kitchen to get ready I heard her say, "Well, since you seem to be the only one able to transport yourself to keep track of him, tell him to write a letter to his mom every once in a while, so she doesn't worry."

The first thing I saw when we transferred were the peaks of the mountains my people named the Three Sisters that overlooked Big Ice Lake. Below us down the hill was the ugly little mining town named Socanna Lake that replaced the trading post and village of earth-covered pit houses that used to be there when I was a child.

The last of the winter's snow concealed much of its hidden squalor, but I could still feel the disharmony seeping up from the ground all about me. Further down the lakeshore several rusting away monster machines stood abandoned and beyond them a tall mound of refuse and pulverized rock loomed as a monument to imperial foolishness and greed.

I didn't need to open my awareness to feel the disharmony seeping into my bones. The wrongness hit me like a hammer blow. The ancestors were crying. The trees and animals who survived were sick with unknown diseases. The land itself was wounded. Polluted with unnatural substances the rich chamuqwani lords had used in their mining and left like discarded garbage to fester in a place they no longer had a use for, now that the yellow gold was gone.

This had been my home once, and now... My heart nearly bursting from my chest I sank to my knees and buried my hands in the snow and pine needles covering the ground. I knew tears were streaming down my face. I let them flow and made no effort to stop them.

Coming up behind me Kotahi put his twig-like hands on my shoulders and squeezed gently, telling me with his touch that he understood.

Letting me cry for a while, he finally said, "You could have made the transfer back here on your own, ever since you returned to your world. Why didn't you?"

That was a good question, and one I didn't know how to answer. When I could speak, I said, "I-I don't know... I thought it would have changed so much with the mining. Coming might bring up too many painful memories.... And then, I was always so busy with my new family. I guess I was afraid of what I might find—I-I don't know."

Covering my face with my hands I let the grief come, my whole body trembling with my sobs. Offering me no further comfort Kotahi waited patiently for me to finish.

When my sobs had drained me out, he spoke again, "If you are ready, there are some people who want to meet you."

Wiping my face on my sleeve, I rose. "Who wants to meet me? Nobody I knew lives here anymore." Giving me a secretive smile, he headed down the slope, expecting me to follow.

We traveled a faint trail off the hillside that skirted the outer portion of the town. Though people still lived here many of the houses were boarded up.Broken windows and trash were being revealed through the mounds of melting spring snow in the yards of the ones left abandoned. A pack of half-starved dogs of all sizes and breeds looked up from their hunt for food and watched us pass, but didn't bark or try to bother us.

Following the bank of the creek where grandfather often came to pray, and the men and boys of our village used to bathe, we came to an old cabin near the creeks mouth. As we approached, the door was opened by a man of middle years with a long hunter's braid starting to gray,hanging down his back. His hands were rough and strong, his brown skin leathery, his face a history of the hard life he had endured to survive in this northern land. It was a face similar to those of the men I'd grew up among. He was a hunter and a man of the land.

"Welcome, Elders, we have been waiting for you," he said in Qwani'Yan and opened the door wider.

Still wearing green hair and looking as much a tree as human, I suddenly realized that Kotahi must have visited here before—and often. He wasn't at all surprised by my brother's odd appearance.

The log house we entered was similar to the one my friend Kutima had lived in with his mother and his chamuqwani father, the head trader for our village. It had a large open front room that served as both kitchen and living area. To the back of the large room were two smaller rooms their doorways covered by blankets that were probably bedrooms. On the wall away from the door and window was an old iron woodstove crackling and popping as Fire greedily ate the wood fed into it.

A woman with her hair twined into two long braids and smiling eyes, welcomed us in my language as well. She had similar family features to the man's and was dressed in men's trousers and a plaid shirt. She motioned us to sit at her kitchen table. The good smells of baking bannoc and some kind of stew made my mouth water and made me remember that I hadn't taken time to eat breakfast before my brother whisked me away.

Knowing already the Kotahi wouldn't drink Kaf-tea she offered us spruce needle tea instead when we were seated.

"Tas," Kotahi said. "These people are your cousin Esuuli's grandchildren." He motioned to them. "This is Tsali Lynx and his sister Luciya Lynx."

"It is good to finally meet you elder cousin," Tsali said. "The ancient, Elder Chumco always told us that if we were patient you would come back to us" he smiled. "And as the Tree Man promised he did bring you home."

Setting my cup down on the table I stared at my brother openmouthed. "How is this possible?"

Kotahi exchanged smiles with our two hosts, then said to me, "Close your mouth, brother, it is very possible. When Chumco and his family left the march south he came back to Big Ice Lake in secret and gathered those of your mother's Qwani'Ya people who were left hiding near the lake to him. He used his Qwakaiva to keep them safe and fed as best he could until his death claimed him."

"Grandmother Esuuli and her first husband Tsali were among those who found and joined his band," Luciya said, taking up the tale.

"And when Tsali was killed by miners while hunting, Ami Esuuli married one of Chumco's sons so that her two children would have someone to provide for them," Tsali said, continuing the story.

As she served me a bowl of fish stew and warm bannoc, fresh from the oven Luciya said, "Chumco always said that his Benefactor had promised him that one day you would come back. With the special Qwakaiva you inherited from your father, you would help us and find your true purpose among us.

"If you can stay with us a few days, honored elder cousin, we would like to take you to a place in the mountains not far from here. It is a place where there was no gold, and so the chamuqwani miners never bothered with it much. "

"It is our dream to buy the land and build an earthen lodge village—like we lived in before. There we would like to teach the young people our language and the bush skills they have lost," Tsali said.

"Even if they chose not to come back here to live permanently they will be stronger for that ancient knowledge," Luciya added.

Their dream was similar to my own thinking—though in truth, I hadn't considered beginning my project so far north. But Tsali's proposal did have its appeal nonetheless. "Your idea is, interesting. Would this school and village be open to just Qwani'Ya people?" I asked.

"No, anyone of good heart could come—even chamuqwani," Luciya said. "In my dreams I have been told by my spirit helpers that our ancient knowledge needs to be shared with anyone who has the ears to listen."

"Hmm, I agree with you on that point..."

"Wasn't this what you were trying to do in Seatown, Tas?" Kotahi said quietly. "Hasn't the Great One charged you with just such a task? If this world is to survive the Crokno threat and the coming storms, the knowledge you have, and could teach with the help of your family and other interested people will be crucial for this world's survival."

"This is a lot to swallow in one mouthful," I said, my emotions in a turmoil. "I will have to pray about this and talk to my family," I hedged.

"Stay with us for a few days, touch the Earth, speak to the ancestors and then decide," Luciya advised. "Tsali can take you to the place we were thinking of, either by dog sled or by canoe. Then you can see the land for yourself and you will know if you approve of our choice."

"If he takes you in his canoe, change into your seal. Dive into the lake as you pray for guidance," Kotahi suggested. "In its cool green depths you may find the answers you seek."

"So you think I should do this?" When I stared at my brother for his answer, like most of my otherworldly kin he gave me no clue as to what he thought about the matter and only shrugged.

I sighed. For good or ill, it was my decision. "Alright I will stay, but I need to let my wife back in Seatown know, so she won't worry," I finally said. "Her mind talk skills aren't very strong, so I will have to use a far-speak." I glanced around the cabin and didn't see one.

Tsali chuckled. "There's one at the northern trading store you can use to call her. Finish your stew and I will take you there and give you a tour of the town—or what's left of it along the way."

His cup now empty, Kotahi rose. "If you are going to stay, Tas, I will leave you now. I have other matters to attend to on your world before I return to my garden in the Beyond."

"Yes, I can transfer home without your help, no problem—go then."

"Good." Then motioning for me to rise and follow him outside, he added, "Walk with me, brother, I have something more to share with you."

Curious and still a bit overwhelmed I followed him back into the yard. When we had drifted into the pines a short distance from the cabin, he stopped and faced me. "Do you plan to take Tsali and Luciya up on their offer? It is what the Great One always saw as a possibility for your future. It is a path I know he would favor if you choose to accept it."

"I'm considering it, true enough. The land here knows my name and is calling to me," I said, staring down at the little creek burbling below us. "I'm just not sure the timing is right. I have to think of my Gahji—and the others counting on me for guidance and protection... I just don't know."

"You shouldn't come alone. Bring them with you; build a community of people around you who want to learn and live in a new way of harmony with the land."

"But can we do that here? The mining has destroyed so much. To restore this feels so—overwhelming—even for the otherworldly powers everybody claims I can use to heal this land. I probably shouldn't have let Grandfather persuade me into stopping my apprenticeship with the man Kunai had chosen for me. Maybe none of this would have happened then." I waved a hand to encompass the rockslide we could see across the lake, a symbol of all the damage done to my home.

"Maybe, but Chumco might have gotten you killed, too. That was another possibility the Great One saw," Kotahi said. "Chumco had his flaws, but he was the one who had the Qwakaiva and was alive at the time, so he was chosen to teach you.

"If you had remained with Chumco as your mentor, or been able to come back north sooner...the mining couldn't have been prevented, but the Land's healing could be further along than it is now. But those possibilities do not matter now.You could still make a great difference if you come back to your northern home—at least for now."

He gave me a secretive smile. "But I foresee that as your reputation grows, you will be asked to travel elsewhere, so like the geese you were watching this morning you and your arms-man—and maybe the young cougar will become travelers, flying on the winds to bring hope and new beginnings to many."

"This is all so overwhelming at the moment," I told him. Then after a bit more reflection, "but I also sense that it is the right path for me and the family, as well. Too much has happened to us while living in Seatown. We all need a change. It will take some time to organize, buy the land with father's money, and get ready, but I believe it is possible."

Kotahi smiled. "I am glad. Now before I go, give me the crystal Kunai gave you for a moment."

Reaching into my shirt I pulled out the pouch I always wore containing the stone and handed it to him. Kotahi took it and holding it between his two hands, he activated one of the facets and when he finished the crystal glowed with a soft green radiance.

He handed it back to me and said, "This I have done for you out of my love, brother. When Kunai created this stone I asked if I could place a small fragment of my own healing gift within it. Neither father nor you speak of it much, but I know the torture you endured, the loved ones you have lost and the other wounds you've suffered in your young life still come at times to haunt you. I offer you this gift of myself in the hope that it will help you when the memories and your grieving become too much to bear."

I held the crystal in my cupped hands for a long moment, feeling its comforting power and knowing tears were once more flowing down my cheeks. "Thank You, your thoughtful Gift humbles me," I said when I could speak again. I put the pouch back around my neck.

Kotahi smiled and then he held out to me another stone that also glowed with its own green radiance. "When you return home make a bag for O'siyan so he can wear this to help keep him safe. Though he is still quite young, and with your permission, of course, the being within the stone and I will begin teaching him. As I'm sure you already know he has inherited your grandfather's healing Gift. We will come to him in his dreams, so he can fulfil his destiny when he is older."

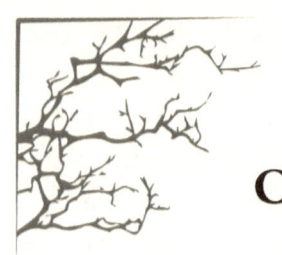

Chapter Thirty-Two

The place the siblings had chosen was beautiful, tucked away in a small inlet off the big lake, with tree covered slopes to shelter us from the worst of the winter storms and a good stream cascading down from the peaks above to give us untainted water. I felt at home and at peace there.

It was also close enough to the little town and the 'outside' world that we weren't completely isolated. I suspected my Gahji would need her own projects to keep her occupied and happy, so when I learned there was a medical clinic in Socanna Lake I had Luciya bring me there to speak to someone about hiring her.

The clinic was only open for a few days each month when a doctor from down south could be persuaded to come in to treat the area's serious cases, people who were too sick or injured for someone like Luciya to handle. With that lack in mind I spoke to a doctor Tomalton, who fortunately was in town during my visit.

When he learned my family and I would be moving to the community and starting up a "tourist" business, and that my wife was a nurse working at the large Seatown infirmarium, he was delighted.

"We have a hard time keeping qualified staff in such an isolated posting. If she meets our requirements I will definitely see about finding money to hire her," he told me.

With Tsali's help I visited government agencies remaining in town and gathered the practical information needed to buy the land Tsali and Luciya suggested. I also looked into purchasing a cabin up the little creek from the Lynx's place. Having the cabin meant we could use it as an office, or a place family members could stay if someone had to be in town.

Promising Tsali and Luciya to keep in touch, I went home after four days, where everyone seemed relieved to see me return—and uninjured.

There were too many practical details to consider for us to just leave in the next month or so, but after discussing my ideas with Gahji and getting her approval, I called a meeting of the family and interested friends, like Tobey, Martin, Rushton and Chief Rickson, to explain the project and discuss the matter.

When we were seated in a large circle on the floor of the living room in Mathrom's house, I laid out my plans, and then passed around a carved and painted wand, asking for their opinions and suggestions. I also was curious to know how many of the young ones might wish to come with me.

As we passed around the wand I wasn't surprised when Mathrom said he wanted to come, but what did surprise me was when Saskina added, "Uncle, it would be so amazing if a young person like me could actually make the same march you did. It would truly help me understand what our people suffered when they were forced to make that journey."

Mathrom chuckled. "Well, since we are already in the south I guess we would have to do the march in reverse, eh?"

"What a wonderful idea," Deillah said, giving us one of her brilliant smiles. "I remember some da stories great granny tell me. I would love to walk da pat she walk, feel her spirit so close to me. it would feel like ma'bee I be bringing her home at last."

I sat back stunned. I hadn't thought about my return in that manner. Feeling the crystal stir within the pouch I wore, I took in a deep calming breath. It would be good for me, too to walk the trail again. I could try to let go my own grief and begin to heal. And someone, like me with Owl's help, did need to bring all the lost ones back home...

Breaking in on my silent reverie, Rushton said, "If you wanted to make the march back north instead of just traveling up the northern highway by mecho-cart I would be willing to help you. I think I would even like to take a break from teaching the same old boring material and come—if that would be all right."

"Of course it would be alright, my friend. All people of good heart would be welcome to come with us—if we actually do what my younger relatives have inspired me to contemplate."

Rushton gave me a smile. "I would like that, and I think great uncle Collin would want me to go with you.

"Between your memories, and maybe with the girls to help me, we could check old imperial records and plot out a course north from the Preserve that would be as close to the old route as we possibly can make it in these modern times."

Reaching for the wand Mathrom's eyes gleamed with his excitement. "Everybody needs to know what our old people suffered. If we tell the media what we're planning I think a lot of people will want to come with us."

Elder Samul chuckled. "At least till the going gets tough for them anyway. But you are right, children, it is a good idea." He chuckled again. "Though Megara and I aren't ready to tackle the march with only a blanket and a knife like you have told me you had to, Tas. We are softys now, so I will drive us in our mecho-camper for most of the way."

I laughed, too. "The soldiers gave us horse-drawn wagons for the old people and women who were pregnant to ride in, Elder, so I guess your mecho-camper is acceptable. Though I may buy a horse and wagon we can use until we get too high in the mountains to carry extra supplies—and anyone not up to the walk who wants a more traditional way to travel."

Mathrom and my arms-man suddenly shared a wicked smile. Still grinning he turned to me and said, "No need to buy a horse and wagon, I plan to go get Pepper. While I'm at the rancha we could do a little creative acquiring at the same time—just like great grandpa might have done if he were here, eh?"

"Mathrom! Mama isn't going to let you take Pepper. She get stud fees for him. He makes a lot of money for her."

Mathrom laughed. "Too bad for her. He happens to be mine, and I got the ownership papers to prove it in my bank downtown. But who said anything about asking her, eh?"

"Mathrom!"

I laughed again and reached for the wand. "Alright, we can talk about this more another time. There are lots of things to do before we decide to leave."

"When were you thinking on leaving?" Martin asked. "I wouldn't mind coming to see where Ati Kutima was born. He told me a lot about the village over the years."

I snorted my disgust. "Well, it doesn't look anything like the village we grew up in now, I assure you. But when I was there a few days ago the land itself spoke to me so the spirit is still there under all the misuse and garbage." I thought about the problem for a moment, before answering his real question.

"I know we could be ready to leave before the end of summer, but winter comes early in the north. I wouldn't want to be climbing into the high country with inexperienced travelers and have a snow storms strand us, like it did to me and the family on our march south. We lost several people during that blizzard.

"No, I think we will prepare and leave while it's still early spring on the coast. By the time we make it North summer will be upon the land. That will give us time to prepare for the following winter."

"That is a very sensible idea," Elder Samul agreed. And the formal portion of the meeting broke up soon after that. Gahji and Aunty Megara brought out big pots of fish stew and pans of scau-bread, and we spent the rest of the evening pleasantly enjoying each other's company.

Though Stakaya had agreed to come to the meeting he had been quiet and withdrawn during the circle. As he was leaving with Denny, who was driving his Elders home I stopped him, and asked if he was considering coming with us.

He shook his head. "No I don't think so. The fishing season will be starting in a couple weeks. I'm going with Denny back to the Smotahlik Preserve up the coast to sign on with an older cousin needing hands on his trawler."

"That sounds like a good plan," I agreed. "But the season will end by late fall. What will you do after that?"

He shrugged. "Not sure, but something's bound to turn up. I plan to stay on the Preserve for the winter anyway."

"Well, you can always come stay with us if you change your mind."

He shrugged and headed for the door.

Gahji was going to be disappointed that he didn't want to come with us. He wasn't saying much about it, but I think Jula's decision to break up with him and end their child's life hit him hard. I suspected the true reason behind his reluctance, was because he was still angry and hadn't forgiven Gahji and the rest of us for forcing him into the ceremonial house and thus leaving Jula to face her family alone.

Staying on the Preserve would keep him away from the gangers in Seatown, but it wasn't without its risks either. I hoped he wouldn't take up smuggling with the chief's shady cousin, if money and a winter job became difficult to find. But Stakaya's troubles weren't my problem. His wolf would call him to dance next winter and if he would let them, there were Elders at the ceremonial House to help him.

As he was leaving, Chief Rickson asked me to walk him to his mecho-cart. As he opened the cart's door he turned and smiled at me. "You may be heading north soon, Old One, but don't forget you are still an enrolled Smotahlik tribal member, and I hope we will see you from time-to-time."

I chuckled. "You will, you will. I am very grateful for all the support you and the Elders have offered me while in your territory. I will be there if you need me."

His smile widened. "Uh, I'm glad you brought that up, because I plan to hold you to the agreement we made, concerning Saint Royston's Live-away school. I hope you haven't forgotten—with everything else that has been happening in your family lately."

Well, actually I had, but now that he had reminded me I felt the Owl on my arm awake. I needed to do this, because singing home the ghosts of our lost ones was also a part of my work.

"No, I haven't forgotten. I will come when you arrange it, but I have a few conditions I need to state beforehand."

Wary now he nodded. "And those conditions are?"

"I won't conduct a ceremony where the imperial media is present. I will show you where the children's bones were buried. What you do with that information later is your business. But I won't be a part of publicity that you, or anyone else plans to use to make the imperials cough up money for future Zacatik programs. What I do, I do to ease the suffering of our people, not to gain a reputation as a great Puhani."

I saw his face harden and I knew he planned to argue my point but I raised a hand to stop him. "I didn't say the money isn't needed. Or that they shouldn't pay us in part for our suffering. I'm just saying I won't be there when you use the information I will give you to pressure the government officials to do that."

He thought about it for a while then nodded and asked, "What do you see as your role here then?"

"My role is to help the dead find their way home and to ease the grieving of the ones left behind. It is that and nothing more."

"I see. But what does that mean exactly?"

"It means that I will come with you and meet with family members who have lost children and think they might be buried somewhere at the school. I will walk the grounds, tell you where to dig up the bones. I will collect the ghosts of the little ones—if they are there to be found. And then at night, as we sit together in circle around a fire and share our stories I will act as a medium between the living and the dead."

He shook his head and sighed. "That will be very helpful and ease many people's minds, but why do you want to do this at night? Some of the people won't want to come to the school after dark."

I snorted a laugh. "Because that is a time when witches are about and they've heard the rumors about me and think I'm a witch?'

Rickson dropped his eyes and mumbled, "Maybe—I don't know."

"It's alright; I've heard the rumors, too. People will believe what they want to believe and I have no power to stop them." Leaning forward, I looked into his eyes as I said, "I am neither a witch nor a saint—whatever those words really mean. What I am, is a man who has inherited special 'Gifts' from my unique lineage. I try to do only good with my power, but like everybody else I'm not perfect and I have made mistakes. I will do the best that I can for those who seek out my help and that is all I can offer."

"But why encourage people's fears? Why do these circles have to happen at night?" he protested.

"Because that is when the night hunter is awake and most willing to carry the lost souls through the portal I will open into the Beyond to be with their ghostly relatives."

"Night hunter? I don't understand."

I raised my arm and tapped the Owl carved into my flesh, releasing her. I gritted my teeth to stop from crying out with the pain as she withdrew herself from my arm for the first time. Perching on my shoulder Owl settled herself and watched the chief with glowing yellow eyes.

Rickson hissed in surprise and put the cart door as a shield between us. "The night hunter," I said, stating the obvious. I stroked her feathers with my other hand. "To use her power is one of the reasons we circle at night. If you recall the ceremony I did for Tommo was in the evening."

"Yes, but that was conducted at Reverend Cal's temple," he argued. "People felt safe there."

Safe? Well, not for me, I thought, recalling the incident. *I'd been careless and that was one of the times Utreal had almost killed me.*

"Yes, and if you can find another priest sympathetic to our needs near the school we can hold a ceremony there," I agreed. "But it would be better done at the school itself. After we pass the talking wand around the circle and all have spoken, both the living and the dead, I will open the portal with my song, and she will fly the souls to our ancestors in the Beyond. That is the task I have been charged with by my Elders. It is the gift I can offer our grieving relatives."

When Rickson had gone, promising he would be in touch when he had a date for me to go with him to the school I walked up to our porch and sat in the old couch rocker, pushing it back and forth with my feet. The night hunter had returned to sleep within my flesh, but my arm now ached to always remind me to use my Gifts wisely. Our neighborhood was quiet for a change only a far off siren wailing in the distance.

Inside I could hear Gahji putting O'siyan to bed and Saskina, Angika, and Deillah cleaning up the kitchen and talking quietly to each other. The two cousins had asked if they could give up paying expensive rent by the Lectorium and move in with us. We said yes. It felt good to be surrounded by family. I knew it wouldn't last. Deillah would be returning to her island home and Saskina and Mathrom would finish their schooling and find jobs elsewhere—eventually. But I would enjoy it while it lasted.

I was nearly asleep when Gahji came out to join me. She handed me a cup of one of my brother's soothing teas and sat down beside me in the swing. After several sips of the brew, she said, "I haven't had a chance to tell you yet, but I talked to that northern doctor again today.

"When he understood that we weren't coming north right away, he suggested that I take a couple classes that will be useful to me once we go north. Will you mind babysitting more often if I do?"

"No, I think that's a great idea. With the girls living here as well, if I am called away I'm sure they won't mind helping out." I told her about Rickson wanting me to fulfill my promise to work with the families at Saint Royston's trying to reclaim their lost children.

I put down my cup and kissed her. When we came up for air I said, "And it will also give you something to do when you have to quit work."

"Quit work?" she thought about my words for a moment then laughed and playfully punched me, "And do you also know what sex the new baby is going to be, oh smart predictor of the future?"

"Ow!" I kissed her again. "Well, if I learned my lesson from father correctly I think we will have a little girl, who will be as lovely as her mother."

She snorted and punched me again. "Well, I might have something to say about that too, you know. But you are right. I do think I carry a little girl this time." And I heard the longing that she was unable to keep out of her voice as she agreed with me. Hugging my wife tight to my side I agreed with her.

I smiled to myself. I was going home at last. With the spring we would have a new baby and we would be travelling north to begin our new life. Saying a silent prayer of gratitude to the Unseen Ones guiding my destiny, I kissed my Gahji and was content. Though my life had been hard and filled with suffering and war I would set the past aside and be thankful for my many blessings.

The End

RUSHTON ARCHIVES: CONCLUSION of Sixth Interview with Zacatik Subject 297

Additional Information for the books telling Tasimu's Story
Words in the Qwani' Ya Language:

Qwani'Ya Tsa'adi, or Fish People, what Tas's human family and the other Indigenous people living by Big Ice Lake call themselves

Qwa'osi the Otter Warrior, a guardian spirit protector of the Qwani'Ya

Co'yeh the Lake Seal, the Otter's rival, a spirit with both light and dark aspects related to Tas's father

Siyatli, a child born to a human woman and a being from another dimension, like Tas's Seal father

Qwakaiva, a difficult word to translate in its full meaning, similar to what we might refer to as magic, chi, life force or shamanic medicine

Qwakaihi, someone gifted with great power that uses their gift for the good of others

Malicer, a translated word from the invader's language, referring to a person who uses Qwakaiva to harm others, (a witch)

Aseutl, a snake-like dragon figure some say lives at the bottom of Big Ice Lake, or in the earth

Kunai, a shape-shifting magical being of great power, and benefactor of Tasimu

Qwa'Nayhi, a shape-shifting being able to travel between many realms of existence, like the Qwa'Nayhi Seal man who is Tasimu's father

Amima, mother in the Qwani'ya language

Appi, father

Ami grandmother

Ati, grandfather

Chamuqwani, a term the Indigenous people use to refer to the Imperial invaders of their land

Asiya, a greeting like hello

Crokno, the name given the enemy from another dimension that Tas and his father battle, because they wish to destroy Tas's world

UNFAMILIAR TERMS IN the Chamuqwani Language:

Zacatik, what the imperials called all the indigenous tribal peoples they encountered on their conquests

Zaunk, a degrading term used by soldiers and settlers from the empire to express their contempt for all Indigenous peoples they discovered

Zaunk-Brotha, a term used by tribal people amongst themselves

Bucki, a derogatory term for an Indigenous man or boy

Buckiyo, a more affectionate usage of the term, used by tribal people themselves

Cloocha or Cloocha-whore, a demeaning term for an Indigenous woman or girl

UNFAMILIAR WORDS IN the Kukiya Language:

Kukiya, what the Indigenous people living in the desert and mountain country out of which the Empire created their Tribal Preserve call themselves

Puhani, a person with magical powers, the same as a Qwakaihi in Tas's people's language

Puwa, the magical power, like Qwakaiva, that a Puhani can use

UNFAMILIAR WORDS IN the West Coast People's Language:

Smotahlik, the name the Indigenous people living on the west coast call themselves

Siiqwah, a spirit guide that a person has throughout life to protect and teach them, often the spirit is connected to a family lineage and can be inherited by an individual.

Bugatzi, masked enforcers, who invoke sacred spirit power to take care of tribal ceremonial affairs when needed

A Drubbing, when the Bugatzi are called to deal with an uncooperative family member, usually family sponsored and comes with family obligations, both to the Bugatzi and the one entrusted into their care.

Don't miss out!

Visit the website below and you can sign up to receive emails whenever Celu Amberstone publishes a new book. There's no charge and no obligation.

https://books2read.com/r/B-A-YGQM-LWMCG

BOOKS 2 READ

Connecting independent readers to independent writers.

Did you love *Memory Reclaimed*? Then you should read *Refugees and Other Stories*[1] by Celu Amberstone!

Shape-shifting beings and magical powers move in the natural world, and curious humans find unexpected roles to play in these stories from a celebrated author. Selkies and dragons have their tales to tell here. Ghosts and aliens with their own agendas and a troll interact with humans in stories that reference myths in new ways. Here, the reader will find reverence and reflection as well as adventure, and even humour.

Refugees And Other Stories is a collection of stories by author Celu Amberstone. Previously available only in anthologies and magazines, these stories are gathered together here for the first time. Drawing on her Indigenous and Celtic heritage, Amberstone writes powerful fiction subtly different from the usual science fiction or fantasy adventures. The introduction to her fine collection of stories is written by author and professor Dr Allan Weiss, whose specialization is in Canadian Literature.

Amberstone integrates her Celtic and Indigenous heritage into these stories. Her characters (whether human, alien, or mythic beings) are strangers in a strange land, at the intersection of the real world and words of magic – and if that makes you think of Heinlein and LeGuin, you are on the right track.

Amberstone's seductive and enthralling stories employ fantastic elements to balance the joy of kinship with the devastating effects of colonialism. A must-read collection! - Dr Joy Sanchez-Taylor, author of *Diverse Futures*, and professor of English at LaGuardia (CUNY)

"Refugees," by Celu Amberstone, throws readers on an emotional roller-coaster ride within a refugee culture that has been rescued, transplanted, and controlled by ambiguous benefactors from a post-apocalyptic Earth. - Quill and Quire

Amberstone's tales reflect real-world challenges and what it takes to overcome them. - Dr Allan Weiss, author and associate professor of English and Humanities, York University.

Also very strong is Vancouver Island writer Celu Amberstone's tale of human refugees living on an alien planet under the supervision of alien Benefactors ("Refugees"). Amberstone does a nice job of painting the shades of gray in her paternalistic society. Humans who have lived on Tallav'Wahir for centuries lead peaceful and happy lives, but they are utterly dependent on aliens to make all the decisions about what is in their best interests. And when a new shipment of refugees arrives from a dying Earth, their assumptions and their security are badly shaken. - Donna McMahon for *SF Site*

The benevolence of an alien race that helped them come to this place, and requires their obedience to rules, is questioned over the course of the story, as is whether harsh decisions aimed at ensuring humanity's survival are an acceptable price to pay. - James McGrath, reviewing "Refugees" for *Journal of Postcolonial Theory and Theology*

Also by Celu Amberstone

Rituals

Blessings of the Blood: A Book of Menstrual Lore and Rituals for Women
Deepening the Power: Community Ritual and Sacred Theatre

Tales of Tasimu

Taste of Memory
When Memory Dies
Abandoning Memory
Bitter Echo of Memory
Reawakening Memory
Memory Reclaimed

Tales of the Kashallans

The Dream-Chosen
The Hunted Kashallan
The Outlawed Bond
Uncertain Refuge
Prey of the Umwira
Blood Magic's Snare
Kashallan Alliance
Treacherous Campaign

Standalone
Refugees and Other Stories

About the Author

Celu is of mixed Cherokee and Scots-Irish ancestry. Celu Amberstone was one of the few young people in her family to take an interest in learning Traditional Native crafts and medicine ways. This interest made several of the older members of her family very happy while annoying others.

Legally blind since birth, she has defied her limitations and spent much of her life avoiding cities. Moving to Canada after falling in love with a Métis-Cree man from Manitoba, she has lived in the rain forests of the west coast, a tepee in the desert and a small village in Canada's arctic. Along the way she also managed to acquire a BA in cultural anthropology and an MA in health education. Celu loves telling stories and reading. She lives in Victoria British Columbia near her grown children and grandchildren.

About the Publisher

Kashallan Press is an independent publisher releasing books by author Celu Amberstone. Among her books are critically-acclaimed works now re-released by Kashallan Press, and new works showcasing her talents in writing both fiction and non-fiction.

www.ingramcontent.com/pod-product-compliance
Lightning Source LLC
Chambersburg PA
CBHW020818260626
47169CB00003B/726